THE BUTLER DIED IN BROOKLYN

MURDER RUNS A FEVER

RUTH FENISONG

Introduction by
Curtis Evans

Stark House Press • Eureka California

THE BUTLER DIED IN BROOKLYN / MURDER RUNS A FEVER

Published by Stark House Press
1315 H Street
Eureka, CA 95501, USA
griffinskye3@sbcglobal.net
www.starkhousepress.com

THE BUTLER DIED IN BROOKLYN
Originally published by Doubleday & Company, Inc., Garden City, and copyright © 1943 by Ruth Fenisong. Copyright © renewed June 9, 1970 by Ruth Fenisong.

MURDER RUNS A FEVER
Originally published by Doubleday and Company, Inc., Garden City, and copyright © 1943 by Ruth Fenisong. Copyright © renewed November 23, 1970 by Ruth Fenisong.

Reprinted by permission of the agent on behalf of the heirs of Ruth Fenisong. All rights reserved under International and Pan-American Copyright Conventions.

"The First Gridley Quartet" copyright © 2023 by Curtis Evans.

ISBN: 979-8-88601-066-4

Book design by Mark Shepard, shepgraphics.com
Cover art by Shootelkora
Proofreading by Bill Kelly

PUBLISHER'S NOTE:
This is a work of fiction. Names, characters, places and incidents are either the products of the author's imagination or used fictionally, and any resemblance to actual persons, living or dead, events or locales, is entirely coincidental.
Without limiting the rights under copyright reserved above, no part of this publication may be reproduced, stored, or introduced into a retrieval system or transmitted in any form or by any means (electronic, mechanical, photocopying, recording or otherwise) without the prior written permission of both the copyright owner and the above publisher of the book.

First Stark House Press Edition: January 2024

7
The First Gridley Quartet
By Curtis Evans

13
The Butler Died in Brooklyn
by Ruth Fenisong

131
Murder Runs a Fever
by Ruth Fenisong

THE FIRST GRIDLEY QUARTET

By Curtis Evans

The first quartet of Gridley "Grid" Nelson detective novels—part of a new wave of modern American detective novels that attempted more accurately to reflect the world as it was, while not sacrificing mystery and its detection—were published, in a flood of productivity on the part of the author, Ruth Fenisong (1904-78), in 1942 and 1943. It is impressive how a neophyte author like Ruth Fenisong hit the ground running with a fully developed world of her own in these books, which she began not long after the House Un-American Activities Committee put her and thousands of other people out of work in 1939 by it effectively shutting down the Work Progress Administration's Federal Theater Project. While an employee of the FTP, Ruth had written marionette plays for Puppet Theater, some of them with a pronounced leftist populist slant.

In the first of the Ruth Fenisong detective novels, *Murder Needs a Name* (1942), "Grid" Nelson is introduced as a privileged yet sensitive gent who "joined the police force to annoy an ambitious father and a snob of a brother. He had a real interest in the motivations of people and no creative talents that might express this interest through the medium of the arts." So Grid became a cop, essentially to advance his interest in the empathetic study of, and personal contact with, the mass of the people. His father, having headed a political machine in some unnamed town, was able to send Grid to elite Princeton University. However, young, idealistic Grid, having inherited a "small income" from his late mother, was able to eschew following in his father's ethically compromised footsteps.

After a few years spent in finding his career footing, in fields ranging "from garage mechanic to little theater*,*" Grid became a rookie cop, rising four years later, when *Murder Needs a Name* was published, to the rank of Detective Sergeant, a position he holds throughout the first four novels. Physically, Grid is a handsome specimen, just under six feet tall, with olive skin, a pointed face, a head of prematurely, but ever so distinguished, white hair and "width in the all the right places—width to his brow, to the space between his sad, deep-dug brown eyes, and to his strong shoulders." He is just like Roderick Alleyn (if you cut the preciosity and tweeness level by about 90%) except that he is conceivably real as a cop.

Grid's boss and mentor is Inspector Waldo Furniss, chief of the Homicide Division, "a tall, active old man with soft silver hair, bright blue eyes, and a great profile," who is "very much in demand as an after-dinner speaker and as master of ceremonies on benefit radio programs." There are other cops detailed in the novels too, like the amusingly named Detective Cricket, my favorite however being Joseph Sugsden, aka "Sugs", a clerical man in the force with the heart (if not the brains) of a hero, who dreams of being on the beat, bravely collaring crooks. (I am rather reminded of actor Ron Carey's forever striving, never achieving Police Sergeant Carl Levitt on the Seventies/Eighties television series *Barney Miller*.)

And then there is Sammy: a "tall Negress" with a "magnificent head," "skin the warm color of apricots" and an expression on her "carved African features ... of dignity and strength." If you have read enough crime fiction from the period, you will know how unusual it is to find a black character so positively described. The treatment of black characters in American entertainment media was starting finally to change in the Forties, but there were still a great many exaggerated comic relief black servant characters, rolling white eyeballs dramatically as they get easily frightened by "hants" and the like and speaking in heavily caricatured, allegedly amusing "negro" dialect. Sammy is a real advance in this regard, as Anthony Boucher noted at the time. (He deemed Sammy an "incomparable Negress.")

Sammy first shows up in *Murder Needs a Name* as a maid working for radio personality Catherine Verney, who hosts one of those sponsor-laden domestic radio shows for housewives from the time. (For example, for many years radio personality Pegeen Fitzgerald, said to have been by Americans "held in holy esteem slightly higher than John Wayne," co-hosted, along with her husband Ed, the at-home program *Breakfast with the Fitzgeralds*.) In this respect the novel reminded me a lot Rex Stout's mystery *And Be a Villain* (1948) as well as Jonathan Stagge's mystery *The Three Fears* (1949). The *Knoxville News-Sentinel* pronounced of Ruth Fenisongs's debut mystery that the author's "smooth technique is a delight." Later in 1942 there followed from Ruth's hand *Murder Needs a Face*, which concerns a murder at a housing project, "Greenhedge." How often do you see a housing project as a setting in Golden Age mystery?

The U.S. the Housing Act of 1937 authorized the federal government to provide subsidies for low-income housing. In New York City this led to a burst of housing projects that are still standing today (some of them historic landmarks), including the Williamsburg Houses, a group of twenty Modernist buildings in Brooklyn (with a total of 1622 apartments). Designed in part by famed Swiss architect William Lescaze, they opened in 1938. The project was highly praised at the time, with President and Mrs. Roosevelt even paying it a visit and Mayor Fiorella LaGuardia pouring the first concrete at the groundbreaking. Prominent modern artists painted murals for the project's common rooms, which by the 1980s were covered over by layers of paint, but happily they have since been recovered and restored and are now on exhibition at the Brooklyn Museum.

In her novel Ruth Fenisong definitely paints a positive portrait of Greenhedge (murder aside), writing through Franca's eyes:

> They walked through Greenhedge, a city of modern units, each with a separate entrance. Thousands of windows gave on precious bits of landscaped courts and gardens. Benches sat smugly on neat paved strips of ground fronting well-cared-for lawns.... Spring would see many baby carriages placed along the paved walks, while mamas sat sewing and gossiping with their neighbors. And children who had outgrown their carriages would come up out of the game rooms in the basements of Greenhedge where real play space had been provided for them the winter long.... Housing experts had labored to give to each tenet the space thought necessary for comfort and decency. And the funds of the tenants had been investigated so that those who earned more than the members of the low-income group for which the project had been designed might not gain entrance. Franca never saw Greenhedge without drawing a breath of gratitude and reciting a silent prayer that she might meet expenses each month and do nothing to incur the displeasure of the management. It was a dwelling place to be proud of, and she wanted no more than to remain there.

Here Ruth definitely voices the social idealism of bright-eyed and hopeful progressives of her era. Greenhedge, we find, is the "darling" of philanthropist G. V. Kuvicek, an eccentric millionaire philanthropist and native Oklahoma oil man. The murder is not actually of him—the traditional rich male victim—but of an unknown man, found dead outside one of the Greenhedge buildings. There are numerous people in the project who seem implicated in the death in some way, however, including: retired Italian puppeteer Peppino Settani and his lovely blonde eighteen-year-old daughter, Franca, a puppeteer herself (she gets her blondness from her late northern Italian mother); the Murtrees, coarse, brazen Julia and careworn husband Henry, aka "Hen" (as in henpecked?); diminutive, bulldog torch singer Mady Cooper and her blind father; and several other, definitely suspicions, characters. Oh, and there's also the project manager, Paul Curtis and his secretary, Arlene Decker. He seems smitten with Franca and she seems smitten with Grid. (But naturally!)

The setting of the novel is strong and unusual, and the puppeteering stuff obviously is something Fenisong knew well. The police are convincingly done, though Franca, who seems like she will be the protagonist of the tale at first, is allowed to fade into the background for most of the story, only to reemerge at the end. However, Sammy reappears early on in the story, to be hired by Grid as the cook and housekeeper as his bachelor gentleman policeman pad. (She will remain with him for the rest of the series.) This happily gives Sammy a chance to butt into Grid's case and help him solve it. "Bless Sammy," thinks Grid: "He wondered what Sammy's life would have been had her background permitted a formal education to supplement native intelligence. Probably just plain unhappy ... in a world that kept dreaming up bigger and better prejudices with every passing moment."

It is asides like that which make Ruth Fenisong's mysteries something commendably different for the period. *Saturday Review* praised the book's "shrewd portrait of life among the lowly—sharp-tongued, colorful and occasionally shifty," while Anthony Boucher enthused: "Novel background and admirable writing recommend this to every type of [mystery] fan." Mystery writer and reviewer Dorothy B. Hughes approvingly pronounced: "Good writing here with some telling points on sweet charity."

After *Murder Needs a Face*, there next came the whimsically titled *The Butler Died in Brooklyn* (1943), the Ruth Fenisong mystery which most resembles a classic traditional mystery, in that it deals with one of those wealthy families imperiously presided over by a domineering, elderly, eccentric relation. The family in this particular novel has relocated from Manhattan to Brooklyn (oh, the humanity!) and, yes, it is their butler, newly laid-off, who gets done in there. (The butler did not do it, in short, but rather had it done to him.) *Saturday Review* praised *Butler's* "brisk and breezy characters" and the *New York Times* its "good puzzlement plus entertainment," while Dorothy B. Hughes contributed an outright rave of the book, with an eminently blurbable conclusion:

> "Ruth Fenisong has a man's attack in her writing, which is, as all men know, a high compliment. Moreover, she can handle dialogue so that it sounds like conversation, whether it's the police brand or out of the mouths of more bizarre folk. She can even handle dialect-like conversation. She's one of the better writers turning out mystery today for my money. 'You can't go wrong on a Fenisong.'"

Murder Runs a Fever, from later that year is a full-scale wartime mystery, dealing with the FBI and suspected Nazi spies; yet there is also a legitimate murder problem to be dealt with too. Shockingly a man, popular radio war commentator Captain Orrin L. Shay, is found strangled in the apartment of Louise Cotter, an old childhood friend of Grid Nelson, with whom he has long been more than half smitten. Louise didn't marry Grid, of course, who is ostensibly a confirmed bachelor in the traditional fashion of Great Detectives (even ones on the force), but rather Charles Cotter, a jeweler who has joined the Army and is stationed at a base in Texas. Charles has just come home on leave when Captain Shay is found slain in his apartment, making him a suspect in the crime (for Shay seemed to show quite a bit of interest in Louise)—even though Charles has come down with a rather serious illness: the "fever" of the title.

Also present at the scene of the crime and viewed suspiciously by the police, especially Waldo Furniss, are Louise and Sammy herself (!), the latter having been on hand to cook a dinner for Louise and the returning Charles. Oh, and let's not forget, there was on the scene as well Louise's young, blondely beautiful cousin, Kyrie Martens, who happens to be making a visit to New York from Washington, D. C. Under the alias "Madge Carter," Kyrie is an FBI agent (Do such females appear much in wartime American crime fiction?); and a goodly section of the novel is devoted to her activities, which eventually merge with Grid's (as do his and Kyrie's personal fates). And Sammy provides a key clue.

Saturday Review called *Murder Runs a Fever* a "lively yarn of murder intrigue with [a] personable sleuth, much action and [a] pleasing dash of romance" while the *New York Times* opined that it was a "cleverly constructed tale of Nazi espionage." Anthony Boucher chimed in as well, as was his wont where Ruth's fiction was concerned, lauding the "skillful story-telling," though he also conceded the presence of "a couple of pretty fearful coincidences."

All these early Fenisongs have the precious quality of sheer readability, not always present in mystery fiction (or mainstream fiction for that matter). And the best news is, the author only got better!

—June 2023
Germantown, TN

....

Curtis Evans received a PhD in American history in 1998. He is the author of *Masters of the "Humdrum" Mystery: Cecil John Charles Street, Freeman Wills Crofts, Alfred Walter Stewart and British Detective Fiction, 1920-1961* (2012) and most recently the editor of the Edgar nominated *Murder in the Closet: Essays on Queer Clues in Crime Fiction Before Stonewall* (2017) and, with Douglas G. Greene, the Richard Webb and Hugh Wheeler short crime fiction collection, *The Cases of Lieutenant Timothy Trant* (2019). He blogs on vintage crime fiction at The Passing Tramp.

THE BUTLER DIED IN BROOKLYN

RUTH FENISONG

Chapter 1

Nearly a hundred years ago, before Brooklyn Heights was a center of fashionable life, the Canarsie Indians had grown corn on the tract that stretches between Fulton and Joralemon streets. This tract was then known as the Maize Lands of Meryckawick.

Much later a different brand of corn had sprouted there in the form of pretentious apartment houses overlooking the harbor and casting perpendicular shadows upon the small conservative mansions of early residents.

Brooklyn Heights was fat with old legends, heavily laced with the supernatural. There was, however, nothing supernatural in the scene taking place on the twelfth floor of the newest house in Furman Street, and the scene's protagonist was far from ghostly.

Hastily he interrupted his activity and turned to face the door of the room. Like a quick-change artist he covered his guilty expression with a smile. "Well?" he said.

The man who advanced upon him was not formidable. But spirit made up for his lack of stature. The shock of what he had just witnessed unhinged his jaw, but that impudent "Well?" snapped it back into place. He took an impulsive forward lunge. He tried to grip a shoulder that was high out of reach. Failing to connect, he assumed a fighting stance and launched a series of ineffectual blows.

His target thrust out an arm, successfully preventing further offensive operation. The smile on his face showed signs of wear and tear.

"Now look here, it doesn't do to jump to conclusions. If you'll stop jigging for a moment and take a look for yourself you'll see that all is as it should be. Stop it. I don't want to hurt you. You're making it very awkward for me, and I assure you that all your zeal is misplaced." Dexterously he wheeled the smaller man about. One of his hands served as a clip to fasten the fragile wrists behind the squirming back. "Naturally I admire your loyalty, but—There! Are you ready to listen?"

He received a frustrated nod. Released suddenly, his captive toppled, striking his forehead against the brass fender. That took the fight out of him.

The leading actor looked down. "I'm sorry." He sounded sincere. "You brought this on yourself, you know." His voice was gently reproving. "Let me have a look. Hmmm—a nasty fall. Can you walk? I'll help you." He half carried, half supported the helpless weight out of the room and down the door-lined corridor. "You'll be all right after you've stretched out for a while.

He felt the quiver that ran through the wilted body and was halted by it. He pushed a door open silently, locked it from the inside, and placed his burden on the neat white bed. His eyes wandered about the small interior. Not bad, he thought. Beulah surprises me sometimes. She has her points. His grin was angry. And well she should, with all those angles. Tough about this. But no real harm's been done. If there hadn't been so much on my mind I wouldn't have—Oh well! I can talk myself out of it. I'll convince him that he's been a fool, and when I'm through he'll be glad to say he tripped over a rug or something. I'll tell him that I—

A moan came from the bed.

"Tone it down. There's a good fellow. We seem to be alone, but just in case we're not, you don't want the family to know what an ass you've been. You see—I—"

The man on the bed fluttered his eyelids. He managed to shape a two-syllabled word.

"Sure." Water flowed into a glass from a thermos jug. But before the glass could be held to the pale lips thirst was gone. Everything was gone except the faint echo of the death sound.

There was no expression at all on the face of the living man. He said, "Hell," mechanically, and repeated it several times, almost as though he were reciting an incantation to start the machinery of his brain.

Then he knelt and felt for the dead man's pulse. Gone all right. Oh lord—a nice note! His heart must have been weak. Not my doing. Murder's not as easy as all that. If it were I wouldn't have to—I wish his pockets were stuffed with money. Then at least he'd have died to some purpose and I'd have no more problems. As it is, I don't even dare to investigate for fear—

He could scarcely believe in his own ill fortune. His thoughts shouted so loudly that he clapped a hand to his mouth, as though he were silencing the spoken word. The senseless gesture brought him back to reality, to the solving of the moment. What do I do now? What is there to do except let well enough alone and look shocked when the time comes?

But he couldn't let well enough alone. That was his trouble. He had to gild the lily. His pocket comb was in his hand. Mechanically he was rearranging the dead man's sparse hair. When he had done, the forehead's livid bruise was hidden under a Hitler lock. He put the comb back in his pocket. He thought, I wasn't seeking any special effect, but that ought to trade in for at least a penny's worth of confusion on the part of the police. Just what *am* I trying to accomplish? Oh yes. Suicide. It won't stick, of course, but it will gain time. I need time.

He opened the dead man's collar and removed his tie. He knotted the tie about the thin throat and arranged fingers so that they gripped the loose ends. He worked quickly, and when his self-imposed task was done he used his own white handkerchief to remove prints from all the likely places.

He paused for a moment to estimate the result of his efforts. It seemed perfect. A suicide as ever was. Now if there's no one in the library I'll do another spot of house cleaning, though it's unlikely they'll sense the connection. Still, it pays to be careful.

Just as he was about to quit the room he heard one of the doors in the corridor open. He began to perspire. So he wasn't alone! Someone had been in the apartment all during the incident, or someone had entered while he was too busy to take notice. Who? He hoped that he would never find out. If he did it would force him to more unplanned activity. He had enough trouble, enough ill luck to last a fellow for the rest of his natural life.

He stood listening. He heard no footsteps. Someone had apparently been on the verge of leaving his or her quarters and had thought better of it. Sure enough. There was the door closing again.

He shrugged. I can't stay here. Been here too long as it is. I have an appointment that must be kept. It was stupidity that led me—No use brooding about that. I've got to risk it.

He risked it. Luck was with him. Or seemed to be.

Chapter 2

Marianne rang the bell. She waited impatiently for a moment or two. Then she tried the door, and it was open. She went into the dining room, where the sherry was kept. She poured some and sipped it slowly.

A voice said, "Boo!" and she jumped.

"Dwight! How did you get here?"

"A sensible question. I mushed it all the way from civilization just for five minutes of wishing you luck in your new hogan."

Marianne laughed. A row of uniform white teeth marched gaily across her vivid little face. Her mouth was like the uncertain line a child might draw to depict a spread-winged bird. She settled it and faced the dark young man. "You *are* a fool."

"Then kiss the fool. He's got a business appointment. He wants to snare himself a job so that he can amuse you permanently."

"A business appointment?" Excitement lifted her voice. "Oh, darling, it's just got to jell this time. I feel it in my bones. Tell me—is it for a good job? The kind you really want, I mean. And will you have to go out of town or can we—?"

"Hush. I'm not going to talk about it until it's actually in the bag. I've made the mistake of shooting off my mouth too often. And then—pffft!"

"*You* hush. You mustn't even think defeat. It's going to be all right. See? I'm keeping my fingers crossed." She studied him hungrily. "You look awfully tired."

"I'm nervous is all. I'm always nervous, before an interview."

"Have a glass of sherry. It will pick you up."

"Nope. Just a kiss. I refuse to jeopardize my chances by waving a liquor breath before a prospective employer. Not that yours isn't becoming. Mmmmm."

She was kissing him, standing on her toes to make the grade. He buckled his hands behind her slim straight back. He murmured something that was muffled by her mouth, but she heard it. "Me too. Now let me go before I eat you."

He released her. "That's a smart hat. Been shopping?"

"Yes. I just got in. Beulah will have to do something about the doorbell when she gets around to it. This is really two apartments thrown into one, and the bell doesn't seem to carry into the second half. Either that or Shepard's hearing isn't what it used to be."

"Maybe he's protesting against butling in his new surroundings." Dwight's eyes took inventory of the dining room. "Not that the surroundings look new. Two apartments in one, huh? If it weren't for the fact that the ceilings here are slightly lower, I'd swear you hadn't moved at all. Just when was this unique job of remodeling started?"

"More than a year ago—before priorities set in and made workmen and materials scarce."

"That accounts for it. Not that I wouldn't put my chips on Booming Beulah, war or no war. The old axe has certainly managed to create a reasonable facsimile of the home place on Gramercy Park, right down to the placing of the last chair."

Marianne said severely, "Don't speak so disrespectfully of Grandma until you're really one of the family." Her delicate face grew wistful. "I hope you'll be a member of the family soon, Dwight."

"I can't do more than I'm doing to speed the day."

She sighed. "I know."

"What is it, lovely? Did you mind leaving the Gramercy Park house as much as all that?"

"Of course I minded. It was the only real home I ever had. But it isn't that. It's—it's the twins, mostly. I'm worried about those brothers of mine."

"Forget it. They're swell guys, both of them. They'll manage to get exactly what they want out of life, in spite of Beulah. Are they in?"

"I haven't had time to find out. Hale might be. I think Clement's taking an afternoon course."

"Which door is Hale's?"

"Third down the corridor, to the left."

"If he's there I'll chat with him for a moment before I go to my interview. So long, lovely."

"So long. Call me the moment the job's definite."

"Bless you for your faith." He was kissing her again when Grandma, née Beulah Fitch, came into the dining room.

Grandma, the one-time toast of two continents, whose current name was Mrs. Leonard Roberts, parted the pair with a knife-like gaze. She said, "I won't have it," in a voice that brought to mind a passing calliope.

Marianne leaned against the Sheraton sideboard. Dwight assumed a forthright stance near one of the long windows that faced the harbor. He said aloofly, "I beg your pardon."

Beulah glared at him out of slaty eyes whose narrow lids were tinted with green paste. "And well you should. How old are you, Dwight Cannon?"

He said, "Goody, we're letting our hair down. You tell me your age first."

The calliope was deafening. "Answer my question!"

"Twenty-nine. But if you're thinking of sending me a gift it's too late. My birthday was last month."

"It's too late for more important things than presents. You've been calling on Marianne for nearly a year. If your intentions were serious you'd have got a job long ago instead of frittering away your time. You're nothing but a loafer."

Dwight's face went red, but his voice was pale enough. "I'm an architect, Mrs. Roberts."

"Same thing. Architects are a dime a dozen these days." Her tone was as searing as a blast furnace. "Presumably, too, in spite of your rather handsome figure, you're not even a perfect physical specimen. The fact that the draft board hasn't bothered you would seem to indicate that there's something wrong."

He opened his mouth. Her words blocked his. "I'm not going to argue with you. I'm just going to tell you to leave this house. You're not to see Marianne again. She's wasted enough time on you as it is."

Marianne cried. "Beulah, this is nineteen forty-three."

"I'm aware of that. You're the one who forgets. You ought to busy yourself with war work instead of waiting for this somewhat uncertain apple to fall into your lap."

"For a person who's so concerned with war work you're taking a mighty peculiar stand where Hale and Clement are concerned. How do you reconcile your—?"

The uncertain apple cut in evenly, "Skip it, lovely. I won't come to the house anymore if it raises Grandma's blood pressure. There are plenty of good meeting places outside, even if we make up our minds to exclude the good old private dining rooms and questionable hotels. Of course in a pinch—"

Beulah stuttered without achievement.

Dwight took a leisurely stroll to Marianne's side. "Goodbye for the moment. As long as I'm here I'll make hay." He made hay robustly. "There! And now I'll have a little visit with Hale before I never darken this door again. See you on the way out." He bowed to Beulah and was gone from the room before she could arrange her victory-red mouth for another blast.

She wheeled on Marianne but was halted by the young girl's eyes. Uncertainly she touched her dyed feather bob with almost matching finger nails. She was sixty and did not look a day younger.

After a slight pause she said brightly, "It's a chilly day, isn't it? But I suppose that's to be expected in February. However, there's a nice fire laid in the library. After you've freshened up a bit wouldn't you like to come in and meet Dr. Silk? I've just brought him back from a tour of the warehouse, and I've asked him to stay for cocktails."

Marianne exploded: "To hell with your Dr. Silk and your cocktails. Let's have this out."

"Have this out? Whatever do you mean, child?"

Marianne said with deliberate cruelty, "I mean not all of us can have or even want more than one husband. And not all of us can reach your age and buy the luxury of a fourth mate who was still in bibs when you had just reached the peak of your female-wolf act. And not all of us can afford to set a succession of bargain-counter misfits up in business nor keep creatures like Dr. Silk in the background in an effort to stimulate interest and prove to ourselves that we're still in the running."

Under its lavish cosmetic art Beulah's high-boned face had turned yellow. "How dare you call Leonard a misfit? He's an idealist, and though he may be lacking in practicality, he knows more about antiques than—"

Marianne said, "He should."

"Why, at this moment he has a deal on that will—What was that you said? Oh, you wicked, wicked girl!"

Marianne was alone in the room. She heard her grandmother's

sharp heels dotting the corridor. Childishly she kicked out at a chair that stood on slender reeded legs against the corniced wall. Then she pulled it toward her and sat down, leaning against its perforated baluster. She closed her violet eyes, feeling ashamed and sick. Her thoughts crawled to the surface of a deep self-anger.

So I had to hit below the belt. But that's the only way to get at Beulah—the only way to reach her. And for her whole hectic life she's been guilty of practicing the same technique, getting away with it too.

The shamed feeling was still there. Marianne began to invoke a past, part hearsay, part memory, to justify the scene that had just occurred.

Kind Grandpa Casey, the first and most successful of Beulah's marital essays. The only one that had borne fruit. An industrial Croesus, he had chosen for his mate Beulah Fitch, who stood out angular and smart in an era of opulent flesh. Terribly ambitious, she had thankfully seized Mike Casey's coat tails, using them as a derrick to swing her high above her unaristocratic beginnings. She had married him at seventeen, and whether under bribery or coercion or impatience to have done with such trivia, she had, as soon as possible, catered to his intense desire for a family by presenting him with a daughter. That ended Mike's time of harvest, and with its lonely yield he had to be content until his daughter grew up and produced Marianne and the twins, Clement and Hale ... How good he was to us, thought Marianne.

Mother she hardly remembered, except as an oil painting on the wall of Grandpa Casey's den. Father was also but dimly recalled.

The two had died of influenza within a week of each other, their deaths followed by a nondescript period during which a hazy sense of loss hung over Marianne and her brothers, and Grandpa Casey's was the hand to which they clung.

Then the swift, sharp blow of his sudden death. An infected cut whose poison spread through his entire body because Beulah said that men were babies and shamed him out of calling a doctor until it was too late.

Beulah had recovered quickly. Beulah, freed of the reins, left with a huge fortune. Champing to start again. She was forty-six years old then but seemed scarcely over thirty, even in a strong sun. It was not until just lately, Marianne reflected, that her years had begun to catch up with her.

The exodus to Europe. Marianne, a panic-stricken little girl of eight, shunted off to a boarding school on the outskirts of Paris. Deprived of the companionship of Clement and Hale because Beulah thought that charming male twins would lend an original flavor to her debut in Parisian society. Other smart angular women that year had walked through the Bois sporting pet panthers and kinkajous and other unlikely fauna. But Beulah ended all competition with her brace of human pets.

Faint rumors of the trio had penetrated the walls of Marianne's school. "Beulah Fitch Casey, modern young grandmother, seen at the races with the golden-haired twins." ... "Beulah Fitch Casey becomes Mrs. Morgan Potter" ... "Mrs. Morgan Potter, formerly Beulah Fitch Casey, seeks to divorce her second husband." ... "That chic young grandmother, the ex-Mrs. Morgan Potter, accompanied by the twins and the young Count Gigino Danelli, paid a visit to ..."

Then the return of the Count and Countess Danelli to America, along with the twins and Marianne, whose existence had been remembered just in time. Marianne, a shy, overdisciplined introvert of thirteen, brought back to normalcy by her eleven-year-old-brothers, whose sophisticated sojourn had miraculously left them unspoiled. A lull, until presently the roving eye of the count had won for Beulah the right to cast him aside.

For a good long period after that Beulah must have found the hunting hard. Only this could account for the children's extended time of contentment in the gracious Gramercy Park house. Yes, they had been happy there, even though it had been cleared of all traces of Grandpa Casey and completely refurnished by Beulah. Collecting antiques was one of the occupations of her restless between-husband stages. And she accorded to it far more care and discrimination than she gave to her marriages.

The stalking began again with the advent of Leonard Roberts. He was nearing forty when Beulah flushed him out of a small moribund antique shop in Brooklyn Heights. She had wandered there in search of a pie-crust tilt table, and she had remained to prey.

From the start he couldn't have offered her much of a chase. Her money was the only ammunition she needed. It hit him square on his weak chin. He was near bankruptcy. A man whose fingers ached with penny pinching didn't sweep luxury off his doorstep. So Leonard Roberts had become Grandpa the Fourth. And from all the signs it seemed as though Beulah would hold him to that high office for as long and perhaps longer than he cared to stay. She'd gone so far as to buy into his shop and to expand it to a flourishing business, complete with warehouse in Brooklyn Heights. She'd gone farther than that, preparing to move herself and her chattels, including Marianne and Hale and Clement, to the neighborhood of the new enterprise. In the first flush of conquest, more than a year ago, she had chosen several apartments in a large building on the upper level of Furman Street, supervised the tearing down of partitions, replaced jerry-built doors and windows, and converted the whole into spacious dwelling quarters. And now, at dreaded last, the remodeling was completed and the occupants installed.

Marianne caught her breath. How she and the twins had pleaded with Beulah not to leave the Gramercy Park house. Home to them. But Beulah had insisted that they were in a rut; that change was good for them.

Oh well, all things considered, the actual wrench was less painful than months of dismayed anticipation had foretold. Brooklyn Heights was nothing more or less than a stop-gap, a transitory phase. Clement and Hale had just registered for the draft, having turned eighteen after the new bill went through. If they weren't called by the time the semester at Columbia was over they intended to enlist anyway, in spite of Beulah's continued resistance. And Marianne had Dwight. Job or no job, Beulah or no Beulah, she had Dwight. And he *would* get a job. And until then she'd see him every day, even if meeting places did narrow down to private dining rooms and questionable hotels. Dwight was happiness.

The twins had met Dwight at the home of one of their classmates. In spite of the discrepancy in age they'd become friends with him immediately and invited him to the house. And he'd kept returning again and again because of Marianne. He'd managed to walk a straight line right to her heart, and he was there to stay. No question about that. Bless him.

Marianne, her eyes still closed, heard his voice overflowing from Hale's room. It was as warm and as comforting as a blanket, and she drew it around her and spun dreams for what seemed like a brief moment.

She did not hear the door open. She did not start until a hand slid gently over her small wrist.

"Dwight," she said without opening her eyes.

The voice that answered was desperate. "I must talk to you, Marianne. I can't go on this way."

Chapter 3

At that she opened her eyes wide to take in the expensive tweeds, the sleek black hair, and the untidy mouth of the man bending over her. His slack face was flushed. He was like the central menace in a nightmare. He was Leonard Roberts.

She sought for words that would make him disappear. His

fingers were still clinging to her wrist. She tugged sharply, and he removed them. She said, "Since when are we on private speaking terms? What way can't you go on—and how does it concern me?"

"Marianne, don't look like that. I'm not the black plague."

"That's only one man's opinion."

Bitterness tightened his mouth. "All right. I don't hold it against you. People, especially young people who've never felt want, can't be expected to show tolerance for—well, I know I've been nothing but an object of contempt from the moment that you and your two smug brothers laid eyes on me, but—"

Marianne said, "You've been more than an object of contempt. You've been a messer-up of all our lives. If it wasn't for you we wouldn't be here. We'd be back in Gramercy Park where we belong."

"Believe me, that wasn't my fault. Beulah acted too hastily. I did all I could to prevent the move."

Her voice was unbelieving. "Why?"

"Because I—because I didn't expect to—I didn't expect to be here long."

Marianne said slowly, "You didn't expect to be here long. That makes it worse. You married my grandmother, knowing that she hands out alimony with all the aplomb of a Tommy Manville, and you—"

"No, no. I married her in good faith. I couldn't be expected to know how it would end."

"And just how will it end?"

"Don't make it hard for me. Surely you've guessed. You must have felt my eyes on you hundreds of times. You came into my life right on the heels of the greatest mistake a man ever made. I'm paying for that mistake, but I can't pay forever. I've found a way out. Even at this moment there's a letter in my pocket that will solve everything. And then—all I ask is that you—Please don't turn away."

She made her eyes meet his. She made herself say dispassionately, "You're mad."

"Yes, I'm mad. I'm mad with hunger." He swooped suddenly and gathered her into his arms.

For a space of seconds she was so still that his hold loosened automatically. His surprise was almost tangible. As though, Marianne thought numbly, he'd prepared to lay siege to some object his own imagination had endowed with life and then found his planning ridiculous in the face of its inanimateness.

She could at that point have made her escape without struggle, but in her eagerness to be rid of his touch she struck at him. As though the blow were a waited signal, his arms pulled her close. His mouth crawled over her neck, her cheek. A moment later his mouth spurted blood and he lay sprawled at her feet. And Dwight stood over him.

Dwight said, "From me to you," and dusted off his knuckles. He went on in a polite tone, "The hazards of family life are terrific, aren't they, lovely? But never fear. There'll always be Jack Dalton to ride to the rescue just in the nick of time." His dark, strongly featured face was neither polite nor conversational. It was an unexpurgated edition of one of the lustier writers. "Or maybe I didn't come to the rescue. Maybe you liked it. If you say the word I'll pick him up and he can start where he left off."

Marianne looked at him. She started a weak giggle that changed midseason to a freak storm. She shouted, "I'm not crying because I'm frustrated—or fr-frightened. I'm just angry. I'm going to take a bath."

Leonard Roberts had regained his feet. He was holding a handkerchief to his lip to stanch the blood, and he was making unsteady progress toward Dwight. He halted as Beulah's bellow came from the doorway.

"So you're back, dear boy. Just in time for cocktails. Why, Lion, what have you done to yourself?" She advanced upon him, relentless as an element.

She was wearing green formalized slacks drawn tight as a drum over her meager posterior. A green bandanna covered the violence of her hair. There was fresh green paste on her eyelids, fresh black hair on her lashes, a fresh layer of crimson on her lips. There was nothing in her retouched face to indicate that Marianne's treatment of her had even scratched the surface.

She said brightly, "Don't tell me, Lion, I know. You've been practicing on that new bicycle I gave you, and you've had a nasty fall. Come along and I'll bathe it for you." She led him from the room, somehow creating the illusion that his neck was surrounded by leather and that he was at the end of a leash. She called back over her shoulder, her words hitting Dwight: "Young man, you appear to have an extremely short memory. I thought I ordered you from the house."

Dwight muttered, "Too bad you don't say that to all the boys." The smile he gave Marianne was a little strained. "Poor baby. How long has this been going on?"

"It's spot news," Marianne cried. Or practically, she thought.

He took a few steps in her direction, changed his mind. "Don't brood about it. Any of it, I mean. Comfort yourself with the pretty thought that if that bastard tries again I'll break every bone in his body. No, I won't kiss you. You've had more than your ration.

Besides, I don't like mixed flavors, especially skunk. Go wash yourself nice and new and we'll meet tomorrow at one for lunch at the Russe. But you'll have to pay the check. A date?"

Marianne nodded.

"Wish me luck, lovely."

She wished him luck. She stood quietly until she heard the outer door close upon him. Then she went to her room.

She shed her clothes and made for the bath tub, but the warm scented water did not relax her. She soaped herself moodily and tried to sort things out.

A fine state of affairs? Spot news? Not exactly. She'd caught Leonard staring at her intently more than once in the past few weeks. She'd been too busy to give his newly accented gaze more than cursory thought. Besides, since the coming of Dwight, something had obviously underlined her appearance, so that male eyes quite often turned her way. Not that she minded. A little open admiration was a nice change after years of being just an unwanted child among many unwanted children, consigned to oblivion for most of the year and remembered sporadically by cold, expensive gifts. She'd even, she thought, developed quite a Narcissus complex after Dwight had insisted her deep violet eyes and white skin made her the nearest thing to a woodland flower he'd ever encountered. She'd spent long moments at her mirror, trying to discover just what it was he meant. So that Leonard, for all the attention she paid his silent wooing, might have been a passing stranger who liked her face and paused for a second look. She'd never stopped to think he might be entertaining any real ideas.

She molded her ardent young lips into a grimace of disgust. She stepped out of the tub and began to dry herself slowly. She saw the sleek black hair again, the overlarge humid brown eyes, the untidy mouth. Like a prematurely old boy, she thought and shivered. Dwight's got to take me away. He's got to take me soon. Please God, let his interview pan out. Dwight's sweet. Another man finding us that way might have thought—

She heard the door of her bedroom open, and her heart set up a painful clamor. She shook herself. Idiot! Get hold of your nerves. Quivering like an animal because a broken-down weakling made a pass at you. The episode's been upsetting, all right, but not that upsetting. He wouldn't dare to come to this room. Anyway, he's with Beulah.

She picked up an atomizer and sprayed her small fine-boned body with fresh smelling cologne. She put on a dressing gown and began to sing in a low, hoarse voice. The sound she made reassured her, especially when a familiar tenor took up the tune and carried it to completion.

She laughed a little shakily and stepped into the bedroom. The twins were there, large and fair and sane as daylight. Hale was on the bed comfortably pillow-propped. Clement stood with one foot resting on the dressing table bench. There was no discernible difference between the pair, except that Clement had a small scar on his chin. He was fingering it absently, a sign that his world could stand improvement.

Hale had embarked on a melody of his own, his lung power unimpaired by his half-reclining position. He ended it abruptly when he saw Marianne. "Will some kind lady tell me why we're singing when tears are the order of the week?" He studied her. "Or maybe you've run out of tears. Your eyes have a washed look."

"Soap," Marianne said. "I've nothing to cry about."

"Then Dwight couldn't have been serious when he mentioned in passing that Beulah had given him the bum's rush."

"The bum's rush from Beulah isn't a serious matter. If it came from me he'd really have something to worry about." She removed Clement's foot from the bench and sat down at the dressing table.

"Good girl. Stick with it. You have our blessing."

Clement nodded. He stopped fingering his chin and lighted a cigarette. "We don't know very much about Dwight, but on the surface there doesn't appear to be anything wrong with him that a little money won't cure. As a matter of fact, the same goes for us. Beulah's cut off our allowance."

Marianne turned, lipstick in her hand. "Oh, Clement, why?"

"I wish I knew the answer. If only for my own private satisfaction." Clement sat down on the edge of the bed. "Did you ever know Beulah to have a rational reason for doing anything?" He was eighteen, older by an hour than Hale. Sometimes that hour seemed to extend itself to years of seniority. "It's just a continuation of the old story. We wanted to go to an officers' training school in Baltimore instead of Columbia, but she put the lid on that fast. She couldn't have her little chicks straying too far from the nest. And now she's giving us the same routine about enlisting. 'Wait a bit, dear boys, until your wings are stronger. Even if you should be called I'm sure I can arrange to have you deferred. The Army recognizes the value of education. I don't say there aren't a great many youngsters of your age who *are* equipped to cope with grown-up problems, but I'm afraid I've cosseted you so much you've had no real opportunity to become hatched. And men are wanted, not fledglings. Nobody can accuse me of being unpatriotic.'" He raised his broad shoulders, "*Ad nauseam.* Oh, what's the use? You've heard it all before. You'll hear it all again."

Marianne put down the lipstick abruptly without applying it.

She pushed the powder box aside without lifting the puff to her small straight nose. She brushed the set coiffed look out of her curly hair and took one swift glance at her reflection in the glass. The clean, unglamorous face of a nice child returned that glance. She got up and went over to Clement. She put her arm around his shoulder.

"You've got to cheer up, fellow. You're going into the Army anyway. Nobody can stop you. And until then my allowance will split three ways."

He hugged her. "Aside from Hale, who rates only as a carbon copy, you're my favorite Ramsey. Never mind. Beulah's thought up a mighty tough combination this trip, but I'll manage to puzzle it out."

Hale said. "Who's consoling who?" He added gloomily, "That combination's got me down too. No dough, and leaving Gramercy Park, and—"

Marianne had returned to the dressing table. "Forget Gramercy Park for the time being. Places don't really count. Only people. We'll be together for a while at least. And then, when the war's over, Dwight and I will buy the Gramercy Park house from Beulah, and you and Clement will come to live with us, and we'll be happy ever after."

Hale said, "Dreamer. You still haven't heard the worst. In addition to everything else, this morning Beulah up and gave Shepard a month's notice. With her usual bludgeoning tact she told him he was too old to be useful any longer—and that in these days of sacrifice she thought it a bit ostentatious to employ a butler in an apartment."

Marianne stiffened indignantly. "He's only a few years older than she is, and he's been a part of the household ever since Grandpa Casey's time. He'll be lost without a job, and it isn't likely he'll get another. Can't we do anything?"

"Can we ever? At least it's a comfort to know that economically Shepard has the jump on us. She's given him a fat pension, and Grandpa Casey left him a little something in his will. Funny the way Grandpa Casey provided for everybody but us."

Marianne had often wondered about that herself. She said, "I guess he thought Beulah would do the right thing when the time came."

Clement arose. He looked down at Marianne from a considerable height. "Paint your face, Sis, and get dressed. Beulah sent us here to persuade you to come to the library for cocktails. Dr. Silk's on tap. If you're a good girl he might even cast your horoscope."

Marianne made no move. "From what I've gathered, he's the character who can't make up his mind whether he's a dentist or a soothsayer. Beulah does get to know the queerest people."

Hale sat up. "You say that sight unseen. But we've just had a squint at him, and queer isn't the word. I hope this is one friendship she doesn't push too far. Grandpa the Fourth ain't a prize package, but at least he's the known evil. Where'd she pick Silk up?"

"Mean to say you ducked that story? Beulah's told it over and over again with variations. It was fate. Right after Dr. Ganz retired to Westchester she got a toothache. She happened to be driving near Columbus Circle and she saw Dr. Silk's sign. She took a chance, and that was the beginning."

Clement said, "Yep, and it developed that dentistry is only a side line with him. When he's not pulling teeth he interprets dreams and casts horoscopes."

"No kidding?" Hale yawned. "Well, you could hardly expect a lady of Beulah's temperament to be proof against such a screwy blending of talents. Get a move on, Sis, or I'll fall asleep. This is the most relaxed I've been for a long time."

Marianne hesitated. "Is—is Grandpa the Fourth in the library too?" It wouldn't do, she thought, to give the twins even an inkling of what happened. They'd murder Leonard, or at least perform some drastic action that would shove them farther into the doghouse that Beulah had designed for them.

Hale said, "That athlete will put in an appearance later. At present he's brooding over a split lip on account of he fell off his new bicycle. And that's the one bright spot in this black day."

Marianne went to the closet. She stared for a few moments at the rows of smart, brightly colored clothes. Then, as though she had arrived at an important decision, she reached far back and brought out an oiled-silk garment bag. She hung it over a chair while she rummaged in the shoe rack. "Wait for me in the hall," she said. "I won't be long."

Chapter 4

Clement and Hale set their broad shoulders against the wall outside of Marianne's room, as though they were twin Atlases. Their stance implied a real burden. Hale broke the silence of moments with a determined chuckle.

Clement said, "If it's really funny I'm in the market."

"I was thinking of Grandpa the Fourth falling off his bicycle."

"Then I rescind the offer. Any other day I might buy, but now it only leads me to reflect that Beulah's sacrificed all our cars to the war effort."

"So what? We won't fall. We're bicycle riders from way back."

"Sure, but ours were disposed of long ago, and the way things are we can't depend on Beulah's generosity anymore." He sighed deeply. Away from Marianne he did not trouble to keep up a pretense of lightness. His handsome, sensitive face looked drawn and unhappy. "What we really ought to do is quit school right now and work up a newspaper route so that we can keep our heads above water until we're called or enlist."

Hale said, "I doubt if we'd make the grade. Peddling papers requires more brains than are supplied by a formal education. It looks like our mistake was in not getting jobs long ago, before luxury had time to set in. Remember how we used to plan to run away and make our fortunes, the way Grandpa Casey did?" He looked at his brother anxiously. "What's the matter, Clement? You've been thwarted before, but you've always managed to take it in your stride. What makes this instance so special? As Marianne says, we're going into the Army even if Beulah gets brain waves from here to Easter. Look—I'm your twin. I can't help knowing there's something else on your mind, and I wish you'd break it in half and let me carry my share."

Clement cleared his throat. He said, "I've got something on my mind, all right, something—" Then he said loudly, "Here's your very special sister—the one who offered to split her allowance three ways." He turned to Marianne, framed by the doorway of her room. "That split didn't include your clothes budget. So you can stop practicing for a shortage. Go right back inside and—"

Hale stared at Marianne. He blinked his gray eyes and said, "Hey! This is none of you. Oh, I get it. A baby party. Wait here while I put on my Indian suit."

Marianne raised her unpainted lips in a guileless smile. "I've decided to donate my sophistication to the war effort. I had this orphan-child costume left over from the role I played in the Junior League's Free French benefit. The material's too good to scrap."

"Taking woolen from a moth," Hale said.

Clement studied her suspiciously. "There's more to this than meets the eye. Beulah won't like it, you know. A sense of humor isn't her strong suit."

"I'm not doing it for Beulah," Marianne answered truthfully. "Anyway, not exactly, though she might profit by it in the long run." She took a few dance steps, holding out the cumbersome pleats of the heavy serge skirt. "What's the general effect? Would you say it could be counted on to kindle passion in the male heart?"

Hale snorted. "Paternal passion, maybe. The kind that itches for a hairbrush. No right-thinking male would pause for a second gander. You look every bit of a gawky twelve. I wouldn't try it on Dwight if I were you. Even if he's big enough not to trump up a sudden call to distant parts, he's likely to be jugged for cradle snatching. Go on back and make with the lipstick. There's a lamb. Something about you takes me back to a painful scene in my childhood when Beulah made me play gentleman to the richest and dowdiest little girl in all Europe."

Marianne said in a satisfied voice, "I'm afraid you'll just have to get used to me. Hurry, before Dr. Silk drinks us out of cocktails."

As they entered the library Beulah was turned on to full volume. "Yes, it is a lovely room, isn't it?" she was saying to Dr. Silk. "The only thing in it that isn't an exact duplicate of the Gramercy Park library is the fireplace. I didn't want to have that transported because it would impair the value of the property, so I just searched and searched until I found another that would fit in with the rest of the *décor*."

It was indeed a lovely room. The eight-foot brick fireplace had probably been lifted intact from a country house, but it did well enough here, flanked by deep cream walls half lined with bookshelves. Above the shelves carefully placed mezzotints of court ladies made mellow survey of highly waxed treasures. Soft blue drapes clothed the mullioned windows.

Dr. Silk sat in a fireside chair, one well-shod foot neatly placed on an eighteenth-century open-work brass fenders. In deference to Marianne he rose, placing his cocktail glass on an inlaid mahogany desk. Wrought by Oeben and Riemer, Marianne thought mechanically. Artisans of the Louis Quinze period. And Beulah doesn't even set up a squawk about liquor stains. Gosh! If she hasn't made him a present of her own precious jade cigarette holder! She looked at Dr. Silk with interest.

He caught the look and smiled a bit sheepishly as he placed the jade holder in his pocket. Standing, he crowded out every beautiful thing the room held. He was a giant. The hand he extended in the general direction of the trio was red-haired and vital and lovingly groomed. He presented an ingratiating face featured with small humorous eyes, a big crooked nose, and a wide clown's mouth.

Beulah performed introductions from her place on a fauteuil covered with *point d'Hongrie*. "Dr. Silk—Marianne, Clement and Hale Ramsey, my grandchildren."

"Your grandchildren, Mrs. Roberts? I can hardly believe it. Then surely you couldn't have been much older than this dear little girl when you married."

Beulah said acidly, "I was a great deal younger, I assure you." Her slate-colored eyes went to Marianne, and she boomed,

"Marianne, wherever did you get that highly original costume?"

"It's a uniform," Hale said quickly. "She's just joined a branch of the W.A.A.C.s, spelled Wacks. Going without make-up is her own idea. She's taking a skin cure."

Beulah decided to laugh. She produced a very false titter. "I must ask you to excuse them, Dr. Silk. A private little joke of their own, no doubt."

Someone coughed. Beulah wheeled toward the sound. "Why, Cromwell, how rude of me. You were so quiet you made me forget your presence. Not that you need an introduction to my little brood."

The little brood exchanged glances. Marianne looked at her brother reproachfully. They made barely perceptible signs to disclaim foreknowledge of Beulah's second guest.

Cromwell Proctor emerged from the shadows. He was known to most of his acquaintances as Crummy. His friends had no name for him because his friends were non-existent. The scion of social registrates now living in Havana, he looked like something out of Saki, by Wodehouse. He was very tall and very thin, and his shoulders merged with the rest of his body without declaring themselves. He was Beulah's choice for Marianne, but her campaigning, though loud and insistent, had won for him only the office of Chief Household Joke.

There was no expression at all on Crummy's long bony face as he bent over Marianne's hand. If it weren't for the fact that his words made note of her appearance, she would have sworn that he saw no difference between present garb and usual chic.

What he said in his bloated high voice was, "I'm not sure I don't like you better this way. It lends a certain piquant flavor to my—er—shall I say regard for you?"

She shrugged, without attempting to translate the curious statement. She decided upon an early escape. She knew from experience that Beulah would somehow manage to plant her at his side and that after a short preamble of hemming and hawing, he would start to hark back to his boyhood. His reminiscences always made her feel slightly sick, though on the surface they seemed harmless enough.

"Do sit down, children," Beulah said. "Clement, suppose you play bartender. Dr. Silk mixed the first round—and very good too." She raised her glass in Dr. Silk's direction, smiling apologetically. "I don't usually put my guests to work, but because of the apartment's space limitations I've had to let most of the staff go. And the maid and the cook worked so hard to facilitate our moving that I permit them to take an extra afternoon off whenever possible. So we just struggle along as best we can."

Marianne said abruptly. "Where's Shepard?"

"Sulking, I'm afraid. I gave him notice this morning." She addressed Dr. Silk again. "Somehow I can't help feeling that butlers are a bit out of place in wartime."

Dr. Silk murmured in a silken voice, "Quite understandable."

"Oh, I'm so glad you agree. Shepard seemed to take his dismissal as a personal insult. But even if we hadn't left the Gramercy Park house he'd be forced to go sooner or later. He's really too old to work."

Marianne said, "Nonsense. He was sixty-two on his last birthday." She scowled at Beulah. "Some people don't consider that old. Some people even embark on new business ventures when they're sixty."

"Now, child, don't excite yourself." Beulah spoke through a heavy veil of patience. "And do sit down. It's very inconsiderate of you to keep all the men standing. You and Cromwell must have lots of things far more interesting to discuss than the servant question," she simpered, "though I'm sure that topic, too, will find its place in your conversation in good time. Why don't you—?"

"No, thanks. I think I'll leave Crummy and the servant question to you. I'm going to talk to Shepard. That will give you one less drink to mix, Clement. So long, Crummy. Remind yourself to tell Beulah that thrilling saga of the day you shot the nasty song sparrow who woke you up mornings. It was nice meeting you, Dr. Silk."

As she went from the room she heard Beulah say, "Such a tempestuous little thing. But she *does* have a kind heart."

Yeah, thought Marianne. And what kind of a heart do you have?

She did not really want to talk to Shepard. He might see in her visit to his room some form of reprieve. And, barring a bagful of consolatory phrases, her hands were empty. Damn Beulah! If there was anything at all to this retribution stuff, she was certainly piling up a nice mess of returns for herself. Ever since Grandpa Casey's death Shepard had known no interest in life but the Ramseys. He had kept the Gramercy Park house well in order against their return, had even carried on a fatherly correspondence with the child, Marianne, all during her loveless stay in the French school. For Beulah to dismiss him now was sheer cruelty.

Marianne paused outside his door. Well, I'm here, so I might as well see it through. Perhaps it will relieve him to pour out his woes. She knocked and opened the door without waiting for an invitation ...

She halted upon the threshold. She did not scream. Her voice had suddenly been pushed down her throat where it struggled to untie itself from a series of strongly fashioned knots.

She did not move. She stood in a block of ice, waiting for the warming power of locomotion to free her. And when she was free she turned and ran. She ran straight back to the library, straight to Beulah.

She gripped Beulah by her thin brittle shoulders and shook her until Hale and Clement intervened and pried her loose and pinned her on either side. Then she began to weep, and the tears melted the knots, and her voice came back. "He's killed himself because you fired him. Now are you satisfied? He's killed himself."

As from a great distance she heard a combined intake of breath. Then she heard Beulah quaver, "The child's gone mad. Hale, get a doctor."

Then Clement was shaking her as she had shaken Beulah and shouting, "Stop it at once, Marianne. Talk sense."

"I am," she sobbed. "Shepard's dead. She made him kill himself. He's dead." Suddenly the whole group of incredulous faces printed themselves upon her blurred vision, and she was angered beyond endurance and pulled together by that anger. "You damn fools! Come and see for yourselves."

That emptied the room. They followed her down the corridor to where Shepard's body lay upon Shepard's neat white bed. They looked down and saw his hands gripping the ends of the tie about his throat, mutely confessing to the way in which he had made his escape.

Beulah said on a high, defiant note, "I don't believe it," and Hale did an unprecedented thing. He went to her and wound his fingers around her clenched cold hand.

Dr. Silk stooped over the body, making professional gestures. When he arose he coughed and said, "I'm afraid there's nothing to be done. Very unfortunate. The poor fellow has indeed shuffled off this mortal coil."

Clement spoke in a voice so loud that a flicker of surprise crossed his set face. "He used your tie, Hale, the one you gave him a few weeks ago."

Cromwell Proctor licked his lips and gave tongue with rare enthusiasm. "Won't that be a bit awkward for Hale, old man? I mean—no, of course not—I take it back. If he were really responsible he wouldn't have been such a stupendous fool as to employ a weapon that would implicate him." He added with syrupy sympathy, "I'm sure the police will arrive at the same conclusion."

Clement looked blank. Beulah, leaning heavily against Hale's arm, screeched like a siren, "The police?"

Hale winced as though the sound she made had scraped all his nerves. "I think so, Beulah," He addressed the room at large. "Does anyone know what the procedure is when a man commits suicide? Do we report it direct—or do we get a doctor and let him report it?"

There was a moment of silence. Then a curious thing happened. All eyes turned in their sockets and focused upon Cromwell Proctor. He had let out a short "yip," as though the question were a bone intended solely for him. He seemed prepared to extract every ounce of nourishment from it.

Hale said in exasperation, "Do you or don't you know?" and the others waited.

It was Crummy's hour and he loved it. "I'd advise you to call the police at once. Because this isn't suicide, you know. It's murder."

They were staring at him now, as scientists might stare at some microbic find unwarranted by the amount of research involved. He met the stares with a bland arrangement of his horsy features. "Your butler was a fragile creature, wasn't he? I doubt if he could have summoned either the will power or the physical strength to strangle himself in just that way."

Clement said in bitter anger, "Too bad you didn't confide your doubts to him before he made the attempt. It might have given him pause."

From the doorway Leonard Roberts called petulantly, "What is this—a mass meeting?" Robed in rust-colored brocade, he entered the room on matching slippered feet. The body on the bed served as a strong magnet. It drew his humid brown eyes before a single mouth could release a single word.

Beulah made a dash for him, seized his arm, and cried hoarsely, "Oh, Lion, don't look! Isn't it dreadful? He's committed suicide. But Cromwell says he was murdered."

"Murdered," Leonard repeated. He bit his lip and grimaced with pain. The wound inflicted by Dwight stood out like a small black bug.

Crummy came into the limelight again. "It's obvious, isn't it? To us, I mean. Not to the fellow who did it, of course, because he couldn't have been very familiar with cause and effect. You see, when a person's strangled his face gets purple, and your butler's is as waxy as a candle."

Dr. Silk slapped his gargantuan thigh. He roared so lustily that there was a concerted movement of cringing away from the sound. "By George, he's right! No trace of a cyanotic condition. How dull of me not to notice it. Belonging to a branch of the profession myself, I should have—"

Clement cleared his throat. He addressed Beulah huskily. "Your precious guests are talking rot. No one would murder Shepard.

He was a harmless old man and he took his own life for obvious reasons." His voice became a riderless horse, galloping out of control. "You know yourself that it isn't necessary to murder servants when you want to get rid of them. You just—you just—" Beulah's face stopped him. He made a helpless gesture. "I'm going to call the police. Get everybody out of here, Hale, but don't let them get out of the house—with special emphasis on our two experts. It would be a great pity if the authorities weren't given an immediate opportunity to plumb their unexpected depths."

Cromwell muttered, "Oh, I say," in a deprecatory way. Dr. Silk assumed the quasi-sad attitude of a performing clown. "There's no need for you to take that tone, young man. We were only trying—"

Marianne had been staring numbly at Shepard. She cried suddenly, "His hair. He never did that to his hair. Fix it. It's horrible."

Chapter 5

Detective Sergeant Gridley Nelson braked his car in front of headquarters, and sat there thinking. He had a chip on his shoulder. And because it was an unaccustomed object for him to be carrying around, he regarded it with loathing and determined to be rid of it at the earliest possible moment.

He was a man in the early thirties, with a pointed olive-skinned face and an astonishing bonnet of white hair that came up in curly wires, as lively as antennae. He had sad deep-dug brown eyes and a plastic mouth, and his brow was good and his chin was good and his nose excellent both in form and utility.

He had graduated from Princeton and engaged in various activities, ranging widely from Little Theater to the laboratory of a criminologist. Yet none of these occupations had satisfied him. His need was for direct contact with people. Not contact across the footlights or through cold research, but face to face. So he had kept on seeking his niche, for although his mother had left him a comfortable income and he did not have to work at all, an idle life was untenable to a man of his disposition. And at last, by process of elimination, he had joined the Homicide Squad.

There in four busy years he had gone from raw rookie to detective sergeant. He had no quarrel with his present status. Nor did he wish for further promotion. During his childhood ambition for high office had encountered an early frost while he watched with mounting distaste the machinations of his politician father. He was content, a round peg in a round hole. He could reach out and touch people and by his inordinate sympathy and understanding discover what it was that made them fall out of line.

The chip had been placed upon his shoulder by the absurd behavior of Inspector Waldo Furniss, chief of the Homicide Squad.

The inspector had been his friend ever since the time that Nelson had first braved his office for an interview. Until that meeting the inspector had embraced three loves: his work, the limelight, and food. And to this list the young white-haired rookie had almost instantly been added, his position cemented by common interests and much good talk when work was shelved for the day. From the outset Nelson had been accorded far more license than is generally granted to an underling by a superior officer. He grew to have a warm regard and a definite respect for his chief, who twitted him for his university background, his hoary locks, and his unorthodox procedure in handling a case. The old man boasted that he himself was a public-school man, not in the English sense, but in good old American slum tradition. Yet he often surprised Nelson by the evidences of self-education that put more formal methods to shame.

Not once in four years had Nelson been dropped from the inspector's preferred list. The trouble was that another item had slipped. The old man's work no longer held first place. Or, for that matter, any place.

The war had taken many lives and altered many more. Police departments throughout the United States had been asked to cooperate closely with the FBI. And that, thought Nelson, was as it should be. It was the inspector's interpretation of cooperation that was wrong. He was so busy pushing his handsome hawk nose into matters which, under ordinary circumstances, would have been outside his realm that the murder of a stray civilian here and there seemed suddenly beneath his notice. Always in demand as an after-dinner speaker who'd never been known to refuse to project his personality at a benefit, his days were now filled by trips to Washington, making appeals for sundry relief funds, selling war bonds, and giving morale talks over the radio. He was rarely to be found in his office, and more and more the onus of the shorthanded department descended upon Nelson.

Something's got to be done about it, Nelson thought grimly. I've not even managed a conference with him in several weeks ... He left his car and began to climb the steps of headquarters.

The world's mass slaughter was having its effect upon private aberrations. It seemed to foster the idea that life was a thing of no great moment, after all, and that the only way to settle a personal feud was by total extinction of the adversary. Thus, crime in the city had taken an upward curve, and Nelson had more than he could handle. But it was not because of the extra work that he was so angered. It was because of the increasingly hostile criticism being directed against the oblivious old man. He had heard plenty of it this afternoon when he visited the district attorney's office to wind up a case. He would have to set the inspector right—and fast—before the cries for blood turned to action and the conveniently extended neck fell beneath the political ax.

The policeman at the outer desk looked up as Nelson entered the building. "In the nick of time, Sarge. There's a call just came for you. Will you take it here?"

Nelson came into the grudgingly circle of light cast by the desk lamp. He said, "Damn," without force. Then he shrugged and said, "Maybe it's a personal call, Jerry."

Jerry's voice was sympathetic. "You don't get much rest, do you, Sarge? Clean up one mess and fall right into another. But this time you're in luck. It's a colored lady—says she works for you."

Nelson reached for the telephone. Sammy's voice came through, peaceful and warm. "Is this you, Mr. Grid-dely? I hope you going to excuse me calling your place of business, but you ain't been home for two nights and I worried you sick or harmed."

"Sorry, Sammy, I meant to call, but I didn't get a chance."

Sammy's voice was pitying. "That job sure keep you jumping."

"It sure does," Nelson said with fervor.

"You get home tonight, Mr. Grid-dely. I going to cook you something really fine."

"I'll try, Sammy. But if I'm not there by eight, you leave. Meantime, keep your fingers crossed that nothing comes up to detain me."

"I good and crossed all over. I like to lay my eyes on that Mr. Chief. I like to tell him he ain't acting right. I read in the papers about them speeches he keep making and I know good he leaving you to do all that dirty murder business by your own poor self. You going to mess up your health if you don't get some eating and sleeping. You come home tonight. Hear?"

Nelson grinned as he replaced the receiver. He had a three-room housekeeping apartment off Lexington Avenue in the Fifties, and it had been a pretty catch-as-catch-can affair until he persuaded Sammy to take charge. Persuaded, because it had been necessary to overcome her vast distaste for minions of the law and her fear that her social status in Harlem might be impaired if her connection with Nelson became known.

Sammy had been left over from a case successfully brought to conclusion by Nelson and Furniss in the days when Furniss was, above all else, a sleuth. Her simplicity and her dignity and, not least, her supreme artistry in the kitchen had won both men. And she had so far conquered her aversion to their chosen work as to lend occasional aid when it seemed to her that they were being blocked by nothing but a lack of plain common sense. Furniss had gorged himself upon many of her excellent dinners ...

A gleam entered Nelson's brown eyes. He said to Jerry, "Do you happen to know where I can reach the chief?"

"Believe it or not, he's in his office. But busy. He gave orders not to be disturbed by anyone short of J. Edgar Hoover. You know how it is with him these days. He's a one-man war effort. He—"

Nelson heard only the first part of Jerry's speech. His long legs had carried him out of earshot. He made a right turn and strode down a gloomy hall. Without breaking his speed he turned again and entered the office of Inspector Waldo Furniss.

The old man's silvery head was bent over his desk. He seemed to be memorizing something. One hand waved a typewritten script. The other was spread out against his heart. No sound issued from his lips, but they were wrapping themselves around words at a furious rate. He looked like a ham actor in a silent movie.

Nelson slammed the door behind him, and Furniss dropped the pose. He shouted angrily, "I gave orders not to be disturbed."

Nelson said, "Excuse it. I heard rumors that you'd resigned. I just wanted to check."

Bright blue eyes fastened themselves on Nelson's face. Furniss smiled cordially. "Well—well! Come in, son, come in. We haven't had a get-together in weeks, have we?" He sighed theatrically. "In this chaotic world a man hasn't much time for his friends."

"A man doesn't seem to have much time for his job either," Nelson said.

Furniss managed to look as though he had been unexpectedly bitten by a house pet. "I'm inclined to think you're overstepping, Grid."

Nelson did not answer.

Furniss continued uncertainly, "Is there something on your mind?"

"Nothing special. Of course I've had little opportunity for sleep lately, and I can just vaguely remember the size and shape of my own living quarters, and together with a much-depleted crew I've been piddling around with five or six small murder cases in the last few weeks, but outside of that there's not a great deal on my mind."

Furniss cleared his throat. "I'm not exactly fiddling while Rome burns, Grid. I'm engaged in important—"

"You're engaged in something that thousands of others without previous commitments could tackle cheerfully and well. You always said you intended to die in harness, Chief."

"And so I do— and so I will."

Nelson shook his white head. "That isn't the way I heard it. I just came from the district attorney's office. What I said to you about being engaged in matters that others could do as well would be almost a direct quote if I added that they could do it without breaking their oaths as public servants."

Rage blackened the handsome old face. "So they're at it again!"

"Yes. And this time it's not just talk—and it's not unjustified talk. They mean business."

"The hell I care what those zero brains mean!" He lowered his voice suddenly, dipping it in pathos. "I suppose it might appear to the uninitiate that I'm neglecting my job, Grid, but I should have expected better understanding from you. After all, I know your capabilities. I know the work of the department is in good hands. I'm the one who groomed you for it, and if it wasn't for the fact that you've so mulishly resisted promotion I could have fixed it so that you'd—"

Nelson decided that if ever there was a time and place for lying, this was it. "Could I count on your understanding, Chief, if I told you that I'm seeking promotion of a different sort. That I've decided to accept a commission in the Army Air Corps?"

"Grid!" It was a howl climbing right up out of the old man's chest. "You can't do that—it would be—it would be shirking. You're needed here. What you're doing is specialized work—a far greater contribution than anything any Tom, Dick or Harry could accomplish in the armed—" He came to an abrupt stop. The telephone rang, and he seized it as eagerly as he might seize the hand of a friend in need.

"Hello?" Then he grunted, "Yes, hold on." He spoke to Nelson without lifting his eyes from the phone. "Jerry's got a call for you. Want to take it here?"

Nelson ran a strong-fingered hand through his hair. He said tonelessly, "It's probably just another small murder. Are you sure it won't disturb you?"

Furniss muttered, "All right. You've made your point."

The telephone receiver gave out a series of inarticulate sounds, like a patient under ether. Nelson ministered to it without tenderness. Jerry's voice said, "You're in again, Sarge. Some excited citizen wants to discuss a brand-new stiff with a responsible party. He's all yours." With a click he bowed himself off the line.

Nelson said, "Detective Sergeant Gridley Nelson speaking ...

Yes ... Yes ... Repeat that address slowly ... Your name? ... All right ... See that the body isn't disturbed. Close the room. No one's to leave ... Yes ... Right away." He hung up.

He waited a moment. Then he took the receiver up again. "Jerry? Rustle up Sugs. Tell him to drop what he's doing and bring a fresh notebook. Get Dr. Perry. I'll meet them at the desk." He started for the door.

Furniss said, "Grid?"

"Yes, Chief?"

"Anything juicy?"

"A butler in Brooklyn Heights."

"Oh. People have no business with butlers these days."

"Someone else evidently had the same conviction."

"Whose butler was he?"

"A lady named Mrs. Leonard Roberts. Her grandson put in the call."

"Mrs. Leonard Roberts? Sounds familiar." Then Furniss whistled. "I've got it." He recited rapidly, "Née Beulah Fitch, known to the sophisticated public on two continents as 'Booming Beulah'—before you started taking notice, Grid. The young grandma—twins." He seemed excited. "I remember mooning over her career when I was a shaver. She spelled glamour to me—stuff that doesn't exist nowadays in spite of moving picture advices. She—"

Nelson said casually, "You wouldn't care to continue your reminiscing en route?"

The look that crossed the old man's face was one of genuine regret. "I'm due on the air in less than an hour. Can't help it. I promised. But—"

"But!" Nelson said. At the door he halted. "The Army grows more tempting every minute—especially since I expect what personal life I have to be disrupted by Sammy's departure."

"Sammy's departure?" Furniss repeated. He sounded hungry and homesick. "I thought she was anchored for all time. Why should she leave?"

"Because she can't cook to an empty house, and that's just what she's been doing lately."

Furniss licked his lips. He said sheepishly, "I don't seem to recall my last square meal, Grid. Nothing but worn-out melba toast and the discouraged chicken they dish up at benefits." He took a deep breath. "How's about inviting me to one of Sammy's spreads?"

"When?"

"Tonight? After dinner we could discuss Beulah's butler."

"All right. I'll phone and tell Sammy to expect you." He whisked his broad smile out the door before Furniss glimpsed it.

Chapter 6

Beulah said nervously, "I think I heard the bell. Yes, there it is again. It must be—"

Hale broke from the group and ran down the long hall. He opened the door upon the party from headquarters. He had been expecting uniforms, so he blinked when he saw the three men in plainclothes. One was large enough to make the black bag he carried look like a child's toy. One was so patently an ex-harness bull that not even rompers and a long blond wig would have submerged his calling. The third had startling white hair, a well-tailored suit, and a cultured voice. He seemed to be top man of the outfit.

Hale led the newcomers to the library. There the white-haired man's eyes focused upon the raised strained faces for an instant, and the click of his mind's shutter was almost audible as it snapped the picture. He asked who had put in the call, and when Clement stepped forward he motioned him to one side. Then pleasantly, without attendant fuss, he herded everybody else to a small sitting room that Beulah had designed for her private use. He requested them to wait there until he returned, and with Clement as guide he and his entourage went to the room that had been Shepard's. They closeted themselves within.

Presently Clement rejoined Beulah and the rest. They swamped him, and when he could lift his head above the morass of questioning he said, "They call it murder. They've sent for the photographers and the fingerprint men."

Beulah looked stunned. Marianne sat down. Chalk was added to Leonard's pasty cheeks. Dr. Silk just didn't say, "I told you so" and Cromwell dressed his face in a smug smile. Hale looked at his brother out of his brother's clear gray eyes, almost as though he were engaged in submitting a problem to his own subconscious.

After a few moments Hale's ex-harness bull appeared. "The sarge wants to ask you folks a few things. He says he'll take you separate, and would the one who found the stiff come first?"

Marianne identified herself. Her nervousness was so apparent that the twins advanced protectively. The policeman gestured them back. "She don't want no escort but me," he said, and offered her his arm. "Nothing to be afraid of, little lady. The sarge won't bite." Almost tenderly he steered her to the library, where Detective Sergeant Gridley Nelson waited.

Oddly enough her panic bowed itself out at her first consciously recorded impression of the man. First she saw that he was built like a tall V. Then she saw his hair, as white as whitewash, over a clever pointed face. Young, she thought, in spite of that hair. Young and nice and not a bit official. And her heart unloaded some of its cargo, and she smiled an involuntary smile.

He answered it, introducing himself in a deep, reassuring voice. He asked her to sit down while the policeman looked uncertainly about the room, discovered the Oeben and Riemer desk, hesitated, then took the plunge. The stenographer's notebook that he placed upon the beautiful inlaid surface was like an ugly invader of a peaceful land.

She could have sworn that the detective sergeant opened his expressive mouth to object to the sacrilege but what he said after a slight pause was, "Don't let the note-taking disturb you. Sugs is one of the department's best clerical men, and he has to keep in practice. May I have your name, please, and your place in this household?"

"Marianne Ramsey. I'm Mrs. Roberts' granddaughter." Her violet eyes were on Sugs's moving pencil. She continued in a clear voice, as though she were dictating to him: "We moved here three days ago because Beulah—because Grandma wanted to be near Grandp—her husband's business. He deals in antiques, and his shop and warehouse are in Brooklyn Heights." She stopped. Then she said, "I'm telling you this because it—it kind of explains—"

He nodded and she continued: "Shepard was our butler. He'd been with the family for years, but when we moved to the apartment, Beu—Grandma decided that he wasn't necessary anymore, so she told him this morning. And I guess he couldn't stand it, so he—" She broke off. She raised both hands to her forehead and pressed with the tips of her fingers. She said helplessly, "But he didn't—did he? I mean Clement said it wasn't suicide—it was murder. So what I'm telling you has nothing to do with it."

Nelson answered gravely, "We're both starting from scratch, but it's been my experience that most crimes have phenomenally long tentacles that reach out and touch everything within a radius of miles. So I find that the more I follow the loops and twists of those tentacles, the more hope I have of arriving at a solution." He smiled suddenly. He said, "I shouldn't be surprised if I'm talking way over your head. You've been expressing yourself so well that I've forgotten you're just a little girl."

"A little girl?" Her widened eyes doubted his sanity. Then she understood. "Oh—this dress! I put it on for—for fun. I'm twenty. You're not talking over my head. You want me to tell all, even if I can't see its significance. But there's nothing more to tell. I've finished."

He did not, she was thankful to note, pursue the matter of her costume. He couldn't be a very good detective, in spite of his far-reaching tentacles. He said, "Then suppose I tell you a few things—just to keep this from being the shortest interview on record."

She sat at attention, her hands clasping in her lap.

He studied her. "I'm taking a chance, you know. Detectives aren't supposed to give information to suspects. And you're as much a suspect as anyone else."

"I—suspect!" Shock made the words taper to a squeak.

"But if everyone's conscience is as clear as yours seems to be there's no need to adhere too closely to the rules of my job."

She relaxed. She said earnestly, "Of course there isn't. I can tell you right now that the only one of us whose conscience isn't clear is Beulah—and that's understandable." She shook her head. "Now I'm confused again. But surely there must be a mistake about Shepard being murdered."

"There's no mistake. Dr. Perry, our medical examiner, is a very precise man. Like most scientists, he hates to give an opinion that isn't substantiated by laboratory work. But his stand of the moment is that Shepard's death was caused by a blow—a blow which might not have resulted in death unless Shepard had a weak heart."

"He did have a weak heart. He's been receiving treatment for the past few years. That part's true enough. But the rest is fantastic."

"You saw the bruise on his forehead, Miss Ramsey."

She began to tremble. The words shook loose from her lips. "Not at f-first. I saw his hair—c-covering it—and then Crummy leaned over and pushed the hair back." She did not seem able to stop. "Crummy smiled. His teeth showed."

Nelson put a cigarette into her hand and lighted it for her. After she had taken a few puffs he said, "Crummy?"

"Cromwell Proctor." She set the cigarette down carefully. "Why should anyone want to kill Shepard? He's not—he wasn't a man who quarreled with people—or asked for violence. Besides, even if some maniac did want to hurt him, how could he possibly sneak into his room to do it?" She searched Nelson's face. It wasn't legible. A thought made sudden and welcome visitation. She voiced it eagerly. "Perhaps Shepard just bumped his head himself, by accident, and it ached, so he went to his room to rest and died because the blow was too much of a shock for his heart to stand."

"An acceptable theory. I wonder it didn't occur to the murderer before he went out of his way to set the stage for suicide. Unless Shepard knew he was going to die and knotted the tie about his own neck to punish your grandmother—make her feel guilty for firing him after so many years of faithful service. Would you say he was a man to dramatize himself in such a way?"

"Oh no—never."

"Then we're back where we started." Nelson sauntered over to one of the bookshelves and made leisurely inspection. His long fingers moved restlessly, as though they might be aching for contact with the leather bindings. When he returned his attention to Marianne he slid the interview back to a question-and-answer basis so smoothly that she did not notice the shift.

"Can you tell me why Shepard should write a letter to your brother Clement, Miss Ramsey?"

She was interested but not startled. "Lately, you mean?"

He nodded.

"No, he used to write to all of us when were in Europe, but now that we're home why should he?"

"I don't know. The only reason I can think of for writing to someone under the same roof is not being on speaking terms with him."

"What do you—? *Did* Shepard write to Clement?"

"He started to."

She said scornfully, "Then you'll have to find another reason—or ask Clement. He'll know. He was Shepard's favorite. Shepard would never stop speaking to him."

He did not give her a chance to think about it. "Were you at home all day, Miss Ramsey?"

"Not all day. I left the house at about nine-thirty. I had an appointment for a shampoo and set."

He was looking at the natural sweep of her dark curly hair. He said casually, "A very artistic job. It hasn't the set look I've come to associate with beauty salon products."

She blushed. "I didn't like it. I combed it out." She rushed on. "When I left the hairdresser's I had lunch at the Marengo and then I did some shopping. I came back here about a quarter after four."

"Was anyone home?"

"No—that is, yes. Hale was, but I didn't know that until later. I rang the bell and nobody answered." She swallowed. She said, "Do you think Shepard—?"

Nelson nodded. "According to Dr. Perry's best judgment, he died somewhere between the hours of three and five. That's a confidence I wouldn't want you to carry further."

"I don't run around revealing confidences." But her vehemence had a puzzled note.

"Did you have a key to the apartment?"

"Yes, only I haven't been using it. Shepard's always—"

"Did you use it today?"

She shook her head. "The door was open."

"And yet you asked how anyone could have sneaked in to kill Shepard?"

"But I've told you what Shepard was like. Why should he be killed?"

"Any number of whys. He might have intercepted a burglar. There are quite a few valuables lying around loose, aren't there?" His eyes came to rest upon an ornate gilded corner cupboard. Its shelves bore a variety of small ornaments wrought in silver and gold and jade. He went a little closer to it. He called to Marianne over his shoulder: "Would you mind coming here a moment?"

Marianne got up and moved to his side.

He looked down at her. "Do you know this cabinet pretty well?"

She said precisely, "I know that Beulah attributes it to Boucher, one of the foremost of the rococo artisans."

His eyes were amused. "Very instructive, but not exactly what I had in mind. I was referring to the contents."

"Oh." Then she said resentfully, "I've been hearing so much stuff about furniture ever since Beulah went into the business that I say things like that in my sleep. Yes, I guess I know the contents pretty well—if it's the same as it was in Gramercy Park. And it isn't likely Beulah's changed it much. She hasn't had time."

"Would you say offhand that anything's been disturbed?"

"I don't think so. But then, when you've looked at a thing day in and day out for a long time, you get so you don't see it very clearly." She leaned toward the cabinet. "Wait a minute. It's odd that the little gold man isn't beside his little gold horse. They belong together. I've seen Shepard dust these ornaments many times, and he's always been most particular about the way he replaces them." She looked at Nelson.

"Is anything else wrong—anything missing?"

"Everything seems to be there, but that little gold man looks awfully strange standing by himself. I'm sure any one of the family would notice that he was out of place. You must be right. Someone did get in and try to rob us, Shepard caught him at it. Someone we've none of us heard of—a common ordinary burglar." Her eyes climbed to his, pleading for confirmation.

He did not respond. He walked over to Sugs and whispered something. Sugs stopped writing for a moment and muttered, "Yeah, sure."

Nelson came back to Marianne. "What did you do after you got in?"

She answered mechanically, her thoughts still occupied with the burglar theory. "I was a little tired. I went to the dining room and drank some sherry. And then Dwight—" She bit her lip. She wished she had left Dwight out of it. He had troubles enough of his own. She didn't want him to be bothered by detectives.

"Dwight?"

"He—he's not here now. He left long ago."

"But he was here today?"

"Yes." She made up her mind quickly. This man had said she was as much a suspect as anyone else, which boiled down, which must surely boil down, to the fact that nobody connected with the household was suspect. Well, she wouldn't give him reason to change his mind by creating the impression that either she or Dwight had a thing in the world to hide. So she made her voice calm and slow. "Here are a few of your far-reaching tentacles served up on a platter. Dwight is Dwight Cannon, and I'm going to marry him."

He waited.

She said, "I'd only been here a few minutes when he dropped in to wish me luck in my new home."

"Did he ring the bell too?"

"No, he got in the same way I did." She went on defiantly, "He liked Shepard, and Shepard approved of him, just in case you're entertaining any foolish ideas." She searched his face again. She decided that behind it foolish ideas would receive no courtesy at all.

"Will you tell me just what you and Dwight did up to the time he left?"

After that she smiled faintly. She couldn't help it. But he seemed to ignore the smile. He said, "I mean roughly, of course. And carry your recital to the moment when you discovered Shepard."

Marianne's smooth forehead wrinkled. "I was with Dwight for a little while. Then he went to Hale's room to see if he was there, and they had a talk. Then either Leonard was in or came in, because he stepped into the dining room—" She paused, expecting Nelson to ask who Leonard was, but he did not interrupt. "And—and Dwight came back to say goodbye, and—let me see—oh yes, Beulah came home. She'd been showing Dr. Silk through the warehouse—and Cromwell Proctor, too, I guess. And she invited them to the house for cocktails, and they were waiting in the library—that's this room. Beulah went off with Leonard to—to talk to him, and Dwight left, and I went to my room to bathe. While I was dressing Clement and Hale came to get me, and we went to the library for cocktails. Only Cromwell was there and I don't like him, and Beulah has plans for us, so I excused myself and said I was going in to console Shepard for being fired. So I—so I found him."

Until the end of her recitation she had been pleased with herself for skirting the details so neatly. But a sudden vision of Shepard's body made her carefully guarded words seem cheap and unimportant. Tears came into her eyes.

Nelson took out his own handkerchief, looked at it absently, and replaced it in his pocket. "You knew he was dead at once? You didn't touch him to find out?"

"No, I didn't touch him. I knew. He was waxy, and there was the tie around his throat—and his hands gripping it. I ran back to the library to tell the others. And when they believed me they came."

"Did you see anyone touch anything in the room?"

"Dr. Silk touched the body. And then Crummy did. That was all."

"Who suggested that it might not be suicide?"

"Crummy did—and Dr. Silk backed him up."

"Let me see if I've got you all straight. The twins are—"

"My brothers, Clement and Hale. Clement is the one who phoned you."

Nelson said, "Yes. Clement has a scar on his chin which might almost have been put there deliberately to set him apart from Hale."

"You really are a good detective after all." She colored. "I mean—"

He chuckled. "You mean you've been entertaining doubts?"

She said quickly, "You're right about the scar. Once when they were kids they got mad at each other, and Clement said he wouldn't have people calling him Hale by mistake, so he nicked himself with Grandpa Casey's old razor as a kind of distinguishing mark." Then she said, "That was just kid stuff. He hasn't a bad temper anymore. He's sweet."

Nelson did not comment. "And the thin lady in slacks is your grandmother?"

Marianne's "Yes" was not enthusiastic.

Nelson said, "But I can't seem to settle upon anyone who might be your grandfather."

"That's because you're probably looking for a long gray beard. Don't you ever read the scandal sheets? We are now in the reign of Grandpa the Fourth, otherwise known as Leonard Roberts. He succeeded Grandpa Danelli, who succeeded Grandpa Potter, who succeeded real Grandpa Casey."

"Oh," Nelson said. She could almost hear him rummaging in the closets of his memory, see him emerging with an armful of facts concerning Beulah. He did not air them. Instead he asked, "Is Leonard Roberts the bony horse without shoulders?" Then he grinned apologetically. "I'm something short of poetic when it comes to description."

She was entertained. "You muffed that one. It's apt enough, but it applies to Crummy—Cromwell Proctor. Leonard's the old-young man with the coal-black hair."

"And the newly minted cut on his lip. How did he get it, by the way?"

She answered innocently, "Beulah said he fell off his bicycle. You see, our cars have been sacrificed to the war effort." She continued with no pause, "The red-headed giant is Dr. Silk, Beulah's dentist. That takes care of everybody."

There was a rather long silence during which Marianne hoped that he had dropped the matter of Leonard's cut lip. She was not ashamed of Dwight's action, but the affair seemed too sordid to become the property of a stranger. And this man *was* a stranger, even though he had somehow mastered the dangerous trick of appearing to be an old friend. Dangerous, she reflected, for if a person really had something to hide—

He dismissed her with pleasant finality. "Thank you for your cooperation, Miss Ramsey."

As she went from the room she heard him tell Sugs to call Mrs. Roberts.

Chapter 7

It was seven o'clock when Nelson and Sugs left the Roberts apartment. Dr. Perry had departed about an hour ago, hitching a ride on the morgue wagon that came for Shepard's body.

Nelson had paused in the lobby for a brief conversation with the switchboard operator. She had just come on to relieve the day girl. She told him that they were the only two employed. There had been a couple of doormen, but first one and then the other left for war jobs. The manager was finding it difficult to replace them. He had advertised, but—Lucky for him that the elevators in the house were automatic. Yes, Nelson could take a look at the switchboard chart showing the location of tenants. What was it all about? Sure, she'd be glad to cooperate ...

The first lap of the drive to headquarters was silent. Sugs had a healthy respect for Nelson's thought processes and did not wish to disturb them. So he squirmed and fidgeted, manfully suppressing the talk that was an ache behind his lips. Finally he burst forth in spite of himself.

Nelson returned from his abstraction like a man whose attention had been torn from the pages of a thoroughly engrossing book. "Did you say something?"

Sugs repeated, "The kid's the only one I'd give a clean bill of health."

"The kid?"

"Yeah—the little lady. Sure—I know she's twenty. I got it right here in my notebook." He patted his coat pocket. "But the way I seen her first is what sticks in my mind. She didn't look more than a scared sprout who'd just had a run-in with the bogeyman." He spat compassionately. "Do you suppose she was really sporting that getup for fun?"

"What do you suppose?" Nelson's interest was flattering.

Sugs said in a pleased voice, "Well, I dunno. Maybe Grandma dresses her that way to make her own self look younger. Some of them rich dames would go through hell and high water to give old age the miss."

"If this deep thinking on your part has a bottom to it how do you account for the fact that the twins aren't wearing Buster Brown collars and short pants?"

"Boys is different. They'd squawk. Especially those two."

"From what I've seen of your little lady, I'd expect her to do a bit of squawking herself."

"Well, I dunno. Say, Sarge, one of them twins took it mighty big when you questioned him."

"That's true enough," Nelson said. "But I hope his behavior was due to nothing more than the usual queasiness of the average citizen for the police."

Sugs took a deep breath. "You wouldn't want this to be an inside job, would you, Sarge, on account of they're your kind? College and stuff. But, like the chief always says, you gotta take crime where you find it. Not that I'm holding out for an inside job, myself, but still and all barring the kid, I wouldn't put it past any one of the others." His round knobby face took on an avid listening look, as though he could not bear to miss even the echo of his own voice.

Nelson, watching him, thought, Poor Sugs. It's so seldom he's allowed to air his deductions that rare opportunities have an almost alcoholic effect. Sugs, born Joseph Sugsden, of ambitious parents, had once been described by the chief as the only clerical man in captivity without an ounce of grammar to his make-up. He hated his stenographic job and laid his status in the department to the door of his mother, who had marched him off to business school before he reached the age of consent. "Only for that," he made repeated complaint, "I'd be a first-class detective, but the chief thinks my pothooks is so elegant he won't ever let me try my hand at the real McCoy." On one occasion, much against his better judgment, the chief had permitted Sugs to participate in "the real McCoy." After the repercussions died down the chief seemed to appreciate the pothooks more than ever. But Sugs intended to die trying for further chances to prove his latent genius as an up-and-coming sleuth.

Emboldened by the fact that Nelson seemed to be listening, he continued importantly, "You're a funny kind of a cop, Sarge. Firstly, you got a heart like dish of hot mush. Secondly, you got a pre— pre—you got a ready-made picture of murderers in your head. You think they look like that there George Raft in the movies and you're always kinda bowled over when they turn out to be just folks. Now take that case we busted a year or so ago, the one where the classy dressmaker got bumped. You couldn't find a nickel's worth of George Raft in the mob she ran with—and still and all it—"

Diverted, Nelson recognized the speech as a bastardized version of the chief's pet stock lecture. He said, "If you expect me to reform you'll have to go the whole hog and put Miss Ramsey back on the suspect list."

Sugs protested uncertainly: "Aw Sarge, you ain't getting set to pin it on her?" He tried to capture the fugitive glint in Nelson's eyes. Nelson egged him on by lowering the corners of his large expressive mouth.

"You got a hot clue, Sarge? Something I missed? You think she ...?"

"How about giving me your candidate first?"

"Well, course I could-a overlooked something, but take them two twins, especially the one who blew up, or that big redheaded guy—more like a circus barker than any dentist I ever seen—or could easy be the shifty la-di-da feller, or Grandma's husband— on account of any guy who'd marry her is strictly from hunger— or Grandma her own self—"

"That narrows it down considerably," Nelson said.

Sugs sighed, the exhalation causing almost total collapse. "Honest—stands to reason it must be an outside job after all. Why should them rich kids waste their time fogging a plain butler? It ain't like they was after his dough, because a regular head of lettuce was sitting there under some shirts in his bureau drawer, and anybody could-a had it for the taking. I don't get it, Sarge; that's a fact." He sounded injured. He pushed his hat back and raked his head, as though he were trying to burrow through to the works inside.

"Never mind. It's too early to jump at conclusions. Here's headquarters. Did you tell Busch to dust that gold piece for prints?"

"Sure, I sneaked it to him in my handkerchief while you was waiting for Grandma."

"Good. Have that page of instructions I dictated carried out to the letter. Shorthanded or no, I've got to have a few tails. Bad luck that Cricket had to take his tonsils to the hospital. He'd have been invaluable on this."

"How about me pinch-hitting?"

"We'll see. Get that paper work done first."

The two men left the car and walked toward the steps. Sugs said, "I guess you want them notes transcribed tonight."

"It would help. I know you've been overworked lately—"

"You and me both. But I got no beef about that. I only wish the chief—Oh, nuts, skip it. I'll give out with your instructions pronto, but before I dig into the notes could I grab some chow? I'm kinda hollow."

"Sure. Enjoy your dinner." Nelson came to an abrupt halt. "Dinner—Zounds!" The last few hours had completely swamped the problem of Inspector Waldo Furniss. "The chief's waiting at my house." He was back in the car before Sugs's surprised expression had time to jell on his face.

Sugs bellowed, "Hey! "

"Yes?"

"Is that on the level about the chief being at your house?"

His foot on the starter, Nelson shouted back, "At his own invitation."

"Hallelujah! Bring him back alive, Sarge. It's been terrible lonesome around here."

There were six feet of Sammy, and she moved like dark honey poured from a high-held jug. In response to Nelson's urgent knocking she flung the door wide. She raised her heavy eyelids to regard him with full approval. "It sure feel good to see you, Mr. Grid-dely. I told that Mr. Chief you can't help it if you late. Not the way he go on speechmaking and leaving everything to you. I told him—"

Nelson smiled peacefully. "I hoped you'd tell him." He stepped into the small foyer. He sent his hat to join the inspector's on a small table and shucked off his topcoat. The atmosphere was laden with nourishment. He sniffed it.

"You hungry, Mr. Grid-dely?"

"A man doesn't have to be hungry to do justice to your cooking."

Sammy was satisfied. She said in her deep calm voice, "I got ham baked with honey and white wine, and I got my oysters packed in rock salt and ready to put under that broiler while you give yourself a wash."

"You've always gone to town for the chief, Sammy."

"No, Mr. Grid-dely, I gone to town cause you home again. You better hurry now. I think Mr. Chief fixing to jump out of his mind from smelling all them good smells. He so hungry he bound to eat himself fat on anybody's vittles."

Nelson went to the living room that Sammy's touch had transformed into a warm and welcoming place. The long ashwood table was set for two, and in a gray stone vase copper-toned chrysanthemums presided with dignity over linen and silver and glass. Drawn curtains shut out the chilly evening. Subdued light touched upon the disgruntled features of Inspector Waldo Furniss. He was seated in Nelson's best chair, a cocktail shaker at his elbow, a glass in his hand.

His greeting was a groan. "It's about time. For the love of heaven, Grid, wash your hands—or do what you have to do—and let's eat."

"In a jiffy, Chief." Nelson went into the bathroom. He looked at the shower with desire and renounced it out of pity for Furniss. His ablutions did not take more than five minutes, but when he returned to the living room Furniss said, "Did you bring me here to torture me? Sammy's a fiend. She wouldn't even give me a crumb to ward off starvation. She wouldn't even tell me what we're going to have."

"I guess she just doesn't like strangers." Nelson filled the inspector's empty glass and poured a cocktail for himself. He sat down and drank slowly. "Sazerac—and good."

"But hell on the appetite." Nevertheless, Furniss drank his dividend. "What's that crack about strangers? Now look here, Grid, I've taken enough punishment for one day." He half rose, inhaled, and sat down weakly. "No, it's no use. I haven't the strength of character to flounce out. Not with that aroma crowding me. Be a good guy and tell me what it is."

"Oysters Rockefeller for a starter—" Nelson grinned at his rapt audience. "But wouldn't it be more profitable if while we're waiting I outlined my afternoon in Brooklyn Heights?"

"Brooklyn Heights?" Furniss sounded as though the name were completely unfamiliar.

Nelson recited imperturbably, "In 1816 Brooklyn was incorporated as a village. The Heights were then occupied by a number of farms owned by such worthy citizens as Furman, Doughty, Middagh, Clark, Hicks, Remsen. Joralemon, and Livingston, whose names have been perpetuated by the streets which bear them. Because the Canarsie Indians once raised corn on the site it was called the Maize Lands of Meryckawick. Later it received the name of Clover Hill, and prior to the revolution it—"

"Listen, Mr. Encyclopedia, I—"

Nelson looked wounded. "I'm not half finished. Aren't you even going to let me explain about the warehouses built in the excavations in the solid rock beneath the residents' gardens? The Heights rises in an almost perpendicular bluff about one hundred feet above water level, you know. And the place is just crammed with historical interest. For example, there's Love Lane where—"

"Shut up. If I ever get my strength back I'll—"

Sammy had come in with the first course. She said, "I know something about Brooklyn Heights, too, Mr. Chief. Mr. Henry Ward Beecher, he preach there for forty years in little old Plymouth Church. He was a good somebody. He raise money from his congregation to buy freedom for some of them poor slaves."

Furniss said, "Uncle!" He said, "Sammy, you'd better quit this Princetonian before he adds further clutter to your good pure mind."

"It ain't no clutter, and it ain't added by no Prince Tony. A lady I worked for once took me out to that church and told me how that preacher done." She motioned the two men to the table. Her carved African features had sacrificed a little of their dignity. She was smiling as she filled the inspector's plate with oysters.

Furniss said, "Well, enough is enough." He did not mean the oysters. He fixed them with an enchanted blue gaze. "Any wine? Barsac? Fine. What are you waiting for? Pour it out."

Dinner was a success. Nelson respected the inspector's ban against talking shop at table and did nothing to steer the pleasant conversation down forbidden paths. Long after his own appetite had become limp from its healthy workout the inspector was still going strong. In addition to the oysters he had packed away enough baked ham, vegetables, and salad to nourish a large family, and he was now tackling his pecan pie with undiminished ecstasy. Finally, as Sammy poured coffee, he looked up at her, beaming. "Haven't you folks heard about rationing?"

"We got us rationings to spare 'cause Mr. Grid-dely, he ain't been eating here or nowhere else lately."

"Sammy, if I could bring myself to the point of murdering Grid would you come to work for me?"

Sammy said calmly, "Seem like this the first time you put your mind to murder in many a day."

Nelson chuckled.

Furniss eyed him under thick dark brows that contrasted dramatically with his silver hair. He grunted, "I've seen plenty of frames in the course of my career, but this is the first time I've been slap-bang in the middle of one."

"Completely spontaneous and unrehearsed, Chief," Nelson said.

"Sure." He tasted his coffee. "Fine—chocolate added—New

Orleans style." But his praise was mechanical. "What do you say we move to more comfortable chairs, Grid, and let Sammy clear?"

They rose and carried their cups to the section of the room that Nelson grandly called the library. Thinking of his interviews in a library that woman named Beulah had built, Nelson sighed unconsciously.

Furniss lighted a cigarette. He puffed for a moment. Then he said, "You can stop looking like a sick cat. I'm listening."

"I need help—not a listener. The murder of a butler may not be of paramount importance in your current scheme, but the attendant circumstances are complicated. I don't want to go into them just for the sake of hearing myself talk. Unless you're—"

"There's been enough *chi-chi*, Grid. What are you waiting for—a written guarantee? My current scheme is altered as of this afternoon. I canceled all future bookings. I'm chief of the Homicide Squad in the flesh. Make your report." Then he lifted a hand. "Wait a moment. That violent symptom of gloating on your face will lead to indigestion if you're not careful. Besides, you have nothing to gloat about. It was a combination of stuff that led me back to the fold after the band music and the flag waving had carried me away. It was the district attorney's office mostly. I thought I was doing the right thing, but they're a fair slice of average, and it if looks bad to them it must look bad to the round they're cut from. Don't run away with the idea that your threat to join up or that tale of Sammy leaving influenced me." He settled back in his chair. "By the way, that was all my hat, wasn't it? Don't be afraid to speak up. I won't change my mind."

Nelson nodded. "Yes. I had it out with myself, the commissioner, and the draft board long ago, and I decided to stick. And I guess Sammy will stick, too, as long as you turn up occasionally to 'eat yourself fat.'" He added a little awkwardly, "I can't have you ousted, Chief. You've worked too hard to get where you are. You're important."

"Don't worry. I won't be ousted. They couldn't do it before and they can't do it again." He smiled warmly. "Glad to know you, Grid. Quite a fellow." He cleared his throat. "We will now shift to the scene of the crime. Take it from the beginning."

Nelson said, "I'll take it from where I came in. Something tells me it was near the middle of the picture."

Into the inspector's intent focus he brought Shepard, the butler, uncaring, on his neat white bed, dead hands clutching the tie around his neck, the lock of the dictator covering his bruised temple. There was a letter in the single drawer of Shepard's small writing table. An unfinished letter that said, "Dear Mr. Clement, I trust that you will not take this amiss. I have been thinking it over. and it is the only way. You must—" It ended there, never to be continued, the pause too precise to indicate violent interruption, but rather the necessity for clarifying whatever it was that Clement must do. And under some shirts in Shepard's bureau there was a bankbook closed over a packet of new bills, two thousand dollars, drawn yesterday, and not on the morning that Shepard had received his notice. Yet no one had touched the money or disturbed the shirts that covered it, and no one knew why it was there.

He brought the twins into focus. Clement and Hale, pleasant youngsters both, but both worried about something that a butler's death did not entirely explain. Alike in appearance, in disposition not twins at all. Clement with a scar and a temper. Clement who, as Sugs put it, had taken the questioning big, resentfully giving the first answer that came to him, denying all knowledge of why Shepard had been writing to him, wanting only to put an end to a business his attitude said plainly would accomplish nothing. And his thoughts out of bounds and not in the library where Nelson conducted the preliminary investigation.

Marianne, twenty, and dressed as a child. For fun, she said. Anxious to help, but on the surface completely bewildered. Mrs. Leonard Roberts, Beulah, a rather horrible caricature of a woman, shocked, but not out of her wits. By turns cooperative, upset, and personally insulted at Shepard's inconsiderate departure. Leonard Roberts, the husband, nervous and shifty. His behavior due to sudden death or outside matters? It was hard to say. Do anything for money—obviously. Yet there was the untouched cash in Shepard's bureau. Cromwell Proctor, a friend of Beulah's. An unlovable character. His answers were pat, his manner bordering on hauteur. He would bear further notice, even though he had papers on him to prove his exemplary source, a family dating back to the Pilgrim Fathers and reaching across seas to the beginning of the line. Julian Silk, D.D.S. From the look of him a cardsharp or a con man or an evangelist or, to borrow from Sugs again, a circus barker who had acquired taste along the way and scrapped his gay checks for conservative worsteds. But something very new and startling in dentists. He had attended Weatherstone's Institute in New Hampshire, he said. Well, that could be verified. And Dwight Cannon, the man Marianne intended to marry. Dwight could not be brought into focus because Dwight, for the moment was only a name. The cook and Beulah's personal maid, both trusted members of the household, who had returned from an afternoon off to weep for Shepard. Lastly, Nelson mentioned the little gold man and the burglar theory and dwelt again on Shepard's unfinished letter and outlined the instructions he had given to Sugs.

Sammy had hurried with her dishes, returning to the room in time to digest most of the recital. She was engaged in small tasks, so that her fixed ear might wear the guise of fortuity.

Furniss said, "Well done, Grid. I can see it all just as plain. In spite of the arrows pointing to Clement and Cromwell and Roberts, it's the dentist."

"Why?"

"Just because I've never met a dentist outside of his office. He has no conceivable place on Beulah's calling list—or, for that matter, in anybody's social scheme."

Nelson laughed. "I don't object to your candidate, but your reasoning throws me. According to Beulah, Dr. Silk is a highly desirable addition to her social life." He went falsetto. "'Dear Dr. Silk—a man of many talents. He interprets dreams far better than any professional analyst I've ever consulted, and his psychic powers are amazing—to say nothing of the way he casts horoscopes.'"

"Stop blowing that dog whistle. See? I told you so. He's a quack. He's got something on her—that's why he's in. Tell me, Grid, what's Beulah really like? I can't believe she resembles either your description or your imitation of her."

Nelson shuddered. "I didn't do it justice. Her voice would sear the scales right off an alligator, but it's no dog whistle. It has to be heard to be appreciated."

"I'd like to hear it." He was serious.

Nelson said curiously, "From the remarks you dropped this afternoon, you know more about her than I could see at a glance. You tell me."

Furniss said, "Actually I've never met the lady. But when I was a young romantic buck I used to read about her in the yellow sheets. And I developed a kind of a yen. Go ahead, grin. It's ridiculous to me too." He took a deep breath and expelled it in a series of short sentences. "She was a child of the people. Plain Beulah Fitch. Wrong side of the tracks. Then suddenly Beulah Fitch Casey with millions added. Then Mrs. Morgan Potter. Then Countess Danelli. And her fabulous doings were bruited from one continent to another. Yep, even after she buried Mike Casey and moved to wider fields I kept reading about her out of habit. Could she have been what you'd call a *femme fatale*, Grid?"

"Chief, you astonish me. If it weren't that she's safely anchored now, I'd have a new worry." He shook his head. "I'm afraid you're in for a shock. There's little left to bear witness to the legend you've built around her, except maybe her eyes—narrow and slanty and a sort of slate-blue gray. I suppose that, decked out with the original lashes instead of the caked fingers she sports in the winter of her life, they might have played hob with the male ticker. But, judging by Leonard Roberts, she didn't need to be a *femme fatale*. Money was the magnet that drew Mike Casey's successors. When did she take time out to raise a family?"

"She didn't raise one, exactly. Just started the ball rolling. A daughter of Mike Casey. And the daughter grew up, bore one girl and one pair of twins before she and her husband died of the flu or something within a week of each other. And when Mike followed them Beulah took the millions and the kids and picked up life anew. Only more so, because her strings had been cut, and her entertainment budget was practically limitless."

"Are Mike's other two successors alive—or did she bury them too?"

"They're alive. Living off her bounty. She forks out alimony by the carload."

"How did Mike Casey die?"

"What?" He shook his head. "No soap, Grid. She didn't kill him. An infection, if I remember correctly."

"Your memory's astounding."

"Let's face it. Memory's where your heart is." He said briskly, "How about another look at the grandchildren? That girl, is she …?"

"No—nothing like Beulah."

Sammy said unexpectedly, "I'm sure glad to hear that."

The two men laughed, Furniss not quite so heartily as Nelson. Furniss said, "I was only trying to get a clearer picture."

"She's very pretty—without artificial aid. A lovely forehead—and purple eyes. Sugs fell for her."

"That makes a nice change. Have you stopped being susceptible?"

"I don't like the way she dresses."

Sammy's voice was rich with interest. "You ask her why she dress like that?"

"No. Forthright questions are the last things that occur to a policeman." He stood up. He did a little jig step to flex his long legs. He looked at the inspector inquiringly.

Furniss nodded. "End of recess. Phone Sugs. By this time he should have unearthed some sort of working map to chart our course."

Chapter 8

The family had retired for the night. Hale started to read in bed, but his eyes were blind to the printed page. He got up, put on bathrobe and slippers, and went out into the corridor. Light seeped from under Clement's door. Hale entered his brother's room, and sat down on the arm of a chair, "It's been a day, hasn't it?"

Clement was fully dressed. He said, "Damn," to himself, and to his brother he said, "Yes, there's no sense prolonging it any further." He yawned loudly. He stooped over and began to remove his shoes.

Hale looked disappointed. "I wish I were as sleepy as you sound. I tried to read myself into a coma, but it's no go. Too wound up. I thought you might want to chin a little."

"Sorry. I'd like to stick with you, but there's no more talk left in me." He threw his coat on the bed and worked at his necktie.

"You're just being ornery. You hadn't even started to undress until I walked in and gave you the idea." Hale stared at him. "Sure you feel all right, Clem?" his voice was concerned.

"No, I feel terrible. I'm on the verge of collapse." Clement's attempt at lightness petered out. "For the love of Pete, stop goggling at me like a fond old auntie and scram before I—"

"All right, keep it clean." At the door Hale paused and said disconsolately, "Sleep well."

Clement strained for the sound of Hale's door closing. Then he hurried into the garments he had discarded. On the way to the closet to get his topcoat he saw his face in the mirror. He stared at it much as Hale had done. It was a new face, one he had never worn before, but it looked like something that had lain in stock for a long time. It was darkly stained beneath the eyes and hollowed out, as though parasites had sucked away its good quality of freshness and youth. Even the hair above it, usually so crisp and yellow, seemed to have suffered a change. He shuddered, and the glands in his mouth flowed swift and bitter. He took his hat and coat and made undetected exit from the quiet apartment.

The clerk stationed at the desk in the lobby looked at him stupidly and without recognition. He had jammed his hat far down and turned up his collar, unconsciously attempting to obliterate the mirrored face, and as he strode past garish stained-glass windows and unconvincing replicas of the Tudor period he seemed not a healthy youngster of eighteen but a bulking, sinister figure bent on evil errand.

As the subway travels, his destination was three quarters of an hour away. He had reached it in thought many times during the disjointed evening. But Hale had quashed one lame pretext after another, and Marianne had clung to him for reassurance, and he could not escape. Not when his brother and sister took it for granted that his mind, too, was filled with nothing but the unexplained tragedy. For it was tacit that they and he took equal shares in each other's problems. So he had stayed with them, perambulating restlessly from room to room, dogged by their steps, sweating at every ring of the bell, praying that it would not herald the visitor he dreaded. And at last they had gone to their beds and he was free.

He went down into the subway. The dreariness of the train was graphic illustration for the dreariness within himself. Dimmed-out Broadway, when he got out at Seventy-second Street, further expressed his gloom.

The boy glanced at his wrist, remembered, and made a rough guess as to time. Somewhere after midnight! He quickened his steps, walking east for a few blocks. He went into a house whose entrance had long ago renounced all claim to grandeur. Not even imitation stained glass or Tudor here. Nothing but dun-colored stucco walls sprouting dirty electric bulbs in branched sockets, an elevator cage with an iron grille, and a scarred and screaming switchboard, unheeded because its overworked attendant was piloting the elevator somewhere in the upper regions.

Clement did not wait for the car to descend. He climbed four flights of stairs and rang a bell. The girl who opened the door almost felled him with her stored spleen.

"This must be your lucky night, guy. A little while longer and I'd have been the guest in *your* house." Her voice was loud. It clamored for entry at the ears of the other tenants on the floor.

Clement muttered, "Let me come in."

She stepped aside and he was in. She slammed the door and advanced upon him. He sat down, too tired suddenly to speak or move. Numb to his eyes, which went from her to the small room and back again to her.

Beulah, his grandmother, had in lordly fashion caused two apartments to be thrown into one. This—this girl occupied a small fraction of what some architect had intended to be one apartment. Just an ugly cubbyhole into which gas plate, bed, bureau, table, chair, and wilted wearing apparel had been introduced in shabby array. People should not be made to live that way. And if they did live that way, he, Clement Ramsey, wanted desperately to have the knowledge of it erased from his consciousness. He shut his eyes.

She forced them open. "Poor little thing. That college he goes to must be a regular factory. Does he want his mother to sing him a nice lullaby?" She could not have been much older than he in years, but she had been stropped by circumstance to a sharp cutting edge. She was long and sparsely built, except for her breasts. Nothing had been spared there. They seemed to be waging perpetual battle against imprisonment.

Her stiffly waved brown hair needed a washing. The brow beneath it was narrow, and the small brown eyes crowded the bridge of her thin nose. Her real mouth was successfully hidden under a thick red coat. Her chin was sharp too. Anger gave it an upward angle toward the tip of her nose. It would incline that way steadily through the years, the nose drooping to meet it. She said, "Well?" on a rising raucous note.

Clement took a few small bills and held them toward her, his hand unsteady. "I pawned my watch and a few other things. Here."

She did not take the money. She slapped it from his hand. She cried contemptuously, "You can blow yourself to a nice big lollipop on that. It's no good to me."

"I'm sorry." He could not bring himself to call her by name. "I—"

"And you can wrap up the sorry routine and cart it home with you, and I'll go along, too, just for the ride—or maybe just to see your family climb down off their white horses to spread the welcome mat. What happened to your precious butler—or is he part of the sweet little fairy tale you've been spinning to keep me quiet?"

"The butler is dead," Clement said.

"Oh yeah? Was he sick or just tired of the company he kept? Try again, sonny. I'm bighearted. Nobody's going to say I didn't give you at least three chances to knock yourself out."

Clement looked at her hopelessly. He saw a slut holding forth against a background of her own design. He said to himself, I don't believe it. It can't be true. He wasn't frightened by her possible effect upon Beulah. Beaulah was a realist, her outlook strongly flavored by the years she had spent on the Continent. She would know how to deal with the situation quickly and efficiently. She might, being what she was, even extract a certain amount of enjoyment from the aplomb with which she would handle the matter. Nor was he much disturbed by the reactions of Hale and Marianne. They, he felt, would be concerned chiefly with the great lack of fastidiousness he had shown. One thought alone kept pushing him relentlessly toward desperation. The Army! Suppose Beulah used this as an additional weapon in her campaign to keep him home. Would he be accepted if the authorities discovered that he—? His eyes traveled the girl's length. This time he said aloud, "I don't believe it. It's impossible."

She misunderstood him. "So you don't believe it! Why do you think I'm all dressed up and raring to go at this time of night, instead of lying around in my shift and taking life easy? I meant it all right. You fork up or I show up. And I'm not bluffing."

Clement said, "I've done my best. I can't raise the money anywhere."

"Won't raise it is what you mean." She put her hands on her hips. She appraised him coldly, noting his pallor, the stain below his eyes. She altered her tone slightly. "How about a drink? You get more ideas when you're high—like on the night we met." She laughed at his tortured expression. "Anyway, I'm thirsty, myself, and I'm not the solo type." She spun on her high heels and went to a roll-top office desk, strange in the small room's welter. The desk in its own capacity was not, and had never been, a part of her pattern. Former tenants had left it behind. So she utilized it as she utilized everything that came her way. She opened it, and odds and ends spilled to the floor as she rummaged for a bottle. She poured rye into tumblers and gave one to Clement. He took it mechanically but did not raise it to his lips.

"What's wrong now? Not as good as Grandma's brand? Down it anyway—put lead in your pencil. You might as well make up your mind that Dutch courage is the only kind you'll ever have." She tossed off her own drink. She sat down on the bed, facing him. "Now that I've been the perfect hostess let's get back to business. You promised you'd get the money and you have the nerve to offer me a handful of chicken feed. You said the butler wanted to ante up—which sounded phony—only I let it go because who am I to know how the upper half gets along? So give it to me straight. Is there a butler—or isn't there? And if not—"

Clement said, "I told you—"

"Oh, for God's sake! Don't go into an encore. It was corny enough for the first time." Then she paused, as though she were taking time out for deep thought. She leaned over and placed her hand on his knee. Her voice came again, poison-sweet. "Do you know—maybe I've got the wrong attitude about this. Maybe I don't want that money after all. It might be fun to carry this thing through—if you know what I mean. I'm sure if we laid our case before Grandma and told her it was really love she wouldn't stop to muster up any real opposition. She'd more than likely give you her blessing and a nice cushy job in the antique business, so you could support us. Sure she would. Because if you were leveling that night about how anxious she is to keep you out of the Army she'd bust a gut laughing when she found you had two ready-made dependents just panting to plunk down on her side of the scales."

Something happened to Clement. His pallor disappeared, drowned by a violent wave of blood. Anger was good, a better stimulant than the tumbler of whisky he held in his hand. He rose, throwing the tumbler so that it crashed against the molding of the far wall. He towered over the girl, his rage increasing height and breadth. It took strength not to strike her. He invoked strength, pocketing his clenched fists. He said, suppressing his need to shout, and therefore producing a strangled version of his normal voice, "You will not go to my grandmother. I said I'd get the money for you—and I will. Shepard's death has nothing to do with that. I wouldn't have taken his savings, anyway. I told him so. I only mentioned his offer to keep you quiet until I could find a way. I will find a way, I tell you. But you'll have to wait. If you are at all wise you *will* wait."

She was frightened by the change in him. She huddled back on the bed, fully expecting the blow implicit in his stance. When it did not come she rallied. "Look at him!" She *was* looking at him warily. "From panty waist to big shot in two easy lessons. So if I'm wise I'll wait, will I? And you'll get the money for me. When and where from? No, don't tell me—I know. You'll revive the butler—"

"The butler is dead," Clement said. He had mastered his voice. It sounded ominous and even. "The butler was murdered."

Her body went rigid. She sat quite still, staring at him as though he were a snake and she fascinated. She said, "Are you kidding?" But it was not a question, and it was not bravado. It seemed to her that the boy's gray eyes were speculative and cruel as they returned her stare. "Who—who murdered him?"

He shrugged his shoulders impatiently. "You can read about it in the morning papers if you're still interested. I didn't come here to talk about it."

"W-why did you come here?"

He said roughly, "You know damn well why I came. What kind of an act are you going into?"

She had the pallor now. She forced herself to her feet. She was talking. Her talk was like the last nervous spurt of a runner. "I didn't mean to put the squeeze on you, Clement. Honest. When you get to know me I'm not so tough as I make out to be. Ask anybody. They'll tell you. I got a soft heart when it comes right down to it. Look—you take your time getting the money. I won't make trouble. I was joking. Maybe I can even raise enough to see me through, and then you can pay it back when it's convenient. I don't want a nice young fellow like you to be in bad with your folks. You go home and get some sleep, and I'll—Stop looking at me like that. Don't you dare come any nearer. Don't—!"

Chapter 9

All night Leonard Roberts had tossed in his bed. He had turned his pillow over and over, the resulting coolness lasting for only a moment against his hot face. He had kicked off the covers, grown chilly, and replaced them. He had emitted a series of groans, muffling them carefully, so that Beulah, who slept in the adjoining room, would not hear. He had itched and he had scratched himself, but his itch was internal and he could not reach it. At intervals he had looked at the radium dial of the bedside clock and groaned again, repeating the whole routine from pillow turning to scratching for what seemed like a long week of nights. And each time he dared another encounter with the clock it informed him stolidly that time was a mighty opponent to those who deliberately sought to kill it. So at last he gave up the struggle and arose.

He went into the bathroom and took a shower, praying that the sound would not spatter against Beulah's ears. When he had shaved and put on his clothes, dragging out the process as much as possible, the clock made concession by pointing to seven. Early enough. But daylight, thank heaven. A special daylight for him, if all went well.

Moving quietly, he unlocked and opened one of the drawers of an ornate Chinese Chippendale desk, grinning a little sardonically as he remembered Beulah's words at the time he had purchased it. "Dear Lion, you can't really like that thing. A complete deviation from Thomas Chippendale's strong, wonderful craftsmanship. All that fretwork. Such an unfortunate phase of the master's career."

But Leonard had held out for the desk above her patronizing horror. And now as he drew from it a small packet containing several letters and one bill-stuffed envelope he thought of it as an X marking the spot where the worm had turned. Superstitiously he hoped that the letters and the money had by contact taken on some of its symbolic virtue.

Reverently he transferred the bill-stuffed envelope to his wallet. He opened the most recent of the letters and re-read it before he placed it in his pocket with the others. It was typed, and its directions were simple. First the warehouse at nine to meet the man who called himself Matthew Crown. Then to pick up the expert. Then on to complete or forget the whole affair, depending upon the expert's opinion.

Leonard stared down at the cramped womanish signature. Matthew Crown. He was familiar with nearly all of New York's reputable dealers in antiques and with a few who were anything but reputable. And this name was unknown to him.

He shrugged. Nothing strange about that. The whole business was so "hush-hush" from start to finish that it shrieked of illegality. And doubtless the man's real name was "hush-hush" too. Since he had taken pains to ensure secrecy, it wasn't likely he'd give the show away by disclosing his true identity. Obviously, if his claims had foundation, he'd come into possession of his incredible find dishonestly. But what really mattered was that he had come into possession of it at all.

No. What really mattered was that Beulah had actually given him, Leonard Roberts, the specified thirty-five thousand dollars in cash and told him to go ahead.

Beulah had always been generous with him, according to her lights, but her gifts had rarely taken the shape of currency. And as a result his pockets were usually as flat as they had been when he was struggling along on his own. So the thirty-five thousand dollars in his wallet was green burgeoning hope. He would cling to it even if the deal fell through. Beulah would never see it or him again. And she wouldn't prosecute because she loved herself too dearly to swallow such contemptuous epithets as would be crammed down her lean throat should the story of his defection be made public.

If the deal did materialize he had other plans, involving a quick undercover resale at twice the purchase price, the details of which had been carefully worked out. These plans, too, excluded Beulah. Excluded Marianne as well, though prior to yesterday she had been the roots from which they had grown. Roots, he thought bitterly, that needed only a small supercilious breeze to tear them loose.

For a moment the money in his wallet ceased to make itself felt, and cheerlessly he reviewed the scene in the dining room. Merely because she had been a shade less rude than the twins in her treatment of him he'd supposed that sympathy and—Never mind. He closed his eyes against the memory of her frozen little face. When he opened them again she was gone, and the emptiness of his heart proved it.

He knew a sharp stab of fear as he quit the apartment for the last time. He was leaving a deal behind him: security, good food to eat, good clothes to wear. What if his plans went awry? But how could they, with the clever secret measures he had taken to ensure their success? Crooked? No matter. The thirty-five thousand dollars that meant hardly a scratch upon the veneer of Beulah's fortune meant new birth to him.

Just thinking of Beulah was enough to keep lesser worries at bay. And he had reached the point where everything short of

Beulah was a lesser worry. So he squared his padded shoulders, summoned the automatic elevator, and presently stepped out into the cold morning.

Fortified by coffee at an all-night dog wagon, he descended to the lower level of Furman Street. It was lined with warehouses, those on the inland side built in excavations in the solid rock which formed a base for upper-level dwellings. A dim lamp on a thick wooden door identified his destination. The sign beneath it read: ROBERTS–FURNITURE. In the same building, several feet away, was a second door wearing a padlock. Leonard fitted a key to the padlock, opened the door, and stepped within.

His progress was immediately halted, and touch told him that the obstacle was one of Beulah's finds, a screen covered with Genoese velvet. He wondered irritably who had given it such awkward placing and stood on tiptoe to peer over its top. Someone came bounding out of the half-lighted interior down an avenue formed by darkly looming shapes. A torch was flashed full on his face, and the voice of the night watchman rose in high relief.

"It's you, Mr. Roberts."

"Stop blinding me. What were you doing—sleeping?" But the question was good-natured enough. An elaborate system of burglar alarms had been ordered, but, owing to the exigencies of the war, it had not yet been installed. Under other circumstances Leonard would have delivered a pompous lecture on the responsibilities of the night watchman, but now those responsibilities were no longer his affair. Let the old fellow sleep. Let burglars come. Before many days had passed, he thought with unaccustomed humor, Beulah might welcome diversion of any sort.

The screen was wedged in place by a collection of odd bedposts on one side and a heavy chest on the other. The arrangement was strange in the face of the warehouse's planned order, but Leonard's mind was on other things. By shoving he created sufficient opening to emerge from behind the screen. Restlessly he began to walk about. The watchman followed at his heels. He was like an affectionate old dog, left too long alone, trotting carefully in the wake of a newly adopted master.

He chattered without pause. "That big chair's Brazilian, isn't it, sir? The wood it's made of would be called jacaranda. Dark as the devil it is, and hard as steel. I know it for a fact because I spent some time in South America when I was a lad, and—"

Leonard said, "South America?" with sudden interest, and stopped there. He must watch himself. If Beulah should make trouble the night watchman might be instructed to recall this meeting, word and action.

The watchman wasn't being observant. He was engaged in

putting himself through his paces, with nothing in mind but the entertainment value it might give to his master. "This place is a real treasure-trove, sir. Take them silver chandeliers over there, for example. Think of them being the real thing! And worth a fortune. Melvin Beck, the day man, told me—"

Leonard muttered absently, "Yes, I know."

The watchman rambled on: "Doubtless you've heard the tale attached to that little marriage chest. Hope chests, we call them now, and my granddaughter has one herself, all filled with fine linens and lace to cozy a house when the right man says the word. But this one's too small to be more than a toy. It goes back to the time of Looie the Fourteenth, and only the peasants had marriage chests then. But because of its size the King let it stay in court, and they do say it was one of his favorite ornaments. I interest myself in such matters, sir, being right in the thick of them, so to speak—"

Leonard said abruptly, "Melvin comes on at nine, doesn't he?"

"That he does, as a rule. He having to sweep and tidy up in case customers are expected. But last night he told me the madam had given him leave to take an extra hour for some private matter of his own, and he asked would I mind staying a bit longer? I was glad to oblige, though the time passes slow enough as it is."

Leonard looked at his watch. It was just eight o'clock. "That means you still have quite a while to stay." He made his voice hearty. "I'll bet you wouldn't mind leaving right now."

The watchman showed an area of vacant gums. "That I wouldn't, sir."

"Then go along. I'll take over."

When the watchman had left Leonard took out Matthew Crown's last letter and read it through again. Nine o'clock, it said, and no matter how much he gazed at it he could not make it earlier. Almost an hour of waiting. He felt dry and hot with impatience. He pitied himself for the sleepless night he had spent. A night in which Shepard's death, the invasion by the police, Marianne, Dwight Cannon, the white-haired detective, and Beulah had set up a series of quakes to rock the unsteady framework of his being. He wished that he had lingered over his breakfast or taken a walk until it was time for Matthew Crown to appear. He even wished that he had not sent the night watchman away.

The back of the warehouse had been partitioned off, one of the partitions serving as an office. He went into it and sat down at the desk. He picked up a pencil and started to make hen tracks on a blank sheet of paper. Matthew Crown. Beulah. Marianne. Matthew Crown. Beulah. Beulah!

And then the hen tracks suddenly resolved themselves, and he found that he was addressing himself to Beulah, pouring out what he had never dared to say in face-to-face encounter. His hurried sentences were full of hate. The ignominy he had suffered at her hands. She being to him nothing more than a steel trap into which he had been lured because he was hungry and in which he had struggled since the beginning. A detailed account of her loathsome personal habits. A detailed account, even more unsavory, of the women he would take to himself now that he was free. Women of flesh and blood. Women with youth. Not dried-up hags with every feature expressing futile and ridiculous effort to simulate youth.

When he was purged and could produce no further insult the pencil dropped from his cramped fingers. He was about to destroy the unwholesome sheet, but impulse stayed him. He thrust it into a pigeonhole stuffed with blotters, rulers, and other hopeful objects sent out by dealers to cry their wares. Why not let Beulah find it on a future day? Or, better still, let it fall into the possession of someone who would hold it over her head. She was getting off too easy. Let her pay through the nose, as he had paid.

He quitted the office and began to make aimless tour of the warehouse, but the lovingly wrought pieces gathered under one roof with so much care and selectivity might have been no more than a Grand Rapids clearance for all the pleasure his eyes extracted from them. He was gazing alternately and with equal abstraction at Matthew Crown's letter and at a heavy inkstand, vintage 1772, when he felt a breeze. He wheeled toward the Genoese screen. Then he realized that the current of air had come from the other door and he made a half turn.

His first thought was that it couldn't be nine o'clock but that Matthew Crown, eager as himself to see the deal consummated, had been unable to wait until the appointed hour. His second thought was that the night watchman had forgotten something and returned to get it. His third thought came simultaneously with his startled recognition of the figure that was advancing upon him. His fourth thought put a period to thinking.

Chapter 10

The family slept late that morning. Marianne came down to breakfast first, wearing a prim jumper dress and an unmade face. The mental caption which she placed under a mirrored reflection of herself was that Leonard would not only be disenchanted but bilious when next he looked her way.

The dining room seemed strange with Shepard not there to see to her wants. Beulah's personal maid served her. A neat woman of middle age who habitually kept whatever emotions she may have had for what private life her position permitted, Irma now looked like a solid that had been vigorously stirred with a heavy spoon. Her light blonde hair had escaped its hurriedly administered discipline. Her stockings sagged, and her black uniform had taken cover under a torn apron discarded by Cook. Red lids framed her round blue eyes.

Tears, Marianne thought. Either because of Shepard or because of the extra duties she's being called upon to perform. Or both. She glanced at the Claude Ballin wall clock. She said sympathetically, "Ten-thirty. A fine time to be serving breakfast. I seem to be first too."

"It doesn't matter." As she set a half grapefruit before Marianne she took in the young girl's appearance.

Marianne caught her brief flickering of curiosity and was embarrassed. Her silly defense against Leonard's attentions seemed suddenly ugly. It was wrong to be playing rotten little games in a household visited by tragedy. She was about to speak of Shepard, beloved of all those who had ever worked under him, when Irma was blasted from the room by Beulah's explosive summoning.

Marianne laid violent siege to her grapefruit and tried not to listen to the rumbling of the battle Beulah was waging. Irma returned in a few moments, her re-entrance even more distraught than her exit had been. Speech came in a burst.

"I want to say good-by to you, Miss Marianne. I can't wait. I'm going right away. I told her last night she'd have to replace poor Shepard, and she—she scolded me, and when I stuck to it she discharged me for insolence—after twelve years—with a week's notice. And this morning she wants to make out the whole thing was a joke and she says I'm to stay, but I'm going anyway. The work's never been easy, and now—no—I can't. I've had too much. It isn't as though I'm leaving her in the lurch. It's true the agency where she used to hire help has changed over to defense workers, but last night after I thought things over I took it on myself to telephone an ad to the papers, and she's sure to have *some* answers today—but she's saying I overstepped and that I won't have any reference from her unless I finish the month to break in somebody new. But breaking in isn't needed; she'll do the breaking—she'll break—I meant well—I—" She fumbled in Cook's pocket for a handkerchief.

"Here, take mine." Then Marianne said helplessly, "I'm sorry you're leaving, Irma, but under the circumstances I can't think of any good reason for you to stay. Never mind about the references.

I'll write some wonderful ones for you. And don't cry anymore. You'll be sick. Why don't you drink a cup of coffee? I'll bet you haven't had time to eat breakfast."

"Thank you, Miss Marianne. Just knowing you understand makes me feel better. But I won't need the references. I have a daughter your age with a year-old baby boy. Her husband's in the Army, and she's been offered a war job. She wants to take it, but she hasn't been able to because of Jackie. I'm going to live with her and see to things, so she can be free to work. Please say goodbye to your brothers for me. They're fine young men. I hope you all have good luck. No, I'll get some coffee in the kitchen. I don't want to be here when she—when Mrs. Roberts—comes out."

Alone, Marianne served herself to a man-sized portion of ham omelet. The dull feeling of depression experienced immediately upon waking, and now somewhat increased, had created an aching hollow which she interpreted as hunger. Misery, she thought, always makes me eat like a horse. And as always, when she was troubled, she remembered the French school and the never-assuaged pangs she had brought to table there.

What was it that really made her depression so vast? Shepard? No, not entirely, though his death had certainly started it. But, aside from her normal grief for the loss of a friend, there was something else that kept digging away at the void inside, something she could not localize. Leonard? He helped, of course, but she could handle him. And if he continued to annoy her against all discouragement she could, at worst, complain to Beulah. Naturally she'd prefer not to, but she didn't intend to subscribe to self-martyrdom. Besides, Beulah would nose it out unaided if he persisted. Well, then? What—or who? Irma? Irma was Beulah's problem. And may she have many more, Marianne thought. I hope Cook leaves too. It would be worth any amount of discomfort just to watch Beulah coping with the mechanics of living. And who are you to take that attitude, my poor ineffectual little piece of nothing? A fine lot of coping you do. Where's *your* year-old son and *your* war job? Skip it ... To return to the subject, what—or who? Not the ridiculous Crummy or the colossal Dr. Silk. Not the twins, although Clement—No, not Clement. Dwight? Surely not Dwight ...

She was sipping coffee moodily when the twins joined her. Hale leaned over, roughed her hair, noted her lack of reaction, and said, "Wake up, Little Dowd, time to change cars—or do I mean clothes? Say, are you really going to dress that way for the duration?"

Clement muttered, "Why not? It fills our cup to overflowing." He drew a covered dish toward him and peered beneath its metal bell. He replaced it hurriedly, a sick expression on his sick young face. He drained a glass of orange juice, as though he were washing away a bitter taste. He poured coffee and scalded his mouth with the first gulp. He exhibited no sign of annoyance. Rather, his face seemed to welcome the physical pain as a nice change. His unhappiness overshadowed the table. Marianne's unlocalized dejection was engulfed by it.

"Don't you feel well, Clement?"

Clement groaned. "My God, why was I born into a family? Suppose you badger Hale for a change. He likes the limelight."

Hale, too, was making little progress with his breakfast. Finally he set down his coffee cup with a bang, lighted a cigarette, strangled over the smoke, and broke the silence with a high distorted voice. "Well, folks, Shepard's lying in state in the morgue." Startled by the sound he had made, he added hurriedly, "Remind me to buy a mute for that horn."

"Buy one for Grandma's brass section while you're about it," Marianne said. "She's just trumpeted herself out of a maid."

"Irma?"

"Yes—quit cold. Wish we could. Some people have all the luck. She—"

Hale's loud "Chicky!" heralded the entrance of Beulah. She swept into the room in a swishing black taffeta housecoat, a matching bow on her viciously dyed red hair. She boomed a hearty "Good morning, children," seated herself, and began and ended her breakfast with black coffee. She set her cup down, fumbled in a taffeta pocket, and extracted one cigarette which she hung on her outthrust lower lip. Neither Clement nor Hale offered to light it for her, so after an exasperated sigh she lighted it herself.

She took a long drag. "Tasteless thing. I'm looking forward to the war's end, so that I can import some more of those little black cigars I used to smoke." She wriggled in her chair and said coyly, "A woman likes to be stared at, of course, but three pairs of eyes at once are just a trifle disconcerting."

Self-consciously the owners of the three pairs of eyes transferred them to other targets. It wasn't that Beulah, this morning, was any more than a variation on an old theme. It was that yesterday's weight of events had not, apparently, transposed the theme to a lower key or subtracted a few cadenzas for the sake of decency.

Clement said, "We were admiring your mourning costume, Beulah."

"My morning costume?"

"M-o-u-r-n, and so forth."

She seemed to be groping for something. A fan, Marianne thought interestedly. Symbol of her real youth. If she had a fan she'd tap Clement smartly and say something like "Silly boy" in an arch voice.

Beulah performed the modern equivalent to fan tapping. She took another drag on her cigarette and said, "Mourning? What a droll fancy," and looked down at her black taffeta.

Into the ensuing pause Marianne threw a reluctant "Isn't Leonard coming to breakfast?"

Beulah rewarded her by hoisting the corners of her painted mouth. Before she could reply in words Clement said, "Have you forgotten that he's practically an invalid? You ought to call the doctor to operate on his poor little scratched lip, Beulah. It looks fatal to me."

Beulah's smile dropped with a thud. It was Hale who picked it up by saying, "Leonard was awake and about, brother, while you were still snoring. I heard him leave the house somewhere around seven. At least I deduced it was he from the direction of the sound."

Clement looked at him sharply.

Hale added, "It took me until then to drop off. After that I overslept like the dead."

Beulah said, "You need a tonic. I know just the thing." But she immediately canceled his need to reply, her voice like an overstuffed fondant. "Was it really so early? Oh, the dear, zealous boy. He just couldn't wait."

"Couldn't wait for what?" Marianne asked.

Clement drawled, "Something too teddibly important, no doubt. Like attending an auction of Louis Quinze chamber pots." He arose. "Excuse, please. I'm late."

Hale pushed his chair back. "What's the rush? You haven't a course until—"

"You're only my business secretary. You weren't hired to keep track of my personal engagements."

Beulah gestured imperiously with a thin jeweled arm. "Sit down, both of you. I want you to know where Leonard's gone. I want you to realize how you've misjudged him and what a really important transaction he's—"

"Some other time," Clement said. "It's after eleven. I should think you'd be going out yourself. Or are you staying home today in honor of Shepard's passing?"

Beulah's voice was big and calm. "I'm afraid your infantile attempt at sarcasm leaves me undisturbed, Clement. My conscience is clear. That very charming detective assured me that Shepard was murdered, and unless you're accusing me of that, I don't quite see—"

"You don't quite see," Clement said, "full stop. Shepard's been murdered and you're even less interested in the whys and wherefores than we are in Leonard—if that's possible." He nodded to Marianne. "See you later, Sis." He went from the room, an unusually sober Hale dogging his steps.

Beulah looked at Marianne. She said plaintively, "So unreasonable." Then she said, "Oh dear, I do wish they weren't in such a rush. I meant to ask one of them to stop at the warehouse for me."

Marianne said, "Why don't you telephone?"

"I'm waiting for a very important call from Leonard. It may come at any moment, and I don't want him to get the busy signal. Well, never mind. Irma can attend to it."

"Haven't you heard? Irma doesn't consider herself employed by you any longer."

"Nonsense. She's just sulking. She'll get over it."

Beulah looked at her searchingly. "I shouldn't be at all surprised if you've been encouraging that woman." She sighed. "Is there no loyalty anywhere?" Then she said. "She took the liberty of putting an ad in the paper for me. I have no doubt there will be plenty of applicants, defense industries notwithstanding. Servants aren't going to let patriotic reasons stand in their way when an easy, well-paying position such as this is open to them. That's another reason why I'll be unable to leave the house. I can't relegate the choosing of a personal maid to Cook. Besides, sometimes the task of interviewing people of that class is very instructive. I'm quite looking forward to it. About that errand—if Irma can't be prevailed upon to make small return for twelve years of security I don't suppose you'd want to—?"

"I don't want to," Marianne said, "but I will, just to spare Irma another round."

"There's a dear. Tell Melvin I left a large package of vitamin pills in the almond-wood chest, and he's to bring them here. Dr. Silk suggested them for Leonard because I mentioned that he'd been looking a bit peaked. The boys can take them too. They seemed seedy this morning—Clement particularly. Tell Melvin that before leaving he might as well lock up for the day. There isn't much on the calendar, and Leonard will probably be too excited to do anything but come straight home after he completes his transaction. You're such a sweet, thoughtful child sometimes, Marianne. That's why I make allowances for you when you choose to be difficult."

Marianne paused on the dining room threshold. "Maybe you'd like to do *me* a little favor?"

"Of course. An advance on your allowance?"

"No. This time it's the twins' allowance." Marianne faced her earnestly. "Clement doesn't need vitamin pills. All he needs is not to be so desperately thwarted at every turn. Hale, too. Why are you being so horrible to them? And how, in view of the fact that you're serving on several war committees and doing your own bit, can you possibly object to their entering the service? You should be proud—"

Beulah had emptied her high-boned face of all friendliness and shut it tight. "I'm sorry, but I must refuse to discuss the matter. I can only assure you that I've given it considerable thought and I shall continue to do everything I can to keep them home. Really, my dear, I think you're far too young and inexperienced to presume to take me to task. Not that I'm above seeking advice from someone I consider capable of giving it. In fact, I've done just that—only to find my own judgment confirmed."

"Sure you sought advice from someone capable of giving it—someone like Crummy Proctor, for example? Well, don't worry. They'll go anyway. Only they're so bright it's a pity they couldn't have gone as officers. But they're perfect physical specimens and they'll be called, and you can't stop them. The only thing you can do is hold them until they're called—and that won't be long. I think it's a crying shame you wouldn't let them go to that officers' training school in Baltimore to—Oh, why do I bother!" Marianne made an exit. She was so upset that she stopped in her room only long enough to put on her hat and coat and grab her handbag.

In the elevator she thought hotly, Vitamin pills! Let her go to the warehouse herself. Let her run her own errands. By the time she reached the street she had cooled off a little. She had given her promise and she would keep it.

The smell of the harbor was potent and exciting. She walked swiftly, her mood lifting with every stride. On the lower level a pleasant odor of chocolate came out of a small candy factory to swallow the river smell. The narrow street was noisy with lusty-voiced men going about their business. But for one comedian who stopped loading a hand truck to whistle after her, she went unnoticed.

In the midst of all the activity the outside of Roberts' warehouse showed nothing to indicate that it was open for business. Marianne glanced at the door with the padlock on it, found that the one bearing the sign gave to her pressure, and entered. She didn't even need to raise her voice to call, "Melvin," because the emptiness of the interior was almost vocal. Nevertheless, she did raise her voice in a loud, echoing shout.

After a moment or two she thought, Melvin must have stepped out for something. He's been here, because the door is open. Pretty careless of him to leave the place unguarded. Everyone on the street is so occupied with his own affairs that a place could be razed to the ground without attracting attention.

She looked at her watch, and it was five minutes past twelve. She'd better get started soon if she wanted to keep her date with Dwight. He hated to wait even more than most men. She decided to write a note and put it where Melvin would be sure to see it when he returned. She found a piece of wrapping paper and a crayon and printed Beulah's message in large block letters. She signed her name with a flourish and looked about for something that would serve as a bulletin board. The Genoese screen in front of the second door seemed made to order. She secured the note to it with a plain pin. She hoped that the pin wouldn't leave a mark or that if it did Beulah wouldn't notice it. She stepped back to survey her handiwork. The screen rocked a little but seemed in no danger of tipping because of the objects piled in front of it. That's that, she thought. He'll be sure to see it first thing.

On her way out she saw a sheet of paper lying on the floor under a large chair. Stooping to reach for it, her knee encountered a small object that rolled away before she had a chance to determine what it was. She picked up the paper, scanned its typed body, and on impulse put it into her pocketbook.

Chapter 11

The inspector's desk was laden with papers. Detective Sergeant Gridley Nelson added to its burden, looking as relaxed as a small boy with a fishing rod.

Furniss dropped the report he was studying to glance up at him. "Grid, you've been on the go since cockcrow. Yet you haven't the decency to show even a line of fatigue. How do you do it?"

Nelson said virtuously, "I love my work." He grinned at Furniss. "You sound like a verse out of *Father William*." His voice was affectionate. It was old times returned to see the chief knee-deep in a case.

Furniss, reading his mind, disguised momentary embarrassment in a business dress. "That new man seems to be working out all right—the one on Cromwell Proctor's tail. Proctor's certainly a dainty dish for a woman to wish on her only granddaughter." His eyes dropped to the report. "Forcibly ejected from the social register, where his family held firm since publication. Family consists of mother and father, former residents of Manhattan. Now living in Havana, and I don't wonder. Remittance man, Cromwell. Remittances fewer and farther between of late. Doubtless they moved from the scene of the nuisance to avoid open scandal and are gradually washing their hands of it because distance lulls them to security."

"What kind of scandal, Chief?"

"According to this report, he began his career by dismembering insects and progressed to several cat killings and the killing of one very fancy pedigreed dog. The last item opened things up for our operator. He discovered that the owners of the dog had filed suit and were pacified out of court at considerable cost. Proctor had been their neighbor. They knew him like a book and they welcomed the opportunity to review him to our—what's his name?—Hatton."

Nelson contracted his nostrils, as though he were excusing them from duty until the bad odor vanished. "Interesting. But it doesn't give him a motive for the butler."

"He had no conceivable motive for the other killings, either."

"This isn't the same sort of thing, Chief. None of the usual signs on the body to indicate sadistic compulsion."

"Those fellows don't always run true to form, Grid. Proctor could have had other compulsions—money, for instance. No source of income but the remittances—which, according to his bank, are tapering off. Don't forget the wad in the butler's bureau."

"That wad is just what makes me skeptical. If money was the motive, why wasn't it taken?"

"He could have been frightened away before he obtained his objective."

"There's no evidence of a search or of the murderer being in a hurry. Nothing in the room was disturbed, and he took care that everything he touched was wiped clean of prints. The thermos jug and the glassful of water bother me. They don't even show the butler's prints. So it stands to reason the murderer handled them and later removed the traces." Nelson looked puzzled. "Why should a murderer pour water?"

"Maybe he was thirsty."

"Then why didn't he drink? The glass was brimming."

"Now don't get fanciful and go off on tangents, Grid. We've had jigsaws where less explicable pieces jumped into place when the picture shaped up." Furniss pushed the report aside. "I don't say Proctor did it and I don't say he didn't—not yet I don't."

"What about your favorite candidate of last night?"

"The dentist? He's still in the running. I've got him right here. Hey—isn't this Sugs' writing?"

Nelson said apologetically, "We're shorthanded, and he did such a good job with my instructions that I let him name his own prize. He chose Dr. Silk, mainly because I confided that you'd singled him out for first honors."

Furniss groaned. "I hope he doesn't muff it. Having him in the field means I can't uncross my fingers until the end's in sight. I wish you weren't such an incurable Santa Claus."

"Let's hear what he's uncovered."

Furniss scanned the sheet rapidly. "Well, I'll be damned. Maybe he has got the makings of a detective. Of course I'll have to translate it into English as I go along. Hmmm. He had Larchville, New Hampshire, on the phone. Spoke to the deputy sheriff. Silk was born there—so far it dovetails. And he studied dentistry, too, and was graduated from Weatherstone's Institute in 1922, at the age of twenty-three. Later opened an office in home town where he practiced for almost a year. Gave it up to go a-roving. Left a lingering perfume behind him. Small-time stuff—no murders—preying on silly women mostly." Furniss was disappointed. "Still, there has to be a first time."

"Anything about this roving period?" Nelson knew the answer.

"No—too much to expect. But Sugs did pretty well at that. He found out when and where he bought his dental equipment for his present office—it's less than half paid for, by the way—and he got onto a talky individual in the equipment company who spilled that Silk was recommended as a customer by Grant's Dental College in New York City. And, taking it from there, he discovered that Silk had attended the evening courses at the college to brush up on latest methods, et cetera, in preparation for starting his new practice on Columbus Circle. All of which took place three years ago. So the roving instinct seems satisfied, and it looks like he's settled down for good. Business seems to have picked up for him lately. Sugs spoke to his nurse on the phone before she left for work this morning and extorted from her—the lord knows by what delicate methods—that her boss, whom she worships, is being recognized at last and has a very snazzy clientele. She even intimated that, judging by Sugs' diction, he'd do better to have his teeth pulled in the lower brackets."

"Perhaps the snazzy clientele happened since Beulah's advent," Nelson said. "She's undoubtedly recommended him to her prosperous friends."

"Yeah, but he's still in the red. Plenty of outstanding debts. Behind in the rent too."

"Maybe he gambles."

"Could be. Whatever it is, he's short of cash, and that wad in the—"

Nelson said quickly, "Well, Sugs is giving him his best attention. At this moment he's planted in the building where Silk has his office. And he has orders to tail him wherever he goes."

Furniss shuddered. "Hell, Grid. I still prefer Sugs' paper work to his footwork. I'll never forget that Greenhedge mess."

"Neither will I," Nelson said. "But in this case I don't see that we have much choice. Cricket, our best bet, is in the hospital. We stationed a man in Beulah's lobby to supervise comings and goings, and Cromwell—"

"I know. I'm not blaming you. Maybe Sugs isn't so dumb after all. Maybe he's just had bad luck. I've got to hand it to him for this report."

Nelson said guiltily, "What's the dope on Dwight Cannon?" He was thinking that Furniss would be even more uneasy if he knew of the inch-by-inch guidance that he, Nelson, had given Sugs in compiling the Silk dossier.

"Dwight Cannon—Dwight Cannon. Here. Holy smoke—he's in the poorhouse too! Born in upstate New York. Age twenty-nine. Architect out of a job. Lives in cheap furnished rooming house. Bank balance of seven dollars. That's about all. No—wait. Been trying to join armed forces ever since Pearl Harbor. Turned down for physical disability, unspecified here. Wonder if his girl knows. Let's hope it's nothing that will interfere with connubial bliss." Furniss chuckled. "Listen to me—a humanist. I must be catching it from you."

"Anything further on the girl?"

"Let's see—no, nothing shady. Except that she might be slightly neurotic. Well, who isn't? Age twenty. Born in Gramercy Park. Uprooted at eight. School in Paris. Returned to America with her brothers and grandma in nineteen thirty-five. Lived in Gramercy Park until a week ago. Junior Leaguer. All the stuff a young girl in her position might be expected to do."

"Why do you say she's neurotic—or is that a guess?"

"It comes out in a statement you got yourself from the cook. She says— Wait a moment, I'll read it off."

"Never mind. Do you mean the bit about how thin and nervous the child was after Paris—and how they must have starved her because for the first month or so she couldn't seem to get enough to eat?"

"Yes, that and the fact that the family doctor sent her to a psychiatrist."

Nelson said warmly, "Probably all due to loneliness. She was separated from her brothers in Europe and she seems fond of them."

"Don't worry, Grid. She doesn't need your protection. Her brothers might, though. Particularly the one named Clement."

Nelson was silent.

Furniss said, "Much as I hate to bring it up again, both boys are short of money. And although you couldn't pry Clement open when you questioned him, the other one gave until it hurt. All about how they wanted to go to an officers' training school in Baltimore and were fobbed off with Columbia, and about how Beulah is moving heaven and earth to make the draft board turn them down when the time comes. Not that she'll have any luck, I imagine, but she'll try to stave off the evil moment as long as possible." He was side-tracked for a moment. He mused audibly, "Funny thing, that. On the surface she's a patriotic woman—active on various committees for the relief of refugees, and so on. And she's doing without her cars and adhering strictly to ration laws, all of which must be no little chore to a woman who married a silver spoon and has been dipping it in the cream ever since. I don't get it. All that husband hunting must have kept her from lavishing much love on her grandchildren, and she seems to be fairly well occupied with her latest catch. Any notion why she shouldn't be glad to get rid of the kids, Grid, in such a—a glory-reflecting way? Having folks in the Army would provide her with a rare chance for self-dramatization, and that's her meat."

"It doesn't make much sense, but I'm curious enough to want to find out—even though I doubt its relation to the case."

"Yeah—where was I? Clement. It looks peculiar for him, to say the least. The man you stationed in the lobby saw him stumble into the house at five minutes past nine this morning. He'd left around midnight, skulked out with his hat over his eyes like a storybook villain. What business would a youngster of his background have away from home in the wee small hours?"

Nelson shrugged. "The overprivileged have been known to seek the same outlets as their underprivileged kin." He added reluctantly, "That isn't what bothers me."

"You holding something back, Grid?"

"No, just trying to fit it into its proper place. I told you about the little gold figure in that precisely ordered cabinet."

"Yeah."

"The whole family had been fingerprinted for identification purposes in case of air raid. There were prints on the figure. They checked with Clement's."

"I don't see—"

"Neither do I, actually. But I'm tormented by an unpleasant theory that could fit."

"Well?"

"We know from Hale that Beulah cut off their allowance in an added attempt to make them see things her way. Hale seems to have taken the cut in his stride, but not Clement. While everybody gathered in the sitting room to wait for me yesterday I made casual inspection of the rest of the apartment. I found pawn tickets in Clement's overcoat pocket and checked on them. One was for a wristwatch; the others, cuff links, a ring, and some evening studs. And the total of what he raised was thirty dollars. It seems to me that he wanted money for some special purpose and tried to get it in the pawnshop. A debt he was being hounded for, maybe. Anyway, it must have been more than thirty dollars, because surely between his sister, whose allowance still goes, and his friends, he could have managed to raise that amount. Besides, people don't put the pressure on anyone for such a small sum. And a boy of his upbringing would have to be hard pressed to resort to a pawnshop."

Furniss objected: "I can't say I see your point yet, but that last statement ain't necessarily so. I can remember several minor incidents in my lean youth that sent me tripping blithely to Uncle's emporium."

"Yes, but you had no inhibitions and, as you so often boast, you weren't born to the purple. Most human beings approach such places with shame and misgiving. The pawnbroker himself judged Clement's visit to be a premier. He said the boy was sweating and blushing by turns. The pawnbroker was very anxious to cooperate with us to gloss over his own natural feeling of guilt. Because he knew that we knew he'd diddled Clement, the articles in question being worth a great deal more than the sum advanced."

"Maybe that was all the boy asked for, to give him a better chance to redeem them."

"No, Uncle admitted that he expected him to bargain. But he didn't know how. He departed in a fog of disappointment."

"Where does the gold figure come in?"

"I don't say it does come in. I say it might. Suppose Clement returned home, his problem still unsolved, and began to consider further ways and means. Suppose, while he was brooding, his eyes happened to stray toward the cabinet. Suppose, his own marketable possessions exhausted, he decided to pocket the rider, which is solid gold and jeweled, to boot, and of real value. Suppose Shepard caught him in the act. And, having a quick temper and thwarted beyond endurance, Clement struck Shepard. Suppose there was no intent to kill. Suppose that, appalled, he lifted the prostrate but still-living butler, whose heart was struggling to withstand the shock, carried him to his room, fussed over him, tried to give him water, and then watched him die."

Furniss said softly, "If I were a Frenchman I'd kiss you on both cheeks."

Nelson did not smile. "I've given you nothing but a theory that has at least one gaping hole."

"Don't bother to point it out to me." Furniss reached for the telephone. "I'm going to have him brought in right away. There's no hole he won't mend if he's properly coaxed."

Nelson said urgently, "Wait, Chief." He rummaged on the desk. "Look at this picture of the corpse. The lock of hair combed down over the forehead."

Furniss looked. "Well, maybe the lad's a Nazi sympathizer—could have picked it up while he was batting around Europe with Beulah."

"How would that tie in with his longing to fight for America?"

"Could be a blind—or he might be following instructions."

"No Nazi sympathizer would go out of his way to get attention by sticking the fuehrer's hairdo on a corpse—and you know it."

"All right, then he isn't a Nazi sympathizer; maybe he did it to make us think there *were* Nazis at the bottom of our murder. A boy's mind would work that way—full of espionage and stuff."

"Not this boy. He wasn't weaned on penny dreadfuls. The collection of books in his room shows solid good taste. Don't call him in yet, Chief. I could stitch up a theory for every one of our suspects and make it fit with a little alteration here and there. Take Leonard Roberts—"

Furniss eyed him keenly. "I guess I'll have to humor you, Grid, to the extent of letting you try to fit a theory to someone more to your liking—or should I say less? I'll take Leonard Roberts and let Clement ride for the moment, but—"

The telephone rang. He answered it. "Who? ... Oh, sure, Sammy. I'll put him on."

Nelson's brow knitted. Sammy's telephone call of yesterday was the first one she had ever made to headquarters. And she had made it under reasonable provocation. She was not the type to take meaningless liberties. He put the receiver to his ear. His "Hello" sounded depressed. Then he said, "What? You must be joking.... But why?" His tone was hurt now. "I was home last night. I couldn't wait until you came to fix breakfast this morning, but ... Temporarily? ... You ... Sammy, you should have asked me first ... Yes, undoubtedly, but I couldn't have prevented you ... You're not under contract ... Yes ... Yes, I'm listening." His voice changed entirely. "Yes ... I'll look into it ... Sure ... Let me know if anything further ... That's right. Leave a message if I'm out. Goodbye, Sammy. Good luck." He hung up the receiver. The face he turned to Furniss was an overcrowded canvas.

Furniss said, "Now what in hell was that all about?"

"It seems that Sammy's been going over the want ads for a friend of hers who can't read."

"So?"

"She came across one that seemed too good to pass up. She

answered it herself."

Furniss looked shocked. "You're not telling me that P.S. she got the job?"

"That's just what I'm telling you."

"No!" He shook his head. "Grid, so help me, I never would have believed it." He placed a hand on his stomach, as though he were bracing it for a shock. He said softly, "No more of those wonderful dinners." Then he shouted, "She can't do this to us! Get her back! Raise her salary! I'll pay the difference. She— What are you grinning about? If this is a gag—"

Nelson said, "I wouldn't call it a gag, exactly. Sammy decided that we needed assistance. The job she took is that of personal maid to Mrs. Leonard Roberts."

"What?" Furniss began to laugh. He built it up to a minor explosion. He chortled through it, "Remind me to put her name up in lights over the department. She's a headliner."

"Let's hope she doesn't stop the show. And let's hope she doesn't get too steeped in luxury to come back home."

"She'll come home. She's no snob. Grid, can't you just see her personal-maiding Beulah and giving her a few quiet tips on deportment when she gets out of hand? Wouldn't I like to be the invisible man, so—" He was interrupted by a knock on the door. He said happily, "Come in. Oh, it's you, Merkle."

Lieutenant Merkle of the Missing Persons Bureau entered. He looked at them morosely. "I'm glad somebody's in good humor. No, I won't sit down—too busy. But I've got something I thought might interest you, You working on that Brooklyn butler thing— or have you closed it? I don't get time to read the papers."

"Give us another five minutes or so and we'll close it. We've got a real sleuth on the job now," Furniss said. He was still laughing.

"Yeah? Well, I didn't come in here to horse around. I took a call around noon advising me to trace the whereabouts of a girl named Grace Lyons who had disappeared from an apartment on West Seventy-fourth Street. I asked who was calling and if there was any reason to suspect foul play, and the joker at the other end said, 'My name's Legion, and I don't suspect foul play. I'm just calling for the chance to talk to a nice handsome dick.' And he slammed down the receiver. I had the call checked, but it was made from a pay station. I sent a man up to the girl's apartment house. She wasn't there all right, and neither were her clothes. The furniture was there, but that went with the joint. Everything was pretty stirred up, as though she'd made a hasty exit, and maybe an involuntary one. She'd been in the place six months and had paid in advance for another month. So neither the elevator man nor the landlord could make much out of it. Their tenants usually skip before they pay up—not after. But this is where you come in. The elevator man says she had a caller last night. He didn't see him come in, but he saw him go out. And this morning he read about the butler in the *Journal*, and there was a picture of the Roberts dame and her twin grandsons in it. And the elevator man swears this girl's caller was either one of those twins or a triplet. Well, we tried to raise the boy for questioning, but it seems he's in school, and we don't want to be rash because Mrs. Roberts is important people, and besides, nobody but the anonymous phone caller has buzzed us, and we don't really know whether the girl is missing or just playing 'lose me.' So for the moment it's all yours." He stalked out of the office.

Furniss had stretched out his hand for the telephone. Nelson said, "Hold it. There'll be time for Clement later. You didn't give me a chance to tell you the full purpose of Sammy's call. Besides advising me of her change of address, she made her first report. She says that from all the signs, and there are plenty, it appears that Leonard Roberts is also a case for Missing Persons. He seems to have done a skip too. Wouldn't that seem rather suspicious, considering that murder's taken place under his own roof?"

Chapter 12

Marianne was only two minutes late to her luncheon engagement. She and Dwight found a table as far away as possible from the balalaikas as the small gay room stretched. Dwight said, "Are you hungry?" And she said, "Yes, starving," because something was digging away at the hollow again, and, oddly enough; being with Dwight didn't command it to stop. Dwight's dark eyes had fires burning in them. His face was flushed. She was about to ask him if he had a fever or just an extra cocktail when he stared at her with touching concern.

"Don't you feel well, lovely?"

"Sure. As well as can be expected." She told him about Shepard. When she had finished he rubbed his forehead and said, "You're sure you didn't dream it?"

"No, I never dream anything but you."

He smiled a sparse smile. "It's about the queerest thing I ever heard." He seemed to be mulling it over, but when he spoke again it was to dismiss the subject.

Marianne knew a moment of disappointment. Dwight was intelligent, but because she loved him she had invested him with genius. She had hoped that he might employ that genius now, put his finger on some subtle point that they had all missed, some point that would rationalize Shepard's death, make it less frightening. She sighed.

Dwight was saying, "I don't wonder you were in too much of a dither this morning to make yourself beautiful for me."

She was surprised that she could laugh. "If you're referring to this classy outfit, it's called 'Lack of Allure Number 2,' inspired by Leonard, and I wore it to breakfast for a reason. I meant to change later, only Beulah made me so angry I left in a tizzy and forgot all about it. Maybe this is a test. If you can still whisper sweet nothings at me and make them sound convincing I'll begin to believe in my luck."

His brow pleated. So she explained, starting with yesterday's costume and drawing a general map of her campaign to make Leonard wonder what he thought he saw in her.

Dwight was not amused. He spoke with such vehemence that she was startled. "Forget it. He'll never bother you again." He added more gently, "Besides, you'd look soft and come-on-ish in a suit of armor." He lifted her handbag from the extra chair. "Here, put on some lipstick before the waiter comes. Otherwise he's likely to discount your order and bring you a nice bowl of bread and milk."

"I might as well wait until I've finished eating. It will save wear and tear," Marianne said. She could see that his humor was forced.

And I suppose, she told herself, I'd feel exactly the same way if I caught some messy female counterpart of Leonard making a pass at *him*.

She lifted a spoonful of borscht to her lips, swallowed, and said, "Did anyone pay you a visit this morning?"

"I don't know. I left my room early. Why do you ask?"

"When the detective questioned me yesterday your name slipped out, and I thought maybe he'd want to see you."

"Why should he want to see me?"

"Just because he said something about far-reaching tentacles, and you happened to drop in when you did."

"Now that makes sense. Take it from the beginning. My ear doesn't seem attuned to your new line of chatter."

"Never mind. I only wanted to prepare you in case you were bothered. Not that he really was a bother. Young, with curly white hair and a wide forehead and a wide space between his eyes and wide shoulders and—"

Dwight cut in with a word that was not "wide," but it had the same number of letters.

Marianne said with fine synthetic shock, "Why, Dwight!"

"Don't 'why, Dwight' me. Just who is this paragon you've been describing so raptly?"

"Mr. Nelson—the detective."

"You certainly snapped his picture."

"You couldn't possibly be jealous!"

"I could." He sounded more than jealous. He sounded furiously angry.

"You needn't be. I wouldn't swap you for a mattress full of white hair."

"Sometimes I'm not so sure. I wouldn't mind Beulah leaving you a slice of her fortune, but I'd hate to think you'd inherited any of her traits."

"Dwight, don't ever say a thing like that again. Look at me, Dwight. I love you. I loved you yesterday and I'll love you tomorrow."

His grin was crooked. "Tell that to the Marines."

"I don't love the Marines."

"If the waiter heard that he'd have you up for sedition."

He was doggedly humorous until they had finished eating. Marianne was replacing compact and lipstick in her bag when she saw the letter she had picked up in the warehouse. She held it out to Dwight.

"Our Leonard is currently engaged in big doings. Read this."

Dwight scowled. "If it's all the same to you, lovely, I've had an overdose of our Leonard."

"Dwight, sometimes I know exactly the sort of little boy you were. Come on, read it. It's very interesting. Leonard left the house at seven o'clock on the strength of this communication."

"What are you doing with his private mail?"

"Don't be moral, darling. It isn't private. Beulah's been trying to publicize it all morning—only nobody would listen. Here, it's right up your alley. You studied furniture in connection with your architectural courses, didn't you?"

Dwight nodded. He handled the letter as though it were a slug. He read it, looked up, and said slowly, "You don't mean he fell for it?"

"Fell for it? Why do you say that?"

"Well, this—this Matthew Crown claims he's come into possession of a wardrobe made and signed by André Charles Boulle."

"I've never heard that name before. Who is he?"

"He was an artisan famous in the time of Louis Seize, whose customers were Philip of Spain, the dukes of Savoy and Lorraine, and even a prince of Siam. André—"

"All right. You don't have to elucidate further. I get more than enough of that talk where I live."

"You asked for it." Dwight continued with the tonelessness of a student reciting his homework, "André Charles Boulle—1642-1732—born, significantly enough, in the Louvre—famous for perfecting a new kind of veneer called marquetry—"

"Look at you! So now I know. Boulle was an important somebody. I'd fall for him myself. Why shouldn't Leonard—or Beulah, too, for that matter? And stop regarding me with such horrible patience."

Dwight consulted the letter again. He said, "Thirty-five thousand dollars in cash is a lot of money, but it couldn't even buy a piece made by Boulle's sons, who imitated him so closely that they were called *les singes de leur p*ère. In fact, as far as I know, the only places where you can get so much as a squint at his stuff are—or were, before the various blitzes—the Louvre, South Kensington, and the Leningrad museums."

Marianne said excitedly, "You're not just showing off? You're sure?"

"Of course I'm not sure." Dwight hesitated. "Offhand I'd say that the thing was a hoax from start to finish, but you never know. It's just barely within the realm of possibility that some snide character has actually managed to get a Boulle piece into this country." He was folding the letter into small squares.

"Well, I hope it *is* a hoax. I hope Beulah really parted with thirty-five thousand dollars and is properly diddled out of it. It will serve her right, the way she's been treating Clement and Hale. If you could have seen Clement this morning—"

"Beulah won't be diddled. She'd never allow her precious consort to buy anything unless he took an expert along to authenticate it."

"Pessimist! Why can't you look on the bright side, like me? Whoa—what are you doing? I meant to return that letter to Leonard with a sweet sympathetic smile when he came home hoaxed."

Absently Dwight had torn the letter to bits. He said, "Sorry, my little sadist. My mind just won't stay in one place." He reached for the check.

Marianne's fingers closed over his. "You *are* in a fog. Have you forgotten that this is my treat?" Then she squealed, "Darling!"

He had pulled out an opulent-looking wallet and was extracting a bill from it. He said, "Better late than never."

"Dwight, I hate myself. No wonder you've been so disgruntled—so unlike yourself. And I never inquired. Dwight, you got the job, and they were so crazy about you they gave you an advance—and we can be married. And I was so full of all that other stuff! If you'll only forgive me for being such a thoughtless pig as to seem uninterested in the most important thing in the world, you can tear me limb from limb and I won't even murmur."

"That limb-from-limb routine will have to keep, lovely. It might cause comment here." He was grinning, a nice generous grin. It turned on the lights in his dark face. "I got the job all right, but they weren't crazy enough about me to shell out in advance. I borrowed elsewhere on my prospects, which are plenty good." He launched into a detailed explanation. Marianne's mind made a stew of the technicalities and swallowed only the boiled-down facts. Defense work. A building project. A share at last in America's war effort. A small share at first, but it would grow. He'd show them. He was to work in the New York office. Later, after the blueprints were completed, he might be transferred.

Marianne said, as though she could not quite believe it, "I'll get my things ready. Then when you do have to leave town there won't be any last-minute rush. Do you start right away?"

"Not until Monday."

"Wonderful. We can go right back to Brooklyn Heights and throw the good news in Beulah's teeth." She added primly, "I'm assuming we'll be married soon. I hope I'm not sweeping you off your feet."

"Sweep away. Off or on my feet you'll still have to run like hell to catch up with me on the way to the hitching post. But I've so many things to attend to that Beulah will have to wait a day or two for the big scene. Jeepers, you've got beautiful eyes. Stop looking like a spoiled baby. Meanwhile, I can be thinking out bigger and better phrases to dish out. After all, telling Grandma the facts of life is an opportunity that might not knock twice. I want to do it justice."

They sat and discussed the future until the waiter's impatience became an almost physical thing that hurled them out of the restaurant. The weather had turned colder, but Dwight's enthusiasm was a portable furnace.

It was three o'clock when he insisted grandly that she take a taxi and tried to present her with the fare. It cost her a ten-minute dissertation on economics to win that battle and his escort to the nearest subway station. There he drew her to him for a brief high moment, not at all troubled by comments evoked from a small newsboy.

Marianne did not go straight home. She changed her mind and went to the beauty salon and wheedled Henri into sandwiching her between previous commitments for a brand-new reset. From there she went to Saks Fifth Avenue and bought a three-piece suit of soft violet wool and a hat that shunned the greater part of her head. She had to celebrate, Leonard notwithstanding.

It was nearly five when she entered the apartment in her new outfit, there to find herself without heart to give Beulah even a hint concerning Dwight's triumph. Because Beulah was in a state. A real state in which her flare for mock heroics played no part.

Chapter 13

The little world built by Marianne and Dwight had shut out all unpleasant thoughts. Marianne pressed the bell of the Brooklyn Heights apartment. Then she remembered that no one was there who could be expected to answer. She withdrew her hand as from a live coal and tried the door as she had tried it yesterday. This time it did not respond. She searched her bag for a key, but before she had fitted it to the lock the door swung inward.

Marianne looked up. She said in bewilderment, "Excuse me. I guess I got off on the wrong floor," and turned away.

The voice of the tall colored woman arrested her. "No ma'am, you wait. You Miss Ma'yanne?"

"Yes."

"Then you on the right floor. You come in. Your grandma need her kinfolks bad, and the visitor she got in there now ain't kinfolk to nobody."

Marianne tried to sort that out. "Oh," she said, "you're taking Irma's place."

"Yes, I the maid your grandma hire to work here. You call me Sammy. I sure glad to know you. I take your wraps."

Marianne, surrendering her precious new coat and hat, returned Sammy's smile. Beulah's showed sense for once, she thought, liking the neat composed figure, the soft rich voice. I hope she doesn't scare her away.

Beulah was in the library with Cromwell Proctor, and when Marianne appeared her face took on life for a moment. Then died again. Her face was strange. Tears had been shed, causing green paste and mascara to join in ugly union around the region of her slaty eyes. Under nervous compulsion she kept applying her handkerchief to her mouth, and between applications Marianne saw that her carefully delineated lips were a formless crimson smear.

Marianne's emotions fused into a jumble. Impulsively she went to her grandmother and embraced her. To her young arms Beulah's thin frame felt like a bagful of hard candy.

"What is it, Beulah? What's wrong?"

Beulah said dully, "Leonard. I haven't heard from him and I've been waiting in all day for his call. He knows I'm waiting. He'd get in touch with me if he could. He promised. I've tried all the places where he might be, but no one's seen him." She slid out of the circle of Marianne's arms. She said, "He can't call because something's happened to him." Her voice sounded eerie, like the voice of a sibyl.

The cause that prompted Beulah's panic might be entirely false, but the effect was genuine, and Marianne was impressed by it. She had never seen her grandmother so shaken. She said, "Did his business this morning have to do with that Boulle thing, Beulah?"

"Yes—yes, of course. Why else would I be worried? What shall I do?" She began to pace the room.

Cromwell Proctor took her arm and led her to a chair. He said soothingly, "You're upsetting yourself unnecessarily, Mrs. Roberts. There are always a plethora of good reasons why a man can't phone when he's promised. It's so easy to get sidetracked—meeting old friends—that kind of thing. Especially in a city like New York. He'll turn up when he's ready, you know. None the worse, I'm sure."

Marianne thought. The poor ass is actually in the groove.

But Crummy had to spoil it. He ran a limp hand through his thinning hair and continued in quite another key: "Naturally, after yesterday's murder, this business of dear old Leonard does seem a bit odd. I can't say I blame you for being nervous." He moistened his lips. "Shepard's poor dead body with that gruesome forelock haunted me all—"

Marianne planted herself firmly between him and Beulah. "Look, Crummy, why don't you go out and reconnoiter. If you do run into Leonard, just tell him to hurry home—or at least phone."

"Run into him? Why, my dear girl"—he changed key again—" he's probably dawdling in some bar without a care in the world. I don't know his haunts. Really, I came to call on— Why, you're not dressed as a little girl any longer. It attracted me so much—it was so—"

"I'd try the warehouse if I were you. He might have lost track of time there, brooding over his treasures or something." Marianne was steering him gently but inflexibly toward the door. "You were solid as a detective yesterday, Crummy. Here's a chance to keep in practice."

Sammy appeared with his hat just as he seemed on the verge of successful resistance. Sedately she ushered him out after sending Marianne a brief understanding glance.

Beulah took no interest at all in his reluctant exit, but Marianne's mention of the word "detective" had struck a responsive chord. She cried, "Child, please call that detective for me—the one who was here. I've waited long enough. Something's happened to Leonard. Tell him to find Leonard. He's never left me for this long before without telephoning. He knows I insist upon—"

"Don't you think we should give it a while longer? Leonard will feel like an awful fool if you send out an alarm for him. He may have forgotten—"

"He can't have forgotten. This transaction means everything to him. Why won't you realize that?" Her voice shattered. "His appointment was for nine o'clock this morning—hours and hours ago—and he was to call me immediately after—no matter what." She struck at her eyes with the handkerchief, and, like the rod of Moses, it produced a flow. She wept without restraint. She sobbed, "Mr. Crown called at noon. He seemed very annoyed. He said Leonard hadn't turned up. That was when I knew, because nothing could have kept him away—nothing but— And then a few minutes later Mr. Selwyn, the expert, phoned. He—he was angry too. He said he was a busy man—accustomed to—to n-normal courtesy in his work—and he'd waited all morning for Leonard and Mr. Crown—"

Marianne looked at her helplessly. She longed for Dwight. He'd know what to do. Maybe Beulah did have reason for grief. Dwight had said— She touched Beulah's shoulder. "Did you get Mr. Crown's number? Perhaps Leonard was delayed and met him later. We could—"

"No—no, I didn't get his number. Call that detective. Call him and—" The command was waterlogged, but it was recognizable as a command.

Marianne went to an extension telephone incongruously placed on a corner of the Oeben and Riemer desk. She lifted the receiver, hesitated for a moment, then asked for Missing Persons.

Beulah shouted hysterically, "No—not Missing Persons. They'll send a stranger to talk to me. I want the man who was here yesterday. He's sympathetic—he'll—"

So Marianne called Homicide and asked to speak to Mr. Nelson.

Waiting, she felt stupid. Like a child about to deliver an unprepared lesson. Beulah's communicated tension blocked her, and she was still unprepared when after several dead ends an alert voice said, "The sarge ain't in. Can I take a message?" and added instantly, "Wait, lady, he just arrived. Hang on."

She hung on, and presently the detective sergeant's voice came as a calm force that released the tension. She found herself explaining the circumstance of the call quite coherently, in spite of a flow of prompting from Beulah. Not that he demanded much explanation. He seemed to sum up the situation the moment she mentioned Leonard's name. Again she was impressed by his cleverness. Almost clairvoyant, she thought. She overrated him, innocent of Sammy's earlier call and of the fact that he had just returned from the warehouse, where he had been searching for some clue to Leonard's whereabouts. The only details he did ask her to repeat concerned Matthew Crown. These she gave as well as she could, trying to listen to her own words above Beulah's shouted interjections. Beulah took it for granted that she would know all about the deal from start to finish, forgetting the incident of the breakfast table, when the telling of it had been suppressed.

Marianne replaced the receiver as though she were dropping a burden and felt correspondingly free.

Beulah questioned her feverishly: "What did he say? Is he coming?"

"He—he's putting it through the proper channels. You'll hear just as soon as he has anything to report." Marianne was eliding deftly. What he had said was, "I'll hand it over to Missing Persons for the time being. They'll send out the alarm and direct their boys to scour the town. Tell Mrs. Roberts to sit tight." He had not minimized the situation or given any words of comfort that might be passed along to Beulah. In fact, he had scrapped his professional manner for a moment to say surprisingly, "Even if he never turns up again I think Mrs. Roberts is well rid of him." This remark, of course, was not to be relayed. And because Beulah was in such desperate want of comfort, Marianne felt driven to invention. "He doesn't think there's anything to worry about. He—"

For a strangely welcome instant Beulah became Beulah. "Then he's a fool and I misjudged him." She paced the room again. Suddenly she wheeled on Marianne and said, "Why didn't I think of it before? Dr. Silk. He's psychic. Maybe—"

She was in no mood to be thwarted. Marianne called Dr. Silk. She was relieved when a female voice stated flatly that he was with a patient and could not be disturbed and added, "Did you wish to make an appointment? Name, please." Marianne left a message that Mrs. Roberts wished to see him the moment he was free; that it was urgent.

Beulah resumed her pacing. Marianne could not get her to settle anywhere. She thought, If anyone had tried to tell me I'd be longing for the sight of Leonard Roberts before this day was over I'd have laughed in his face. But I'm not laughing now. I'm longing.

She tried to divert Beulah, picking over possible conversational openings as expertly as a sorter of grain. But her labor showed scant result beyond a fictive heap of discarded chaff. She even tried to anger her by again taking up arms for the twins, but all the shafts fell short. As a last resort she spoke of Irma's departure. "So you couldn't induce her to stay after all. Well, you picked a happy substitute. I don't remember that we ever had colored help before."

At that Beulah stopped being an ancient untamed panther and stood still just long enough to say, "Her references were excellent, and she's not afraid of a little extra work either. She's experienced with men's wardrobes too. Leonard will— Oh, Leonard—Leonard!"

By six-thirty, when the outer door opened, Marianne had fully absorbed the contagion of frenzy. She could hardly bear the spectacle of Beulah's hope emerging for a moment naked and begging, only to cower back because it was Hale who made answer to her clarioned "Leonard!"

Hale entered the library, whistling the latest war song. He seemed like an impudent intruder. Marianne thought unjustly, How dare he act as though this were any day in the week—as though nothing had happened? She forgot that she loved him and wanted to hit him hard for bringing normalcy into the demented room.

Hale said, "Things are picking up. Where did you find Sammy, Beulah? She's quite a gal." Then he looked at Beulah. "What's the matter with *you?*"

He was quick to combine and digest the broken fragments that were flung at him. He strained to be matter-of-fact. "You'd better not go to pieces. Most likely Grandpa the Fourth found out something that made him sure the deal was a phony. He's probably walking off a big disappointment. He's going to need you when he does come home."

Beulah only cried, "Don't call him that odious name. He hates it. You're to blame. You've helped to drive him from me. You and Clement and you, Marianne."

Clement arrived while she was still laying about her impartially, dwelling upon forgotten slights which her own flesh and blood and, yes, even she herself had inflicted upon poor, sensitive Leonard.

Unlike his twin, Clement did not enter whistling or carry ill-timed cheer into the room. His gloom had, if anything, been heightened since the morning. He listened and gleaned what there was to be gleaned. Then, like a man who grasps at some reason for being, he turned to Beulah as to a cherished partner in sorrow and tried to take her under his own wounded wing. Perhaps because of urgent need to exchange his misery for another's his ministrations were effective to some degree. He did manage to make her lie down on the couch, but there his efficacy ended. Pacing or reclining were, at this point, all one to Beulah. She burst into a passion of weeping that infected the room like a black plague of sound.

Hale clutched at his throat. Marianne bit through her lip. Clement shouted, "Goddammit, Goddammit!" in a doomed voice.

"What shall we do?" Marianne was sobbing too. "She's got to stop. She's got to—she'll tear herself to pieces. We'd better get the doctor. What's his number? Where's that address book?"

They were running mad circles when Sammy came in bearing a tray. "You don't need no doctor. I going to fix her up good." The tray contained a face cloth, a towel, a basin of water, and a tall bottle of cologne. She set it down on a small table. She propped Beulah's shuddering body with a tight strong arm. The arm seemed to absorb some of the tremors. Marianne and the twins watched Beulah become quieter as Sammy bathed her face and wrists.

She sent Marianne to the kitchen for tea and literally forced it down Beulah's throat together with crooning sedative words. She covered the exhausted woman with a thin blanket of calm which stayed in place until Cromwell Proctor returned to the apartment.

Cromwell ripped off the blanket without ceremony. He addressed Marianne in injured accents: "First I drove over to the St. George Bar because I remembered that Leonard sometimes entertains his clients there. But he wasn't around, and after I'd had a spot I decided to take your advice and drop in at the warehouse. But it was no go. The place is guarded by policemen, and they refused to let me in. One of them began to ask rude questions, as though I were a murderer, but he was just being officious, of course. If he really suspected me I wouldn't be walking around loose, would I?"

The phone rang. Clement got there first. He shouted into the mouthpiece and received an answering shout

Beulah, sitting upright, caught the unembellished message that escaped into the still room. She repeated mechanically, "Leonard Roberts found dead." She fainted.

Chapter 14

Nelson drove with no more conscious effort than is used by a pedestrian in motivating his legs. His thoughts were free to cope with Furniss, who sat beside him.

Furniss said grimly, "Anyway, he's one suspect we can scratch."

"I gather you don't hold with the accident theory."

"Not unless my own eyes prove it—too coincidental."

"Well, we can scratch Dr. Silk too. From last reports, he's been under surveillance all day."

"So has Proctor. Which leaves Clement Ramsey, Dwight Cannon, and the women."

"You can eliminate at least one of the women. Sammy's been with Beulah since—"

Furniss said, "Sammy went out to a booth to phone you. That gave Beulah ten minutes leeway. Not that I'm half anxious to pin it on her. I just want to show you that *I* don't have favorites. I'm strictly impartial."

"I think we'd better find out the approximate time of death before we wear ourselves out."

"I'm not wearing myself out. I've got those eliminations well under control. What I'm afraid of now is a third murder. They haven't found a trace of that uptown mouse. She's either dead or traveling fast."

Nelson said with heat, "If you're strictly impartial what makes you so sure it's Clement? From your point of view we're wasting a lot of time."

"Your fault—not mine. I wanted to pull him in. Someday I'm going to wake up and find I've had too much faith in you."

"He doesn't fit the part, Chief."

"You're not playing Little Theater. We don't deal in stock types in this racket."

Nelson said doggedly, "I still don't believe that Clement—"

Furniss snorted, "Hunches—crystal ball stuff." He himself went into silence.

On Clark Street, Nelson braked near the St. George Hotel. He turned to Furniss. "You took down the directions. Where now?"

"Eh?" Furniss swam out of an abstraction. He said in synthetic wonder, "I thought you'd lead me straight to it. 'Smatter? Did the crystal ball go back on you? Well, never mind. It lends a human touch to your sometimes overwhelming omniscience. Let me see—just how is the warehouse situated?"

"It was on the inland side of Furman Street when I left it this afternoon."

"Hmmm—two miles beyond that, at the start of—" Swiftly he sketched an imaginary map. "We turn left at the corner. I'll sing out directions as we go."

The car slid forward smoothly. Presently Furniss said, "Turn right. Yep. That's it. You're pretty farsighted, Grid. Do you see what looks like one of our arc lights at the corner of the next street?"

"Yes, and I can spot a green-and-white patrol coupé and an outline that might be Doc Perry."

He parked skillfully between a squad car and an ambulance. He and Furniss got out. Two local policemen, strangers to them, barred their way, questioning their right to be there. Furniss blustered but made no attempt to produce his credentials. To save time, Nelson searched his own person, finally producing his badge of office. He cut off profuse apologies, absently slipping the badge into his overcoat pocket. Furniss said, "Why don't you pin it on like a self-respecting dick?"

They bored through what seemed like a concrete slab of spectators and joined the official group in the road.

The night was not yet at its maximum of darkness. Nevertheless, an arc light had been rigged to illumine what was left of Leonard Roberts and a battered bicycle. It showed his body resting on its left hip, the empty eyes turned blindly toward the curb. It showed the knees drawn up to the abdomen, the elbows clamped close to the sides, the forearms raised and crossed over the chest in self-embrace, the finger tips pointing to the shoulders. It showed black hair, hard as a hat with crusted blood.

The blood, Nelson reflected, had poured down the opened head to color and starch the shirt. It had gone no farther. Yes, the shirt had absorbed most of the blood; the shirt and the sponginess of the soft tweed coat. And the fact that the asphalt where Roberts huddled seemed unstained might be attributed to the quick-drying powers of the fresh breeze that blew from the harbor.

Nelson stooped and touched the rigid fingers. He swallowed a sudden flow of saliva. Dealing with death was his business. Yet never, in spite of constant repetition, could he take it in his stride. He set his expressive lips. He straightened and did a little jig step to flex his long legs. Furniss was at his side, crowded by big Dr. Perry.

Nelson said, "It's no accident."

Furniss, the extrovert, nodded cheerfully. "He was murdered all right. If it wasn't for the head wound I'd guess poison. That position looks like the result of sudden seizure to me. No doubt about it being Roberts, is there?"

"It's Roberts."

Dr. Perry said, "I could have told you that. I managed to extract a wallet containing his automobile license, without moving the limbs."

"Anything else in the wallet?"

"Nothing but some business cards. No cash."

Furniss said, "And Beulah made quite a point of the large sum he was carrying to consummate that business deal." He shrugged. "Maybe he completed the deal before he cycled off in all directions."

"He didn't. That's what got Beulah started. The man he was to meet, Matthew Crown, phoned to ask why he hadn't turned up." Nelson added, "At least Matthew Crown said he hadn't turned up. The night watchman disagreed."

"Oh, so now we've got a dark horse. Well, to please you we'll give him a light workout."

"If we find him. We don't know his address or his phone number, and possibly we don't even know his right name."

"Fine. But we do know money's the motive this time. Roberts was tailed to this lonely street, forced to dismount his wheel, knocked out, and rolled for his wad."

Dr. Perry was shaking his large head hopelessly, but he made no attempt at utterance.

Nelson said, "Not so fast. You've observed, of course, that rigor has set in. Since protein doesn't begin to coagulate until at least two hours after death—"

Furniss shouted, "Sue me!" loudly enough to reach the handful of reporters that policemen had been unable to blast out of earshot. Someone tittered nervously.

A car drove up and unloaded Busch, the department's chief photographer. He reached the inspector, took a professional squint at the body, shuddered, and said, "Ain't this an accident?"

"No, it ain't. Get busy." As Busch went off to assemble his equipment Furniss said softly, "What you're trying so patiently to convey, Grid, is that Roberts has been dead for some time and that if he died in this particular spot he'd have been discovered sooner. Because even though this is a deserted street, a few stray individuals would surely pass by occasionally—witness the crowd that's gathered now—and it isn't likely they'd be too blasé to notify the police if they stumbled over a corpse. Besides, the patrol boys have been out ever since Sammy gave us a ring. If he died here they'd have come upon him long before rigor set in, even allowing for the cold weather." He turned to Dr. Perry. "Could I persuade you to give your version, Doc?"

Perry answered with his usual reluctance to offer an opinion not checked by full research. "If I live to be a hundred I'll still find that in my racket a dissecting table has it all over a crowded street." He prodded the corpse's hip gently with the toe of his shoe. "All I can say now is that I think this has been dead of a fractured skull—and perhaps contributory causes—for at least a number of hours. I'm not inclined to lean to poison, in spite of the position, but when I've had time to brood over stomach, lungs, limbs, larynx, liver, viscera—"

Furniss interrupted testily: "All right—all right. I thought you were never going to run out of *Is*. We'll go into the *v* department later. Meanwhile, we'll assume you're right about the fractured skull, but I think he's been poisoned to boot. If that isn't a gastric paroxysm, he was practicing to be a contortionist when the end came. And just what do you mean by 'perhaps contributory causes'?"

"I mean that in addition to the fractured skull our new customer has two broken arms and two broken legs. You'd better let the morgue boys remove him before he gets hurt." Dr. Perry strode back to his car, efficiently tackling the reporters who tried to block him.

Furniss shouted, "Hey, Doc, wait a minute! Are you sure?" Then he muttered, "Hell," and stared down at the corpse.

Busch returned, dogged by an assistant loaded with paraphernalia. He jostled Furniss and tried more or less delicately to move him. But the old man did not stir until Nelson took his arm and walked him out of the camera's eye.

Furniss said hoarsely, "That head blow came from the rear. Yet someone didn't just sneak up behind him and go 'wham.' Someone met him face to face, picked him up, and hurled him a few miles. Because that's the only way I can account for such wholesale damage."

Nelson took off his hat. He rumpled his white hair until it looked like stuffing torn from a mattress and generously, if carelessly, placed upon his well-shaped skull. "Notice his lip, Chief. He cut it yesterday. They said he fell off his bicycle—an explanation I'd have found reason to doubt if there had been any blood traces on Shepard's hands or clothing." He shrugged. "The cut, as you can see, is nicely scabbed over now. Doesn't it seem logical that if he suffered pain he'd have automatically clamped down with his teeth and caused it to reopen?"

"You're as good as telling me the killer advanced from the rear and leisurely proceeded to crack limbs without causing his victim to even cock a snoot." Furniss was heavily sarcastic. "Something wrong with his reflexes, no doubt!"

"I'm telling you the head blow might have killed him instantly, before he had time to react, and that the other injuries might have been inflicted after death."

"Might have—might have! You getting set to pin this on a Frankenstein creation?" Then he said questioningly, "Proctor—maybe?" And answered himself: "Nope, that's going too far even for an ex-cat killer." Suddenly his face took on a listening look. "Shhh—don't interrupt. A little man's hanging on my ear lobe, whispering away like sixty. He says Roberts was tossed from a fast-moving car, bicycle and all. He says that would take care of everything but the head wound."

Nelson smiled. "Tell your little man to guess again. So far as we know, unless someone shifted him before we arrived, his arms and legs didn't hit the pavement at any point. He's resting on his hip, and if that fast-moving-car theory is correct, that should be fractured too."

"Well, maybe it is. You can't expect a hurried guy like Doc to mention every little detail. This has to be thought through, Grid. We've got to take it from the beginning—"

A freckled-faced reporter who looked under twenty had found an opening in the crowd. He elbowed his way to the inspector. "Care to say something for the press, Inspector?"

Nelson interposed his own body, managing to hold the reporter a short distance from his objective. "Don't hound the inspector now. He's thinking."

The reporter murmured, "About his next radio spiel, no doubt." He stepped back a little, pushed by Nelson's scowl. "'Scuse it, Sarge. Glad to see him back on the job. If *you're* not busy thinking how about giving out? Does the dead butler tie in with this?" He spat disgustedly. "Jeez! Why can't we have a dead deb for a change? Butlers! I'm strictly one of the masses, myself. I thought the breed was extinct."

"Maybe yesterday's murder was a step in that direction."

The reporter grinned. "You're a great kidder, Sarge. A great sidetracker too. Be a sport. Spill something once."

Nelson made his voice confidential. "Inspector Furniss is sure the two killings were committed by the same person. He'll be working on the case all night. If you drop up at headquarters later he'll talk to you."

"Honest?"

"Honest."

The reporter dashed off. Nelson returned to Furniss.

Furniss said, "Little squirt. I heard what he said. I heard what you said too. I hope you're not sticking my neck out. Look, Grid, if he wasn't killed here—and I'll ride that far with you—we've got to find out where he was killed. You tell me you hunted up the night watchman and he swore that Roberts turned up at the warehouse before nine this morning. Well, when you cased the warehouse did you come across anything that might point to a killing there?"

"I went to the warehouse because we thought Roberts was a murder suspect, not a murder victim. All I did was hunt some clue that would lead to his whereabouts if he had planned a skip. I didn't get down on my knees to ferret out bloodstains. I just riffled papers and—"

"Well, now we'll have to go back and look for bloodstains. Because if we discovered where he was killed and get Doc to narrow down the time we can check reports to see who might possibly have been in that vicinity. Hell, Grid, we can't win. Your paper search uncovered that billet-doux he'd written to his wife which told that he was planning a skip. So if he hadn't turned up dead he'd still be a suspect. But, dead, he's worse than a suspect. He's an added headache and—Hey! Where do you think *you're* going?"

"To find out what's what. A couple of our boys seem to be having an argument with some latecomers."

Furniss looked. He said, "Tsk, tsk. They ought to get refunds for missing the best part of the show." He caught only a glimpse of their faces between sternly vocal uniforms. He followed Nelson over to the group. "What's this?"

The policeman stepped aside to reveal two men and a girl.

Chapter 15

Hale and Marianne were driven by Cromwell Proctor to the place where Leonard Roberts' body had been found by a cruising squad car. Though considerable pressure had been exerted to persuade Marianne to stay with Beulah, she had refused. Anything, she thought, was preferable to the futility of standing by with no panacea for Beulah's anguish. So after all arguments failed it was Clement who decided to remain behind.

On the way Hale, except for giving Cromwell directions hastily relayed by Clement, addressed himself solely to his sister: "I must have been insane to let you come. When we get there you stay in the car. Do you hear?"

Cromwell neighed, "Rather! No sight for a woman." And his nostrils twitched, as though he were anticipating a rare treat.

Hale paid no attention to him. "I'll be the one to get out. Though they're pretty certain it *is* Leonard, it seems no identification's complete without the say-so of his nearest and dearest. That's a laugh, isn't it?" His sensitive features misted with distaste. "All I've got to do is give a quick look and tell them to go ahead and label him. It will save one of us a trip to the morgue and it won't take more than a few moments. So you stay put. Turn right, Crummy. Clement said it was a few miles beyond the warehouse. Isn't that a crowd at the start of the next street? Yes, that must be it."

Marianne had not been listening to Hale. When Cromwell found parking space she got out of the car automatically and followed her would-be protectors.

Progress was halted by several blue uniforms who demanded a detailed explanation and seemed to reject it on general principles. But the uniforms were overruled by Detective Sergeant Gridley Nelson, who had apparently been attracted to the spot by their loud skepticism. He was accompanied by an older man who gave the new arrivals brief but comprehensive scrutiny.

Nelson looked hard at Marianne, as though he did not quite recognize her. Then he said, "Inspector Furniss, this is Miss Marianne Ramsey, her brother—Hale, I believe—and Mr. Proctor, a friend of the family. I expect they've come to identify the body."

The inspector's response was almost jovial. "Fine. No matter how positive we are, identification can't be official without confirmation from some next of kin. Come along." He led the way, for all the world like a good host about to exhibit a favorite possession to his favorite guests.

Busch and his assistant had just completed their last shot. The ambulance had unloaded two impatient white-coated men who were preparing to fill their long basket.

Furniss said, "Hold it, boys," and stood by, his bright blue eyes intent.

Marianne looked down. Then she shut her eyes. She whispered inanely, "He did fall off his bicycle. He fell off and killed himself." She opened her eyes carefully. She saw that Hale was creating the illusion of trying to maintain his balance on a heaving deck.

"Curled up like a—like an embryo," Hale was repeating, his whitened lips framing the words.

Marianne tugged frantically at his arm. "All right. Tell them it *is*—tell them and come away. Hale!" But she could not make him hear. She saw that Cromwell was breathing fast, like a runner who had reached goal and intended to remain there. She saw that Nelson was standing with the inspector a few feet away from the terrible spot which must not be allowed to stamp itself further upon her vision or upon Hale's, if nights were ever again to be endured. She was about to ask Nelson to help her with Hale, when she noticed that his companion was eying her brother strangely.

She saw him turn to Nelson and say something. Saw Nelson shrug and heard his reply, "No, I'm not wrong. This one is Hale." Then she saw him lift his hand and beckon, his gesture answered by two policemen who nodded knowingly at whatever it was he said to them.

No part of the nightmare made sense to her. She stood bewildered, jostled by a policeman, jostled by a man with a white coat, jostled by someone with a card in his hat who asked her if she was Marianne Ramsey and to whom she made no answer. Isolated voices came out of the pressed-back crowd and broke against her ears.

"They say that both his arms and both his legs are busted. I got it from one of the cops." ... "If that cute trick's his wife he had something to live for, I'm telling you." ... "Must be the work of a fiend." ... "He was rolled." ... "Yeah—a rich guy too." ... "Cleaned out. Not a cent left in his wallet. Some creep hit pay dirt." ... "Whoever done it must've come up from behind and conked him unbeknownst." ... "If he got it from the rear why is he all curled up like a horse had kicked him?" ... "Gosh! A finished job. Both arms and legs snapped like twigs." ... "His skull didn't get bashed like that with one sock—must've hit him again after he was out."

Suddenly Nelson looked her way. He came to where she stood and took her arm gently.

She said without inflection, "Is it true that his arms and legs are broken?"

She felt his fingers stiffen. "Who told you that?"

She said wearily, "Someone in the crowd said it."

"Oh." Then he said, "Come on—I'll get you out of this."

She found herself back in Cromwell Proctor's car with no consciousness of having moved from the seething road. She heard Nelson say, "Your brother will be with you in a few minutes," before he left her.

She leaned back against the upholstery. She touched her forehead and it was damp. "Ridiculous," she kept murmuring. "Mad!" But her mind refused to accept the adjectives, just as years ago her mind had refused to accept her misery in the French school. Her mind was relentlessly comparing the words of the crowd with the words that had been spoken by Dwight Cannon. "Two broken arms and two broken legs," said the crowd. "I'll break every bone in his body," said Dwight. "Not a cent in his wallet," said the crowd. Dwight's wallet was full. They hadn't given him a salary advance. The money was borrowed, he said. "Come up from behind. Pay dirt." ... "He'll never bother you again." That was what Dwight had said. But Dwight couldn't. Dwight was good. How can I marry you, Dwight, if I have no faith? I'm a fool. A neurotic, shivering fool. It started in France. I thought I was cured, but I'll never be cured. This is the way I'll always be.

"Stop it," she cried so loudly that a policeman poked his head in through the open window and stared at her and said, "Sit tight, lady. We won't take long," and withdrew and held conference with fellow uniforms.

The car was shaking beneath her. The policemen seemed to be doing something to it. Incuriously she heard them tinkering at the back, raising the lid of the luggage compartment.

I'll call Dwight, she thought, as soon as we get home. I'm not a neurotic. If there's need for strength I'll be strong—strong and sane. Forgive me, Dwight. But if if there's nothing to forgive, then I'll help you. I'll help you ...

Hale climbed into the car and moved close to her, as though he were warming himself. People did turn green. His color proved it.

Crummy's voice, high and petulant, said, "I'll complain. Why should they search my car?" His face was red. It appeared at the window between the heads of Detective Sergeant Nelson and the inspector.

The inspector motioned Marianne and Hale to the pavement. Cromwell, still protesting, slid under the wheel, and another plainclothesman came up and got in beside him.

As the car rolled away the inspector said to Nelson, "Here's where we divide forces for the time being." He drew him aside and spoke quickly and, to the listening Hale and Marianne, cryptically. They caught the words "Warehouse … bloodstains," and looked at each other with empty faces.

Hale shrugged and summoned bravado. "Well, that's that. But why the business with Crummy? Surely they don't think—"

Marianne prayed silently, Let them think anything—anything but Dwight.

Nelson returned to them. "I'll drive you home."

Hale protested, "No need to put you to the trouble. We can get a taxi. That is"—he was embarrassed—"have you any money with you, Sis?"

She reached absently into the pocket of her smart topcoat. "No, I didn't bring my pocketbook."

Nelson said, "It doesn't matter. I'm going your way."

He deposited them in the back of his car and took the wheel. His foot pressed the starter. He could catch glimpses of brother and sister in the mirror. The green tinge had drained from Hale's young face. It was pale now and very troubled. Marianne stared straight ahead, as though she were trying to search out something in a dark room.

Hale leaned forward. "If you drop us off at the corner of our street it will be all right." He hesitated. "I doubt if my grandmother will be able to see you tonight. She's hard hit."

Nelson said, "I promise you I won't try to see her unless she wishes it. But I know she's anxious to have the murderer of her husband found and punished. It may ease her mind to talk to me."

Hale said, "Is—is Crummy being arrested?"

Marianne shifted her eyes for a moment.

Nelson shook his white head. "No." Then he said, "I think you should take more of a hand in running your home life from now on. Your visiting list could stand a bit of revision."

"I—I don't exactly know what you're getting at." Hale glanced at his sister. Her eyes were again focused ahead on some far-off truth.

"I'll go into it in detail later." Nelson changed the subject abruptly, calling Marianne back from her straining quest. "Miss Ramsey, you went to the warehouse today. At what time?"

"Warehouse?" She fixed her eyes on his collar. "Did you say something to me? Oh—yes. I went on an errand for Beulah. She— she—Dr. Silk had recommended some vitamin tablets for— She wanted Melvin Beck, the day man, to bring them over so that—" Her voice rambled nervously.

"When did you go on this errand?"

"I— About noon. Perhaps a little before. I was to meet—I— About noon, I guess."

The car was crawling along. Nelson said, "And you didn't find Beck there. So you left a note for him."

"Yes, I left a note. I pinned it to the big screen."

"And propped the screen so that it wouldn't topple over. How did you manage to lift those heavy objects with no one there to help you?"

"Lift?" She was attentive now and puzzled. "I didn't lift anything. The screen *was* propped up. It toppled a little when I pinned the note to it."

Hale said uncertainly, "Where does the warehouse come in? Look here!" His voice shook. "What were you doing in the warehouse? You can't imagine for a moment that Marianne is mixed—"

"I'm not accusing your sister of murder or of complicity in murder."

"How can you be so sure Leonard *was* murdered? He's been falling off his bicycle ever since my grandmother bought it for him. Couldn't he have fallen this time and—?"

"When did he get the bicycle?"

"A few weeks ago."

"New or secondhand?"

"New, of course," Hale muttered, "streamlined—nothing but the best for *him*."

"Did you happen to notice the one beside him?"

Hale shuddered. "No—I—"

"Well, it wasn't new. It corresponded to a model-T in vintage. But that's beside the point. He was murdered. You can take my word for it. And the murderer made a halfhearted attempt to dress it up as an accident. He didn't even take the trouble to plant the victim's own wheels beside him. It looks like he was just having fun, because unless he's a moron he couldn't have thought we'd be fooled by it. He gave himself away a bit too. Because I believe the lock of hair covering the butler's forehead was born of the same sense of humor, which means we've only to find one man."

"Only," said Hale. Then he said shakily, "Here's the old homestead. Wake up, Sis."

Chapter 16

Marianne accompanied her brother and the detective as far as the library. Then she lagged behind. Their entrance was marked by confusion, and she was able to turn tail and slip away quietly. She had to speak to Dwight, and there would be no privacy anywhere in the apartment. She would go out to a booth to telephone.

But she needed money to telephone. Her pocketbook. Where was it? Had she left it in the library? O God, please, wasn't there somewhere she could get just one nickel? Perhaps her pocketbook wasn't in the library after all. Perhaps in her room. Or she might have left it on the little table near the door. No, it wasn't there. But sometimes there was loose change in the drawer of that table, kept there for the tipping of errand boys. She began to search feverishly. The new maid, walking down the corridor with someone's coat over her arm, saw her and spoke.

"You want to find something, Miss Ma'yanne? I help you."

"Did you see my pocketbook?"

"Yes, I see it in the room where they all is. You want me to go get it?"

"No." They would ask why it was needed. They would stop her. She said, "Sammy, could you—could you lend me a nickel?"

"Sure, but it ain't going to buy you much. I lend you more than that. I always carry a few small change in my apron just in case I called on with no notice." Silver jingled in Sammy's palm, but her long brown fingers started to close over it.

Marianne snatched at a five-cent piece, clutched it tightly.

Sammy said slowly, "You ain't going no place?"

"Yes. I must." She slipped past Sammy, struggled with the door, and gained the outer hall. The automatic elevator was not on the floor. She could not bear to wait for its ascent. She raced down twelve flights of stairs. When she reached the ground floor her knees were trembling and her heart was wild. She stood still for as long as it took to steady herself. Then she raced through the lobby, through the street, and through the doors of the nearest drugstore. She shut herself into a booth and dialed the number of Dwight's furnished rooming house.

She heard his name shouted by a male voice that answered the telephone. And then she heard him say, "Hello?"

"This is Marianne, Dwight."

His voice smiled. "So help me, it's nothing short of telepathy. I was thinking of you. I hope no one else in your neighborhood got the drift of my thoughts."

"Dwight?"

"Yes, lovely?"

"Could you—could you come?"

"Where? You sound peculiar." His voice stopped smiling. "There's nothing wrong?"

"Dwight, please. I'd meet you at the Clark Street station—please."

"Hold everything. I'm starting now."

She left the drugstore. It would be all right. Whatever it was, as soon as she saw him and touched him it would be all right. He was on the way. He'd take the Eighth Avenue subway on Fiftieth Street. That would bring him to her in a half-hour. Three quarters of an hour at most. She wouldn't go back upstairs. She might not be able to leave again, and she didn't want to lead him into—into— She'd start walking very slowly toward Clark Street.

She started walking. Time was tough. Time was hard to kill. She saw Time in a leathery hide, showing strong teeth. Mocking her.

She stopped to look in half-lighted windows. She passed another drugstore, retraced her steps, and entered it. She asked to see a lipstick and was vague as to brand and color. She remembered that she had no money and turned and left without apology. She resumed her slow walk. Her steps had covered a block when she realized that she was being addressed.

An oncoming car had drawn up at the curb. A hesitant voice said, "Good evening. It *is* Miss Ramsey, isn't it?" And Dr. Silk got out. He took off his hat and bowed. His red hair gleamed under the light of the street lamp.

His small, humorous eyes appraised her. The corners of his wide clown's mouth turned up. "I thought I recognized you, but I couldn't be sure. In fact, I'm not sure now. You've changed so incredibly since yesterday. Do they permit little girls to wear grown-up violet suits in this part of town?"

Her hand lost itself in his great warm grasp. She felt less lonely.

"I'm on my way to your house in answer to a message from Mrs. Roberts. She's been such a benefactress—increased my practice to such an astonishing degree that I'd feel it my duty to come from the ends of the earth if she called me. I do hope the dear lady isn't ill."

Feeling blessedly detached, Marianne told him about Leonard.

Talking to someone, she found, blocked the recently installed machinery in her aching head. She wanted to keep talking until Dwight came and blocked that machinery for all time.

"A regrettable occurrence," he was saying. "Cut off in his prime, when he had everything to live for." His silken voice went on, running the gamut of stock phrases unfailingly produced by sudden death. When he ended it was to say apologetically, "But how inconsiderate of me to keep you standing in the chill night air. And you're headed away from my own objective. Do you think that quite wise under the circumstances? If I make a suggestion will you take it as from a friend? You're shivering, child. You've had a bad shock. Permit me to drive you home and to bed. Youth is so resilient. You'll be surprised at how much better you'll feel in the morning sunlight."

His triteness was healing. Marianne managed a smile, though her lips stiffened against the effort. "No, thank you. I'm—I won't be able to sleep. I think a little night air might help."

The street was full of passers-by. Normal, happy people. She resented them. They kept brushing her sleeve, and she drew closer to Dr. Silk to avoid contact with them.

He said, "Mrs. Roberts is undoubtedly surrounded by her kin. I think your need of me is greater than hers just now. I'm a bit of a psychologist, you know." His voice was deprecating. "If economic pressure hadn't interfered I'd have pursued that career instead of the humble one in which I am presently engaged. Let us sit in my car awhile. Perhaps if you unburden yourself you'll find you can sleep after all."

His hand was on her arm. It was impossible to rebuff him. He was so earnest. Her wristwatch said she had succeeded in wasting fifteen minutes. The rest of the time must be spent somehow. And it *was* cold. So she found herself seated beside Dr. Silk in his long black car.

He's nice, she thought dully. It's really kind of him to want to help.

His large, vital hands lay idle upon the steering wheel. After a few moments of silence he said, "What do the police make of this double tragedy?"

"Mr. Nelson didn't say."

"Oh, you've spoken to him today?"

"Yes, I went with Hale to identify L-Leonard."

Dr. Silk said distressfully, "But they must have been out of their minds to permit that. No wonder you're so unhappy." He added, "Mr. Nelson's the detective with the white hair, isn't he? He seems to be an intelligent chap. I'm sure he'll get to the bottom of this."

"Yes—I—yes. He drove us back to the house afterward. He asked some funny questions."

"I'll wager he did. All policemen do—sometimes just to make their work seem more important." Dr. Silk smiled. "What sort of questions do you mean? Perhaps between us we can work out their possible relation to the case."

Marianne said, "I don't know—something about my being in the warehouse today. I'm afraid I wasn't listening very carefully. My mind—"

"I know. Your mind was where the mind of a pretty young lady usually is—on her sweetheart." He seemed to be trying to divert her. "I saw you glance at your wristwatch. I do hope you haven't come out at this hour to keep a clandestine appointment. I won't say I'm old enough to be your father—vanity, you know—but I will say that sometimes the manners and customs of the younger generation do fuddle me a bit." Then he said, "If silence is affirmation I don't suppose you'll consent to spend much more time with me. And I greatly fear that I haven't been as helpful as I should have liked to be, so perhaps—"

She said absently, "You've been very helpful."

"I do hope that the one you're meeting has been duly approved by dear Mrs. Roberts."

"What?" The tone she used was that of a sleeper waking sharply. She looked at her watch again and started to leave the car. Then she saw that the big well-meaning simpleton had started the motor. She was flung back against the upholstery. She tensed herself for protest. If he took her home she'd miss Dwight, and Dwight would—

He said as the car shot forward, "I do beg your pardon. I didn't mean to shake you up. Why, what is it, little girl? If it weren't so absurd I'd almost think you were afraid of me."

Chapter 17

Sammy had wadded her apron and thrust it into the pocket of Nelson's overcoat. She had the coat on, buttoned up to her chin. In the chill night air it felt warm and comforting. She needed comfort. She put her foot on the running board of the taxi. She said to the driver, "Man, you see that long black car across the street and down a ways in front of that truck?"

The driver thrust his head out of the window and craned. "There ain't nothing wrong with my gloms."

"I want you to follow it. Hear?"

"Oh yeah! That's one for the book. You're asking me to tail a crate which ain't rolling and which, besides, is headed in my direction."

"I ain't asking. I telling. It going to roll. When it start you follow. No matter what directions."

The cabdriver looked bored. "Let's see the pictures on your bank notes, sister."

Sammy swallowed. Without hope she stuffed her hand into Nelson's coat pocket. Hope came surging. Under the wadded apron her hand encountered something that felt like a bill. She drew it out, and it was a bill. She waved it at the driver.

"A fin," he said. "Business is so bad I'd tail a tank across Africa for a fin. Get in, sister. But if the fin runs out, you run out too. No rides on the house."

Sammy got into the cab, murmuring, "Mr. Grid-dely sure got a bad habit of sticking everything into his pockets. I fixing to talk to him about this, so he take more care of his little old fins." Her hands explored the other pocket.

The driver's round head pivoted on his neck. "Did you say something, sister?"

Sammy withdrew her hand, grasping Nelson's police badge. She opened her hand. The badge shone on her flat palm. "I said I a police lady. I on law business. You put your eyes back where they belong on that black car. Else you ain't going to look at the pictures on no fin money. You going to look at the pictures in the paper, and the paper going to shout that you got yourself in the jailhouse for not paying no mind to a police lady."

He laughed. "I guess anything goes in wartime, but I need salt on this one. Where did you get the badge, sister?"

Sammy sighed. She had edged close to the window, so that she could get a side view of the black car. She took her eyes away to lean forward and read the driver's framed identification card. His name was Daniel Glover. She said, "I going to tell you about it fast, Mr. Daniel, but you got to pass me your promise to keep a hushed mouth."

He was still chuckling. "I won't snitch—not unless you bumped a copper."

"I ain't done nothing like that." Returning her eyes to the window, Sammy began to lie. She did not lie very often, and so her words came out labored and tense, giving an effect of deep sincerity. She lied because torture would not have made her discuss Nelson's police activities with an outsider.

"They's a little girl in that car and a bad man. That little girl my little girl. I work for her grandma. Her grandma sick. She don't know her poor lamb go with that no-good man. It like to kill her if she find out. So when I see my little girl I raise from a baby run out, I shake into her daddy's coat, which I taking to my room to sew on a loose button, and I run after her. Her daddy big in the police business. He going to thank you for this 'cause that man she out with, he peddle reefers. That man a dog. He want to harm my little girl."

The driver said, "Reefers, huh?" He clicked his tongue against his teeth. "I'm a father myself. This reefer character—has he got a gun?"

"He ain't got nothing. You walk up and sneeze at him he going to run like a rabbit." She was devoutly thankful that the driver had not seen the size and girth of the stranger with Marianne. She said pleadingly, "Please, Mr. Daniel, that car rolling now. You studying to follow it or do I find another gentleman?"

Daniel put his foot on the starter. "Hold onto your back hair, sister. Here we go."

Sammy said, "I holding." She relaxed and calmly put her trust in Daniel.

When Marianne had made hurried exit it seemed to Sammy that there was only one course to take. Marianne had just returned to the apartment with Mr. Grid-dely and one of the twins, who were not, as yet, separated in Sammy's mind. Sammy's disturbed thoughts boiled down to the strong conviction that the young girl had no good reason to be "taking her sad little face right out again." Her exit was obviously in the nature of an escape, confirmed by the fact that she dared not go into the library to get her own pocketbook and would not allow Sammy to get it either. That meant she feared being detained. And Mr. Grid-dely was the only one in the apartment who could detain her against her will. Trying to escape from Mr. Grid-dely was a bad mistake. Sammy knew that well, because once in the past she had tried it herself. But that was before she had come to learn how good and kind he was—"a fine, solid somebody, always going out of his road to help folks that got messed up."

Sammy regretted that there had been no time to go to the library to summon him. If only she had known that Marianne would provide leeway by taking the stairs instead of the elevator.

Her heart had lurched when she found the outer hall empty. She had pressed her finger on the elevator button with little faith. And then it had descended to her like an angel, from just one story above.

She had stomped into it, as though the extra pressure would hurl her to the ground floor. There she had questioned the switchboard girl, who told her after maddening deliberation that no one of Marianne's description had passed through the lobby. The switchboard girl had looked at her suspiciously and said, "What's it to you? I don't care if you do work for Mrs. Roberts.

There was a plainclothesman on duty here until a few minutes ago, and he saw the head man go up, so he said everything was all right and he went out for some cigarettes."

Just as Sammy decided that it might yet be possible to summon Nelson by telephone Marianne came on the run. So Sammy ducked behind a chair until she was out of sight. Then she gave chase.

She saw Marianne go into the drugstore and drew the right conclusion, thinking, She only want one nickel, so she telephoning. When the girl appeared again she followed her like a detective-born. Not that much caution was necessary. That poor little lump of misery ain't in no state to see what's in front of her, let alone what's behind, Sammy thought. And she so pretty and happy when I open the door this afternoon, it sing out of her. How come she walk so slow? Reckon she meeting somebody and don't want to get there before he do.

She took cover while Marianne went into the second drugstore, but this time she was unable to figure out her motive, since she emerged empty-handed. After that she did not have to take cover again until the black car drew up at the curb. It was simply a matter of clipping her long stride so that she kept a reasonable distance between herself and her newly adopted charge. When the car disgorged the redheaded giant Sammy ducked into the nearest doorway, ready to interfere if he was just one of those "moving-picture wolves" with dishonorable intentions. She could not hear their conversation, but she saw quickly that Marianne recognized him and seemed to welcome him. He, then, must be the person she had telephoned. The one she expected to meet. Wait a minute! Something stirred in her memory. Couldn't he be that dentist Mr. Grid-dely had described last night? And hadn't Mr. Chief fixed upon him immediately as suspect number one?

Sammy did not like it. He was too smooth. She liked it less when the girl permitted herself to be led to his car. His size was frightening, and no pure-thinking man had a right to hair of that sinister shade. Sammy did not mean to let him out of her sight.

Her eyes scanned the block and picked out a pink taxi. Pink was her favorite color. Without hesitation she ran across the street and embarked upon her talk with Mr. Daniel.

Sitting back in the taxi now, she thought, He know his driving good. He going to make out all right. I wish he let me sit in front with him, but I guess that too much to coax for.

Glancing out of the window, she saw that they were passing through a dingy, dimmed-out street and that buildings were becoming scarcer. Leaning as far forward as she could, so that part of her head stuck through the opening created by the slid-back glass panel, she glimpsed the taillight of the black car. "Don't be scared, you little Miss Ma'yanne," she muttered. "He ain't going to do you nothing while I around."

"Talking to me?"

"Don't let that dentist man get too far away."

"Did you say 'dentist'?"

"Maybe. I come from New Orleans, Mr. Daniel. Down there we call everybody who no good a dentist man."

"Yeah? That's rich. I don't like them operators myself. But listen, sister, I gotta keep my distance, unless you want him to catch wise that he ain't alone. Cripes! I don't like this neighborhood. Too many empty lots. If you ask me, you guessed right. Looks like that guy's up to something plenty shady. I'd feel better if you turned out to be a real dick in disguise 'stead of—" He broke off, his eyes squinting into the reflector. "Blow me down! We're being tailed too. I saw it a few streets back where there was more houses and I— But it ain't coincidence." Suddenly he began to swear with mounting distinction.

Sammy had settled back against the upholstery. She thought, That's good. If he swear like that it mean he beginning to take his job serious. He wrong about us being tailed. She turned her head for a quick glance. That don't look like nothing but another little old taxi. It aiming to pass us.

Then brakes screeched. Daniel's cab came to a jolting stop, not leaping forward again until a good measure of minutes had been lost. Sammy asked anxiously, "What for you do like that?" She hurled her body toward the open panel.

The black car's taillight was no longer visible. The second taxi had shot forward in a wide-sweeping curve and was now hyphenating the space between Daniel and his quarry. Daniel had braked to avoid collision.

Daniel said acidly, "So now we're a cozy little threesome. Could be your little girl's daddy got the vine and is taking charge himself."

"That ain't her daddy. Her daddy got his own car."

"Well, do you still want to kiss off that fin or do I take you back to where I found you?"

"Please, Mr. Daniel, don't stop. Keep on going. I suspicion it all even worse now than when we start."

"That's what I'm afraid of, sister. I ain't heeled and I got my family to consider."

"You got a wrinch, Mr. Daniel?"

"Yeah, sure—but—"

"You give it here. I going to use it if I have to. I don't disfavor you none for being scared. If your family—"

"I'm scared all right. No getting away from it. I don't like trouble.

Never did. But I guess I'd rather swing that wrench myself, if it comes down to it, God forbid." Then he said, "Hey, is that driver nuts—or just practicing to be a suicide? Either he's lost control of the wheel or he's trying to pass that black car the way he did us. He can't make it. This street's too narrow. So help me, he's not trying to pass—he's trying to tangle. Wham!"

Sammy's moan was drawn out and desolate. "Stop driving. Stop! That new devil done it on purpose. He study to kill Miss Ma'yanne for sure." She shoved the door open. Her feet slapped the road before Daniel had time to pull up. She saw a dark shadow leap from the crashed taxi to the battered black car. She began to run. Daniel followed her, gripping a wrench.

Chapter 18

Beulah had completely spent herself during her long hours of waiting. When confirmation of her worst fears came she had nothing left but dreadful resignation. In spite of repeated urging on the part of Clement and Sammy she refused to be put to bed. And when Nelson brought Marianne and Hale back to the apartment she insisted upon talking to him, applying his carefully phrased questions as though they were leeches that would suck away the bad blood congesting her heart.

Did she know the man with whom Leonard had the appointment that morning? No, she'd never laid eyes on Matthew Crown. Yes, she had spoken to him when he telephoned that morning to tell her that Leonard had not kept the appointment. Was his voice a familiar one? No, she had not recognized it as belonging to anyone she knew. Yes, she supposed it might have been disguised. Now that she thought about it, it had sounded rather nasal. But she could not swear to that. Her mind had been too fully occupied with what he said to take particular notice of his voice.

Yes, she had seen his letters. The first, she said, had asked Leonard if he would be interested in buying a rare antique. Where had it been mailed from? She did not know. Not a printed letterhead. Just a sheet of typewriting paper stating that the reply was to be sent to the post office, care of general delivery. Unusual? No. They were always receiving communications of that nature, some of them leading to really worthwhile finds. Consequently, Leonard had replied that he was interested.

The second letter adjured him to secrecy if negotiations were to be carried further. And after he had sent the required assurance the third letter came. It had excited him to such a degree that she hadn't the heart to pour cold water. It described the object under sale: a Louis Seize wardrobe, designed and wrought by André Charles Boulle, a piece—if it existed outside of a museum—which would fill any collector's soul with longing. The price, thirty-five thousand dollars in cash, to be paid after Crown had conducted Leonard and any expert he might choose to the place where it was hidden.

The line about the expert had clinched the matter as far as Leonard was concerned. It had seemed to him so eminently fair and aboveboard.

Had it seemed that way to her? She shrugged. She had been skeptical, but she was a rich woman. She could well afford to speculate with such a sum. And she'd been thinking lately that perhaps she had not been exactly fair to Leonard. She had so enjoyed showering luxuries upon him that sometimes she lost sight of the fact that a man might wish to buy things for himself, handle actual cash. So she'd been meaning to present him with a sizeable sum on his next birthday. And though she had not told him so, the money for the Boulle purchase was just an advance against the intended gift. Whether or not he concluded the purchase seemed unimportant in the face of his pleasure at being permitted to follow through without aid or advice from—from anyone.

Had the expert been chosen? Yes. He was a man highly regarded in his field. She knew him well. But he, too, had telephoned to complain that neither Leonard nor Matthew Crown had called for him at the hour agreed upon.

Where were Matthew Crown's letters now? She supposed that Leonard had taken them with him. Hadn't they been on—in his wallet? No? Then she did not know, unless the murderer had destroyed them.

When it became apparent that she had talked herself out it was Nelson who led her to her room. "Try to rest now, Mrs. Roberts. Perhaps a sedative will do the trick. You've been very helpful, and we're going to do our best to clear this thing up as soon as possible. I'll send Sammy to you."

She said, "Thank you, young man. I have confidence in you." For an incredible moment there appeared on her ravaged face a look of coquetry. "You're an extraordinary person. You've even taken the trouble to learn the name of my new maid."

Nelson retreated hastily. But he had forgotten about Sammy before he re-entered the library. There was a strange expression on his olive-skinned face. The name "Matthew Crown" had escaped the underbrush of his thoughts to emerge on his lips. It took shape slowly as he walked to the telephone.

The twins broke off a conversation to stare at him. Hale said uncertainly, "Would you mind explaining about Crummy Proctor?"

Nelson, his hand on the receiver, answered impatiently, "We did some delving into his past in connection with the death of your butler. Proctor isn't fit company even for an animal—especially for an animal." He clarified the statement briefly. The faint sound of the doorbell interrupted him.

Hale said, "I'd better answer it. I guess Sammy is with my grandmother." He went to the door and came back in the impressive wake of Inspector Furniss.

Furniss was bathed in self-esteem. He gestured the twins from the room, as though they were gadget salesmen who had invaded his private office.

He said to Nelson, "It was the warehouse, all right. After what I found there I haven't a valid doubt of it." He proceeded to give the details of what he had found.

Nelson nodded. "Proof enough. I'm sure it will hold water. But why did—?"

Furniss said resentfully, "I know. I haven't worked that out yet. You were going to say why did Mr. X return later to remove the body and dump it elsewhere? I'll take your guess even though we should be past the guessing stage."

Nelson glanced toward the telephone but made no move. He did not want to be questioned about the reason for the call he was itching to make. He knew how Furniss felt about hunches. He said absently, "Mr. X didn't intend to return for the body, but he got to worrying. Maybe he missed some small article from his person and was sure he'd left it at the scene of the crime. So after several hours of deliberation he chanced coming back for it. Then the thought may have occurred to him that if he'd left one clue he might have left others that would point him out. So he changed his plans and conveyed the body to a vicinity less likely to provide leads. Do you like that guess?"

"I love it. It jells without pectin." Furniss shivered. "I could do with a drink. It was chilly in that warehouse. They keep it at low temperature because heat is bad for certain woods."

"Which puts hair on our theory about the broken arms and legs."

"Yep. Where, by the way, is Beulah Fitch-Casey-et-cetera-Roberts?"

"Gone to bed. She's all in." Nelson was amused by the inspector's obvious disappointment. "I didn't think it important for you to see her. I'm pretty certain she told me all she had to tell."

Furniss grinned sheepishly. "I just wanted to get a little firsthand gander to satisfy my boyhood ambition. She's certainly got a fancy layout here. Sammy will turn up her nose at your place after this." A sound turned him toward the door. "I thought I told you two to keep out until you were called."

The twins crossed the threshold, Hale tagging Clement. Clement said, "We have the freedom of this apartment and we have a right to know what's going on." He sat down in an Early Victorian library chair and draped a leg over its stubby arm to show that he was quite at ease.

Hale stood, shifting from one foot to the other.

Furniss said sternly, "Which of you is which?"

Hale cleared his throat. "I'm Hale. He's Clement. Don't pay any attention to him, sir. If you haven't finished your talk I'll get him out of here."

Clement lighted a cigarette. "Stop acting the startled fawn, you ass."

Furniss pounced. "So you're Clement? I've been looking forward to this. I'm the one who has a right to know what's going on, and if I'm not mistaken you're the one who can tell me. What were you doing on West Seventy-fourth Street last night?"

There was a dull, painful thud as Clement's blond head struck the chair's high mahogany back. His eyes glazed, as though the blow had stunned him.

Involuntarily Hale cried, "Ouch." He looked at Furniss. "You must be a bit confused, sir. He was with me last night until he went to bed."

"But he didn't go to bed. He—"

Clement sat forward. He turned to Hale fiercely. "Get out of here. Since you're so sensitive about intruding on other people's private affairs I'd just as soon you took the same stand about mine. Go on—scram."

Hale stared at him. Then he came farther into the room and sat down with an air of permanence. "You're not other people. Where did you go last night?"

"If you don't mind, I'll ask the questions," Furniss said. His voice was less severe. He said to Nelson, "You might take a few notes, Grid, since Sugs isn't on tap." He drew a chair around so that it faced Clement and sank into it. "Now then, son, what have you done with that girl?"

"D-done with her?"

"Let's not make a short story long. She was reported missing at noon today."

"Missing!"

Nelson, making aimless doodles on the back of an envelope, thought he detected a note of relief in the exclamation.

Furniss seemed to catch it too. "Perhaps 'missing' wasn't the word you expected to hear." He pounced again. "Perhaps the word was 'murdered.'"

Clement's response was unexpected. His hand rose to finger the scar on his chin. His voice sounded tired and very young. "I'm not trying to be rude now, sir, but I don't know what you're talking about. You seem somehow to have learned of my—of that girl. Yet I can't see why you should be interested. I thought you were here to investigate the deaths of Shepard and Leonard Roberts."

For a moment Furniss looked completely nonplussed. Then he began to sputter.

Nelson said, "Mind if I step in, Chief? You *do* want to cut this short." He addressed Clement: "We'll have to ask you to tell us the story of that girl. She's become a police matter which the inspector believes is relevant to the two crimes."

"A police matter? You mean I've—? Must I?" The last was a plea that reduced Clement to half his eighteen years. It seemed to have been uttered by a frightened small boy. At Nelson's nod he swallowed.

"We're not concerned with the morals of the situation," Nelson said. "We're just trying to clear up a point. I'd get it over with as fast as possible if I were you. After that I wouldn't be surprised if you could forget the whole thing."

"I'll never forget it." Clement's voice was bitter. But he began to talk fast. "One of the fellows in my class took me to a party. Hale didn't go. He was catching up on his homework that night. We drove out to some filthy joint in New Jersey. I'd expected it to be a drinking party, but it wasn't. It was a smoking party—marijuana, I mean. I'd never tried the stuff before, but a girl shoved a cigarette into my mouth and I took a few puffs just to—I don't know why—anyway, it doesn't make sense now. And I remember somebody giving me a drink, too, but by that time I was feeling very pleased with myself because nobody else was drinking, and I seemed to be getting special service. There were a lot of funny people around. This girl—Grace Lyons—was one of them. I didn't think I liked her, but I must have, because the next thing I knew I woke up in—in her apartment. And then she kept phoning me. And after a few weeks she said she had to see me again. I didn't want to see her—ever—but I went. I had to or she'd have come to see me. And she told me she was going to have a baby." He grimaced. "I didn't know what to do. She said it cost a lot of money for—not to have it—and if she didn't do something quick it would cost even more to support it. She said if I didn't give her the money—lots of it—she'd tell Beulah and Beulah would make me marry her. She might have been right. Marriage isn't very final for Beulah, and she'd do almost anything to keep me out of the Army."

Hale groaned. "If you'd only told me. I'd have robbed a bank or something."

Furniss said, "Is that so? Well, maybe he did tell you. Maybe you're involved too. Shepard was killed for money, and Roberts was killed for money, and—"

Nelson forgot the respect due to a superior officer. "Give it a rest, Chief!" A thought struck him. "Did you tell anybody—Shepard, for example?"

"Yes, I told Shepard. I had to talk to someone or—or go crazy. And he'd always been a sort of father-confessor to all of us. He wanted to help me, but of course I couldn't let him. I'd been heel enough without taking his savings. And then he was killed."

Furniss said, "A likely story. When in doubt confide in the butler."

Clement ignored him. "I went to her place last night with what I'd managed to raise in a pawnshop. I thought it might keep her quiet until I could think of something else to do."

"Like murdering Roberts," Furniss shouted. "Thirty-five thousand dollars would have kept her very quiet."

Nelson said calmly, "But I thought you were accusing him of murdering the girl. If he did that there was no need for him to murder Roberts."

Then Clement began to laugh. He doubled up with laughter. But it was apparent that he was not amused.

Hale yelled, "For God's sake!" and went to his twin and seized him violently. "You big lousy sissy. A fine soldier you'll make. The Army just loves hysterical guys." He pummeled him. Clement began to parry the blows mechanically. Abruptly he seemed to realize that he could not fight and laugh at the same time. He pushed Hale off balance and straddled him as he hit the floor. He said in his normal voice, "You ass, what do you think you're doing?"

Nelson drew Furniss aside, "You, Chief, are barking up the wrong tree. Shepard *intended* to help him. That's why he drew his money from the bank and started to write that letter. It was going to be a delicate task to make Clement accept help from him, and he thought the boy would be more likely to respond to written persuasion than—"

The phone rang. Furniss pushed past him angrily to answer it. He lifted the receiver. He said, "Yes? ... No, this is Furniss ... You can talk to me. He sometimes takes me into his confidence ... Oh ... It's you? But I thought you were ... What! ... Where? ... Well, make it as close as possible ... He ...? Say that name again ... You're sure you've ...? All right—all right ... Yes, we'll find it ... Yes." He hung up. He said, "That, my friends, was Sammy."

"Sammy?" Nelson was bewildered. "I thought she was with—"

"You thought—you thought! You're so busy dragging theories

out of a hat that you don't know what's going on under your own nose. You didn't even take time out to notice that Marianne Ramsey wasn't in the audience. Where the hell is my coat?"

The twins were on their feet. Hale stuttered, "M-Marianne? She— I thought she'd gone to bed because the shock of seeing Roberts was—"

Furniss, striding toward the door, called back, "She's beyond shock now. And this little murder project is on Dwight Cannon. But we have something to shout about. At least they've caught him at it—and no thanks to anyone on my pay roll, either."

"Dwight Cannon!" Hale shouted the name hoarsely.

Nelson shook himself. He joined the race out of the apartment.

Chapter 19

Furniss sat beside Nelson to shout directions, while the twins huddled together in the back of the car. Nelson drove on two wheels in one long weaving thread that was unbroken by traffic lights. The thread ended at a street whose lonely character had recently undergone drastic alteration.

A small, still figure lay on the pavement, its dark childish head cushioned by Sammy's lap. Almost as still as this tableau was the figure that loomed above it, the figure of Dwight Cannon, looking as no young man should ever look. Near enough to reach out and grip his arm stood a policeman, and a few feet away was Dr. Silk, a study in perplexity.

Furniss, Nelson, and the twins rushed out of the car. Clement took root on the pavement near Marianne. His face was stupid, uncomprehending. Hale's face was crawling with tears. He kept brushing them away with his fists, as though they were troublesome insects. Neither of the boys paid any attention to Dwight. Their eyes were on their sister.

A short plump man with a driver's cap on his head and wrench in his hand was leading someone through the small fungus growth of onlookers. He noted the newcomers and chose Furniss as being most outstanding among them. "I called an ambulance, but they said it might take time on account of they're all out, so I picked up Doc here, who was just coming out of the drugstore with his bag of tools."

The doctor knelt beside Marianne. He glanced at Sammy with disapproval and muttered something about the stupidity of moving accident cases.

Sammy said softly, "It too late to talk about that now." She looked up and met Nelson's eyes. "I glad you here, Mr. Grid-dely."

She raised her hand, careful not to shift the rest of her body. "This here badge belong to you. You tell that policeman who you are, and then that taxi driver, he going to explain everything."

Furniss said witheringly, "Remind yourself to collect his salary next payday." He took the badge from her hand and flashed it under the nose of the policeman. "Inspector Furniss of Homicide and Sergeant Nelson, in his better moments. Start talking."

"I don't know much, Inspector. I was going off duty when that tan citizen hauls me out of a coffeepot and says there's been an accident. There are no other officers around, so I follow her here and find this. And from what the hacky tells me, it's not an accident at all but monkey business. As far as I can make out, this man's responsible." He jerked his finger at Dwight.

Furniss said, "Hah!" and eyed Dwight with honest pleasure. He turned to the taxi driver. "Where do you fit, and why are you carrying that wrench?"

"Oh, that? I forgot I had it. I better start from the beginning. My name's Daniel Glover. I'm waiting for a fare when she"—he looked at Sammy—"buttonholes me with a song about that girl"—he pointed to the pavement—"being out with a rat"—he indicated Dr. Silk—"who ain't going to do her no good. And she wants me to tail his car just to see that he don't try any tricks, because she says if the girl comes to harm it will kill her grandmother, who's sick, and I think I better humor her, especially when she flashes the badge and says the girl's old man is a dick and— Are you him?"

Furniss and Nelson exchanged quick glances. Furniss said, "We can skip the family history. So you tailed the car."

"Yeah. And pretty soon I get nervous because we're rolling off the beaten track and it's getting lonely. I happen to squint into the mirror and I see it's not so lonely after all, and the black car ain't the only crate with a tail on it, because there's another cab right behind mine. And then the cab swings out and gets between us and it, and from then on it's a procession, with nobody going nowhere in particular. Me and my fare are getting impatient, and so is the cab, only more so. It suddenly shoots up alongside the black car, tangles, and wham-bang, here we are. And if it wasn't done on purpose I got d.t.'s. So I grab the wrench, just in case, and join the party. The cab unloads the dark wild-eyed guy, and he leaps on the black car and unloads the girl, who's not bleeding or anything; only she's out like a light, and we can't figure how she got that way. First thing we know he's got her in his arms and he's crooning and he won't let her down. Course I know it's against the rules to move an accident case till the doctor comes, but the damage is done, so we manage to stretch her on

the pavement. And my fare goes to get a cop and to telephone, and the other cabdriver goes with her on account of he's hurt—nothing serious—just his lip needs attention. He bit it in half when the wild guy went haywire and jumped through the partition and grabbed the wheel. And I stand guard with my monkey wrench. Not that it would do much good if either of them wanted to make a break. But it seems they don't. The wild guy's in a trance, and the redhead don't seem to understand what's cooking but is mighty anxious to find out. He says he met the girl by chance and took her for a drive. I dunno—that ain't the way I heard it."

Furniss put his hand on Dwight's sleeve. "We'll give you a break. We can't bother to get the wagon. You can ride to jail with us nice and private."

The doctor was beckoning to them. He said to the policeman, "Are you in charge?"

The policeman wanted no part of it. "Talk to the inspector here. No, you better talk to the sarge. The inspector's busy."

Nelson listened to the doctor's calm professional murmur. He whispered something to the policeman, who looked startled, said, "Huh?" and hurried away. Nelson walked after him slowly and with seeming lack of purpose. When he returned, the doctor had disappeared. Sammy was still cradling Marianne's head, but she had somehow managed to worm out of Nelson's coat, which now served as a cover for the girl's limp body. The twins seemed to be pleading with Sammy. Nelson heard Hale say in a shattered voice, "The doctor didn't do anything; he didn't do anything because—"

Furniss was still gripping Dwight, and Dr. Silk had edged a little nearer, looking hesitant, as though he wished to ask questions but could not decide upon a fitting approach. The taxi driver stood by, tiredly clinging to his wrench.

Furniss yelled, "Where the hell did you disappear, Grid? What did it? Concussion? Why doesn't that ambulance come? I can't keep my eyes everywhere at once, and my prime concern is to get this beauty safely housed before he does any more damage. I suppose I could take him in Sammy's taxi."

The driver looked unwilling but resigned.

"Chief," Nelson said. He moved close to Furniss, so that not even Dwight could hear his low, swift rush of words. "Listen, Chief, and don't take any action and don't change your expression."

Furniss listened. Once or twice he nodded casually. His bright blue eyes did not move from Nelson's face. Just as Nelson finished talking a patrol car rolled up, and the original policeman got out with two others. They made almost leisurely approach.

Nelson ignored them. His whisper reached Dwight. "Do you

think you have strength enough to lift her and place her in my car?"

Dwight's lips moved in his numb face, but no sound came. He bent to his task.

The twins advanced like newly wound automatons. "Don't let him touch her. He killed her."

Nelson brought them up short, his voice as obstructive as a boulder. "Stay where you are, boys."

Dr. Silk said, "If I can be of service. It hardly seems proper that this man who—" Then he said brightly, "Oh, I see—enormously foresighted—it will prevent him from attempting to escape."

Dwight rose, with Marianne's head against his shoulder. His voice was muted by her hair. "She screamed. I—"

Nelson nodded toward the policeman. "Take him—don't shoot unless you have to."

Dr. Silk relaxed. He did not struggle against the vise formed by his captors. He said, "I'm afraid you're misinterpreting the sergeant's orders, my friends. I am an innocent bystander. I met the little lady just as I was about to call on Mrs. Roberts." He smiled his clown's smile. "She seemed sad, and because I consider myself a friend of the family, I felt it my duty to cheer her up. I asked her to go for a drive, thinking it might make her forget her troubles. She was apparently a neurotic type, as are so many of her generation. I believe she did scream when that young man's cab swung in behind us. No doubt she feared collision." He raised his shoulders. "But the crash was his fault. I have witnesses to prove—" He stopped talking abruptly. His shrewd, humorous eyes were on the object that seemed to have jumped into Nelson's hand.

"Does this belong to you?" Nelson said.

"No, I don't believe it does."

"Then the gremlins are at work again. I found it tucked between the cushions of your car. You will note that it's still half full. Matthew Crown, I arrest you for the murder of—" He got no further, because the red-headed giant had flexed his muscles, flipped off his captors, and was making a break for it.

Dwight looked on, frustrated, with Marianne in his arms. The twins and Furniss teamed up in a flying tackle. It was Nelson who finally brought order out of chaos by instinctively employing the rest of the liquid in the hypodermic syringe.

Chapter 20

The twins were alone at the breakfast table. They were not discussing the events of the night before. They were not speaking at all. Sammy came in and broke the heavy silence.

She looked down at them. "Would which of you is Mr. Clement please say so?"

Clement said, "I'm Clement." His tone said, "I wish I weren't."

"Then you the one I got a message for—private—from headquarters."

Without looking at his brother, Hale started to rise. Clement pulled him back. "You might as well know the worst."

Sammy took a deep breath. "It didn't sound like no worst to me—not the way Mr.—the white-headed detective say it when I talking to him on the phone before you up yet. He tell me to tell you Missing Persons found a lady named Grace in good health without no baby coming or going, and she ready to forget about bothering anybody no more. Her business seem to be bothering folks, and she work with a partner. Her partner call the police yesterday to say she gone 'cause he think she do him bad by bothering a lot of money out of some gentleman, and he want to know where she at with that money. But she ain't fixing to do him bad. She just hiding with a girlfriend like she scared of something." Sammy eyed Clement anxiously. "You hear what I saying? 'Cause if you don't, that Mr. Detective going to be around soon and he—"

Clement stared at her. "I hear." His face was beautiful.

"That all right then. You eat your good breakfast now. Your grandma calling me."

Clement picked up a hot biscuit and began to butter it. The knife dropped from his hand. He looked at it. Then he looked at Hale. He shouted, "Take a lesson, wise guy!" and pounded Hale on the back.

"Don't think I won't." Hale was grinning sympathetically. His grin closed the subject for all time. "Hey—I bet Cook had nothing to do with those biscuits. I bet Sammy baked them. She's some—some dame."

"If it hadn't been for her," Clement said, "Silk might have got away with it. He could easily have handled Dwight without—"

"Shhh."

Beulah entered the room. She was wearing the black taffeta housecoat. And this time it was mourning. But her face was dressed as usual in varying tints carefully applied.

The two boys rose. Clement walked around to his grandmother's place and filled her coffee cup. "Here, Beulah, drink it."

She looked at the vacant chairs. "I—I thought you'd asked Dwight to stay the night here. Has he left?"

"He's still in bed," Hale said. "We talked until morning." He glanced at his watch. "Gosh—after eleven. Maybe I should call him."

"No, he's earned his rest." She raised the cup to her freshly painted lips, set it down again. "I want to apologize to him. I want to thank him." She studied her fingernails. "Do you think Marianne will have any ill effects?"

"Not a chance," Hale said cheerfully. "After they worked over her and brought her to she sat up and took notice for more than an hour. Then she fell into a normal sleep. She's a young horse."

Beulah said, flaying herself with the words, "That monstrous creature. I can—I can understand the plot against Leonard to get the money, but why should he want to kill Marianne? And how did Shepard ...?"

Clement's face darkened. "Let's not speculate about it. The detective promised faithfully he'd be here this morning. He'll tell us. Drink a little more coffee, Beulah."

She said tonelessly, "You're sweet boys, both of you." She gave a dry little cough. "There's something I—"

Hale said, "Hush."

"No, there's something you ought to know."

"Don't trouble yourself with it now, Beulah."

She said impatiently, "Yes, now—before anyone joins us. Don't treat me as though I were a grieving old woman. I grieved last night. It's over now. Leonard was no good, but I loved him, perhaps more than— Never mind. What I must tell you concerns Mike, your grandfather Casey. Mike wanted to keep us together—at any cost. But he knew me so well—better than any one's ever known me. So he added a codicil to his will. It said that if you lived under my roof up until your twenty-first year I'd receive an additional inheritance, held in trust until that date. If not, the money was to go to charity."

Their eyes were dissecting her. She said lamely, "The same codicil provides for you, without condition. You and Marianne, too, are to come into a considerable sum at that time, whether or not you're still with me."

Clement's lips parted.

Hale said angrily, "That's why you wouldn't let us enlist. What a lot of unnecessary trouble you went to. Surely you must know that the war changed everything. If we enlisted, or were drafted, you could have contested that codicil and won hands down."

She leaned forward, propped by her thin elbows. "You must believe this. It wasn't the money. I have enough—too much. It was that—that dentist. I told him about it, and he cast your horoscope. He said—he said if you did enlist, death would come to you both during your fifth month in the service."

Hale muttered, "That phony!"

Clement said, "I don't get it—unless he just couldn't bear to see good money wasted on charity." Then his face showed sudden awareness. He barely refrained from saying aloud, Or else he wanted you as well padded as possible when he finally got around to being Grandpa the Fifth.

She sighed. "I'll make it up to you. You're to enlist as soon as you want to."

They tried to conceal their indecent happiness. Clement could not hold himself down. He got up impulsively and kissed her. She clung to his hand for a moment. "You and Hale are the only men I have left." She repeated thoughtfully, "The only men I have left."

Clement could feel his scalp tingling. He looked at Hale and saw that he seemed to be experiencing the same sensation. It was as though Beulah had just emerged from a trance and was girding her loins to remedy an untenable situation.

Hale changed the subject hurriedly: "You ought to give Sammy a fat reward, Beulah. She did some fast thinking last night. The taxi driver was all right too. But I saw Mr. Nelson slip him something."

Beulah said absently, "Sammy's leaving. It seems some previous commitment prevents her from keeping this position."

"Hell! Something told me she was too good to last."

"She's sending a friend to take her place. She's certain I'll be well satisfied."

Dwight came into the room. He gave Beulah a self-conscious "Good morning."

Beulah motioned him to a chair beside her. "I hope you rested well, Dwight." Her manner was as tangible as a royal decoration.

He sat down. He said, "Is Marianne—?"

"Sleeping like a baby," Hale said.

"Not me." Marianne stood in the doorway. Except for the violet shadows under her eyes she seemed well enough. She went straight to Dwight. "Have you moved in?" She stood behind him with her hands on his shoulders.

He looked up at her. Tearing his eyes away was strenuous physical exercise. It left him breathless, so that he spoke with effort. "Shouldn't you be in bed?"

"Not under the present circumstances." She moved away, dropped into a chair. She drank some coffee and began to play with a piece of toast. She said, "Could I persuade everybody to stop staring at me so anxiously? I'm all right. The effect of that drug wore off hours ago. I have a faint memory of biting the hand that held the needle, so the shot couldn't have been as big as he intended it to be. That's all I do remember, except giving a yell that was nipped in the bud."

Dwight said, "Don't talk about it."

"But I want to—it's better that way. Any psychoanalyst will tell you the same thing." She stopped playing with the toast, and their eyes met again. The contact formed a bridge to which the others in the room had no access. "There are a few minor details I'd like cleared up."

"Me too, lovely. I keep thanking my stars that you phoned when you did. But what made you so urgent?"

A shadow crossed her face. "Oh, that? Nothing. I— I just had a terrific desire to see you." She smiled and the shadow disappeared. "Tell me how you got there like—like Jack Dalton."

"Well, you stood me up at the subway station, so I started walking toward the house, hoping to meet you. And I did meet you—or, rather, I got a load of you driving off in a black car—only you didn't see me. You were too busy looking bug-eyed at your new boyfriend. You know me—I'm a conventional guy. I don't like my future wife to ride around with strangers. So I hopped a cab and followed. And when I heard that nipped yell I went into action."

It was Hale who broke the enchantment of their locked gaze. "Hey, you two. Stop being such a closed shop. We want in."

Everyone jumped at the sound of the bell. Five mouths opened with perfect timing as Sammy ushered Nelson and Furniss into the room.

Before they could ask questions Nelson said, "This is Inspector Furniss of Homicide, Mrs. Roberts. I believe the others have met him."

Beulah nodded graciously. "Do sit down, gentlemen. Perhaps you'd like some coffee?"

"A good idea," Furniss said. "I think we had some at six this morning, but I'm not certain." Sammy filled his cup while he filled his eyes with Beulah. "Do you feel up to hearing this, Mrs. Roberts?"

"I must hear it."

"Then take it away, Grid. It's your case." He took a biscuit and buttered it pensively.

Nelson said, "My talk with Miss Ramsey the other day makes as good a starting point as any I can think of. I was working on the premise that Shepard had intercepted a burglar and I asked

Miss Ramsey to examine the cabinet in the library to see if anything had been disturbed. She said that for as long as she could remember the gold horse and its rider had stood side by side, and it seemed odd to her that they had been separated, so that several objects were placed between them. So I worked out a fairly logical theory—"

Clement said, "I noticed that, too, when I came in that day. In fact, I picked up the little man to put him where he belonged, but then I was joined by Hale and I guess I forgot about it."

"Yes," Nelson said. "Your fingerprints were on it, and that threw us off the track a bit. No, don't interrupt. We start from scratch, you know. Everybody looks guilty to a policeman. Later I rearranged my theory to fit Dr. Silk, and he corroborated it early this morning when he awoke and realized he had nothing further to lose. Silk came here, Mrs. Roberts, on the day of Shepard's death. I mean before as well as after. You had invited him to visit the warehouse, and he'd got the appointment confused and thought he was to call for you at the apartment. Shepard had probably been in his room since morning. He answered the door, let Silk into the library, and went to see if you were at home. He returned to the library as Silk, unable to resist, was pocketing the gold rider."

"Perhaps," Marianne said, "he wanted to melt it down for fillings."

Nelson smiled. "Perhaps. At any rate, Shepard made the mistake of attacking him, and Silk hit back. A man of his size can't always gauge the force of his blows. I don't think he meant to kill Shepard, but he killed him—though not instantly. He carried him to his room, where he was found later by Miss Ramsey. The necktie arrangement was done in the forlorn hope that it would look like a suicide."

Beulah wet her lips. "Why weren't his prints on the gold figure, as well as Clement's?"

"He'd gone back to the library to wipe them off, but the position of the figure meant nothing to him. He'd only replaced it because he knew he'd be coming back to the apartment with you. If by that time the police were investigating Shepard's death he thought it barely possible that they might hit upon burglary as a motive, and naturally he did not want to have stolen property on his person."

"Oh."

Nelson continued: "Of course we made a routine check on everybody and discovered that Silk's past was far from neat. So we set a man to watch him."

Furniss groaned.

"But Silk spotted our man and gave him the slip yesterday

morning by leaving his combined office and dwelling quarters over the roof tops and emerging five doors down the block. He returned the same way. Later in the day when Sugs, our man, began to get suspicious about Silk's non-appearance he went up to the door of his apartment. It was open, as dentists' doors often are. He heard the sound of a dentist's drill and assumed that everything was under control. He didn't know that Silk had turned on the drill and set his thickest needle in a small block of cement and that it had been boring away steadily all day. Silk had even persuaded two separate women patients who were madly in love with him to swear he'd been working on them should the matter come up. Both of these women are married, and both of them are afraid their husbands will discover their extra-marital activities. So Silk had them pretty well under his thumb. His nurse, also in love with him, would have sworn to anything."

This time it was Beulah who groaned.

Marianne said, "How did I come into it? Why did he bother to be a dentist when—when he was so versatile?"

"He may have thought it would provide a wide field for the rest of his talents. After a varied career he came to New York and opened his present office. Things had been going badly with him until you appeared, Mrs. Roberts. And even though you recommended a great many patients, they weren't sufficient to put him on a solvent basis. He needed money. He was being dunned for rent and he owed a tremendous sum in gambling debts. In addition, his costly dental equipment was due for immediate removal if he didn't pay up. Your coming, Mrs. Roberts, and the wealthy patients you brought made him begin to fancy himself as a fashionable dentist, and he didn't intend to risk his new position for lack of ready cash. So he conceived a rather elaborate hoax. He read up on furniture and, as Matthew Crown, entered into a correspondence with Leonard Roberts. He *did* mean to kill Roberts. Thirty-five thousand dollars, after urgent debts have been subtracted, is no nest egg for a gambler. With Roberts gone he'd be—"

Beulah said, "He'd be free to court his widow with an eye to larger gains."

Furniss stopped eating biscuits to look at her with lush sympathy. She did not notice. Her slaty eyes were on Nelson. She seemed fascinated.

Marianne cried hurriedly, "But me? Why me?"

"I'm getting there." Nelson quickened his tempo. "We know from the night watchman that Roberts arrived at the warehouse before nine that morning. He sent the watchman home and waited alone for Matthew Crown. We know that he was killed in the warehouse because we—or, rather the inspector—found the murder weapon, an iron inkstand which had been cleaned carefully but still smelled vaguely of hair oil. He also found traces where the body had lain—traces of hair oil and dirt from his shoes—far enough apart to indicate that he had been placed full length behind that velvet screen."

"The screen!" It was Marianne.

"Yes. Silk had propped it that way the afternoon before, while Mrs. Roberts was showing something to Cromwell Proctor in one of the back rooms. His original plan was to deposit the body behind it to put off the hour of discovery. But circumstances forced him to revise that plan, so he returned later and removed the body to a lonely street, where we found it."

"You mean the—body was there when I pinned the note to the screen?"

Nelson nodded. "And that note might have proved fatal to you. Silk returned because he thought he had dropped his cigarette holder at the scene of the crime. The holder was there all right, under a chair, but Silk couldn't find it. One of our men picked it up later and placed it on top of a miniature chest. He thought it was just another curio, and so did the inspector, and so did I, when we saw it on the chest. But Silk did not consider that possibility. He saw your note, Miss Ramsey, and remembered that you had noticed the holder in his hand on the previous day. He made up his mind that if you had picked it up you'd never get a chance to recall it in court."

Marianne said, "Wait a minute. I remember something. I remember when I knelt to pick up the letter my knee hit a small object that rolled away. If I hadn't been in such a hurry I'd have—"

Nelson said reassuringly, "You'd have discovered the holder and told us about it when Roberts was found and avoided going for that ride. But never mind. As things turned out, you were playing in luck, anyway. Your costume was as good as a suit of armor."

"I don't understand."

"Silk had two deaths to his credit. And as usually happens, human life was becoming increasingly unimportant to him. He says that he'd have had you safely out of the way if your clothes hadn't delayed him. At your initial meeting you were dressed like a little girl. Last night, in your sophisticated outfit, and with make-up on your face, you resembled that little girl about as much as an older sister might have done. So it took Silk ten precious minutes of riding around the block you were walking to make sure you were you. And those ten minutes allowed your fiancé to catch up with you."

"So it was Leonard who saved my life," Marianne said bleakly.

"Because if I hadn't dressed that way to make him—to—" She became conscious of the weight of eyes pressing against her. "If— well, if I'd been wearing my regular clothes when I met Dr. Silk yesterday he wouldn't have been delayed. He'd have known me right off and—"

Dwight reached over and took her cold hand. He whispered, "Don't be goofy. He was the reason for Matthew Crown in the first place."

Curious himself, Nelson hurried on to relieve her of the room's curious concentrated stare. "Silk removed Roberts' body to make the issue as cloudy as possible. The bicycle at its side was prompted by the same motive. It was an old one he found in the warehouse belonging to your day man. All the way through he had the tendency and the cold nerve it must have taken to overdo."

Hale said, as though he didn't want to know, "What about the broken arms and legs?"

"That also was dictated by circumstances. By the time he returned to the warehouse rigor mortis had set in. He had to fold the body in the position in which we found it to make it fit into the luggage compartment of his car. Bones cracked during the process. He flung a rug over it and carried it out, so that anyone noticing might think he was carting home a purchase. People don't notice much on that street, though. Too busy with their own affairs."

Marianne said, "So that's why you searched Crummy's car—for signs—that it had carried—"

"Yes. I think that's all—except that your Melvin Beck didn't show up that day because Silk had sent him an anonymous note containing a twenty-dollar bill. He'd taken the trouble to investigate his habits and he knew just where twenty dollars would land him. It did—in a poker game that made him forget his job for about six hours."

Dwight spoke. "How was it I didn't come in for suspicion?"

Marianne said in a small voice, "No one would ever suspect you."

Nelson smiled. "No stone's unturned's our motto. We found that you had just succeeded in getting a swell job and that the service had turned you down because as a kid you fractured your right arm at the elbow and it never set properly, making it out as far as a gun's concerned. But you proved last night that you still have full use of it for all other purposes."

Marianne said, "You never told me that, Dwight."

"Couldn't bear to have you know I wasn't a perfect physical specimen."

"Silly. I'd marry you if you didn't have a leg to stand on."

Dwight blushed. He said to Nelson, "What I don't understand is why he didn't make a break for it before you arrived. He must have known he was licked."

"He didn't know it. And a break then would have admitted guilt, with you and Sammy and the taxi driver to testify to his presence. He had complete confidence in his ability to brazen it out. Even this morning he tried it on by swearing the hypodermic needle was yours, but Marianne's teeth marks in his arm weakened that story a bit."

Nelson and Furniss rose as one man. Furniss cleared his throat, but the graceful exit speech he had prepared for Beulah's benefit froze.

Beulah was addressing Nelson, her voice stuffed with charm: "Dear Mr. Nelson, how can I thank you? I realize that you're a very busy man, but I sincerely hope you will find time to call upon me at some not-too-distant date, so that I may further express my gratitude. I intend to move back to Gramercy Park. You'll love my house, I'm sure."

Sammy came to the rescue, firmly steering the two men from the danger zone.

Out in the corridor Sammy said, "This the first time I know you gentlemen to call on the folks in a case after that case all tidied up."

Nelson grinned. "We came because the chief wanted to lay a ghost."

Furniss said sourly, "Your chances in that direction seem much more likely to succeed."

"Sammy, the chief needs cheer. How about coming back tonight and cooking him a fine big dinner?"

"Yes, Mr. Grid-dely, I going to be there." She sighed. "I wish you rich so you could buy us some of this here Chickendale and Sheridan furnitures. I going to miss it bad."

As they rang for the automatic elevator Furniss said suddenly, "Grid, did you suspect Silk before that doctor said the girl had been drugged?"

"Yes, I suspected him before we left the apartment."

"Why? Sugs is a damn fool, but you were the one who trusted him, and his reports seemed conclusive enough."

"I had a hunch, Chief. I can't help it—I know you hate hunches. But they come to me just the same. Silk's subconscious played him false. Some people associate the word 'Crown' with royalty. I associate it with teeth."

THE END

MURDER RUNS A FEVER

RUTH FENISONG

Chapter I

Detective Sergeant Gridley Nelson walked out of the Chinese laundry. There was nothing more that he could do. The three young hoodlums who had murdered Chin Goon were behind bars. They would never be given the chance to spend the sum of seven dollars and twelve cents, sole yield of the ugly crime. The three dry-eyed stoics who had survived Chin Goon, his wife and his infant sons, were left to carry on. Nelson's part in the sordid affair was ended.

He thought, I should phone headquarters and report to the chief. He strode down a dingy chain of side streets and turned at Madison Avenue. He hesitated for a moment in front of a corner drugstore but permitted his long legs to carry him past the entrance. The harsh hangover that was his unfailing visitant after every case weighed him down. He felt an urgent need for something in the nature of a pickup before he could bring himself to swallow the chief's usual brand of raillery. Not a drink, but a good dose of sanity administered by a friend who would prove to him that wartime psychology blinding the callow eyes of juveniles was only one of life's facets.

His pointed olive-skinned face smiled at the association induced by the word "facets." Louise. Louise Cotter. The Cotter Jewelry Store was just a short walk up the avenue. He would visit Louise. He hadn't talked with her since Charles, her husband, had left for the Army. Hard to prescribe a more efficacious cure than Louise for the sadness that filled him.

She was a product of Nelson's own hometown. And although she was about three years younger than he, the age discrepancy had never, even in their earliest stages, been a bar to friendship. He could remember himself as a man of ten spreading out for her warm interest the splendid map that was to be his future. A map which showed no indication that at thirty-odd he would find himself a detective on the New York Homicide Squad.

What a lovely child she had been. Large for her age, and wise and poised beyond it. He wondered why he had never fallen in love with her. But he had not, nor she with him. Though even now, gone separate ways, their liking for each other ran deep, and the well-spaced intervals of renewing their friendship presented no great bridges to cross.

Louise had been almost as swift as he to leave the stuffy town, the credo of her pioneer family as violent an impetus as the dicta of Nelson's politician father. Nelson went to Princeton, she to some Eastern finishing school, and they wrote to each other sporadically and then lost touch for a while.

His formal education completed, Nelson came to New York, too steeped in his quest for a niche to be haunted by ties of childhood. Because his mother had left him a comfortable income he had traveled slowly, with no economic pressure to urge him on. He had sampled a variety of occupations ranging from the stage of a Little Theater group to the laboratory of a criminologist. But in the end his need for direct contact with people, not across footlights or by way of theories, had led him to his present position.

And during his sure trek toward the enviable goal of being at last a round peg in a round hole Louise had given up whatever fleeting notion of a career she may have housed to marry Charles Cotter. A choice of which Nelson approved from his first meeting with Charles.

Charles had inherited Cotter's at the death of his father several years ago. And since his induction Louise was running the business and running it well. It was a considerable business, not to be judged by the modest front before which Nelson halted his steps. The fashionable world went to Cartier's for their jewels and their wedding presents, but when there were stones to be reset or precious possessions to be repaired the *cognoscenti* brought them straight to Cotter's.

There was nothing to dazzle the eye in Cotter's one small window; nothing, in fact, but an eighteenth-century bonnet-top clock above whose metal face paraded the phases of the lunar day. Since Cotter's did not sell antiques, this one had obviously been left for repairs. It stated that the hour was twelve-thirty, and Nelson, comparing it with his wristwatch, noted that the clock was now ready and waiting for its owner to claim it. He wondered who, in the absence of Charles, had done the work, and how efficiently. For Charles came of a long line of jewelers, and his hands were precision instruments that had taken watches apart since his childhood. His craftsmanship would be hard to equal.

Nelson walked into the shop. It was larger than the front indicated. He knew that behind it there were two good-sized workrooms, one the private quarters of Charles, the other devoted to the general activities of the shop's employees.

He took off his hat, and the small bright eyes of the gnome behind the counter climbed and settled upon his vital cap of curly white hair.

The gnome said, "Good day, sir," in a high-pitched voice. "You have brought your watch to us?"

Nelson said, "No," and for a fleeting moment mused upon the

question, shrugged, and smiled in self-disdain. His job, he thought, was beginning to exceed bounds. The recent press of work had been overstimulating, detection growing from habit to nuisance. He must guard himself or he would become too highly keyed for comfort. He seemed, of late, unable to resist running down the source of even a chance remark. This one, for example, caused him to speculate that Cotter's handled other objects besides watches. They knocked the dents out of old silver, replaced broken handles, glossed over scratches. Witness the floor-to-ceiling shelves upon which were stacked cutlery, soup tureens, cream pitchers, and flat plates, all newly restored and ready to take up their duties. Why, then, was the greeting so specific? Simple. Nelson was carrying no package. Naturally the little man had assumed a watch, because a watch would not bulk in the pocket or show upon the wrist. Yet Cotter's reset stones too. A ring would not bulk.... Impatiently he commanded himself to have done.

"I would like to see Mrs. Cotter. Is she here?"

"She is here—but at the moment engaged." The gnome actually seemed pleased with the words he was saying.

Nelson was disappointed. "Oh. Well, never mind. I'm just making a social call. Please tell her that Gridley Nelson dropped in." He turned to leave as the back door opened and Louise appeared on its threshold.

Louise said, "Grid," and went to him with hands outstretched. "You weren't going without seeing me?"

"I'd heard by grapevine that you were busy." Nelson looked at her and, as always after a long absence, caught his breath.

She was an abundant woman, with shiny dark hair wound around her head like a black halo. Perhaps she was not beautiful. Having grown up with her, it was hard for him to tell. But he did know that her voice was beautiful and that the way she moved was beautiful. And once again he was startled into awareness of the fact that her face never came into its own until she smiled. Her face was firmly and classically carved so that the bone structure was there to be seen, but her smile made mobile the classic lines, transforming it to the face of a gamin or a schoolgirl or a mother or a great lady, depending upon what it was that had caused her mouth to tilt and her eyes, somewhere between gray and blue and green, to shoot little rays at the corners like a child's drawing of stars. She was the schoolgirl now, contemplating an unexpected treat.

Nelson took both her hands and held them warmly.

She whispered with unwonted self-consciousness, "Mind your manners. It's very rude to stare." And then he noticed the man who had accompanied her from the workroom and recognized him before she had time to complete her introductions.

"Captain Shay, Detective Sergeant Nelson. Grid's an old friend of the family, Captain. I knew him when he had no thought of being a police officer."

Three separate gazes were directed at Nelson, including the sudden sharp scrutiny of the gnome behind the counter. Captain Shay said, "Glad to meet you, sir," and followed the politeness with a hearty chuckle. "May I add that no one would ever suspect your line of work?"

Nelson felt that his appearance, from the good cut of his suit to the good leather in his shoes, was undergoing careful inventory. He said pleasantly, "You're not the first to make that observation. I find it more of a help than a hindrance."

"Yes—yes—undoubtedly. You can probably mingle with the best of them without fear of discovery." And then, as though realizing that he was not being entirely tactful, Captain Shay rushed on: "I'm sure we have friends in common—other than Louise, I mean. I know quite a number of your co-workers. What branch are you attached to?"

"Homicide," Nelson said.

"Ah?" Shay chuckled again. "I take it all back. Let it be said to my credit that I've had no dealings whatever with that particular department."

So this was Orrin L. Shay, previously known to Nelson only as a picture in a newspaper or a voice on the radio, neither of which manifestations had attracted him to any degree. Yet grudgingly he was forced to concede that the man had a type of urgent charm which might call forth liking if one were exposed to it long enough. At any rate, if Shay's publicity was to be credited, women were not immune. It was bruited about that they sat up and begged for notice. And small wonder. His voice alone was a battering ram designed for the destruction of sales resistance. It remained the voice of a public speaker even without benefit of platform. He had a large rangy physique and large rangy features, adding up, although he was past fifty, to a peculiar sum of ugliness which so many females found irresistible. Did Louise find him irresistible too? Where had she met him?

His mind touching on Charles for a moment, Nelson thought resentfully, No Army for Shay. Too old. But, a veteran of the last war, his experience had evidently qualified him to act as a self-styled military expert. He broadcast, analyzing the news for a nationwide radio audience. He arranged programs to be sent out over the shortwaves. He made speeches and participated in bond drives. He was wealthy. He was athletic....

But Louise? Nelson caught her eyes. They twinkled. And that

was reassuring.

She said, addressing Shay, "It was kind of you to pay me a visit." And so dismissed him.

"A pleasure. Are you sure you won't reconsider and take lunch with me? No? Well, perhaps when I return. Don't work too hard or I'll be forced to report you to your charming husband. I'm sure he'd hate knowing you were too tied down to indulge in a bit of harmless relaxation. Good day, my dear. Good day to you, sir." A military carriage bore him from the shop.

Nelson heard Louise's sigh synchronize with the door's closing. She went to the counter. He heard her say calmly, "In the future, Mr. Loth, if people come to the shop and ask expressly for me, please let me know before you send them away. It might be important."

"But certainly, madam." The gnome's brown nutcracker face was expressionless.

Nelson took a dislike to that face. No self-respecting nose would end in such a ridiculous cleft. He said to dilute the atmosphere, "It *might* be important, huh? Puts me in my place."

Louise came back to him. "Oh, Grid, it's so good to see you."

"And you. I was about to suggest a bit of harmless relaxation myself. Lunch, in fact. But if that tied-down business is on the level—"

"Wait here. I'll get my coat."

"Permit me, madam." Helpful Mr. Loth rushed into a back room and rematerialized carrying her coat. He held it for her ceremoniously, and when she had fastened it he offered her handbag with the air of a man who forgets nothing.

"Thank you," she said, unsmiling.

"You will be gone long, madam?"

"No—less than an hour. Then you can have your lunch."

"Please, there is no need for you to hurry. Midday never finds me hungry. And everything in the workroom is being attended to, so I am at liberty to spend my time out here in front."

"Did you have any message from Alex this morning?"

"Yes. His wife called. It will be quite a while before he is able to come to work. But never fear. I assume full charge."

She walked through the door that Nelson was holding, onto the busy sidewalk.

"Winter's getting a foothold," Nelson said. "I can smell it—crisp and clean. Or is it you I smell? Anyway, I like it, which is more than I can say for those smudges under your eyes. You don't get out enough." Nevertheless, he eyed her approvingly. "Sensible girl never to wear a hat. A touch of conceit, that. Because you think no milliner in town can duplicate the effect of those braids."

"You're trying to cheer me up. You suspect I feel low."

"I feel low myself. That's why I came to you. I hoped we could swap miseries. Want to choose a restaurant?"

"Somewhere near. I hate to leave the shop for too long."

"Why? Really busy?"

She nodded. "I guess people are being infected with the conservation bug at last. Taking care of what they've got for fear there'll be no replacements."

"Are you doing any of the repairs?"

"No. Charles taught me the anatomy of watches and I was getting good. But my new man won't have it. Apparently he thinks I should sit home and do fancywork."

"Funny little squirt. Where did you dig him up?"

"Do you remember Alex, Charles' assistant? Well, he met with an accident. So I advertised, and Loth was the only possible applicant. A good jeweler with good references. But—I don't know."

"My suspicious nature advises me that you'd better check on Alex yourself. Maybe Loth is falsifying messages to keep his job."

"There's no need for him to do that. I don't like him personally, but I don't have to. He stays on when Alex returns. If business keeps booming there'll be enough work for six men. At the moment we're employing only three besides Loth—old Ben Seeger, who's been with Cotter's since Charles' father was a boy, and two silversmiths."

"Oh well, let's forget about stuff for the time and fuel up. We'll try the Hotel Benedict. My chief, who's an epicure, recommends it highly."

"I'd like to meet your chief, Grid. You've told me such a lot about Inspector Waldo Furniss that he's as familiar as a favorite book. Is he still so much in demand as an after-dinner speaker at benefits?"

"Yes, but he can't accept as many invitations as he used to." Nelson's face clouded. "We're that rushed." He brightened. "Tell you what—some night when there's a letup I'll have you both for dinner. He doesn't need any urging for a chance at Sammy's victuals."

"Grid, could I borrow Sammy for the first night Charles is home on furlough? He's due in two weeks."

"Sure, if she's willing. And I know she'll be. Sammy likes you." It was great praise. "What happened to your own cook?"

"She left at about the same time Charles did. She was offered a better job, and I encouraged her to take it. I eat out most of the time. It's no fun being served at home in solitary splendor."

The dining room of the Hotel Benedict was large and sunny. Most of the lunchers, male and female, wore uniforms. Nelson and his companion attracted an equal share of attention from both sexes. Separately, they were figures who commanded second looks. Together, the effect was doubled. Nelson stretched to man's full length, and he had width in all the right places, width to his shoulders, to his mouth, to the space between his deep-dug brown eyes, and to his brow. The premature topping of white dramatized his appearance, just as Louise's dark crown brought out the creaminess of her skin and the changing colors of her light eyes.

A waiter seated them at a table near a window, as though determined to place them on display.

"Unless you've changed your tipple while my back was turned, you're in the market for one scotch sour," Nelson said. He ordered two.

She was looking at the menu listlessly, and that was a bad sign. She had always taken a healthy interest in food.

Nelson found himself sharing her apathy. "Too bad it's a meatless day. We'd each of us be better for a thick slab of beef." Guiltily he nodded to the waiter's recommendation of goose liver casserole, without permitting him to finish his prose poem on the excellence of the wine sauce. He grinned, thinking of how revolted the chief would be at this summary treatment of an all-important matter.

When the waiter had set the drinks before them Nelson said, "Skoal." They clicked glasses. He waited until she had swallowed deeply. Then he said, "Want to tell me? Or do I knock myself out being funny to make you forget whatever it is that's gnawing at your vitals?"

"It isn't fair, Grid. You came to shed burdens—not to take them on."

"Sounds like something out of *Julius Caesar*." He saw with concern that her eyes were wet. "Nix," he said. "Nix. You've never done that in company. You're not going to start now. Blow your nose."

Obediently she took a handkerchief from her bag. She looked at it and said, "You haven't altered a scrap, Grid. You're an awfully bossy guy. But my nose doesn't need blowing. That moisture you haven't the tact to ignore is the beginning and the end. I'm not going to cry."

"Good. You've always been my best tonic. I don't want my tonic watered." After a moment's wait he began to probe patiently for the source of her unhappiness. "When did Captain Shay first start to darken your doorstep?"

The question did not take her by surprise. She said, as though connecting it with her gloom-freighted thought train, "We met before Charles went away. Shay brought in an old hunting watch to be repaired. He discovered that he and Charles had many interests in common, and the first thing we knew he was in Charles' private workroom, gloating over that ham radio set Charles had built. After that he invited himself to the apartment. He seemed to like us because he kept turning up."

"He seemed to like *us* or you?"

She said wearily, "I can't answer that. He's never made a false move and he knows how I feel about Charles. A blind man would sense it, and he's far from blind."

"Then what's with the tragedy routine? I don't recognize you."

"Charles," she said.

"But you tell me he's coming home in two weeks. That isn't so long to wait."

The waiter brought food, served it, and went away. They began to eat without appetite and without conversation. Finally Nelson said, "The sporting thing at this point would be to stop stalking that mushroom around your plate and concede defeat. What about Charles? Doesn't he like the Army?"

She put down her fork. "Charles makes the best of things. He doesn't enjoy having his life invaded any more than a lot of other very private citizens. But he's a patriot and he accepts what he feels to be essential to the country's welfare. After his aptitude tests had been gone over he was put to work adjusting airplane equipment. Yes, I guess he likes it well enough. He doesn't complain." She added, "He did mention that he'd caught cold, but only because he wanted me to have his special prescription filled and sent on to him. He's always been subject to colds, but he takes this one hard because he doesn't want it to slow up his work. That's the kind of a man he is."

"Am I to conclude that you're like this because you miss him and Texas is a long way off?"

"Oh no!" Then she said resentfully, "Of course I miss him, but I'm not exactly a weakling. I can bear it. I can even consider myself fortunate that he's much too valuable in his present post to be sent overseas at the drop of a hat. Most of my friends are in the same boat, or in leakier boats. I don't expect special dispensations. It's his letters. They're strange. Not like him at all. They're the letters of a man in a delirium who sees everything he wants relentlessly slipping out of reach. Even his handwriting's changed. It's weak and sick. I'm afraid."

"A cold can do a lot to impair a man's morale. Do you have one of the letters with you?" He said it because he did not know what else to say.

She shook her head. "I don't keep them. I tear them up. And even if I did keep them I wouldn't show them—not even to you. It would seem like a betrayal."

Nelson spoke slowly, coating each word with as much comfort as it would take. "Charles has Celtic blood in his veins. He's given to black despair from which he can shoot up at nothing more tangible than the right word at the right moment. Sometimes his moods last for a period of weeks. You confided that much to me yourself in the first stages of your marriage. Look, Louise, if there was anything seriously wrong with him they wouldn't permit him to keep on with the delicate work he's doing. He's just lonely for you. Also, he's got a rare streak of jealousy. It stems from humbleness. I'm speaking from my own observation. Intelligent and swell as he is, he can't force himself to believe that a big broth of a girl like you will stay satisfied with the little sandy-haired, blue-eyed specimen he sees in his mirror." He thought for a moment. "Maybe he's bothered by the fact that someone like Captain Shay is right here in New York with you, trying to beat his time. But as soon as he gets his furlough and has you on tap everything will be all right. Believe me."

Louise said, "I can believe the Shay part. It seeps out between every line. Somehow Charles cooled toward him after his second or third visit. He couldn't explain why, but it was there just the same."

"Then the whole thing's simple. If I were in your shoes I wouldn't go back to the shop this afternoon. I'd go home and sit down and write a nice long letter to my love. And I'd lie like hell. I'd say, very casually, that Captain Shay has been called away for an indefinite period of time. I'd say that business is good, that all's well, or would be if my love were here, and just wait till I get him home, et cetera. I'd offer him the most beautiful bouquet of sweet-smelling sentences ever gathered together, and I'd put lots of ferns around it to set it off."

"Actually, Captain Shay *is* going away for a week or so. His interests take him off on trips constantly. I didn't mean to give you the impression that he does nothing but camp on my doorstep."

Nelson smiled at her. "So you won't have to lie, my honest buxom wench."

"I'm not buxom—just generously built." He could almost read the letter taking shape in her mind, easing the strain. She leaned toward him. "Do you think it will do the trick?"

"Depend upon it." So far as he knew, neither Louise nor Charles was capable of creating teapot tempests. He wished he were as confident as he sounded. But for the moment there was nothing more to be gained by further pursuit of the subject. He started to reminisce, invariable accompaniment to their meetings. "How's your uncle Henry—still a pillar of the church?"

"His nose is out of joint. Our town has a new preacher who won't listen to suggestions. Remember the time Uncle Henry coaxed you to sing in the choir and your voice cracked?"

"I'll never forget. It shook the foundations of the building, and your cousin, the Martens brat, laughed so uproariously she had to be removed. I was always scared stiff of that one. She got under my skin. Do you still keep in touch? Somehow I can't believe she's grown up. I keep picturing a little towheaded string bean with a passionate will, but from all reports she must be quite a person."

Louise had gone back to the composition of her letter. She said absently, "She writes to me occasionally. Huh? What do you mean by 'all reports'?"

"I should have said 'report.' The last time he wrote my father intimated that the rest of your family had washed their hands of her."

"I wish they'd wash their mouths of her. She's worth the whole slew of them with premiums thrown in. Whatever nasty rumors they circulate come to them in dreams."

"What's she been doing to raise their blood pressure?"

"I don't know. Deep mystery. She hasn't even given me a real address—just general delivery. But I do know that whatever she's doing she's doing well and with a clear conscience. She's a darling. No towheaded string bean either. More like a gold willow tree, Grid. You ought to see her. She'd take that bachelor heart of yours and stuff it to bursting point before you had time to cry 'Uncle.'"

"Hmmm. Probably just your family pride speaking. Is your grandmother still going? Now there's a girl to stuff a man's heart—by force, if necessary."

Louise laughed. "She used force on you several times, but it wasn't aimed at your heart. Are you having dessert? I think I will."

Chapter 2

There were about forty girls pounding typewriters in the outer room of that particular government bureau. They ranged in age from eighteen to fifty and in appearance from slim showgirl to stout matron. They dressed as well as they could on the salaries they received, which was not very well. But an American girl can do a lot with a little, and in most cases the effect of the cheap ready-made clothes they wore was pleasing enough. In the case of the typist called Madge Carter the effect was almost too pleasing for comfort. She was an ash blonde with a tall, supple body and a face designed for connoisseurs. She glanced at her wristwatch without breaking the rhythm of her fingers.

The girl seated next to her whispered, "Tell me the bad news."

"Not so bad. Just ten minutes to go."

"Cheers! I can see a silhouette on the glass door of the private sanctum, and it's too big to be anyone else but your boyfriend. Looks like his interview with the boss is finished. Gee, I envy you. Don't bother to look innocent. Everybody in the joint has been keeping tabs on your secret romance. Why not make like you're going out to powder your nose? Then you can meet him in the corridor and wangle a dinner date."

The ash blonde smiled. "Thanks. It's not a bad idea." Unobtrusively she flowed out of her chair and into the corridor.

She had not long to wait. The door opened, and great hands were on her shoulders. "Clever little girl," he said. "You were waiting for me."

Her head declined modestly upon its lovely neck. "Yes." She hesitated. "I—I missed you so much."

"Poor child. Well, as soon I left the plane I made straight for this place, and my hurry wasn't due entirely to business either." His eyes sucked in every part of her. "We're dining together tonight."

She seemed overcome. "Oh. You'll—you'll call for me?"

"All right. Though I can't say I enjoy that zoo you live in. I want to take you out of it, Madge. Out of this too." He indicated the closed door of the office. "You're like a wonderful little flower wilting in a harsh climate. You have only to say the word—"

She said nervously, "I must go back. They'll miss me. Tonight?"

"Tonight. At seven-thirty." He raised her hand to his lips.

She withdrew it, placing it upon her heart. A little unsteadily, conscious of his avid gaze, she opened the door and went back to her typewriter.

Her neighbor whispered, "Any luck?"

"Dinner."

"Swell. Ask him if he's got a friend—a little younger than he is, if possible. Not that you can pick and choose in this burg. Hurrah! There's the bell—we're free!"

The girl called Madge Carter got her hat and coat, but she did not leave the building. Hidden in the washroom, she waited until the last of her co-workers had departed. Then cautiously she made her way to another floor. She knocked twice upon a door and entered.

Though it held only two men, the small office seemed overcrowded. Everything in Washington seems overcrowded, she thought drearily. Not only seems but is.

Both men greeted her warmly. The older one, known as Mr.

Price, was seated behind his desk. He stopped writing and said, "You look a bit tired, child. Sit down and tell us about it."

The younger man, Gene Holden, sprang to his feet. He moved a chair for her, placing it close to his own.

She shook her head. "I've been sitting all day." She leaned against the wall. "He's turned up on schedule. He was closeted with Major Riffey for about an hour. On the way out he invited me to dinner. He'll call for me at seven-thirty."

"Good. How did he act?"

"Not suspicious of me, if that's what you mean. To him I'm still the small-town girl he condescended to lift out of a herd of small-town girls. Since he hasn't an inkling that I engineered his first look at me how could he think otherwise? A man of his type would find it hard to believe that anyone who didn't have to would choose to live the life I've been living for the past month. Especially after he saw the rooming house."

Mr. Price clicked his tongue sympathetically. "We know it's unpleasant for you, but it's doubtful you'll have to put up with it much longer. Meanwhile—under the circumstances—a hotel is impossible, considering the rates being charged and the influence it takes to get in. Unless you"—he hesitated—"unless you care to enter one under his protection, but I hardly think that will be necessary."

Gene Holden cried, "Hey!" It was born of shock.

The girl sat down suddenly. Her vocal cords played her a trick, acting before she could censor the words they sent into the momentary silence. "I'm sick of Washington. I wish I didn't have to see it again until cherry blossom time."

Mr. Price smiled. His smile was as involuntary as her speech. "Impatience can be an asset. Your eagerness to conclude matters might help you to stumble upon the right approach. I trust you, however, to look before you stumble."

Gene Holden leaned over and patted her hand. "And you shouldn't mention cherry blossoms, K-k-kid." He took a deep breath. "They reek of the Rising Sun. First thing you know you'll be jugged for a spy, and the jig will be up."

Mr. Price retracted his smile. He said pompously, "Within these walls Miss Carter has earned the right to say what she wishes. It's you who should guard your tongue, my boy. If you were to hesitate over her name in public there might well be trouble. Practice saying 'Madge' until it comes natural."

"Check. But Madge doesn't suit the girl. Every time I get as far as M-a, Mata Hari pops into my mind and I'm stymied."

Mr. Price twisted the one long lock on his large pink pate. "A sense of humor is a fine thing—sometimes. Sometimes it's deadly.

You're young." His alert eyes included the girl. "But not too young, I hope, to sense the full importance of your undertaking. Watch out. Your quarry has everything to lose. It will react like a wild animal if it so much as smells interference. I can't caution you too much."

"You needn't worry, sir. We don't laugh while we're working."

The girl said bitterly, "Anyway, I don't. Not on this job. Keep telling me that it's important, because if I stop believing it I'll either destroy myself or that big ape the next time he lays a paw on me."

"And she doesn't mean me," said Gene Holden.

Mr. Price said, "Important? Doesn't your own intelligence tell you that unless we discover the leak we'll pay through the nose—not with money but with human currency? I'm sorry I can't give you a written guarantee that your man is the one we're after, but I do know that we can't afford to neglect him." Then he changed his tune. He pantomimed distress and said falsely, "Perhaps we're asking too much. If—"

"Please—you needn't go on. I'm sorry. The truth is that I'm hungry. I don't dare to eat a decent lunch these days for fear it will look too opulent. And when I'm hungry I lose my sense of values. I offered my services. I didn't expect a bed of roses."

Gene Holden scowled. "You didn't expect any kind of a bed."

She ignored him. "So you're not asking too much. You're not asking nearly enough."

Mr. Price said briskly, "Your spirit is fine. Did I mention that one way or another you'll soon be given that long overdue vacation?"

Her face lit up. "Wonderful. And it will be one way—not the other. I'll see to it."

Gene Holden moved impatiently. "We've got our respective roles down pat. Is there anything else, sir?"

"No. I just wish we were employing a less clumsy method, but it seems the only way to get tangible evidence—if tangible evidence exists. So do your best. Report to me as soon as you can. And at the first opportunity I want you to take your co-worker out and buy her the best dinner to be had. My treat."

"Thanks. But that's one bill I don't mind footing myself. Coming, lass?"

Gene Holden was a few inches taller than his companion. Just the height to make walking with her a pleasure. And it was easy to see that he was more than pleased. Out in the street he spoke casually, as though being her squire was an everyday affair.

"That old so-and-so runs neck in neck with the world's biggest hypocrites. To further the cause he'd sell his ten-year-old grand-

granddaughter into worse than death."

"I know it, but he's a great guy. I love him."

"Any left over for me, Kyrie?"

"Haven't I heard that song before?"

"Yes. I use the same tactics as radio announcers. I think that constant repetition is bound to sell you in the end."

"Not me. I just get irritated and buy something else."

He looked at her unhappily. She was fragilely built. It seemed as though a breeze would sway her. But he knew that she had a dark strength that could, when she summoned it, be counted upon to keep her on her feet.

"You're a cruel woman, Kyrie. In your own way you're as cruel as—well, never mind." He shrugged. "Hell! Whenever I spend time with the old man he has me too scared to mention even my own handle above a whisper."

"Your own handle doesn't matter. You're new to the game and no one knows you. But he's right about my handle. You've used it twice in the last few minutes. I'm Madge. Madge Carter."

"I wish I could take an active dislike to you, Madge Carter."

"I wish you could." She sounded sincere. "Or just be indifferent."

"The way you are to me?"

"Yes. The way I am to you."

"God, you're cruel."

"I'd be cruel if I led you on, Gene." Her voice was so lovely that even when she strove to be matter-of-fact the intention was lost in its warm tones. "And I'd be subnormal if after several years of being at large I was unaware of the effect I have on men. 'You're beautiful. You're devastating. You're a blonde with a brain. You're a *femme fatale*. Your body is like a young slender birch. Your eyes are changing autumn leaves.' I could quote endlessly, but I won't bother. If I'm not mistaken you'll recognize some of the phrases as your very own. And all of them are worn thin by too much use. Men stand in queues for me. I'm not smug about it. Just bored."

He said roughly, "You talk like a fancy lady."

"So far it hasn't been difficult to resist even the initial step toward being a fancy lady. And that, my dear, is what's really got you down."

"I want to marry you."

"That's not startlingly original either."

He sidestepped, putting a short distance between them.

She reached out and touched his arm pacifically. "But at least you didn't trot out the good old stock piece. So you're one up for my money."

"What good old stock piece?"

"It goes like this: 'Is there anyone else? Because if there isn't I'll keep on hoping—and someday—'"

"Stop it." He had been assembling a version of "Is there anyone else?" in his mind, and had been on the point of launching that version. He said explosively, "So help me—if I ever make another pass at you may all the rats in—"

She whispered, "Gene, are you mad? We're on the street. There are people all around us."

His voice was sulky. "You could have let me finish. I was only invoking a childhood oath. I wasn't going to mention—"

"It seems to me that you haven't left your childhood far enough behind. Perhaps you *are* too young."

"Perhaps you're too old—in spite of your years. Too bad Grandpa Jitterpuss Price is so well mated. You'd have been ideal for him. You could sit and feed each other nightmares all day long and grow fat together." He lowered his voice dramatically. "If you think the spies surrounding us can make anything out of that, just slap my wrist and send me home for blabbing."

Kyrie laughed. "I'd like to send you home to lick your wounds, but there are chores to be done, and you're needed."

"Yeah—chores. Equivalent to filling the wood basket and collecting the eggs. Big manly stuff."

"Listen to me, Gene. You weren't railroaded into this. You came of your own accord. And you were taken because you have all the necessary qualifications. So it stands to reason that you believe in the importance of what you're doing. Or you wouldn't be doing it."

"I believe in it, all right. But not this special job. Aside from the fact that I'm nothing more than a looker-on while you do all the dirty work, the whole thing has a dash too much fantasy for me to swallow. It's practically impossible—not to say insane—for a man in— Take that brake out of your eyes. You don't need it."

"You must believe in every job. You must be certain that whatever orders you receive are more important than anything else in the world. Because those orders are weighed to an ounce before they reach you. And as soon as you start to put them on your own private scales you lose out. You've got to accept them blindly, without question."

"I was prepared to accept them blindly. Before I met you I could have gone in eye-deep. But—well, even if you were just any female I wouldn't like the assignment that's been handed out to you. The old man has no right to go at it that way. It's sheer melodrama. Surely he could find other means."

"Other means have been tried, without result. I'm going strong. I don't mind it at all. I get a boot out of it."

"Sure you do. Right where it hurts. That's why you kept asking for reassurance back in the office."

"Oh, pooh! I was just blowing off steam." She looked up into his angry eyes. Then deliberately she made her voice soft, sent it out to embrace him. "Very well, Gene. You don't like this job because of my part in it. You can't believe in its importance or in the method used to get evidence. But you *do* think I'm important and you don't want anything to happen to me."

"Right. Not even if you *are* indifferent to my peculiar allure."

"If you could only remember that personalities have no place in our pattern."

He said, "I notice that you're not above dragging them in when everything else fails to soften the brute."

Her voice was still soft. "All right. You win, I'm not indifferent to you. I like you. You have personality and you're smart. Maybe sometime—"

His eagerness was painful. "Sometime?"

Kyrie could not carry through. She said in exasperation, "Oh, drop it. I can't promise anything."

"Don't get sore. You needn't promise. I'll stop all this. I won't falter by word or deed from now on. You can be easy about me. And—and—" He finished it defiantly, "I'll keep on hoping."

He took her arm. They walked down the next street in silence. When they reached the corner he said, "I won't coax to go any farther, though I'd sure like to get a load of your rooming house. From what you've let slip it must be a collector's item. Not that mine is any slouch. It has the new double-breasted sleeping arrangements specially designed for these brisk Washington nights. See you later, partner. Watch for me. Meanwhile, shake."

She smiled and gave him her hand. "That's the talk."

"Just one more thing. Jitterpuss wants me to take you to dinner at the first opportunity. You heard him. Don't forget it in the press of your other duties. We've got to follow orders blindly, you know, without stopping to weigh them."

"At the first opportunity," she said and left him.

He raced after her. "I forgot. I picked up your mail at the post office. Here."

"Thanks." Absently she put the envelopes in her pocket. "Don't mention it. We can't have you jeopardizing your incognito by calling for it yourself."

It occurred to her as she walked toward the rooming house that, for all his qualms, Gene Holden was far more optimistic than she. Because an opportunity for her to dine with him or with anyone other than the central figure of her current enterprise seemed too far off to glimpse through a powerful telescope. She was not "going strong," in spite of her brave assertion. The affair just kept dragging on through countless lunches and dinners and dances whenever the prospect was in Washington. But after the bulk of the accompanying conversation was put through a strainer it yielded scarcely enough juice to make a small teardrop. So help me, she thought, if I fail after all my talk I'll turn myself into a lady hermit and live in complete isolation until I sicken and die of my own rotten company. And my covey of ardent swains will have to take what comfort they can by comparing notes at my funeral. Then she grimaced at herself and made scoffing appraisal. Cute little Kyrie, the whimsey spinner!

Someone behind her broke into a run. Gene, she thought impatiently. He forgot something else. But the man who drew abreast of her was a stranger. He took off his hat and smiled and said, "I'm shameless. I've been following you and biding my time until your Romeo departed. I work in the same building you do and I've been trying to arrange a meeting for days."

She said, "I must admit you lay your cards on the table. Why did you want to meet me?"

"Did you ever look at yourself in the mirror?" She could not see his features plainly, but his bared head was pale and his teeth gleamed with a light of their own on the dark street.

"I don't like blond men, Mr.—?"

"Edward Long. And don't believe that 'opposites-attract' stuff. It's been exploded ages ago. I did it myself. Never looked twice at a brunette in my life. What do you say we have a drink somewhere, Miss—?"

"Carter. But I wouldn't bother to memorize it if I were you. It isn't worth your while. I have an engagement now and every night for the next twenty weeks."

"Ouch." He took her arm. "Is that nice? You might give me a chance. This is a democracy, isn't it?"

"We have to draw the line somewhere. Let me go."

He held on. "I know a swell place for cocktails."

"Take your hands off me or I'll call for help."

"You wouldn't do that."

"Wouldn't I?" She was a little frightened.

"All right." He relinquished her suddenly. "My mistake. I'll bet you *are* dated up for the next twenty weeks—with a different guy every night." He turned on his heel and hurried away.

She wanted to laugh. It was not the first time she had sent a would-be Lothario about his business. Yet ... She walked on so rapidly that she was breathless when she reached her destination.

She climbed the veranda steps of a low broad building whose right wing was almost completely devoured by a spreading copper beech tree. Years ago the building had been the property of a long-forgotten senator. Confident of his power to brave the tide of future elections, the senator had chosen a residence large enough to shelter not only his family but its far-reaching tag ends. And, judging by the confused interior, even his wife's fifth cousin's second husband had been permitted a say in the furnishings. Kyrie had been living there for a month, and she was still startled by the heterogeneous jumble that oozed out even into the entrance hall.

Miss Abbott, the present owner, had added to the jumble, her contribution being mostly cots. Miss Abbott was a sweetish spinster whose fluttery mannerisms did nothing to jar the steadiness of her business sense. She rented rooms to females garnered from the host that had flocked to Washington to supply the government's need for file clerks, typists, stenographers, pamphleteers, and defense workers. And it seemed to Kyrie that this lady Simon Legree would continue to accept all corners until the last available cot had been purchased and the last space had been created to receive it.

She had been steered to Miss Abbott's because it was so innocent-seeming, a place where a lowly typist might well be expected to hang her snood. She had fondly believed that the cubicle for which she paid full room rent was to be her very own, but twice during her stay she had returned to find that she was sharing it with a real white-collar worker who took the arrangement in stride.

When Kyrie protested Miss Abbott stopped fluttering for a moment and braced her voice with sugar-coated steel. "We're at war, dear. We mustn't allow ourselves to complain about small discomforts." And Kyrie vowed inelegantly that the next person who saw fit to hand her that routine would receive a good sock in the kisser. So tired was she growing of those who used the war as an excuse to cover personal greed, inefficiency, or intent to swindle.

None of Miss Abbott's paying guests had keys. And that, if anything, Kyrie thought, belonged in the category of necessary war measures. Because keys for everyone who slept under the Abbott roof would make serious inroads upon the country's supply of metal. She raised the knocker on the door and gave it extra impetus for its downward swing, repeating the action several times, taking imaginary aim at her landlady's corseted diaphragm.

After a few moments an old colored man responded to the clatter. He smiled at her in spite of his obvious weariness. "Good evening, miss."

She smiled back, ashamed of the intemperate means by which he had been summoned. "Good evening." She added impulsively, "Don't you ever get just too tired to go on?"

He said gently, "We're at war. Can't get tired in wartime."

She did not sock him in the kisser. She gave him fifty cents and was conscious of his surprised eyes following her as she climbed the stairs to her cubicle.

I know—I know, she told her guilty conscience. Not in character. Clerical workers who are supposed to be living on their invisible wages don't hand out fifty centses. I won't do it again, but I couldn't help it that time.

She entered her cubicle, discovered with thanksgiving that for the time being at least she was its sole occupant, and shut the door. Miss Abbott called it the yellow room. It looked to Kyrie like a swollen and jaundiced telephone booth. The wallpaper was patterned with glaring overblown tea roses that reached out and slapped her face when she was unwary enough to glance at them. A bilious yellow carpet hid the floor; yellow spreads covered the twin Army cots, and yellow throws protected the scarred surfaces of two giant bureaus and one rickety table. A yellow cushion softened the seat of an ancient rocker.

She put me in here because I have yellow hair, Kyrie thought. A dark woman would supply a false note. She undressed quickly and carefully, experience having taught her that the furniture was ready to rear up and bark her shins at the first opportunity. She put on a robe, armed herself with the paraphernalia of the bath, and went out into the long dim hall, praying devoutly as she started toward her objective. Her prayers were answered. The bathroom was empty, the tub dry and clean.

Ten minutes later she was back in the yellow room, making up her face more from memory than from the grudging reflection thrown back by the dingy wall mirror. No rouge. A slash of lipstick. A touch of eye shadow on her long lids. To hell with mascara. Her lashes were several shades darker than her hair and curled back upon themselves without aid. Now the dress. She pulled it on, thinking with longing of other remembered dresses that her knowing escort would surely recognize as beyond the grasp of a typist. If I could wear my own clothes, she thought, I wouldn't have to pry his tongue loose with liquor. I'd make him so drunk on just me that he'd tell all. But she was not too concerned. Her view of herself was entirely realistic, and she realized that she gave the clinging line of the bargain special a value far above its sale tag. Its delicate pastel green brought out the translucent quality of her skin, deepened her eyes. She would do. It wasn't as though he would take her to an ultrafashionable restaurant where her poise might be undermined by the oblique glances of perfectly turned-out sisters. He did not care to exhibit his new find in places where he was known. And he was widely known. But, she thought, cheered suddenly, he likes good food, and even the drab spot he calls our rendezvous has plenty of that. I wasn't fooling. I'm hungry.

She was ready and waiting, engrossed more in the planning of the meal she would get him to order by subtle hints than in the ordeal to follow. She sat down on her cot and previewed that meal course by course. She had reached dessert when someone knocked upon her door.

"Come in," she said.

The old colored man entered, stood on the threshold. He said apologetically, "With so many coming and going I get the rooms mixed up sometimes. You Miss Carter?"

"Yes, I am."

"I thought you was. You got a face to remember. I won't forget the name that belongs with it no more. Your escort, he waiting down in the reception room. He seem mighty impatient."

"Thanks. What's your name?"

"Andrew."

"Thanks, Andrew." She picked up her evening wrap gingerly, hoping it was proof against the chill outside. "I'm ready."

He advanced a few steps to stand firm in her path. He said, "They was a man here today asking about Miss Carter. I didn't know he meant you. I had to look in the register to find out did we have a guest by that name."

She stiffened. "Yes?"

"I figure he somebody checking up for the government where you work. The government keep checking up all the time." He hesitated. "Then when he pass me a dollar bill I naturally figure he ain't somebody from the government."

"What did he want to know about me?"

"He want to know how long you been here and how long you fixing to stay. I didn't have no information like that, and my lady was out, so I couldn't ask her. Pretty soon he say he from your hometown and he can't leave his name because he want to surprise you. He describe you good to show he telling the truth. He want to know where your room is so he can leave a private note for you. I tell him leave it with me 'cause I can't read, but that don't satisfy him. My lady never lets menfolk upstairs, but I ain't starting an argument, so I say I new here and can't tell which room you got. And he laugh and tell me to find out so he can pass me another dollar next time he come."

"What did he look like?"

"He dressed real good. He not so tall and not so fat but kind of thick. He got hair most as light as yours."

"Next time, if you can slip him past Miss Abbott, let him come up. Maybe I do know him. If he leaves a note I can tell." She thought, And if he finds anything in this room besides a nervous breakdown he's welcome to it.

Andrew said doubtfully, "Yes ma'am."

When he had retreated quietly an unpleasant thought struck her. His description of the visitor applied too closely for comfort to the man who had accosted her on the street. She ran to the wardrobe where hung the coat she had been wearing. She searched its pockets. The letters that Gene Holden had collected for her were gone.

So that was it! The enemy was playing the same game that she and Gene had planned for the evening. Her right name was on the envelopes of the letters, and she had barely glanced at them to judge their contents. Should she call off the dinner date? If the stranger was working with Rex he would give the show away at the first opportunity.

She descended the stairs, her mind busy. She wanted to telephone the old man and ask his advice. But she had to pass the reception room to get to the public phone booth, and Rex was there, facing the door.

He saw her before she could slip by. Too late. She smiled seraphically as he rose to meet her.

Chapter 3

Awaiting their own escorts, at least six females occupied the straight-backed chairs lining the walls of Miss Abbott's cluttered reception room. It was plain from the covert glances they cast his way that Rex was the subject of their pre-dinner conversation. He almost leaped upon Kyrie, so great was his eagerness to escape.

"Rex," she said softly.

He had asked her to call him "Rex" at the outset of their acquaintance, explaining that it was a nickname given him at school and used now only by specially privileged friends. She assumed correctly that this category was reserved for his rather widespread harem. But her role was that of a simple, unsophisticated girl who knew nothing of such matters, so she had thanked him prettily and transformed the sharp syllable into a caress that sent his blood pressure up each time she proffered it.

"Let's get out of here," he said.

On the street he mopped his forehead. Partially restored, he bellowed for a taxi.

Kyrie said, "Couldn't we walk? I'd rather."

"My dear little girl"—he beamed at her—"how many times must

I tell you that there's no need to consider the budget when you're out with me?"

"It takes a lot of getting used to, Rex. You see, I've been so poor all my life that I feel guilty when money's spent unnecessarily. And we're not going far." Reading from left to right, her mind presented quite another argument. In the first place, Gene is standing in the shadows across the street, I hope. And if we take a taxi he'll miss out. In the second place, you won't talk in a taxi. You'll just grunt and paw.

He humored her. "Well, as you say, we're not going far. Sure your wrap's warm enough? I wish you'd let me buy you a proper one. You'd be marvelous in furs."

She gathered her mouth together primly. "But I couldn't let you do that. I couldn't." Then she cried, "I wish you were poor, Rex. It would make us closer. I could plan for you—save for you. Sometimes I lie awake nights thinking of the fabulous sums a man of your talents must earn, and I seem so inadequate that I get scared."

"Radio doesn't pay such fabulous sums. It's just that I've been a bit fortunate in my investments. You mustn't fret. Spending a man's wealth is the easiest thing for a girl to learn. If your beauty didn't walk hand in hand with the most incredible combination of naïveté and unselfishness a man ever had the good fortune to witness, you'd have learned long ago." He pressed her arm. "Not that I want you to change. The day I collided with you in the hall outside your office was the luckiest day in the world for me."

"Oh, Rex, thank you." She added shyly, "I'm the lucky one. All the girls in my office have crushes on you. They'd be green with jealousy if they knew—of us, I mean. They're always raving about you. Of course I never join in because the moment I said your name they'd be bound to know how I felt."

"That's a good girl. Let it be our secret for a while. What do they say about me?"

"Well, they say you're terribly attractive, for one thing, and that you must be really important or a man like the big boss of our bureau wouldn't receive you so readily. They seem to think you're engaged in things aside from your regular work—like—like being a—a secret agent for the government, or something."

He smirked. "I have a few side lines."

She was wistful. "You have? I suppose you can't discuss them with me, but I wish you could. Then it would seem as though I were helping you—if only by listening. You know. The way some of the women in history helped their men." She sighed. "Since we've met I've become so restless—changed. I go crazy just sitting and typing all day. It seems so useless. Sometimes I think that if

I have to type one more report on scrap metal or industrial diamonds, I'll end it all. Rex, I hate to ask favors, but isn't there some real work you—?"

He reproved her as one chides a fractious child. "You're depressed, Madge, and small wonder, but you mustn't talk of ending it all. The life you're leading is enough to give anyone the blues. I do wish you'd let me—" He broke off. He said thoughtfully, "There might be a job for you at that."

"Rex!"

"I'm not promising, mind you. It's nothing that can be arranged at the drop of a hat. It has to be gone into thoroughly—thought out."

Her eyes were shining. "I'll do anything, Rex. Anything if I can work with you."

"I'm sure of that. But unfortunately there are others who remain to be convinced." He made the practiced self-deprecating gesture that he considered to be no small part of his charm. "I'm not the whole show, you know. Now let's forget work and enjoy the evening. You're shivering. I knew that wrap wasn't warm enough. The little place we tried last time is right down the next street. Suit you?"

"Oh yes. That restaurant seems so essentially masculine—like you. Do you know, Rex, the steaks they have there remind me of the ones we used to get at home on special holidays. Mmmm."

"Then you shall have another tonight, child. Better than the ones at home. A plank steak with all the trimmings."

She almost swooned with pleasure.

He took note and made complete misinterpretation. "Madge, you're so responsive. It makes a fellow want to do everything for you. I've been lonely, though, considering the life I've led, that might be hard to swallow. But it's true. And through all my loneliness I've dreamed of a dear companion with your beauty and charm. I only hope you're going to be kind to—" He broke off. He began to quicken his steps. "Not a sign of life on this block."

Kyrie said in a small voice, "It *is* deserted. I'd be frightened if you weren't with me."

"Frightened?" He was walking very fast now. He said with nervous gallantry, "You need never fear anything. One glance at you and the most hardened criminal would duck into the nearest church to pray to your plaster replica. It's men like me who are endangered. Public figures are constantly making enemies through no fault of their own."

"Not you, Rex. You're too fine, too sensitive to make enemies." She clung tightly to his arm, keeping up with his long strides. Suddenly she said, "We *are* being followed, aren't we? You hear it too."

"Eh?"

"Those footsteps—I noticed them a little while after we started, but I didn't want to say anything. It seemed silly."

"Nonsense. I've infected you with my own fears." Nevertheless, he wheeled, taking her with him. "Sheer imagination."

But it wasn't imagination. The sharp turn brought him face to face with a man who halted his own steps abruptly, without giving ground.

Kyrie made a frightened sound.

The man said, "I'm following you all right. So what?" His breath injected alcohol into the surrounding air.

"He's—he's intoxicated," Kyrie said.

The man addressed himself to her. He was tall and dark, and his hat was pulled down over his eyes. "I'm drunk—plain drunk—but I know what I'm doing. I know you, Madge Carter."

"Are you familiar with this person, Madge?" Rex's nervousness had vanished. He spoke as a presiding judge who has the situation well in hand.

"She's not so familiar as I want her to be, but I'm the persistent type."

"Do you know him, Madge?"

She nodded miserably. "He comes from my hometown. He's been a disgrace to himself and his family ever since I can remember. Last week he came to Washington and looked me up and he's been pestering me, but I never—"

"Sure you never. How's about making a start? How's about ditching the duke and starting in right now? I bet the duke can't even dance. He's too old for you, Madgie. Your mother wouldn't like it. Come on—be a sport. I can dance. I'm a jitterbug. Think of the rugs we could cut together." He did a few steps to illustrate. One of them sent him off balance. He reeled, putting his arms around her for support.

She cried out in distress.

Her escort yanked the man loose. He shook him. "What's your name?"

"Let me go, stoolie. I know your game. You want to find out where I work and get me canned. Well, try again. I don't work, see? So you can't hook me that way. You're a fox, mister. Or maybe a wolf. You're maybe even the vice-president of wolves on account of everybody in Washington has some kind of office. So take this, vice-president of wolves, right on your sticky snout."

Kyrie saw her escort dodge the blow. She saw his attempt to pinion the younger man's arms, saw the two bodies lock in close embrace, cast a rocking shadow on the lonely sidewalk. It was a prize fight without a referee to break the combatants apart. It seemed as though it might continue forever in one endless round with no points for either side.

Fascinated, she watched for an unrecorded interval that might have been a moment or an hour. Then she found voice and raised it in one thin, distinct call. "Police!"

And that was all the referee the younger man needed. He broke away violently, ran, and was out of sight before Rex had time to straighten.

He stared at her reproachfully. His first words were so unexpected that she engaged in her own brief struggle, winning quick victory over the giggle on her lips. It gave ground, replaced by a credible sob.

He said, "You must have encouraged him, Madge. Surely he couldn't have taken it for granted that—"

She sobbed again.

"There—I didn't intend to be harsh. I realize the encouragement was unwitting, of course. Take my handkerchief. We'll pretend the whole unpleasant incident never happened. We won't let it spoil our evening."

"You're not hurt, Rex. Please say you're not hurt."

"Good as new. I'm a man who has always managed to take physical violence in his stride. I don't go out to look for it, but I don't dodge it when it comes."

She smiled tremulously. "I'm sorry, Rex. I wish it hadn't happened. Part of me thinks it's my fault, and part of me doesn't. You see, I—I always find it so hard to rebuff people so that they believe I really mean—"

He was magnanimous. "Poor child. Never mind. We're going to forget it. Now not another word. Into the final sprint." He took her arm. "On your mark—get set—go! This ought to work up an appetite."

Kyrie thought a bit hysterically, Some fun. What will he think of next? Resigned, she sprinted at his side until they reached their objective.

"Well, this is it. How's your wind?"

Not so good as yours, windbag, she thought. She said breathlessly, "You're not even puffing, Rex."

"I keep pretty well trained. Never smoke too much or drink too much."

Remembering how often she had prayed for him to take just one above quota that her ends might be served, she groaned inwardly, Don't I know it, brother.

They entered the restaurant. It was modeled on the lines of a London chophouse, heavy and dark and solid. They were greeted simultaneously by the heartening smell of food and by the bowing manager.

"Good evening. Glad to welcome you again. Your table is ready and waiting." Few people were dining, yet he led them to one of the unoccupied tables with the air of having held it against all odds.

When they were seated Rex said sheepishly, "I thought we might land here, child, so I took the liberty of phoning for a reservation. You never know. Now for that plank steak. Waiter! Oh, there you are."

Kyrie paid little attention while he dictated the impressive order. She was thinking, We'd have ended up here even if I sat down in the gutter and bawled for sea food. He's probably given this address in case anything turns up. I wonder if Gene's luck was as good as the blond man's. Funny that both sides should use the same tactics on the same night. I wonder what was in those letters. Rex isn't the only fool. I was completely off guard. I hope—

The waiter had taken his instructions to the kitchen, and Rex was turning to her for approval. "How did that sound to you?"

"Perfect, Rex."

He seized her hand. He said ardently, "That's what I mean about you being responsive. A fellow likes appreciation when it comes from the heart, as yours does. No one's looking. Have you a kiss for your Rex? I'll find it much more of an appetizer than anything on the menu."

Appetizer to you. Emetic to me. She leaned toward him with what might have been reluctance due to modesty. It was just reluctance. She was saved by the arrival of the Rum Collins.

Subsequently she was saved by each course in turn. But nothing tasted as it had tasted in anticipation. And that, she thought, is because he keeps staring at me with that ravening expression. For heaven's sake, eat up, she told him silently, and stop putting me in the same class as the food on your plate.

He wouldn't talk either. Or, rather, he wouldn't talk sense. He kept plowing a path through her gambits to make way for his emotions. By the time coffee arrived she had gone down under a vast wave of discouragement. I'm no use, she decided. This can go on forever. What I need is a bona fide clairvoyance sharp enough to pierce that thick hide.

"Why so pensive, my darling? Your lovely clear eyes are searching right down into my soul. Sometimes you seem so all-knowing that you awe me."

I wish I were all-knowing enough to awe myself. She sugared her reply busily, wondering if the cloying thing she had become could really hold savor for any man. It could, she concluded. He was swallowing it whole when the manager walked over to the table.

"There's a telephone call for you, sir. You can take it in the booth near the entrance."

"Thank you. Excuse me, Madge. I won't be long." But he was away for at least ten minutes.

And now all I need, she thought, is a pocket wiretapping device that works by remote control. The blond man tipping him off? Oh no—please don't let it be—please. But if it is I'll be able to tell by his face. And then? If not, I'll get on with this thing—someway—somehow.

She waited for his return, trying to whittle out an entering wedge that would be foolproof against caution or stupidity or whatever it was that protected him. Still weaponless, she saw him approach.

She raised her eyes sympathetically. "Poor Rex. Was it business? They don't give you a moment's peace, do they?" She could tell nothing by his face except that some sort of activity was going on behind it, because his features were stiff with the effort of concealment.

His voice was reassuring. "Nothing of importance. At any rate, nothing that will interfere with our plans." He sat down and finished his coffee. "Did I tell you that I have tickets for that new show they're trying out in Washington? Yes, I thought it would please you. But first, if you'll bear with me, I must stop off to pick up some papers—as a favor to a friend of mine." He called for a check, glanced at it with less than the usual attention he paid such matters, and put his hand in his pocket. He looked blank for a moment. Then he began a methodical search through his clothes.

"Is anything wrong, Rex?"

He nodded. "Your young man was not so drunk after all. That little encounter cost me my wallet."

"Oh no!"

"Oh yes." He smiled at her. "Don't worry. There was nothing of importance in it except money, and I always carry a few spare bills. See?" He produced one and covered the check with it.

Her voice was forlorn. "Rex, I can't tell you how I feel." She was not acting. Nothing important except money, she thought bitterly. Poor Gene. Poor me.

"Ready to start?" He helped her into her coat. She noticed that his hands were not quite steady. And I'd give everything I own to know whether that's due to the wallet or the phone call, she thought lavishly.

Outside the restaurant he signaled a passing taxi, muttering something about not wishing to risk a second adventure with one of her admirers.

"Rex," she said reproachfully.

"Just trying to be funny, my dear."

She took it for granted that the papers were to be picked up at his hotel, and she assumed, chary as he was of exhibiting her to acquaintances, that he would ask her to wait in the cab. As it drew up she was engaged in trying to devise a scheme that would make it seem logical for a modest maiden to be smuggled to his room. There she might be seized by a sudden thirst. Water would do. She could contrive to spill it on his trousers. He would go to the bathroom to mop up. And she would make quick survey. Clumsy—but what else was there to do? As it turned out she could have spared her mind the exercise.

She knew that on his brief trips to Washington he stayed at the Shoreline Hotel. His room had been visited and searched on several occasions, uncovering nothing that provided a clue to his suspected activities. He traveled lightly, and if Mr. Price was on the right track he carried nothing incriminating aside from the perfidy in his own head. Or that had been the case to date. Well, perhaps she, Kyrie, would be more successful than her predecessors.

She stepped into the cab. He followed, crowding close. Too close. His thigh pressed heavily against hers. He's preoccupied, she thought, but not too preoccupied to neglect the moment's largesse. He gave her temporary relief as he leaned forward to direct the driver. He was back in his chosen position before she had time to digest the fact that their destination was not the Shoreline Hotel. What had he said? It sounded like "dock basin."

He made brief explanation. "This friend of mine, an eccentric fellow, is fed up with the red tape attached to getting accommodations. So whenever it's necessary for him to stay in Washington he sleeps on his yacht. That's where my errand takes us."

She permitted a reasonable amount of her real excitement to enter her voice. "A yacht? How romantic. I've never been on one. The nearest I've ever got was in the movies."

"Well, I'm afraid you won't get much nearer than that tonight. There won't be time for me to show you around if we want to make the first curtain. So you'll just have to be a good girl and wait in the cab. I won't be more than a moment or two."

There was an undercurrent to that shallow speech. She felt its warning tug but could not understand why it should be there. He was not suspicious of her. That much seemed patent in his attitude, in his fussy talk of theaters and first curtains. Therefore, the phone call had not been made by the blond man. Yet it seemed strange that a man like Rex should pass up such a perfect opportunity to stage a big seduction scene. He had made attempts before, on far less auspicious occasions. So it might be that the yacht contained something not for the public eye.

Her long-curved lips were not designed for pouting, but she did her best. "Rex," she pleaded childishly, "can't I get on board just for a few minutes? I've been to the theater before, but this will be a new experience. Please. I want to pretend that the yacht is ours, yours and mine, and that we're going on a long cruise together."

He capitulated. "All right, little girl. You know I can't refuse you anything. Come here."

There was no timely interruption to save her from his kiss. His mouth felt ugly and urgent. Heat seeped through his clothes and penetrated her own flimsy garments. Self-discipline was a potent force. She did not scream or even shudder. She was commanding her body to be a cage strong enough to confine her wild distaste.

Even the abrupt cessation of wheels did not end the embrace. After a preliminary cough the taxi driver used his voice as a tool of leverage.

"I can't go any farther, sir. The *Angela*'s moored out a ways. You'll have to get a tender if you want to board her. Do I wait?"

She was released. Rex got out and offered her assistance. She stumbled as her feet touched ground. She recovered and stepped clear of his steadying arm. He turned his attention to the driver. She drew in the commingled odors of water and paint and hemp and tar, all freshened by the night's crisp breath. In that moment nothing was so important as this healing feast of air.

She barely noted the uniformed man who came out of the shadows to approach Rex, to examine the contents of the envelope he held in his hand, speak pleasant words, and disappear again. She was barely conscious of Rex leading her to a small shed, of the further exchange of pleasantries, and money too. Boarding the tender was only half recorded, as was climbing a ship's ladder, setting foot on the lazy-moving deck of the *Angela*. The small light of the departing tender awakened her. She breathed sharply.

Rex said, "Excited, child? Tell me, how does a first experience feel? It's been so long since I've had one."

Her hands clenched upon an invisible checkrein. Pull yourself up sharp. This is what you wanted, isn't it? Then look alert. Stop behaving like the ravished maiden in her post-maiden scene.

She laughed. "Wait until I've seen more. Does it have a bar and a luxurious salon and staterooms and everything? Is there anyone aboard besides us?"

"Not a soul. My friend is in New York at the moment. The call I got was from his man, asking me if I'd mind doing this errand."

It sounded thin, even for the naïve creature she was impersonating. She said guilelessly, "I'm glad he managed to reach you at the restaurant. I wouldn't have missed this for the world."

"Naturally I always leave a number at the hotel where I can be reached." He added quickly, "What were you saying about bars and staterooms? Oh yes. Well, I guess the yacht has all the things you mentioned. Just follow me. Be careful of the steps."

He wasn't guessing. He seemed to know his way. He fumbled in his pocket and produced a small torch. She followed its beam down a companionway that gave on to a good-sized oblong. He switched off the torch, and she stood still a moment, keying her eyes to the dark. She distinguished the outlines of chairs and tables and something that might have been a piano.

"This is the salon. I don't want to light it until I make sure that all curtains are drawn. Regulations, you know. We'll come back to it later." He guided her into a corridor. "I'll show you a stateroom first and get what I came for at the same time. Don't expect movie gadgets though. My friend doesn't go in for that sort of thing."

He passed one door, opened a second one. He stepped inside. The porthole was a pale round glow. He pulled a cord, and curtains slid along a rod and the glow vanished. She heard him say in a satisfied tone, "There now. We're completely blacked out." His hand rose to the electric switch.

The light made her blink. He looked at her. "Disappointed, Madge? Well, this is the way most yachts look in real life. No great movie minds to add the nice touch of satin bedspreads and deep pile rugs." He was watching her face. "Come in," he said and took her arm and pulled her over the threshold.

"It's sweet, Rex. Clean and bare and—and shipshape. A real berth with plenty of drawer space beneath it, and a reading lamp, and a comfortable chair, and a desk." Under the cover of her rambling she was telling herself that she had *not* heard the door close behind her, had not heard the sound of a drawn bolt.

The battle of the taxicab had left her a little shaken. It had been nasty but not fatal, and she did not doubt her ability to keep further skirmishes out of the fatal class. She knew a trick or two. But she wished the big fool had not chosen this time and place. Or did he imagine she had been the chooser? Did he, in his stupendous ego, think she had contrived to board the yacht just to—?

Adjectives to describe the small cabin petered out. She gave a last lingering inspection, wondering as to the hiding place of the papers he had come to get. In the desk? In one of the drawers under the berth? Surely they couldn't be important after all, or they would be kept under lock and key. But perhaps there was a wall safe. That panel over the washstand looked movable.

He said with calm amusement, "I think you've taken it all in."

She sighed raptly. "But there's still the bar and the salon and the bridge and the stern and the bow and the galley. So get what you came for and let's finish the tour."

"You know a lot about ships, Madge. What you don't seem to know is a lot about men. I mean to remedy that. Yes, I'll get what I came for." He caught her to him.

"Rex!" The syllable was stripped of caressive quality. It came out naked, born of his sudden transformation.

He performed a shocking parody of laughter. "Don't struggle. You can't win." There was no tenderness in the way he held her, nothing that spoke of a lover whose chivalrous control has broken at last in spite of himself. His hands were not just rough. They were intent on hurting. "In England they call it leading a man up the garden path. Well, this time the victim has balked midway. So you thought you had me fooled. What would come next—breach of promise? Just an innocent girl, eh? So sweet—so pliable." He snorted. "Sooner or later you must have expected to meet your match. Not, I imagine, that you haven't been called upon to pay up before this—and liked it too. You walked right into it, didn't you?" He was forcing her toward the berth and he was talking as though he could not stop, deliberately whipping himself up. "Tart" was one of the names he called her. The rest were companion names, an angry stream of them.

She was fighting him off almost mechanically while she strove for understanding. Then she knew. That telephone call had been from the blond man. This angered bull did not believe any of the things he was saying. He was merely using them as false justification for the revenge he meant to take. He dared not give voice to the real reason because after this was over she would go free. And, free, she must carry no substantiation, no hint of proof that he was anything but what he seemed.

She was lying across the berth now. And he was leaning over her, pinning her arms. His mouth was distorted.

She tensed herself. She closed her eyes, then opened them. I have to, she thought, sickened. Here goes. She brought her knee up, unerring and sharp.

He had loosed her. She raised herself to sitting posture. She heard him groan. She saw him doubled against the wall, his face twisted with pain. She ran to the door and unbolted it. She groped her way along the corridor to the salon, to the companionway, to the deck. She leaned over the rail, staving off nausea.

Night's loudest sound was her heart. She waited for its drumming to subside, trying, as she invariably did try when in a predicament, to summon humor. Why am I standing here? The correct procedure would be to jump overboard and strike out for the shore. But it's too cold for heroics. And, besides, the dock inspector would be sure to show a pardonable amount of curiosity. So I'll just have to stick it out until my charming companion recovers enough to join the ladies on deck. Madge Carter and me, both. He must have ordered the tender to return for us at a set time. I was too fuzzy-witted to pay much attention to his goings on. And when the tender comes we'll take our last sad voyage together and then part. He won't risk any more snide tricks on dry land because he has his pristine reputation to uphold and he isn't anxious to be caught with his— Oh well. But my work's finished. I've failed. I've not only failed, myself, but I've probably gummed it up for whoever follows after. He'll be doubly cautious from now on.... She caught her breath. I was so cocky—so sure. Letting myself be taken in. God knows what those letters contained. She flayed herself. Shame! How can I face Price? He was confident of me. Price—hell! I deserve whatever he says— whatever he does. But me—how can I face me? What can I do to wash this out?

Chapter 4

Louise straightened a picture, moved a chair, took flowers out of their wrappings, shoved a book back into alignment with its fellows, and shifted a rug on the polished floor. She moved about unaided by her mind which was on none of these matters. Her mind was on Charles, tracing his journey from Texas to New York, halted every so often by irrelevancies that kept interfering with his progress.

He would be seated in his Pullman chair now. She closed her eyes the better to see him there. An annoying little question intruded itself, blocking out the vision she sought. Were privates permitted Pullmans? It sounded like a tongue twister. Pullmans for privates. Privates for Pullmans. Well, anyway, he would be seated somewhere on the train. He would be reading or trying to keep track of the racing scenery or just thinking. And presently he would go to the diner. Another annoying question popped up, dealing with the time element. What time was it where Charles was? Lunch time? She sighed but did not attempt to figure it out.

She just hoped that he would eat or had eaten a substantial

lunch. On second thought, not too substantial. Grid, true to his promise, was sending Sammy over to prepare a meal suitable for a soldier on his first furlough. So she telegraphed a silent message to Charles. Don't eat too much, darling. All your favorite dishes are on tonight's menu.

She looked without judgment at the flowers she was arranging in a copper-luster bowl. Perhaps she should call Grid and remind him that this was the day. Halfway to the telephone she stopped. Nonsense. Grid would be at headquarters. She couldn't call headquarters and go into a song and dance about household affairs. Besides, Grid didn't need reminding. He remembered things that were far less important to him. He had been almost as pleased as she when he heard the good news.

She went back to the bowl of flowers. Absently she set it on the radio cabinet. A yellow peony fell to the floor. She knelt to pick it up. Her face was on a level with the radio dial. Her hand forgot the flower. It closed over a knob, freeing the thin nostalgic voice of a blues singer. Her own voice, too joyous for blues, went out warmly to join the invisible guest. She supplied an impromptu variation to the song's lyric. "I know my baby's coming home tonight."

She wrinkled her nose. "Baby" had a vulgar ring to it as applied to Charles. She did not like songs with "baby" in them or people who called each other "baby." She turned off the radio with a decisiveness she did not feel. She had no permanent room for any feeling but the happiness that was in her. She made another attempt to organize her wits by checking off what had been done and what remained to be done. She interrupted herself to admire the room. It looked just the way she wanted it to look. It looked as though a sharing man and woman had done a large part of their living in it; as though the man had left it for only a brief interval of work and would return gaily to celebrate some festive occasion.

Her heart responded alarmingly to the sound of the doorbell. Be still, she scolded it. That's not Charles. He isn't due for hours. And, besides, I'm going to meet him at the station. Sammy, probably.

She made herself walk sedately to the door. She opened it with a greeting on her lips for Sammy. She got as far as, "I'm so glad you could—" and swallowed the rest.

"Well, aren't you glad?"

Louise stared for a moment at the unexpected guest. Then she said incredulously, "Kyrie Martens."

"Black sheep me in person. You might say a few words to put me at my ease, even if you were preparing to welcome someone else."

"Kyrie!" Louise swooped and hugged her. "Why didn't you let me know you were in town? Where are you staying?"

"I won't talk unless you ask me in."

"You surprised me out of my manners." She stepped aside to let the girl pass. "The desk clerk must be slipping. He didn't even bother to announce you."

"I didn't give my name. I just stepped into an elevator and came on up. Mind?"

"I'm livid. March straight to the living room and make yourself comfortable. I'll be with you in a moment. There's Sammy now—knocking on the service door." She lifted her voice. "Come in this way, Sammy. The kitchen door is locked."

The tall handsome colored woman moved toward her, speaking over a delicately balanced structure of packages. "Good morning, Mrs. Cotter. I a little late 'cause I doing some shopping for extras Mr. Grid-dely say you bound to need."

Louise was touched. "He thinks of everything. It was swell of him to let you come and swell of you not to mind."

Sammy said in her deep, peaceful voice, "I pleased. I going to cook your soldier man a fine dinner."

"I know it. He's eaten your fine dinners before and never stopped talking about them. I'll show you where the kitchen is. Yesterday I ordered the stuff on that list you sent. It's in the refrigerator."

She led Sammy down the hall to the compact sunny room. Sammy's heavy-lidded eyes made approving survey. "It mighty handy."

"Yes. I hesitated over it at first because of the three doors—the one we came through, the service door, and the one leading to the dining room. But the remaining wall gives enough shelf space to make up for it."

"Yes'm. If you please tell me where I rest my hat and coat I going to get started."

"There's a dressing room you can use, right off the hall as you come in." Louise stood watching her efficient, unhurried movements as she lined her purchases on a porcelain-topped table. She spoke involuntarily: "I wonder if Grid knows how lucky he is."

"He sure living kind of scattered before I hire to work for him," Sammy admitted, smiling. "Now just you leave everything to me. I think you got company on the way up here."

"Company? Do you mean my cousin? She *is* here. She arrived a moment before you did."

"It ain't no she I talking about. I talking about a man. I hear the desk clerk give him your apartment number."

"That's funny. Maybe he's someone from the shop. What does he look like?"

"He very big and he wearing a sharp overcoat."

"Sharp? Oh. He doesn't sound like anyone I know. I guess the desk clerk made a mistake. Call me if you need help." Louise left Sammy and went to the living room.

Kyrie had taken off her hat and slipped her arms out of her beaver coat so that it hung from her slim shoulders cape-fashion. She was walking the large room aimlessly, an unlit cigarette in her hand. She turned abruptly at Louise's entrance. It seemed a gesture born of nerves.

Louise said, "Looking for matches? Sit down and I'll get them for you. You've grown thinner. How do you do it? We could act out a charade together—the heifer and the zephyr."

Kyrie smiled charmingly. "I'd rather be a heifer than a zephyr if it meant looking as happy and beautiful as you look. What makes you so wound up?" She came to rest on the couch. She took Louise's hand and drew her down beside her. "Never mind the matches. I'll just play like I'm smoking for a while. I've run over my quota lately." She glanced toward the flowers. "Seems to me as though I've barged into something. The place looks that gala. Want me to leave?"

"You'll have to fight your way out. I'm expecting Charles this evening. I haven't seen him since he joined up." She tried to be matter-of-fact, but her voice soared.

"Oh! That explains everything. And you've imported a new cook for the occasion. What happened to Flora?"

"She left. She said she had a better job, but I think the real reason was the loneliness around here. Sammy's only temporary. She works for Gridley Nelson. Remember him?"

"Sure—the object of my first hero worship. He joined the police force, didn't he? I can't imagine a policeman with a cook. In fact, I can't imagine Grid Nelson as a policeman. Once when I was a kid I hit him over the head with a cookie dish just as a bid for notice. Then I was scared to death because I expected him to retaliate in kind, but he just stood there looking puzzled, as though he were trying to figure out what made me tick."

"That may have been the detective in him starting to sprout. Anyway, he *is* on the force and he has a cook plus. He met her on one of his cases, and later she walked in and rearranged his life. I saw his apartment before and after, so I know. He'd been pigging it, with only a sloppy landlady to do for him, but Sammy changed all that. She keeps an eye on his job too. He swears that his chief consults her whenever the going gets tough." She became aware that Kyrie was not listening. She changed her tone deliberately to one of sprightly observation. "I'm such a bore."

"What?"

"You haven't heard a word. By the way, are you hungry? I can't ask you to stay for lunch because it might hinder Sammy, but I'd be awfully pleased to take you out and feed you."

"I had a late breakfast. Besides, I made a lunch date."

"Balked at every turn." She saw that Kyrie had gone back into the silence. "How would you like a good shaking?"

Kyrie answered mechanically, "That would be nice." Then she turned to stare at Louise. "What did you say?" She put the cigarette between her lips. "I guess I will smoke after all."

"Good. It might wake you up. The matches are at your elbow." Louise waited until the cigarette had been lit. "Kyrie, I suppose you realize you're being exasperating."

"Stop badgering me. You used to be the least talkative person on my list."

"But you can't suddenly drop out of nowhere and expect me to hold my breath while you commune with your thoughts. I want to know things—what you've been doing, why you're in New York, how long you intend to stay."

Impulsively Kyrie leaned over and kissed her cheek. "You sound just like Aunt Tillie."

"What's wrong with Aunt Tillie?"

"Nothing that distance doesn't cure. You found that out for yourself. But I didn't come here to discuss the family."

"Did you come here to discuss anything?"

"No—I came to see you."

"Then you might have the decency to look at me. What's the matter, Kyrie? Why are you so edgy?"

"I'm not. Anyone who wasn't bursting with joy would seem edgy to you today." She blew an accidental smoke ring and watched it disappear. "If I'd known of the homecoming I wouldn't have intruded my earthbound presence. You must have loads of things to attend to. I'll be in town for a few weeks. I'll leave in a moment, but I'll drop in tomorrow and say hello to Charles."

"No, you won't. You'll stay. I'm going to call your hotel and tell them to send your bags over. There's no reason why you can't bunk here."

"And be a glaring nuisance? Never."

"Don't be silly. We've plenty of room. You're not an everyday occurrence, you know."

"Good thing. I'm no bargain. But thanks for wanting me."

"Kyrie, is this couch hot? Stop wriggling. There *is* something wrong with you. You're not the fidgety type."

"I'm not any type. Let me alone."

"All right. I won't probe. But I'm your favorite cousin, and you love me and you're going to stay here."

Kyrie laughed. "I didn't mean to be ungracious or make mysteries. There's nothing wrong. It's all very simple. I've been in Washington doing clerical work for the government and I'm taking my vacation because I didn't have one last summer. I'm a little tired, and when a gal's tired—"

"Is that all? What's the name of your hotel?"

"The Gascony."

"I'm impressed. If I take a clerical job will I end up at the Gascony?"

"Yes, if you still have your share of the money we inherited from Grandpa Martens. And end up is right!" Kyrie bit her lower lip. "Don't mind me. I've got a Washington hangover. Living there's been a strain. I'm going to relax now and forget about it. And you're going to help me. How's Charles, aside from being on furlough? I can't imagine him as a soldier any more than I can imagine Grid Nelson as a cop."

Louise looked troubled for a moment. Then she said resolutely, "He's fine—or will be. I've been a little upset about him. His letters sounded so dreary. But as soon as I get my arms around him—"

"You're pure mother, Louise. Even when you were in bibs it manifested itself. How come you haven't a few dozen kids lousing up the house?"

Louise said seriously, "I'm going to do my best to have at least one this go around. It'll be the first real vacation Charles has had since our honeymoon, and I mean it to be a memorable one." Then she laughed.

"You ought to be blushing instead of laughing. I hope those two thoughts are unrelated. How's the jewelry business?"

"Flourishing. Don't you read your mail?" Louise made her generous mouth severe. "If you weren't so tired here's where I'd really do an 'Aunt Tillie.' You never bothered to answer my last letter. Don't put on that innocent look. I obeyed your instructions and sent it to general delivery." She saw Kyrie's expression change. She said hurriedly, "Never mind. You're answering in person, and that's much more satisfying."

Kyrie said slowly, "I don't remember getting a letter from you that I didn't answer. What was in it?"

"Nothing much. Just family news, including a suggestion from Grandma which she asked me to pass on to you. Something to the effect that if you insisted on living away from home you ought to stop flibbertigibbeting around and get in touch with Uncle Paul, who has a big job in Washington. She said he could put you onto something respectable. Why don't you get in touch with him, by the way? It's a shame for a girl with your brains to do plain clerical work when you might be in the intelligence department or secret service or whatever they call it."

"Did you say that in your letter?"

"Maybe. Why? Kyrie, are you sure you had breakfast? You look faint."

Kyrie shrugged impatiently. "I'm cold." She drew her coat around her to prove it. "You've got too many windows open." She said hurriedly, "Paul Martens is a big shot. Everybody in Washington knows him and tries to take advantage of knowing him. I wouldn't want him to subscribe to nepotism."

"You *are* an independent creature." Louise dropped the matter. She got up off the couch and crossed the room. She took a bottle and two glasses from a small portable bar. "Sherry?"

Kyrie nodded. She accepted the glass and took a long drink. A little color showed on her high-boned cheeks. "What time is your lunch date?"

"One o'clock."

"Good. That will give you a chance to work up a fresh appetite for Sammy's dinner."

Kyrie shook her head. "No, I draw the line there. I'll accept your invitation to stay because you're a darling and I want to. But I won't horn in on your first dinner with Charles. I'll come later in the evening. That will give you both a chance to get over the first ecstasy."

Chapter 5

He looked ordinary sitting there in the crowded coach. He was blue-eyed and sandy-haired and thin, with a long Celtic upper lip that had been designed to express humor. At the moment it expressed nothing. He seemed neither quick-witted nor imaginative nor sensitive. He might have been summed up as a drugstore clerk, lifted out of his milieu and poured into khaki, or a harassed small businessman brooding quietly on the debts and responsibilities he had left behind. He was Charles Cotter.

His thoughts were swifter than the train that carried him toward Louise. His thoughts were with Louise. She had strong arms, and he could close his eyes and feel the firmness of them. And he could feel the texture of her hair. He could close his eyes and— No, he must not close his eyes.

He lifted the magazine in his lap and forcibly stretched his lids apart so that the pupils showed in strained dark rounds. But moisture gathered like a veil between his vision and the print, and reading was impossible.

Presently he transferred his gaze to the window. He started to count trees as people count sheep, and for the opposite reason. He could not concentrate. Isolated houses kept creeping into the count, scattered here and there without logical plan behind vast stretches of naked track. Lean houses, unnourished by the life they sheltered, sending forth an occasional figure to reach toward a line of clothes, to chop wood or otherwise add homely patches to the pattern of a sparse existence.

Charles turned away and sought comfort from his fellow passengers. Having traveled with them so many miles, he knew them by heart, and nothing fresh manifested itself to divert him. There was the lady executive still serene and smug, the old man and his grandson, the troupe of radio entertainers homeward bound from a tour of Army camps and loud with professional enthusiasm, two Army officers, one whose potbelly had held out against all methods of reducing, one tall and broad with a face that advertised well-being.

His interest held momentarily by the second officer, Charles thought, He has no doubts or fears. I wouldn't have either if I looked like him. He's a younger edition of Orrin Shay.

But Louise chose me. She did not choose Orrin Shay or any of his numerous counterparts. And I'm on my way to her now, and the trip is cutting a large chunk out of my first furlough. But it doesn't matter, because we'll crowd everything into the time that is left. So to hell with him and whatever it is that makes me suspect him of— Of what?

Of what? he repeated to himself, and his mind set out on one of its endless futile excursions. He was lost again, because there was not even a faint light in the distance to give him direction.

His eyes dropped to his delicate well-shaped hands that were two separate entities divorced from the rest of his insignificant physical being. I'm jealous, he thought, and that's natural—for me. Whatever I feel about Orrin Shay is at least one part jealousy. He spends a great deal of his time in New York with her, and I'm in Texas, or was. And he has all the things I lack, including stature and assurance. But she was exposed to men like him before and since she met me, and I survived. She loves me. God knows why. But she does, and I'm sure of it. So in my saner moments I can rationalize my jealousy and reduce it to nothing. But I can't rationalize the rest of it, no matter how hard I try. He has his pick of women—of friends too. Then why us? Why has he singled us out? As his values go we're little people, and he's an opportunist. That much is obvious in all he's done and is doing to climb to and hold to his present position. What does he want of us?

Louise accepts the advances of all kinds of people as her due because she's warm and giving, and her ego is as strong and healthy as her body. She doesn't have the urge to search out hidden motives. But I have that urge, and perhaps even a sixth sense to pursue it with, as compensation for my wretched humbleness.

He smiled then, inwardly, no seepage of it appearing on his taut face. Charles, the fey. Sixth-sense Charlie. If it comes down to it, why in this instance does the urge persist? Aside from Louise— and I'm sure of Louise—what remains to be lost to Orrin Shay? Am I accusing that fine public figure of intent to rob? Do I imagine that he is after the furnishings of my apartment, the jewels in my shop, when I know there's been nothing of importance in either place since we set the Santa Elena diamond? If my misgivings lie in that direction I'll have to import something for him to steal. Which puts me in the same zany class as the Marx brothers and the non-existent house next door.... That's right, fellow. Laugh it off. Think about the Marx brothers. Think about—

Suddenly he forced himself to sit up. He was hot with fright. It was there again—that compulsion to sleep. He labored to keep his eyelids raised, his facial muscles rigid with the effort. He stared glassily ahead, his thin face immovable as a death mask. He felt like a furnace, and the people in the car had become distorted shadows, and he wanted to cry out against their nightmare quality, but his mouth was stiff and would not take orders.

For weeks now the curse had been upon him, making sudden visitation at the worst possible times. It swooped when he was engaged in work upon which hinged other lives, while he was attempting to remedy the hairbreadth of difference that went to make an instrument one of succor or destruction for its wielder.

He could not go on this way. He would see his own doctor immediately. He had hoped to effect a cure with the medicine sent on by Louise, but it had failed to work this time. He had swallowed a large dose just before he went to the diner, but— flu, probably. It always came at low ebb. Those first days of strenuous drilling before they had assigned him to his present post had been too much for a man of his sedentary habits. He should have succumbed at the onset of the symptoms and gone to the infirmary. But he was stubborn where work was concerned. And there was so much work and so much gold-bricking that he had—

Someone was tugging at his khaki sleeve. His head ached violently as he awoke to dusk, to the immobility of the wheels under him, to the anxious face of a conductor.

The conductor smiled with relief. "You sure can sleep, Private. That Army's got you all tired out. We're in. Grand Central."

Except for Charles, the train had emptied. He stumbled to his feet. Dazed, he huddled into his overcoat and pulled on his cap. He made an ineffectual gesture toward the rack that held his light bag.

The conductor swung it down expertly. "What's the matter—no pep? Say, you look kind of peaked under that tan. You're the first soldier I've laid eyes on that don't advertise Uncle Sam's cooking."

Charles forced himself to smile. "I'm all right. Just excitement. I haven't seen New York for a long time."

He left the train. He followed the tail end of the crowd up the long ramp. He walked with the dogged, weary persistence of a mountain climber who knows that if he can endure but a short while longer the view will be his.

The view was his. Louise was there, waiting. He saw the mask of anxiety lift from her face to reveal pure welcome. Ignoring the presence of a few less fortunate stragglers, she opened her arms to him. He set down his bag and went home. He inhaled her good smell, and the tension flowed out of him.

They separated and stared at each other. Louise spoke. "I've been putting in a bad few minutes, but it was worth it. I'd begun to think you'd either missed the train or got off somewhere between Texas and here to visit another wife."

Charles's mouth was working. He steadied it with words. "You're twenty wives rolled into one."

"I hope that's not a subtle reference to my size. But never mind. You're going to take on poundage, too, as of tonight. I've got Grid Nelson's Sammy to cook dinner." Her first glimpse of him had been a shock. He seemed to have shrunk. She took his arm. She felt as though she could not hold him close enough. "Oh, Charles, we're going to have such a good time."

"I know. Let's get started—unless you've rented Grand Central for the celebration."

In the taxi it was she who did most of the talking. He was content to look and listen. He was really content. His head no longer ached. His eyes felt eased and rested. Either that sleep in the train did the trick, he thought with relief, or Louise is all the medicine I need. He touched her hair.

She said in mock reproof, "Charles, look out of the window. This is your own Fifth Avenue. See all the shop windows—no sign of war in them."

"Fifth Avenue will keep."

"Are you afraid I won't? Not very flattering. Speaking of shops, don't you want news of Cotter's?"

"How's the new assistant?" he asked tepidly.

"A fusspot. Men—pooh! Ever since you've left I've been swinging around to the conclusion that a man's place is in the home."

"Hallelujah!"

"Tell me about you and the Army, Charles. Your letters were so—so sketchy. Do you hate it?"

"I'd hate heaven if you weren't boss there. Otherwise I've no valid complaints."

"Would you like me to go back with you? I could get an apartment near enough to camp to absorb all your idle moments."

"God bless you, darling. But what about Cotter's?"

"It runs itself. Just ask Loth. He doesn't let me lift a finger. Besides, Alex will be back on the job soon, and between the two of them they can certainly do without me."

"Is business as good as you keep saying it is when you write?"

"Better. I didn't elaborate because I wanted to leave room for the X's."

"Do you love me?"

"Love you? I only wish I were Elizabeth Barrett Browning so I could count the ways."

"There's a sonnet in every move you make."

"Then let's change the subject until I can move more freely. Guess who's in town?"

"Orrin Shay?" The name flew out of him. The smile he had been wearing froze on his mouth.

Her indifference was thawing. "He might be. I haven't seen him for weeks. Guess again."

"I can't. Tell me."

"Kyrie Martens."

"Oh," he said, "that's nice. You've always been fond of Kyrie."

She nodded. "And now I've joined the family in worrying about her. She dropped in this morning without notice, all tired and jumpy. She put it down to the work she'd been doing in Washington and the fact that she needed a vacation."

"That sounds plausible enough."

"I know. I'm just a natural busybody. I asked her to stay with us. Do you mind? The spare bedroom's completely private and—and the walls are soundproofed and everything."

Charles grinned. It made his face boyish and mischievous. "If I minded would you rescind the invitation?"

"Of course." She was relishing the grin. It was a part of the Charles she knew. It routed the stranger she had met at the station.

"Well, I don't mind, provided you give me most of your attention. Is she there now?"

"No, but we are. Charles, we've arrived."

He felt queer to be entering the familiar lobby in his private's uniform. The new doorman stared at him, then at Louise, but could not seem to figure the combination. The desk clerk had not been replaced. He came forward with hand extended. He said, "Welcome back, sir," and added wistfully, "I guess it will be over before they call men of my age and responsibilities."

"Pray God," Louise said.

They stepped into one of the elevators. A girl was running it. She smiled at them good-naturedly and let them off at the right floor.

Louise said, "We won't tear Sammy away from her preparations," and handed him the key.

He fitted it into the lock as though not many hours had passed since his last performance of the same task. He put his cap on the hall table. He put his arm around Louise, and together they went to the living room.

"Well?" she said.

"Flowers too. Yellow flowers in my own house." He embraced her. She felt strong and vital to his touch. With no one there to see, his lips made tour, resting in a hollow of her neck.

"Now me," she said, "this way."

As they drew apart Sammy entered, carrying a tray. Her carved African features expressed all of benevolence. She set the tray down and said, "I glad to see you, Mr. Cotter. Dinner ain't for two more hours, so I thought maybe you want to pick yourself up with cocktails and canopies."

"Thank you," Charles said. "And thank Mr. Nelson for making the supreme sacrifice." His knees were trembling. He sat down suddenly. "How is he?"

"He keep his health, but he working a little harder than he got a right to." Sammy regarded Charles for a moment. She said delicately, "I guess you doing the same thing. After you drink your drink you ought to catch yourself a catnap. You going to enjoy the victuals better if you fresh for them."

When she had gone Louise and Charles toasted each other with dry martinis. Charles ate a canapé without tasting it. He ate another. Louise kept pace with him. "These are wonderful," she said. "I wonder what Sammy uses for seasoning. I must ask her."

The canapés were cardboard squares to Charles, but he did not say so. His eyelids were beginning to droop again. It's natural that I should be tired, he told himself fiercely. And natural that the tiredness should affect my palate. That trip is enough to knock anyone out. Seeking stimulus, he drank a second cocktail. He joked feebly: "If Sammy weren't a pal I'd suspect her of slipping me a Mickey."

He heard Louise say in a voice that seemed to be separated from him by a thick wall, "I think she's got something with that catnap idea. Why don't you go inside and stretch out for a while?"

"Bed," he said longingly. "But you must come too. I can't afford to lose you at this point."

She laughed. "Charles!" She stood up. She tugged at his hands until he rose from the couch. She escorted him to the bedroom. "Your personal effects are all where you left them. Your robe is hanging in the closet. Make yourself comfortable and I'll be back in a few moments."

But when she returned to the room her husband gave her no welcome. He was stretched out on top of the bedspread, sound asleep. He had started to undress. One of his Government Issue shoes, lying beside the bed, testified to that. Gently Louise removed its mate. Then she loosened his collar and covered him with a light blanket.

His face was flushed. His forehead was hot to her palm. She stood looking at him for a few moments. Loneliness swept over her. Sighing, she left him and went to the kitchen.

The atmosphere was a warm, spicy blend. It should have been heartening. Sammy was mixing something in an earthenware bowl. Louise broke in upon the rhythmic beat of the spoon. "Did you make those cocktails extra strong? They were awfully good, but I don't imagine my husband has been doing much drinking lately and—" She broke off.

Sammy said with slow dignity, "I taste them drinks myself. They just right, same as always." She gave Louise a measured look. "Don't you worry none. He so happy he home, it too big for him. After a little rest he going to be like new."

"Oh, Sammy." Then she said, "I knew the cocktails were all right. I was just talking. What's in that bowl?"

"Chopped mushrooms and onions and shallots and things. I binding them together with egg yellow. Then I fix my *artichauts farcis*." She pronounced the French words with a Louisiana accent.

"May I watch?" Louise felt a strong need for company.

Sammy pulled out a chair for her. She said with complete understanding, "You sit here at the table, and while you watching maybe you skin some almonds for me." She placed a cup of hot water and a dish of almonds on the table.

It was peaceful and comforting to be sitting in the warm kitchen blanching almonds. It reminded Louise of her childhood when she had insisted upon helping to prepare for company. Dreamily she watched Sammy fill the globe artichokes, tie their petals together, top them with thin bacon strips, and bathe them thoroughly in a vinous liquid.

She said, "You know a lot of French dishes, don't you? Gridley Nelson said he'd pay money just to dream about your *tournedos à la Béarnaise.*"

Sammy smiled. "You going to do better than dream about it. You going to taste it for true later on. Before I come North I work for a French lady in New Orleans, and she school me good." She stopped talking to listen. "That your phone ringing. You want me to answer it?"

"No, I will." Louise got up and went to the hall where the telephone sat on its small square table. She did not bother to pull out the nesting chair. She lifted the receiver to her ear and said, "Hello."

An unfamiliar voice spoke an unfamiliar name. "Could I speak to Madge Carter, please?"

"You must have the wrong number. There's no Madge Carter here."

"Excuse it, lady." The stranger severed the connection.

Louise put the receiver back on its hook. She went into the bedroom. Charles was still sleeping. As she gazed down at him he shifted his position, muttered something, and coughed spasmodically. She whispered, "Charles," several times, but could not reach him. She pulled down the blind, purposely making a clatter. He slept on. She reproached herself. I'm a selfish pig. There's no hurry.

In the living room she picked up a book. The going was hard at first, but presently her attention was caught. Engrossed, she gave herself to the experiences of a woman war correspondent....

She had become vaguely aware that the room was darkening when Sammy called to her from the doorway. "Everything about ready. I think you better rouse up Mr. Cotter."

Louise switched on a lamp, blinking against its violence. "What time is it?"

"Most half-past seven."

"Good heavens! I meant to make myself beautiful."

"You beautiful enough," Sammy said sincerely.

"Why, how nice. You get ready to serve. We'll be at table in about ten minutes."

But that was optimism. Sammy came running in answer to her call.

Chapter 6

"What happen, Mrs. Cotter? I here."

Louise was kneeling by the bed. She said, "I can't wake him."

Sammy knelt too. Her large capable hands fastened around one of Charles's wrists. "He mighty warm," she said. Then she crooned persuasively, "Mr. Cotter, you scaring us bad. Open your eyes a minute."

As though she had woven a spell, Charles did open his eyes, but they were sleeping eyes. They touched the white face of his wife. He muttered, "Reflections of everything," and his lids dropped again like heavy curtains. His flushed face had a painted masklike quality.

The two women looked at each other. Louise said numbly, "Will you call the doctor? That index on the hall table—Dr. Purcell—tell him he must come at once."

Sammy left the room. When she returned five minutes later Louise was still on her knees. Only her lips moved. "What took you so long?"

"Your doctor man busy with an emergency operation. His nurse give me the name of two others, but they ain't home. Then I try the one in the house, but he can't be raised neither, so I leave a hurry-up message all around, and one of them bound to be here soon." She laid her hand on Louise's shoulder. "You got to help me get Mr. Cotter out of his clothes and under the covers so he all ready."

The words were a release. Stiffly Louise rose to her feet. "I'll undress him. You—you can go home." She added a forlorn "No dinner tonight," as though it summed up everything.

Sammy said heroically, "That dinner going to be just as good tomorrow when it touched up some. And maybe Mr. Cotter eat it too. Seem like he only caught him a cold on the train. Soon as we get him in his nightclothes we going to cover him good and put a wet cloth to his poor head, 'cause he got it bunched up like it hurt."

She assumed full command, her calm strength infusing strength and steadiness to Louise. Together they eased Charles out of his Army clothes.

Surely in the middle of all this he will awake and talk, Louise thought. But he handled limp as a stuffed doll and with as little response. Now his left leg, now his right. Left arm, right arm, into the fresh pajamas whose gay stripes seemed as jarring as false notes in mournful music. They laid his head back on the pillow and smoothed the covers. Louise sat holding his hot hand. She listened for the arrival of the doctor, any doctor, and tried to stem her rising panic.

Sammy went into the connecting bathroom and completed the project of the cold cloth. Her heart was uneasy, haunted by Charles's stricken face. On her way back to the kitchen she was inspired. She would phone Mr. Grid-dely. He might be able to send the police doctor, but if that was impossible he would surely think of something else to do. She had boundless faith in her employer's ability to control any given situation.

First she dialed his apartment, and when there was no response she called headquarters. She identified herself to the police clerk, who was expansive. Everybody on the squad had heard of Sammy.

"The sarge? He just stepped out with Inspector Furniss for a bite. Something I can do?"

Sammy sighed, her mind relinquishing its problem for a moment. "And I left him a nice supper all ready to eat."

The clerk clicked his teeth in sympathy. "Ain't that too bad? I wish you could wrap it up and send it over. What'll I tell him when he comes back? He *is* coming back on account of he and the chief was talking about cleaning up some work."

Sammy said, "Just you tell him I at Mrs. Cotter's and I think we going to need the police doctor." She hung up.

She went into the kitchen and gazed sorrowfully at the feast she had prepared. She sampled a few of the dishes and nodded with detached approval. Then she prepared a tray and carried it to Louise.

"You got to keep up your strength. Who going to nurse Mr. Cotter if you get took?"

Louise, because she could not withstand kindness, forced herself to eat. At intervals she would hold her fork suspended, the expression on her unlit face an easy one to read. She seemed to be trying to bring the doctor into the room by sheer force of concentration.

Sammy took the tray away, tidied up the kitchen, and made several repeat phone calls. At nine o'clock she could take no more of the waiting. She returned to the bedroom and said, "I going out to fetch us a doctor. I find one somewhere or other."

Louise looked at her hopefully. "Oh, please!"

Just as Sammy was putting on her coat the bell rang. She hurried to open the door. Accusingly she gazed at the slim figure of Kyrie Martens.

"You ain't the doctor."

Kyrie said flippantly, "No, but I'm just what he ordered." Then something in Sammy's attitude sobered her. "Doctor? Is anyone sick?"

"Yes'm." Sammy hesitated. "I don't think Mrs. Cotter ready for company right now."

"I'm not company. I've been invited to stay here."

The house porter had approached, a suitcase under each arm. Kyrie said to him, "Use one of those to prop the door with so you won't have to knock when you bring the hatbox." She turned back to Sammy. "Where *is* Mrs. Cotter?"

"She in the bedroom."

Kyrie darted past her.

Another bell sounded. Bewildered, Sammy could not trace its source. The porter said, "You must be new. That's the house phone."

"Where it at?"

"Right outside the kitchen."

Sammy retraced her steps. She cried into the mouthpiece, "This Mrs. Cotter's apartment.... Yes.... Sure she want to see him. Send him right up."

She removed her coat and took up a stand near the door. She had barely heard the announced name. She tried to remember it so that she could give tactful greeting, but after a moment she shrugged and stopped trying. She had phoned so many doctors that it was impossible to sort them out.

Soon an elevator stopped on the floor and a large rangy man walked toward the apartment with an assured step. He look like he been here before, Sammy thought. I guess he Mrs. Cotter's own Dr. Purcell. She said the name tentatively and saw by his expression that it was a wrong guess. When he spoke she knew with sinking heart that any guess would have been wrong.

"I'm Captain Shay. I'm expected."

Louise came quickly down the hall. "I heard the house phone a moment ago. Is—?" She broke off and looked blankly from the visitor to Sammy.

Captain Shay said loudly and pompously, "I announced myself. I was told to come up. If there's been a mistake I'll go."

Louise regained her poise. "Forgive the reception. You see, Charles came home on furlough today and he's ill. We've telephoned every doctor in town, and they're all busy. When the house phone rang I thought that one of them had turned up at last."

Shay said, "Oh, so Charles is home—and ill." He stepped into the apartment. His tone grew brisk. "Well, perhaps I'm an angel in disguise. I just left my own doctor starting a bridge game at the club. I'll be glad to call him if the occasion warrants it."

Louise said eagerly, "I'd be so grateful—"

"Think nothing of it. But first let me look at the patient. I've had considerable experience with sick men. An officer had to be jack-of-all-trades in the first World War, you know."

"I'll show you where the phone is," Louise said.

"Wait a minute—the patient first. Undoubtedly you've got yourself wrought up without reason. Women are apt to do that." His vigorous laugh was whisky-flavored. He put his arm around Louise. "My dear, I'm sorry about Charles. I had so hoped to spend a pleasant evening with you."

Louise was on the verge of screaming. She thought with sudden clarity, I hate this man. She said, "Your doctor might leave the club. I wish you'd call him before you see Charles."

"Don't worry. He was well settled when I left, and I wouldn't want to break into his game unnecessarily. Lead the way, fair lady. Let's have a look."

Louise led the way. She had left Kyrie with Charles when she went to investigate the ringing of the house phone. But Kyrie was no longer in the bedroom. She wondered about that for a moment, then dismissed it in her renewed anxiety. Charles was lying so still that he seemed hardly to breathe. Unhappily she saw Captain Shay look down, saw him lay the back of a thick heavy hand on Charles's neck. She gritted her teeth, thinking of how strongly Charles would resent such cold clinical interest from one for whom he had no liking. It was a betrayal to expose him to it. Damn Shay. Why was it necessary for him to act the great healer? If he was sincere in his desire to help, let him call the doctor without further delay.

Shay cleared his throat and said, "Does Charles take drugs of any kind?"

"Of course not."

He bridled at her indignant tone. "I'm not displaying vulgar curiosity, my dear. Tell me, did he write anything in his letters about feeling under the weather?"

"He said he had a cold."

"Hmmm—well, I don't like the look of him. He's febrile. I'll have old Randolph here in short order." He patted Louise's shoulder in a proprietary way. "While I'm telephoning you might ask your maid to mix a drink for me. I'd advise you to have one too. Nothing like alcohol to stave off possible infection."

She followed him into the hall. He pulled out the chair and seated himself with maddening deliberation. He dialed a number. She heard him make the connection and ask for Dr. Randolph. She felt a draft and noted abstractedly that the door to the apartment was propped open by a suitcase. She started toward it, changed her mind, and walked to the kitchen. She called out to Sammy, "Please give Captain Shay a whisky and soda."

Receiving no reply, she went the rest of the way. As she entered the kitchen she heard Shay say in a crisp military voice, "I tell you it's urgent.... Hot as fire.... I'd say that one hundred and three ... Yes, I'll wait for you.... What?"

The porter was in the kitchen talking to Sammy. She said severely, "Don't make no matter how many parties is going on in the doctor's apartment. Something wrong with him if he won't leave a little old party to do right by a sick man. You go get him. Hear?"

The porter scratched his ear. "But doctors don't figure like that these days. It ain't as if Mr. Cotter's a patient of his."

Louise said, "Never mind, Sammy. Captain Shay's doctor is coming."

Sammy shooed the porter out through the service door and faced her. She said, "I feel better when I see that for my own self. I sure wish Mr. Grid-dely get a move on." It was evident that Shay's personality had not endeared him to her.

"The captain wants a whisky and soda, Sammy."

"Yes'm. I put the liquor ready in the dining room case you all wanted to sit for a while after dinner. I go get it."

"Is my cousin unpacking? She might like a drink too."

"I don't know where she at," Sammy said. She went into the dining room.

Louise stood for a moment near the hall door. Shay was giving his voice a rest. She assumed that he had completed his call. She hoped that Dr. Randolph would arrive quickly and thought with distaste of the intervening period to be spent with Shay. His attitude had changed since their last meeting. Perhaps he had been drinking too much. Yes, that would account for it, though she had heard him boast often of knowing exactly when to stop. She did not like the way he had touched her, nor did she like the informality of his visit. Well, no matter. If he was the instrument of bringing help to Charles she would put up with him. Reluctantly she headed in his direction. No....

She returned to the kitchen, went through it to the dining room where Sammy was setting out a siphon and a bottle of scotch. Without halting her steps she passed from there to a small foyer that connected with her bath and with the spare bedroom.

The door to the spare bedroom was open, but it was untenanted. One of Kyrie's closed bags stood on the floor. Louise entered the bathroom, glanced at her face in the mirror, and winced. She splashed it with cold water and rubbed color into it with a towel. She powdered her nose and picked up a lipstick with some vague idea that she must make herself presentable. She noticed without interest that the lipstick was not her own but used it anyway.

Kyrie's, she thought fleetingly.

She walked through the other door that led to her own bedroom. She looked at the pillow, and so vicious was her heart's sudden clamor that heavily booted feet seemed to assault her ribs.

Charles's head was not on the pillow. It was hanging over the edge of the bed, dark-tinged, as though all his body's blood had rushed to fill it. The covers of the bed were thrust back. She thought numbly, He awoke alone and tried to rise.

His eyes were closed, and in that moment before she ran to him and felt his shallow breathing she was sure that he was dead. She tried to lift him, but his inert weight was too much for her. She managed to control her voice, to shape Sammy's name. And simultaneously she heard a crash and Sammy's voice, not in answer, but panicked and scarcely human. Long moments passed before Sammy stood in the doorway, trembling and talking.

"He dead, Mrs. Cotter. He dead."

"No, Sammy, no. He just tried to get up and fell. Help me."

Automatically Sammy went to her assistance. The necessity for immediate action steadied her. She lifted Charles back into bed. Then she spoke quite normally.

"You got to come with me, Mrs. Cotter. I got to show you—"

"I can't," Louise said firmly.

There was fear on Sammy's face. "Why can't you?"

"I'm not going to stir from here until the doctor comes. He woke up when I left him before. He might do it again—hurt himself."

"But that Shay gentleman—he—"

"Damn Shay."

"Yes'm." Sammy shuddered.

Louise looked at her. "I can't stand much more of this."

Sammy sat down suddenly. "I can't too. I—I called Mr. Griddely just now. He say he be along soon. Likely he bringing the police doctor with him."

"Sammy, why don't you go home?"

"No. Mr. Grid-dely tell me to wait 'cause I—" She gave it up. She sat with her eyes fixed straight ahead on nothing in particular. Presently both women started.

"There—that the bell for sure. The doorbell. And this time it really something."

It *was* really something; neither timid nor casual, but persistent and authoritative. Charles stirred uneasily. Louise murmured, "At last." And Sammy seemed flung from her chair down the full length of the hall.

The new arrivals were already in the apartment. They were definitely divided into two separate groups and an outsider. The first group was composed of Detective Sergeant Gridley Nelson,

Inspector Waldo Furniss, a uniformed policeman, and a plainclothesman whose lack of uniform did nothing to understate his calling. A cameraman, his assistant, and a burly individual with a black bag made up the second group. The outsider was a youngish, fair, stocky man with an expression of puzzled annoyance on his face. He, too, carried a black bag.

He spoke first. "Is this the Cotter residence?"

Sammy's eyes were on Nelson. She nodded.

"I'm Dr. Randolph. Will you please take me to Captain Shay?"

Nelson said abruptly, "Where is he, Sammy?"

At that she made a right about-face. The others dropped into single file and followed her to the telephone table. Their marching feet trod glass into the carpet where lay a shattered tumbler and a siphon. Whisky was the predominant smell.

Dr. Randolph said, "Good God!" The others uttered no sound. Just a new job, their silence said.

Orrin Shay's close-cropped head was pillowed on the telephone table. His elbows were out at right angles. His hands were at his own throat. His scarf was crossed at the nape of his neck, the ends trailing loosely down his no-longer-military back.

Dr. Randolph and the police doctor moved at the same time like dancing partners, their steps synchronizing.

Nelson cut in, breaking the rhythm. He said to Dr. Randolph, "This patient is in good hands."

"They's a patient inside needs attention," Sammy said shakily.

Inspector Waldo Furniss groaned. "Another corpse?"

"No, Mr. Chief. I talking about Mr. Cotter. He sick. That why I—"

Nelson said, "All right, Sammy, show the doctor the way." Dazed, Randolph permitted himself to be steered to the bedroom.

The cameraman was setting up his paraphernalia. Careful not to shift the body, Dr. Perry was making his preliminary examination. He turned to Inspector Furniss. "Dead on arrival, Chief."

"Strangled?"

"I'd say so. Slugged first—there's a lump on his head."

Furniss shoved his hat back on his silver hair. He fixed his bright blue eyes on the plainclothesman. "Sugs, the door was open when we came in. Go lock it. Then get out your notebook and start with the D.O.A. entry."

Sugs went off. Furniss gestured in the direction of the body, his fine old face gloomy. "An important guy. That always means a hurry-up job for us, Grid. Sammy said Captain Shay, didn't she?"

"Yes."

"I would have recognized him anyway. We were on a radio program together once—a Red Cross blood donor rally. I must say he looked more chipper then than he does now. What's he doing here?"

"He knew the Cotters."

"Hmmm." Furniss addressed Dr. Perry: "How long has he been dead, Doc?"

Perry said cautiously, "Not very long. Maybe not even an hour."

"Hear that, Grid?"

"Yes, I hear it."

"Well, don't just stand there hoarding your thoughts. What do you make of it? Just as we got back to the police station Jerry started to tell us Sammy called and wanted a police doctor. Then the phone rang and it was Sammy again with the news. More than an hour had passed since she called the first time. If it was anyone else but Sammy I'd say she was telegraphing her intentions."

"It *isn't* anyone else but Sammy, Chief."

"Then why should she want a medical examiner before a murder was committed?"

Nelson said, "She didn't want a medical examiner. She wanted a doctor. That's easily explained by the fact that Charles Cotter seems to have been taken ill."

"Why call us for a doctor? She knows we're not running a private hospital. Besides, she's got a doctor—that fellow who came in with us."

"Dr. Perry could be wrong about the time of death. He always says it's impossible to establish it exactly."

Perry looked up and said tersely, "The body's still warm."

Furniss shouted a triumphant "Hah!"

Nelson said calmly, "That seems to indicate that we can all pack up and go home. Sammy's your man, Chief. She killed him because she didn't like his face."

"Now, Grid, would I want to pin anything on Sammy? All I'm trying to say is that the surface of this business has a roiled look."

"One way of getting below the surface is to ask Sammy a few questions."

"Don't take that patient tone with me." He gave a series of orders. "Hurry up with those pics, Busch, so we can give him the once-over. Spiegel, dust for prints. One of these days, if you're real industrious, you might find one that's a clue. Charlie, stand by the door. Sugs, you scout out a place with a desk or a table and reserve it for us. Grid, go pry Sammy loose from the sickroom—and don't let that doctor leave. I want a word with him and with whoever else is tucked away—sick man included."

Chapter 7

Three reporters had nosed their way to the Cotter hall and were unsuccessfully attempting to bait an opinion from Nelson. Dr. Perry, on the verge of departure, tried to catch Nelson's eye. Busch, the cameraman, and Thumbs Spiegel had gone off to develop their findings. Inspector Furniss and Sugs were not in evidence. Nor was the body of Captain Orrin L. Shay. It had been deposited on a couch in the little room near the kitchen to await the arrival of the morgue wagon.

The reporters were eying the carpet which showed a drying pool and a few shards of broken glass.

"You didn't mention there'd been a struggle, Sarge."

"There was no struggle. The maid was carrying a drink to the captain. Quite naturally she dropped it when she discovered what had happened."

Sammy came out of the bedroom, and one of the reporters deserted Nelson to block her way. "You saw it first, sister. What have you got to say?"

Sammy glanced down at him from her six-foot length. "I got to say, 'Excuse me.'" Firmly she set him aside and continued on her way.

Dr. Randolph appeared, steering a course for the telephone. He saw that it was overlaid with a powdery substance and hesitated. Nelson said, "We've finished with it. You can make your call if it's necessary."

Dr. Randolph blew his nose, dropped his handkerchief into a whisky puddle, picked it up, and put it in his pocket. He seemed very upset. "I want to phone the Parkside Hospital to send an ambulance."

"Mr. Cotter's condition is serious, then?"

"In my opinion, yes. He has symptoms of influenza, but under the circumstances I can't offer a full diagnosis."

Nelson said courteously, "Unless it would endanger him, we'd prefer that he remain here. Would you permit a consultation before you call the ambulance?"

"Consultation? Just what is your authority, sir?"

Nelson introduced himself. Then he presented Dr. Perry. Randolph said, "I wouldn't advise delay. I'd be glad to have your opinion, of course." The two men disappeared, closing the bedroom door behind them.

The reporter who had tackled Sammy took a handkerchief from his pocket and placed it carefully over his nose and mouth. His words came muffled. "Influenza, huh?" Then he removed the handkerchief. "Nuts, I've got it. Not influenza but an angle. Jealous husband. Makes like he's sick. Gets up—garrotes—goes back to bed. Finis. This bird Shay was a noted ladies' man—"

"I'll let you know if you're right," Nelson said and cursed himself for the sharp quality that had entered his voice. All of the reporters noticed it. They looked at him speculatively.

He smiled. "I always do let you know, don't I?"

"Sure, Sarge, you play nice."

"Well, then, the sooner you leave me to it, the sooner the scoop." He kept talking rapidly, herding them before him. "You've plenty for a starter. Captain Shay was strangled with his own scarf by person or persons unknown while calling his doctor to attend a soldier acquaintance whose feverish condition had alarmed him. The door to the apartment was open, like this." Nelson held the door wide. "Shay was a man in the public eye, a patriot of considerable service to his country. It is suspected that some Fascist sympathizer wanted him out of the way, followed him to his destination, and killed him. A quiet murder could have been accomplished easily due to conditions prevailing in the troubled household. The soldier's wife was closeted with her husband while Captain Shay telephoned, and the maid was busy mixing a drink. See you later, boys." He shut the door in their skeptical faces.

He stood for a moment, leaning his broad shoulders against the jamb. He passed a long-fingered hand through his vital curly white hair. He saw that the two doctors had emerged from the bedroom and were deep in conversation. He went to join them. He heard Perry say, "That stuff he muttered might mean diplopia."

Nelson had never known the big medical examiner to be so animated. It was as though he had been granted unexpected holiday from everlasting contact with the dead.

Dr. Randolph was drawing on his gloves. He said weightily, "I'm not prepared to attach significance to delirious mutterings. Still, I've seen cases before—"

Perry nodded. "That deep rapid respiration—the cough—the rigidity of the facial muscles—as fair an example of the Parkinsonian syndrome as I've ever witnessed. If we had a history of—" He looked up and saw Nelson. "Dr. Randolph is right. The man needs immediate hospitalization."

Poor Louise, Nelson thought. He said to Randolph, "All right, Doctor, make your arrangements. But after you've phoned I must ask you to remain here for a short while. Inspector Furniss will want to talk to you."

Dr. Randolph made no comment. He shook hands with Perry. "Glad to have met you, Doctor." Then he went to the telephone.

Perry picked up his bag. "Well, I'm off." Usually he could not wait to exit from the scene of the crime. Now he sounded regretful.

Nelson said, "What?" but did not finish the sentence. The voice of Inspector Furniss was raised in peremptory summons. He hastened to answer it.

Furniss had set up office in the dining room. He was seated at the head of the long bare table which only a short while ago had been spread for a feast. Sugs was on his right, his round legible face gloomy, his notebook opened to a blank page. Sugs, often characterized by the inspector as the only clerical man in captivity without an ounce of grammar to his make-up, blamed his present status in the department on his mother, who had literally dragged him off to business school before he attained the age of valid objection. He wanted to be a detective and was convinced that only his indispensability as a stenographer stood in the way. His conviction was unshared by Furniss, and Furniss had grounds for doubt.

Sammy stood before Furniss as before judgment, her handsome face a blend of torment and resignation.

Nelson said, "Sit down, Sammy," and drew a chair for her.

"I think Mr. Chief want me to stand."

"The chief's your friend. He wants you to be comfortable."

Furniss said irritably, "Oh, sit down."

Sammy sat, her eyes on Furniss. Nelson looked at Furniss inquiringly.

"I'm not getting anywhere, Grid. I'd be blessed with more than human understanding if I could take that first phone call to you—before the murder was committed—on faith. Sammy insists she called you to bring Perry to Mr. Cotter, and she knows as well as I do that medical examiners don't have a private practice on the side. She wanted Perry here all right—but not for the reason given. And if that call didn't indicate foreknowledge of—"

Sammy said, "I didn't have no fore nothing. Mr. Grid-dely can do anything he got a mind to do is why I phoned. I couldn't get no other medical man, and Mr. Cotter, he—"

Furniss shrugged. "That's her story, but I'm not stuck on it. She thinks I'm some kind of a louse just because I'm trying to do my job. You take over."

Sammy said deeply, "No sir, I don't think you nothing like that, but you get me messed up when you shout questions at me."

Nelson grinned at the expression on the chief's face. "All right, Sammy, tell it your own way."

She told it her own way, beginning with her arrival at the Cotter apartment. If the chief's impatient attitude was an indicator, she could have omitted much of her recital. But Nelson listened carefully, only shifting his attention to spur Sugs on with a nod each time he stopped to rest his rebellious fingers.

Once or twice Furniss interrupted her. "Skip the preparations for dinner. Do you want to kill me? All I ate tonight was a piece of horse meat badly disguised as roast beef."

Sammy's eyes twinkled for a moment. "They's plenty gone begging in the kitchen. You want me to—?"

Now it was Furniss who looked tormented. "Never mind trying to change the subject. You say you heard a man inquiring for the Cotter apartment, but he didn't come up. Would you recognize him if you saw him again?"

"No, Mr. Chief. I only see his back. He wearing a check overcoat with a belt to it."

"Well, maybe the desk clerk can furnish a description if we decide it's important. Go on."

"We put Mr. Cotter in bed," Sammy continued, "and I call up all the doctors. They don't come and they don't come." She paused.

"Yes?"

She said hesitantly, "But somebody else come—Mrs. Cotter's cousin—the same lady that visit this morning. She walk in bag and baggage, and she tell the porter to prop the door open so he can bring the rest of it without disturbing nobody."

Both Nelson and Furniss said, "What?" Furniss followed it up: "You didn't mention this cousin before."

Sammy said firmly, "'Cause she ain't around when that gentleman get himself killed."

"You mean she moved in and moved right out again?"

"No, Mr. Chief. I mean her bags is here, but she gone. She talking to Mrs. Cotter in the bedroom when the gentleman come. After that she gone."

"Didn't you see her leave?"

Sammy shook her massive head. "I too busy waiting for doctors to mind what else go on."

Nelson said, "Which cousin was she, Sammy? What was her name?"

"I don't know, Mr. Grid-dely. She a right kissy young lady. She just tell me she Mrs. Cotter's cousin and she here to stay awhile."

"Are you sure she's gone? I suppose Mrs. Cotter told her what room she was to have. Perhaps she's in there."

"Sure," said Furniss. "Sound asleep—and her conscience too clear to be disturbed by the noise we've been making."

Sammy was silent. Nelson's forehead pleated.

Furniss decided to sing a different song. He stared at her reproachfully from under his heavy brows. He filled his accomplished voice with pain. "Ever since you came to work for

Grid, Sammy, I've looked upon you as practically one of my squad because you've taken such an intelligent interest in past cases. And now, when you're in at the death, so to speak, you let us down—suddenly refuse to cooperate."

Sammy cleared her throat. "That cousin didn't do no murder, Mr. Chief."

Furniss almost leaped out of his chair. He shouted, "Now we're getting somewhere. She bribed you—she gave you money to keep her name out of it."

Sugs murmured deprecatingly, "Aw, Chief."

Nelson, torn between anger and a desire to laugh, saw dignity descend upon Sammy.

She stood up. "You believe that too, Mr. Grid-dely?"

"No, Sammy."

She studied his grave face. She nodded at what she read there. "That's good, 'cause then I don't need to find me another job. I going to keep right on cooking for you." There was just faint emphasis on the final pronoun. "That bell ringing some more. I see who—"

Furniss said, "Not necessary. A policeman's on the door. Stay put." His voice was still raised, but not for the purpose of shock tactics. He was trying to make himself heard above the noises taking place outside the room. "Captain Shay was announced, and you thought he was one of the doctors. You told him to come up, and Mrs. Cotter received him. What was her manner like?"

Sammy addressed herself to Nelson. "Her manner disappointed is all. She tell him Mr. Cotter sick, and then he say maybe he going to fetch his own doctor on the phone. He say he left him playing bridge at the club. But first he march her to the bedroom. I don't know what go on there 'cause I back in the kitchen, and pretty soon Mrs. Cotter come along and tell me the gentleman want a drink, so I step in the dining room and fix it for him. But when I tote it out to the hall he don't want it no more 'cause he dead. I scared and my hands let go the tray."

"Didn't Mrs. Cotter go back to him after she told you to fix the drink?" Furniss asked.

Sammy was sending all her answers toward Nelson. "She—" Her voice swelled with relief. "Here Mrs. Cotter now. She going to tell you about it."

Louise came into the room, her body taut with distress. She went straight to Nelson. "Grid, they've come to take Charles to the Parkside Hospital, and that policeman at the door won't let me go with him. Please—"

Furniss sat up. "What's this? Who said he could go to a hospital? No one's leaving the apartment until they've talked with me.

Sugs, stop them."

Nelson explained patiently, "Chief, both Dr. Perry and the other doctor agree that Cotter needs immediate hospitalization. He's unconscious, so you won't be able to question him anyway." He put a comforting hand out to Louise. "The chances are that if he receives the proper care he'll be able to talk to you tomorrow—provided he has anything to tell."

Louise cried, "How could he have anything to tell? He's been asleep for hours. He doesn't even know Captain Shay is dead. Grid, don't let them keep me from him."

"Sorry," Furniss said. "Murder's been done, and we're stretching a point by permitting your husband to be removed. But you'll have to stay for a while at least. Then perhaps you can join him."

"I won't—I won't." She was beside herself. She turned on Furniss passionately. "So you're the man I've heard so much about—the one I wanted to meet—"

Nelson caught her arm. "Listen to me, Louise. You can't help Charles by going with him now. If I thought you could I'd defy Inspector Furniss myself. I'll do this—I'll go out and speak to the ambulance men and then I'll call Parkside and give further instructions, and I'll see that they telephone bulletins to you at short intervals. Then as soon as the inspector's through with you I'll drive you to Parkside. All right?"

She drew a deep breath. "All right, Grid, but I—I'll go with you while you talk to the men. I—I want to say goodbye." With a defiant glance at Furniss, who made no move to stop her, she followed Nelson from the room.

Sugs chuckled.

Furniss glared at him. "What the hell's so funny?"

"Nothing, Chief, except you're sure crawling into a lot of doghouses tonight." He added hurriedly, "Well, that's life."

"Never mind the philosophy. Go get that doctor in here. And while you're about it, case all the rooms and see if you can turn up the mysterious cousin."

"Sure, Chief, sure." He made a hurried exit.

Furniss assumed a mournful expression for Sammy's benefit. He coughed several times, but she would not look at him. Finally he said, "I'm an old man, Sammy, and sometimes I speak out of turn. You made me angry by failing to mention there'd been another woman here, when you know as well as I do how important every little detail is in regard to a crime of this nature. Are we friends?"

Sammy said aloofly, "You the law, and I got to answer to the law, but I don't got to be friends with it."

Sugs came back into the room. "There ain't a cousin in the place.

Nothing but some bags to prove she ain't a dream. I even looked under the beds for her. About that doc—he'll be here directly. He's locked up in the bathroom with cramps or something."

"Have they taken the sick man out yet?"

"Practically. Them interns are just carrying the stretcher through the door, so I guess the sarge and the dame will be with us in a minute. Jeez—she's some looker. I go for the big girls myself. And does she care! She's hanging over that stretcher like—"

"Save your strength for your notes. There'll be plenty of them." He addressed Sammy again. "To return to the subject, you've been here ever since this morning, and whether you know it or not, you must have observed something that bears on Captain Shay's death. The attitude of Mrs. Cotter, for example. How did she—?"

"I told you Mrs. Cotter ain't got no attitude. She mighty happy when she let me in today. And she keep happy till Mr. Cotter catch his spell. I hear her talking and laughing like big music. She got a laugh I rather hear than eat when I hungry. She ain't mixed up with what happen out there."

Furniss restrained himself. "I'm not saying she is, but—"

Sugs said, "Chicky!"

The warning heralded Louise and Nelson. Furniss decided to make a new start. He arose and personally supervised the seating of Louise. Then he gave her an ingratiating smile and said, "Please try to relax. I know you've had a difficult day and I regret the necessity for this. Our mutual friend, Grid, has often spoken of you, so I can dispense with preliminaries. I'm acquainted with your background, Cotter's, your husband's induction into the Army, and so on. The questions I'm going to ask now are just routine. I'll get them over with as quickly as possible."

Louise said nothing. Her beautiful eyes said, Get them over with, then.

"How long have you known Captain Shay?"

She answered quietly, "About six months. He brought a watch to Cotter's for repairs. After that he became a regular visitor."

"To your home or to the shop?"

"Both."

"And he kept these visits up after your husband went away?"

"To the shop, yes."

"On business?"

"Sometimes. He'd recommended quite a few customers and wanted to know if they had appeared. But more often than not his calls were purely social."

"Yet he was not in the habit of making informal calls to your home?"

"No."

"Had he come tonight by special invitation?"

"No."

"I see. You'd make a good witness, Mrs. Cotter, but you're not on the witness stand now. If my questions should happen to start any train of thought, please feel free to elaborate."

"There's nothing to elaborate," Louise said. "He just dropped in. I wasn't expecting him."

"He knew your husband was home on furlough?"

"I think I mentioned that Charles was due, several weeks ago. He probably forgot."

"You mean he wouldn't have come if he knew your husband was home?"

"That isn't what I meant."

"Did your husband like Captain Shay?"

Louise said, "My husband isn't a man of wide friendships. He likes very few people and bothers to dislike even fewer. He accepted Captain Shay."

"You're a very beautiful woman, Mrs. Cotter. If your husband was inclined to jealousy—"

Louise said evenly, "Is this part of your routine, Inspector?"

"Of course. It comes under the heading of eliminating suspects."

"Then consider my husband eliminated. He knows me too well to think seriously of Captain Shay as a rival for my affections."

"I gather you weren't particularly keen on the late gentleman."

"Not particularly. Our relationship was quite pleasant and quite shallow." She glanced at her watch. She turned to Nelson. "Do you think they've reached the hospital yet, Grid?"

"Hardly." Nelson sent her an encouraging look. I'm proud of you, it said.

Furniss resumed briskly, "Not much farther to go, Mrs. Cotter. Tell me in your own words when and how the death of Shay was brought to your notice."

She swallowed. "I was in the bedroom. I knew vaguely that something was going on, but nothing seemed important except Charles. I didn't know about Shay until Grid came in and told me."

Furniss shot a quick glance at Sammy. Her face was impassive. He said, "I'm afraid you're a bit confused. I sent Grid into the bedroom to tell Sammy I wanted her. She had discovered the body. Surely she must have thought it worthwhile to mention to you that a man had been strangled in your apartment!"

Sammy spoke. "I helping the doctor. Mrs. Cotter hard off enough without my giving her more misery. I know she going to find out soon anyways."

Furniss flung his hands ceilingward. The shout he launched became in transit a wounded wail. "I've been insulted. They think Furniss is a moron. Good old Furniss. Feed it to him fast and he'll swallow anything. Well, I don't swallow this—not by a long shot." He pounced on Sammy. "You were fixing a drink for Shay. Meanwhile, he was telephoning his doctor. You—"

Louise said, as though she and Nelson were the only ones present, as though Furniss were a gramophone record that they could listen to or not, as they chose, "Grid, I haven't much confidence in that doctor. I don't want to continue with him. Dr. Purcell knows Charles. Will you ?"

Nelson nodded. He said, "Shhhh."

Furniss banged his fist on the table. "Go right ahead. Make your plans. Don't mind me. Were you paying attention, Sammy, or have you something else you'd rather talk about? The night is young. Nobody's in a hurry."

"Please," Louise said, "I—"

Furniss bowed to her. He said, "Thank you," his voice heavy with sarcasm. "Now then. Sammy, you carried the drink to Shay and found him slumped over the telephone table—dead. You were mildly shocked—not enough to run to Mrs. Cotter with the news, but at least enough to drop the tray. Let's assume that the tray wasn't equipped with a silencer—that it made some kind of a crash when it hit the floor. Did you hear that crash, Mrs. Cotter?"

"Yes, but I—I tell you, nothing registered."

"You weren't tied to your husband's bedside, were you? You had left him when Shay was admitted, attracted by the sound of the bell, no doubt. But the more unusual sound of a heavy crash didn't even stir your curiosity?"

"I didn't want to leave Charles again. He—" She pressed her hands to her head.

Furniss said shrewdly, "Your husband hadn't taken a turn for the worse at the moment of Sammy's discovery? Or should I say a turn for the better? He hadn't regained consciousness?"

"No—no!"

Sugs looked up and said, "Here's Doc," before the others noted the man's presence in the room.

Randolph pulled out a chair and sat on the edge of it. He looked very temporary. His words underlined the pose. "I hope this won't take long. Terrible thing, Shay's sudden demise. A great loss to the country. I'm anxious to cooperate, of course, but I'm equally anxious to go to my patient. Service to the living, you know."

Louise opened her mouth and closed it in response to Nelson's warning eyes.

Furniss said, "Just how well did you know the dead man?"

"I've been his physician for years, and we're members of the same club. As a matter of fact, I doubt if I'd have come out to oblige anyone else tonight. I was rather busy."

Sammy muttered, "Busy at bridge games."

Randolph gave her his full pale-eyed attention for a moment. The smile that touched his rather coarse lips was quite synthetic. "Er—yes." He shrugged apologetically. "We doctors have so little opportunity for recreation these days."

Nelson exchanged glances with Furniss. Furniss inclined his head slightly. Nelson said, "You were with Captain Shay earlier this evening, Doctor. Can you describe his general manner?"

Randolph took his time. "Quite normal. Nothing to indicate that he had anything on his mind—or any premonition of an untimely end."

"How old are you?"

Randolph looked startled, "Er—I'm forty-three. Aren't you becoming unnecessarily personal?"

"Perhaps. But I was curious because you said you had been Shay's physician for years. I'll be even more personal and pay you a compliment. You don't look your age." Something was trying for a foothold in Nelson's brain. It had a fantastic shape. He quashed it. "Where were you when he called tonight?"

The two women, Louise and Sammy, moved impatiently. Randolph's eyes went to Sammy. "I was playing bridge—at the club."

Nelson switched abruptly. "Would you mind telling us something about Mr. Cotter's condition—just to reassure his wife? Naturally she's beside herself with worry."

"Yes, yes, of course." He cleared his throat. "I'd like nothing better than to reassure the lady, but until the patient has been under observation I'm not prepared to venture a definite opinion. Your police doctor agrees with me that certain aspects of the case point to influenza. However, there are a few symptoms—" He smiled. "As laymen you wouldn't understand. Just let me say that I'm certain the patient will pull through."

The hands of Louise were locked in combat on the table top. She tore them apart. Nelson rose. He said, "Thank you, Doctor. That will be all for the present. Just leave your address with the inspector's secretary and I'll see you out. There's a policeman stationed at the door, and he might be unwilling to let you pass without an official okay."

Randolph mumbled an address to Sugs. Then, as though some comment were demanded of him, he said, "I appreciate your courtesy and—er—brevity. I'm confident that you'll reach a quick solution of this tragedy." He aimed a "Good night" at large and followed Nelson from the room.

Before the door was opened it became apparent that he had something further to say. He looked from Nelson to the uniformed policeman. He hesitated, placed a hand on Nelson's arm, and drew him aside. He tilted his head back to meet the taller man's eyes. He spoke softly. "I expected this to come out during my interview, but due to the presence of the man's wife, delicacy forbade my offering it. Your police doctor seemed to be both intelligent and observant. But, should he have overlooked it, I'd feel guilty if I neglected to mention—er— After all, Captain Shay was my friend, and though it may have no bearing, as a citizen I wish to assist the police in every possible way—because—"

Nelson decided that he shared Louise's lack of confidence in Dr. Randolph. "You mentioned that you were in a hurry. Will you please come to the point?"

Randolph's confidential tone stiffened. "I'm not accustomed to dealing with the police, and although I don't expect you to appreciate it professional etiquette makes me extremely reluctant—"

"I'm not asking you to violate professional etiquette," Nelson said and meant it. He had a sense of foreboding. As a friend of the Cotters he did not want to hear what this man so patently wanted to say. As a detective he knew that he must listen.

"You're not making it any easier for me," Randolph complained.

Nelson said nothing, knowing that here was no witness to be cosseted, nursed along with encouraging words. Randolph, with his air of furtive excitement, suddenly resembled a malignant type of gossipmonger who would somehow manage to be heard through a gag.

He said triumphantly, "When I examined the patient I noted that there was a stain on the edge of his pajama leg—a wet stain that smelled of scotch whisky."

Chapter 8

To Kyrie Martens it made no sense at all. Of her own volition she had dashed out of the Cotter apartment by way of the service door. She had gone into a drugstore and ordered coffee, and presently her foolish panic had abated. She scolded herself for turning tail. The thing to do was to get back there immediately. So she had started to return.

And now she was sandwiched between two men in the back of a small green coupé. And one of the men was either dead or very near to death. She felt a shiver of repulsion every time a jolt threw her into contact with his limp left shoulder. She had never seen him before.

The man on her other side was a stranger, too, a comic strip character, little and thin and droll-faced. Yet his actions were not born of a comic strip. This she had reason to know.

He had materialized out of the shadows near the entrance of the house to call her Madge Carter, make the small, almost imperceptible sign used by Price's men, and ask for a moment of conversation. Without pausing to demand further proof she had rushed to the conclusion, perhaps because she so wished it, that he had come to summon her back to work. Her lack of caution was partially justified. There was no reason for the other side to be interested in her, since temporarily at least she was out of the running.

"This is important," the comic strip man had said, "and not to be discussed here." And she had agreed with him. Willingly she had allowed herself to be led along the darkened sidewalk.

She rubbed the arm that still hurt from the unexpected judo hold that had been used upon her, a hold ending in her present position in the traveling car.

"Sit still," the comic strip man ordered nastily. Nothing about him, she decided, was consistent with his appearance.

She dropped her hand to her lap to join its mate. She let her eyes play for a moment of speculation on the thick, unpromising neck of the car's driver. She had neither glimpsed his face nor heard his voice. The visible portion of him did not indicate a better nature to which she might appeal.

She turned her head toward her conscious neighbor. "What do you want of me?" she asked calmly.

He answered in precise English, "Nothing more than information."

"Why the violence? I'd have gone with you anyway because I thought—" She stopped.

"You thought what I wanted you to think. If you are a sample of the operatives now being used I have little cause for worry." She could feel his sharp stare cutting through the dim light. "No doubt," he said, "your beauty dulled their judgment."

"Could you open a window?"

"No. You must endure the stuffiness for the time being. There will be air for you later."

She said to herself, He's trying to frighten me—deliberately. But I'm not frightened. The palms of her hands were clammy. She ran them along the warm dry fur of her coat. She said aloud, "I'm a reasonable person. If you give me some idea of the information you're after we might be able to cut this short."

He looked across at her neighbor. "We will cut it short enough. But we will do it in privacy."

"Are you afraid you'll bore *him?*"

"You have a charming sense of humor. I have none. Keep your mouth shut until it is time to speak."

She closed her mouth, partly because of a certainty that he was capable of further violence and partly because she wanted to think things through. A huge, dancing question mark blocked her. It kept getting in the way, no matter how she tried to peer around it. He was the enemy all right. But she was no longer on the case, and, having ferreted her out, he must know that. One way or another her failure in Washington was a fact far easier to glean than—well, say, for example, the means of contact practiced by her co-agents. Why?

The question mark dissolved in self-occasioned pain. Kyrie had been biting down savagely on her lower lip.

Her captor lit a cigarette. She sniffed it hungrily and made instinctive motion toward a pocketbook that was not there. In her hurried exit she had left it behind. That really worried her, smoker that she was. For the moment it seemed the most important thing in the whole bad dream. Furtive exploration of her coat yielded only the small jingling of coins, change from the stray quarter with which she had paid for her coffee in the drugstore. Had I but known, she thought, I'd have squandered my all on cigarettes. She muttered aloud, "'Kyrie Martens, or Slave to the Foul Weed.'"

Comic Strip moved threateningly. "What's that you're saying?"

"Nothing. Less than nothing."

She craned past the silent figure on her right, attempting to read the street signs as they slid by. She caught one by sheer force of will power and concentration. Eighteenth Street, it said. She did not recognize the avenue. Sixth, it might be, or Seventh.

She thought, On the whole they've been stingy with the melodrama. I'm neither bound nor blindfolded. Shame on them. The Emily Post of accepted procedure for kidnapers will haul them over the coals for this.

But the omission did nothing to cheer her. They're not cautious because they don't think it worthwhile to cover their tracks.... Again the question mark appeared, not dancing now. Quite static. It was easy to read the answer that lay behind it. Too easy. She shut her eyes, refusing it. She shook her head slightly. Now I'm the one who's spreading on melodrama. Of course they're not going to kill me. This downtown destination we're heading for is a temporary hideout, one from which they're planning a quick getaway. That's why my eyes are free to look. They don't care whether I see it or not because by the time I'm able to pass on the information they'll be far out of reach.... She wanted to believe it. Covertly she put her hand under her coat, laid it over her heart. The strong beat reassured her. They can't stop that, she thought bravely. They're not big enough to tackle so much life.

The comic strip character said, "I told you to sit still," and gave her a shove. She could feel fire climbing to her hair. I must control myself. I must not invite abuse. He's a little man. He would welcome provocation—enjoy hurting me. His kind doesn't get opportunities often.

The car was turning, rolling down a dark narrow street. The Village, she thought, past Abingdon Square. Then the car stopped.

Fingers dug into her arm. She said through her teeth, "I'll come quietly," but the fingers did not loosen.

The driver got out first. In the shadows his face was as featureless as his neck. "Go ahead, Max. I'll bring *him*."

Kyrie made no resistance. Carefully she matched her captor's steps to avoid being dragged. The shabby gray stone house was third from the corner. The ground floor of the corner building was a saloon. There was activity in the saloon: people and music of a sort. The music rushed out to the pavement, but the people stayed inside. Even a scream would not have brought them forth. Screams in that neighborhood were natural phenomena. So the hand rammed suddenly against her mouth was doubly useless. Because she would not have screamed anyway. Not without a publishable story to offer in explanation.

She was partnered up three flights of dusty stairs. Her iron-fingered companion fitted key to lock and pushed her over a threshold. She heard a slam, followed by the click of a switch. An old-fashioned central chandelier functioned dully. She saw that she was in a dun-colored square, a combination dining room and kitchen furnished with a round table, several straight chairs, and a radio on a wooden stool. A gas range, an icebox, and a sink lined one wall. The other walls were broken up by doors, the entrance door and one that led to a room behind.

She seemed to be alone with the comic strip character. She supported herself against the low icebox and looked at him meekly. Busily, behind the dejected stance, she schemed. He was tricky. Bedroom tactics would not work here. She could not hope to handle him without a weapon, at least not long enough to serve her ends. She had noticed a few empty bottles on the shelf above the icebox. If she could reach one of those bottles, wield it, and hide, she might be able to wage a surprise attack on the driver....

Enemy number one had wedged a hand under his belt. She thought he was scratching himself and felt a hysterical urge to laugh. His hand emerged holding a flat pistol. He juggled it carelessly.

Heavy steps approached. The door opened, and the driver was there. He seemed enormous. His flat, amateurishly modeled face had features now, but no expression. Obviously he chose to express himself by the clothes he wore, a suit of lozenge weave, a green shirt, and colors that hurt in his flashing necktie.

He shifted the body in his arms and said in a businesslike voice, "Inside, Max?" At a nod he continued to the inner room. She heard a thud before he reappeared without his burden. She wondered if the man was dead. If not he needed aid. She was stricken by the knowledge of her own helplessness.

The driver sat down at the table and leaned upon his elbows. He looked at her with unflattering disinterest.

The silence held for minutes. It became as wearing as strenuous physical exercise. Kyrie tried to while it away by memorizing in detail the face of little Max. He had button-bright eyes in a brown leather skin. His ears were outstanding, his nose long and ludicrous, his mouth a crooked red seam above a bladelike chin. She could not see much of his hair. The gentleman, she thought, keeps his hat on.

Presently, pointing the gun in her general direction, he took a few steps toward the table. He spoke to the driver. "You had better go down and put the car away."

"Don't I wait till the boss gets here? He's sure to want me, Max." The driver's gaze was still on Kyrie, surveying her coldly, as though she were some object he might soon be called upon to alter.

Because there was no humane quality in his eyes, she shivered.

"He won't need you, Walter. I am capable of managing the situation." Kyrie's shiver had not gone unmarked. Max was tasting it, licking his lips. "He will be very angry if he finds that car downstairs."

Walter rose reluctantly. "Why did he have to pick my place? Now maybe I'll have to move, and I was just getting used to it here. What do you suppose is keeping him so long?"

The red seam split, showing teeth. "Maybe he's sitting up with a sick friend." He bowed toward Kyrie. "I find I have a sense of humor after all."

"Ha, ha." Walter did not laugh. He pronounced the syllables gloomily. He went out slamming the door.

There was more silence. Max sat down and watched Kyrie. It went on forever, she standing until her slim feet seemed to overspread her high-heeled shoes, he sitting and watching.

At the start of it she had moved toward a chair, to be stopped by his foot. She was conscious of the ache of it on her instep. And once she had set her lips for speech, but he had stopped that, too, not with a blow or a kick but with his eyes. He feels taller sitting, she thought. He doesn't slap me because it would detract from his sense of power to have to stand up to it. When the "boss" arrives Max will sit me down so he can take his fun with comfort and dignity. Meanwhile, this cat-and-mouse business is commonly termed the "softening-up process."

Bitterly she admitted that the softening-up process was beginning to take effect. Then finally she thought, I must be mad to let him get away with it. Whatever I do, he won't shoot. He thinks I can give him information, and information doesn't come from a corpse.... She acted before she had time to doubt her own reasoning, making a sudden rush for the chair farthest away from him. She sat down. The hard wood felt like luxury's lap. She steadied her trembling legs.

"Get up," he said.

She did not answer.

"Do you hear me?"

Her mouth curled.

"Damn you—speak. Move."

"You told me not to talk until it was time. Is it time?" Her voice was small and cool.

He leaned forward but could not reach her. The table was between. He jerked out of his chair and ran around the table. That part of it was funny....

Her eyes streamed. Not tears, but a smooth flow. There was no time for tears to form between the intervals of his stinging openhanded blows about her head and face and neck. She could do nothing but kick out at him, because instinct had belatedly raised her arms to shield her bruising flesh.

She was hardly conscious of pain. She was praying a confused and feminine prayer. Don't let him break my nose. Just don't let him disfigure me. Let me get at him. Let me kill him....

She managed to make contact with his shin. That seemed to sober him, to blunt the edge of his loose rage. He jumped back and wheezed breathlessly, "Only a sample. Wait a little."

She touched a cut place on her cheek. She outlined strange puffed lips with a fingertip. She saw him through salt. He had changed. He was breathing evenly now. He was sleek and suave. Satiated.

He stared at her. He said with the air of one who pays a compliment in recognition of past favors, "You have very pretty hair."

Her stomach turned over.

He glanced at his watch and frowned. "It grows late. He must have been detained. I think I will let you talk after all. Perhaps he will be tired. Perhaps he will prefer that the spadework is accomplished before he arrives. I will ask a few questions and you will answer them. Is that understood?"

She nodded with difficulty. She was afraid that if she dropped her head too far she would not be able to lift it again. She brushed her fur sleeve across her eyes.

He said with horrible kindness, "Have you a handkerchief?"

She took one from her pocket and used it gingerly. When she drew it away her vision was cleared. She looked at the handkerchief. It was red with her blood where his ring had cut her. It was a flag calling her to action. She acted, taking him by surprise, leaping from the chair to throw herself upon him.

She did not know how long the struggle lasted or whether its result upon Max was worthy of the clean wild anger that had inspired it. Later she remembered the point at which she had been tripped. And she remembered the sickening sound of metal against her skull. But those memories came slowly and with much striving after she had recovered consciousness in the squalid bedroom of the squalid little flat.

She came back to life in anguish, hearing nothing but the noise of her own physical suffering. She seemed to be lying on the prickly sands of a limitless desert with the sun beating down upon her face and head. It was a peculiar desert, because there was water on it. Her dress was wet with it. If she had only strength to reach and bring the wet cloth to her hot eyes there would be ease for her. She made the effort and went down in defeat under a wave of dizziness. She lay quite still, waiting for the wave to spend itself. Her teeth began to chatter, and she discovered with surprise that she was cold in spite of the sun. She groped for a fur coat that was not there. Coat! Inside. She had thrust it off when she—

After a little while she dared to open her eyes. The sun was nothing but a naked electric bulb suspended from a cracked, discolored ceiling. And the desert was the rough, scratchy surface of a blanket. Step by painful step she retraveled the path that had led to this room.

The Cotters. Louise. Charles. Fretfully her waking mind struggled with Charles. He had come home. He was sick. Poor Charles. Poor Louise. No doctor. She must do something. But who was that at the Cotter door? Whose voice was that? No, it couldn't be. That voice had no connection with Louise or Charles.

How hard it was to think with the sun—the electric bulb—

glaring down at her. She moved slightly. Thank God she could move. She lifted her hand to her head. She searched out the wound under its silk matting of hair. It hurt, but she could bear it. It couldn't be dangerous, because she was conscious and she was thinking. Go on thinking, Kyrie. Think.

The voice. Unmistakably the voice of Orrin Shay. Orrin Shay in the Cotter apartment. Louise had gone to meet him. And she, Kyrie, what had she done? The wrong thing. She knew that now. It was easy to know that now....

But to know it then? To give the show away? Hatefully he would call her Madge. My dear Madge.

In the lobby another man had called her Madge. And he had brought her here and had his fun while awaiting the arrival of the "boss."

But she had been brave. She had given him fight, forced him to resort to a weapon. Proved to him that bare hands were not enough to subdue such a redoubtable adversary as Kyrie Martens. And what had her bravery accomplished? Her poor mouth tried to smile. Brave! Brave as a fool all the way. What next?

Again she became uncomfortably aware of her wet dress. Just another puzzle to be solved. She found an answer that would do. The "boss" must have come while she was "out." Must have tried to revive her with splashings of water. Yes, her hair was damp too. But her cheeks had been dried by the heat from within, and her throat was dry, and her tongue had withered in her dry mouth.

She thought, I'll continue to play possum for as long as it will work, and maybe then the "boss" will be the one to talk. And what he says while I lie here thwarting him might be the thing I've come all this hard way to hear. My luck is due for a change. But after I hear it—what? How will I manage to escape with it to the right quarter? Oh well—sufficient unto the day—

But I must have water to drink or I won't have to play possum. I'll go under again. She listened. She heard voices coming from the outer room. Then one voice. The radio spouting from its wooden stool. A news broadcast. She hoped that it would be interesting enough to hold them. She heard something else. A closer, more frightening sound. A moan.

She pulled herself to a sitting posture. The room wavered, then settled. She looked over the foot of the brass bed at the man lying in a crumpled heap on the floor. He had been that other unwilling passenger in the green car. He was alive. As she looked his eyes opened and fixed upon her. They were bewildered but completely sensible.

She whispered, "Shhh. I'm going to help you. Try not to make any noise."

He stirred slightly, seeming to comprehend. Perspiration crawled from under his graying hair. The moaning stopped.

It was a remarkable effort that dragged her to her feet. She saw the washstand with thanksgiving. Grimly denying her head's throbbing protest, she made for it. There was a tumbler on its edge. She held it under the tap and let the water fill it slowly. She glanced toward the man hesitantly, but succor was there in her hand, and she could not resist the pull of her own crying need. The water was blessedly cold. First she swished it around in her mouth. Then she drank. She filled the basin, but bending her head to it was more than she could accomplish. A soiled towel hung from a rack. She wet a corner of it and washed her aching face. Septic as hell, she thought, but this is no time to be fastidious. She rested from her labors, her eyes on the closed door. The radio was still playing above all other sounds. Good.

Now she felt better. Now she could minister to her fellow victim. She brought water to him and managed to support him while he swallowed. Aside from a great lump on the back of his head, he had no visible injuries. She wanted to arrange him more comfortably with pillow and blanket but dared not for fear of a visitor from the other room. He seemed to understand. He whispered faintly, "They hit me—I felt the blow."

"How do you come to be mixed up in this?"

"I don't—know." He closed his eyes. He had a thin, well-bred face. He was middle-aged.

She rubbed his wrists desperately. She said, "Listen—try with everything you have to listen. They may be back in a moment. They mustn't know that you've recovered consciousness. If they do they might tackle you again—for keeps. We've got to play for time. I can't explain in detail—or guess why they want you—but they think I have information for them, so they won't kill me. I'm going to lie down just as I was. And I'm going to think of something that will help us both. So please—don't by any sign let them know that either of us rallied."

He opened his eyes. Through the gaze they flickered with something like interest. "Your head is bleeding. Let me—"

"It will have to bleed. Will you do as I say?"

"But your head—" Then he said weakly, "Yes."

An idea struck her. She smiled painfully. What does the maiden in distress do to summon help? She said, "Have you any money—and a pencil?"

He moved his shoulder helplessly. She searched him. No wallet. A fountain pen clipped to his vest. And in an inner pocket an isolated dollar bill.

"My lucky piece," he whispered.

"Good. Just what I need." She left him. She opened one of the drawers of a drunken bureau. It was empty but lined. She tore off a small piece of the brown paper, put it on the bureau's top, and wrote a shaky message. She made a twist of the bill and the paper, took a ring off her little finger, and used it to girdle the twist. She tried the window cautiously. The lower half would not budge, but the top was open about an inch. Somehow she managed to climb up on the narrow sill. She rested the message on the top half of the window and flicked it out with her thumb and forefinger. Almost immediately she heard it land. It had not reached the ground but had been intercepted by another sill. She said, "Damn," softly and climbed down.

She replaced the glass on the washstand and rehung the towel. She looked at her wristwatch, but it had stopped at ten-thirty. She could not gauge the hour, though she walked to the window again and lifted the dark shade to peer out. The room was on a narrow court faced by a blank brick wall. She could see neither sky nor ground nor any sign of life. The gray light told her nothing. Day or night would present little difference in that court.

She whispered, "Is your watch going?" but received no answer. She dared not press for one or investigate for herself. The radio had just been silenced.

She went back to the bed and lay supine under the wicked glare. She waited.

Chapter 9

It was a quarter past eleven when Nelson escorted Dr. Randolph to the door. He watched him make for one of the elevators and felt oddly at a loss as he disappeared from view. But he could not translate this sense of loss into any reasonable terms, so he shrugged it off. He did not return immediately to the Cotter dining room. He stopped in the hall to telephone. When the Parkside Hospital answered he asked to be connected with the room of the newly arrived patient, Charles Cotter.

There was bitter protest at the unorthodoxy of the call at such an hour. Nelson was forced to outline his own history before the request was honored, and a professional female voice told him that Mr. Cotter was resting nicely.

"Are you the nurse assigned to him?" Nelson asked.

"Yes. I'm usually placed on Dr. Randolph's cases." Then she said warmly, "Dr. Randolph is a wonderful man. The patient couldn't be in better hands. May I ask who you are?"

Nelson said, "I'm Nelson of the Homicide Squad."

It was plain that this rang no bell. Evidently the news had not traveled with Charles to the Parkside Hospital. The nurse said, "Oh?"

"A man was murdered at Mr. Cotter's apartment," Nelson said and heard her gasp. He went on hurriedly, "Mr. Cotter was ill in bed at the time, so in all likelihood he won't be able to throw any light upon the crime, but routine makes it necessary for us to question him as soon as he is able to speak."

"I see," the nurse said, not seeing. He could have sworn that she took time out to cast an anxious glance at the bed and that the sight of poor helpless Charles reassured her. She spoke again, bravely: "Dr. Randolph is the one to decide when you will be permitted to visit the patient."

"Naturally." Nelson's voice was an asset. He capitalized on it now, deliberately adding charm. "I've never met you, of course, but you sound very much the sort of person I'd enjoy knowing. I have a feeling that you're going to prove of great service to both Mr. Cotter and myself. Aside from my official capacity I'm a close friend of his."

She sounded less professional, more conscious of her sex. "I'm sure I'll be very glad to help, as long as I'm not asked to do anything that will interfere with my duties."

"I promise you won't be. I needn't ask *you* to promise that this talk between us be kept in strictest confidence."

"Oh no."

He dropped his voice conspiratorially. "For a starter, will you tell me what Mr. Cotter is wearing?"

"Why, he's wearing a hospital gown."

"He had on pajamas when he was received."

"Yes, they're here. They'll be laundered, and when the examinations are over he'll wear them again."

"They're in the room?"

"Yes, but—"

Nelson said, "Don't let them be laundered. Wrap them up just as they are. I'll send someone in the department for them."

"But why?"

"Believe me, it's important. Can I depend upon you?"

"Yes, but—but perhaps if they're so important I should keep them for the police. I—"

"But I am the police."

"Oh—I forgot—you don't sound like a policeman."

"The man who calls for the pajamas will be in full uniform. That should reassure you."

"Yes, certainly, but—"

"Thank you, Miss—?"

"Miss Hartshorn, but—"

"Thank you, Miss Hartshorn. I'll be in to see you as soon as I can." He hung up. He called softly to the policeman at the door.

"Yes, Sarge?" The blue uniform came quickly.

"Tired?"

"Nah."

"Do you know where Parkside Hospital is?"

"Sure, Sarge. I was born in this town."

"All right. Run over there—Room 617. The name's Cotter, in case you forget the number. Tell the nurse in charge that I sent you and ask for a package."

"What's in the package—a clue?"

"I don't think so, but we're playing safe. Put it in the big drawer of my desk at headquarters. Then send someone to relieve you here and go home. This is a confidential errand. Keep mum."

"You bet. I'll take care of it. So long, Sarge."

Nelson further delayed his return to the others by going into the spare bedroom. It was in good order. Two suitcases and a hatbox stood undisturbed upon the soft gray rug. The bags were locked, but there was a woman's pocketbook fallen between them, and this was open to investigation. Nelson went through it rapidly. It contained a handkerchief, a compact, a cigarette case, a lemon-colored slip of paper, War Ration Book Number Two, and a purse filled with small bills and change. "Hotel Gascony" was printed across the top of the lemon-colored slip above a written message stating that Mr. Holden had called. The day's date and the hour, five-thirty, filled the spaces left for them. War Ration Book Number Two had no stamps missing from it. "Madge Carter" was penciled on its cover, followed by an address in Washington.

Nelson regarded it thoughtfully before he pocketed it along with the hotel memorandum. Then he went back to the dining room.

The atmosphere there had not improved. Furniss was eyeing an unlit cigarette as though he hated it. Sugs had dropped his pencil and was quietly putting his large right hand through a series of exercises. Sammy sneezed three times in a row. Then she sat back, still as an idol. Louise seemed on the point of collapse. Nelson's appearance revived her. She started up.

"Grid, may I—?"

"I just spoke to Charles' nurse. He's still sleeping. I'm going to drive you over soon." He sat down and took her hand. It was cold, and he rubbed it gently between his as he spoke. "Which of your cousins came today? One I know?"

Louise nodded. "Kyrie Martens. She's on a vacation from Washington. I asked her to stay."

Furniss snorted. "I've learned that much myself, Grid, but very little else."

"Perhaps there isn't much else to learn from this quarter, Chief."

"Then again perhaps there is. Your dear friend, Mrs. Cotter, is holding back, and our dear friend, Sammy, is aiding and abetting her."

"I think it's just that they're both too tired to see things in their proper light."

"Who isn't?"

"Exactly. Let's call it a night."

Furniss gave him a searching glance, squinting his bright blue eyes. "I'll have a moment's private conversation with you first. Sugs, remove the ladies. While you're waiting you'd better get into your hat and coat, Mrs. Cotter."

Sugs jumped to his feet, scrapping an unfinished yawn. He steered his charges out.

Furniss said, "Grid, I don't blame you for being loyal to an old schoolmate, or whatever she is, but you've got a job to do, and I'm afraid she's part of it."

"I'm not forgetting my job, Chief."

"You love that dame. Now wait a minute, son, don't interrupt. I'm not accusing you of coveting your neighbor's wife. You love her like a sister, I mean. So do you honestly stand there and tell me that if she's involved you're going to help hang it on her?"

"You've seen her—talked to her. Do you honestly stand there and tell me she *is* involved?"

Furniss said gently, "I think so, Grid. Not directly, maybe, but she's covering for someone—her cousin, or her husband."

"I'll get to the bottom of that, Chief." It was a promise. Nelson's expressive pointed face showed the effort it had cost him to make it.

"I could arrest her this minute as a material witness, but I won't. I'll give you time. But use your head. Both Cotters, the cousin, and Sammy were in this apartment while Shay was murdered. If we exclude Sammy that leaves three. And it stands to reason that one of—"

Nelson said hurriedly, "If you're so ready to exclude Sammy, Chief, why have you been riding her? Her integrity has been proved to you over and over, and it's not likely she'd shed it suddenly out of loyalty to Louise Cotter. She hardly knows her."

"Sammy's loyalties are where she happens to be at the moment."

"Granting there's some truth in that, she doesn't swap them for old ones. She just adds them on, and in a showdown the old ones win out."

"Then why hasn't she come clean? Her account of events leading up to and past the tragedy is full of holes. I don't believe she took a bribe from that cousin—or anybody else. I only said it to make her angry enough to—" Abruptly he switched his train of thought. "There's one thing I'm going to do, whether or not you object to it. I'm going to send out an alarm for Cousin—Cousin—what's her name?"

"Madge—I mean Kyrie—K-y-r-i-e Martens."

Furniss looked at him curiously. "Kyrie Martens. Is her middle name Madge, or is Madge a disappearing act you haven't seen fit to mention?"

"Excuse it, Chief, I was thinking of something else."

"Do you love Kyrie like a sister too?"

"I haven't seen her since she was a little kid." He added hopefully, "I can't even furnish a physical description for you to broadcast." As soon as the words were out he thought of the description given by Louise at lunch not so long ago: "Like a gold willow tree, Grid."

Furniss said, "Too bad. That means I'll have to tackle Mrs. Cotter again."

"Not tonight, Chief. I'll have the description for you tomorrow." Anything for a delay. He was thinking of the Martens family, of the effect of such publicity upon it.

"Hmmm." After a slight pause Furniss said slowly, "Grid, there's plenty of other work in the department that needs your good cool headwork. Perhaps it would be better for all concerned if I took you off this case and got an unbiased assistant to help me."

"No use, Chief. I'd devote all of my spare time to it anyway."

"I'd see that you had no spare time."

"Then I'd be forced to resign and set up as a private sleuth."

"Blackmail. You know you'd resign only over my dead body."

Nelson smiled. "Trust me, Chief."

"I'll have to—but just remember that I'm not noted for my patience." He arose. "If you're driving Mrs. Cotter to the hospital Sugs and I will have to take the subway. Unless you want to drop us off."

"I'd like a chance to talk with Louise on the way. She might recall something if you're not present."

"Very well. All the rope you want—up to a certain length. It might not be a bad idea if I offered Sammy safe escort to a Harlem-bound train. A bit of air might help her to recall something too. Good luck, Grid."

Out in the hall Nelson saw that the relief policeman had arrived. He hoped that Furniss would be too preoccupied to investigate the substitution. Louise was waiting. She took his arm. "Come on—hurry."

He felt an ache of pity. She was so white and strained. He hugged her close for a moment. "Poor kid. Too bad this had to happen to you."

As they quit the apartment he heard Sammy saying with unshakable conviction, "I don't need no air, Mr. Chief. 'Specially night air, 'cause I been sneezing and I think I fixing to catch me a cold. I going to stay here case Mrs. Cotter want me when she come home. No, I ain't afraid—not while you leaving that big fine policeman behind. I going to warm him and me both a nice supper and then I going to lay down and shut my eyes until I needed."

He heard Furniss groan.

In the lobby a little man whose livery was only three quarters filled hurried to open the door for them. He sent a half-admiring, half-curious stare toward Louise, who walked on ahead.

Nelson stopped and said, "How long have you been on?"

"Just about twenty minutes, sir. Isn't that the lady who—?"

Nelson shook his white head. "No, that's not the lady."

He caught up with Louise and led her to his car. She entered it blindly, stumbling on the running board. He went around to the other side and climbed in behind the wheel. When they had traveled for a few blocks he said gently, "I'm in a spot, Louise."

"*You're* in a spot. Oh, Grid, that would make me laugh if I *could* laugh."

"The inspector wants to take me off this case and put someone else on."

"I wish he would."

"Why?"

She did not reply.

He said, "It isn't because you think I know you so well that it would be hard for you to conceal anything from me?" He waited for a moment. Then he said, "Let's get this straight. You have nothing to conceal unless you murdered Shay yourself."

Her answer shook him. She said coldly and surely, as though she had been rehearsing it over and over, "I'll confess when and if it proves necessary."

His foot had pressed hard on the gas pedal in automatic effort to outdistance an unexpected foe. He slowed down and laughed. It was not a good laugh, but it was a good whip. He saw her shrink from it.

"If I didn't know you better, Louise, I'd say you'd been glutting your brains with cheap movies."

She said stonily, "What's that supposed to mean?"

"I thought that making a phony confession to shield a loved one had gone out with the bustle."

"I'm not shielding anyone. I don't have to."

"Agreed. You don't have to. Charles would go out of his way to avoid stepping on a cockroach."

"But, Grid, he—" She pressed her lips together.

"Tell me about it."

"I did. Don't make me go through it again."

"All right. Just tell me the part you left out. Or I'll tell you. Charles was alone during part of the time that Shay was in the apartment. When you went back to the bedroom you saw that he was awake."

"No, he wasn't awake. He—he'd just fallen half out of bed."

"As though he'd come to and tried to rise and couldn't make it. So you and Sammy lifted him in again, and one of you or both of you jumped to the conclusion that he had made a round trip to the hall where Shay sat telephoning and—"

"No—no. That's not the way it was."

"What way then?" The structure rising between them was all but tangible. He had to wreck it before it became indestructible. "Louise, look at me. I'm your friend. I'm afraid that I'm much more your friend than I am an officer of the law." But the structure stood strong. When she spoke at last he was unhappily aware of a too-long lapse of time. Louise was one to whom the truth came quickly, instinctively.

"I couldn't have jumped to any conclusion, because when I found Charles lying that way I didn't even know that Captain Shay was dead. I called out to Sammy to help me, and almost at the exact same moment I heard a noise that must have been the crashing tray. I didn't care what it was or why. I just waited for Sammy. I guess she phoned for you before she came."

"And she helped you with Charles and didn't say a word about what had happened outside?"

"She did say something like 'He's dead,' but I thought she meant Charles because I'd got such a shock myself when I saw him. And then I remember that she said she wanted to show me something, but I was afraid to leave Charles again. He seemed so feverish—delirious—I—I thought that in his delirium he might hurt himself."

"I see. Well, it makes more sense than the way you told it to Inspector Furniss. But of course it cancels out this confession you've been mulling over in your mind."

"Grid!" Then she said in a small, lonely voice, "This morning was so beautiful."

He became a one-armed driver. He put his other arm around her, drawing her head to his shoulder. The structure toppled. In a little while she said, "I know you're my friend, Grid. Ask me anything you like."

"We're practically at the gates of Parkside. I'm about through with my inquisition, except for one relatively harmless question.

Did you ever hear of a person named Madge Carter?"

"No—I— That's funny. Let me think. The name sounds familiar. I could swear I heard it somewhere—and not so long ago."

He felt that she was honestly trying, not attempting to cover. "Take your time. It will come to you. And when it does, tell me."

"I will. What's the number of Charles' room?"

"Six seventeen."

There was no more talk for the remainder of the drive. As they left the car Nelson's long legs sprinted to keep up with Louise. In the subdued elegance of Parkside's entrance hall he stopped to present his credentials to the capped receptionist. When he turned around Louise had disappeared.

He took an elevator to the sixth floor. He found the room and paused for a moment outside the open door. He did not see Louise because the interior was partially blocked by a screen. He heard a recognized voice say, "Your husband is lucky. I don't believe he'd have been admitted for anybody but Dr. Randolph. We're so crowded. As a matter of fact, this room has only been unoccupied since five o'clock today. The poor lady who had it passed away and—"

He entered hurriedly. The nurse stopped talking and looked up at him, her cheerful gray eyes smacking with an almost audible plop against his curly white hair. He saw with relief that Louise had not been listening to her. She was kneeling beside the bed, alone with Charles.

He smiled at the nurse. "Are you Miss Hartshorn?"

Lowering her gaze to the region of his mouth, she said tentatively, "Yes?"

"I spoke to you on the phone a while ago. I'm Nelson." He glanced toward Louise, then shaped a silent question. He placed a finger on his lips.

Miss Hartshorn's plump face took on a look of great knowing. She nodded eagerly and went into such a remarkable pantomime that an empty-handed policeman materialized and made stealthy exit with a package. Nelson shook his head in congratulation. She flushed with pleasure.

Louise tore herself away from Charles. "Why have they left him lying here without any attention? Where's that doctor? He was in such a hurry to get here. Where is he, Grid?"

Nelson said, "Miss Hartshorn, didn't he call to give you any instructions?"

"No, but if he said he was coming tonight, he'll come. Perhaps he's stopped off to look in on some of his other patients. He's a busy man, you know." She added reprovingly, "Besides, the patient isn't lying here without attention. His temperature has been taken, and he's been made comfortable. In cases like this there isn't much else can be done until certain tests are made. We may know more when the cerebrospinal fluid—"

Louise said, "In cases like what?"

Miss Hartshorn hesitated. "Why, *encephalitis lethargica*. I understood that Dr. Randolph—"

Nelson began to curse under his breath. He looked at Louise anxiously. She said, "What?"

He stepped between her and the capped matronly figure. "A form of sleeping sickness, Louise, but Nurse has Charles confused with another patient who was admitted at the same time. Charles' entrance card has 'influenza' written on it, and that only because they have to write something." To himself he added fiercely, A fine thing to spring with no firmer basis than a snap diagnosis! He thought fleetingly of a man he knew who had been pronounced cured of encephalitis lethargica. He moistened his lips and said, "I'll find out if Dr. Randolph is in the building." He lifted the bedside telephone and spoke softly into it. After a few moments he hung up.

Louise looked at him. "Well?"

"He doesn't seem to be in the building. But one of the nurses thinks she saw him a few moments ago on the third floor. They'll—"

Louise said imperiously, "Call Dr. Purcell."

Miss Hartshorn came out from behind Nelson. "Would that be Dr. Vivian Purcell? I believe he's a member of our staff, too, but it's extremely unlikely, unless Dr. Randolph calls him for consultation, that he'd be willing to—well, professional ethics make it im—"

Louise cried, "Dr. Randolph is a stranger to us; he came because of—because of an emergency. But Dr. Purcell's our family physician, and I want him here at once—no matter where he is or what he's doing, Grid. He's got to come; he will if I speak to—"

Nelson caught her. "Take it easy. Please get her some water, Nurse. She's all in."

Miss Hartshorn became efficient. She seated Louise and forced her head between her knees.

Nelson lifted the phone again and asked for information. Grimly he called Dr. Purcell.

Chapter 10

Dr. Purcell was awakened and impelled to action by the urgency of Nelson's summons. He came to the hospital and took over. He looked and acted like a country practitioner, but there was a blend of shrewd intelligence and common sense behind his bluff bedside manner, and he was not an alarmist. His presence canceled out a large portion of the day's horror for Louise. Nelson saw her straighten as she transferred some of her load to the man's willing shoulders. Even Miss Hartshorn, resentful of Dr. Purcell's usurpation, unbent when he said to her, "I'll be pleased to have you carry on with me, Nurse, if it doesn't inconvenience Dr. Randolph."

He pinched Louise's pale cheek. "That's one way to produce color, but a better way is sleep. This fellow will be needing everything you've got when he begins to sit up and take notice." He shook hands with Nelson. "Get her a hot drink and see that she's tucked in. Don't take any nonsense from her."

Louise said, "Can't you tell me—?"

"I can tell you what anyone with half an eye could tell you. The poor lad's been overworking. He's so worn out that Nature got disgusted and decided to do for him what he didn't have sense enough to do for himself. If you want me to spout out a pretty list of Latin complications you're in for a disappointment. Now scat. I'll see you tomorrow."

Nelson took her home. She was so quiet on the way that he thought she had dozed off. He was startled when she sat up suddenly and said, "Grid, it's just come to me."

"What has?"

"Madge Carter. It was a phone call—a wrong number. A man asked to speak to Madge Carter. I repeated the name after him. I said, 'There's no Madge Carter here,' and he excused himself and hung up."

Nelson was interested. "And that's the only time you heard the name?"

"Yes, until you mentioned it."

"You're sure? I don't mean about the phone call—I mean associating it with the question I asked. You're so tired and you want to help so much that the two things might be confused in your mind."

"But I wasn't trying to think of it, Grid. It just popped up. Why did you ask, anyway? Who is she, and what has she got to do with all this?"

"I don't know myself. I saw the name penciled on something in Kyrie Martens' pocketbook." He spoke absently.

"Kyrie's pocketbook?"

He sent himself a message of hate. "Everything in the apartment was gone through, Louise. The police do that as a matter of course."

Louise said, "I understand. But women don't run out without their pocketbooks unless they're coming right back. Kyrie wouldn't. She's so well groomed, her pocketbook is a part of her costume."

Nelson hedged. "Women have extra bags, don't they?" Kyrie's pocketbook had stated plainly that it was the one in current use, but Louise had enough to worry about. He became inventive. "I think Kyrie's exit is easily explained. When she realized that Charles was ill she decided that you were in no shape for house guests. So she went back to the hotel without waiting for the arguments she knew you'd present. She'll probably send for her luggage in the morning."

"That doesn't sound like Kyrie, somehow. I should think she'd have wanted to stay to see if there wasn't something she could do to help. But you may be right. If she hasn't returned to the apartment since we left I'll call the hotel and see if she checked back in."

"I'll call. You're going to obey Dr. Purcell's orders and go to bed and let Sammy bring you a hot drink. Here we are." He got out and helped her to the sidewalk.

But Sammy was not on call to furnish the hot drink. She was stretched out on a couch in the little dressing room. She was sound asleep in her neat clothes. She had not even troubled to remove her shoes.

Nelson called her name. Then he leaned over and shook her. She murmured something and turned her face to the wall. His feelings were a mixture of worry and resentment. Ever since Sammy had come to work for him he had looked upon her as a tower of strength, and with reason. When she was needed, or thought she was needed, he had seen her skip a night's sleep without so much as a yawn of protest. This wholehearted renunciation of care was entirely out of character. Once more he tried to awaken her. "Sammy, are you ill?" She shifted her position again, but there was no change in her even breathing.

Puzzled, he took upon himself the task of heating milk for Louise. He added a sedative to it and brought it to the bedroom.

Louise, wearing gown and robe, was seated at the dressing table, staring blindly at her reflection. Her loosened black hair hung to her waist in a soft, glistening shawl.

"Come on, Ceres, get into bed and drink this."

She tried to laugh. "Ceres was the goddess of fertility, wasn't she? I don't know whether to be flattered or go on a diet, starting now." She looked at the milk distastefully.

"You can diet on your own time. This is my time."

She threw off her robe and got into bed. He sat down beside her and waited until she had emptied the cup.

"That's the girl. Now flat on your back."

"Did Sammy go home, Grid?"

"No, she's here—taking a nap. She's got sense." Invoking the power of suggestion, he yawned deliberately. "Close your eyes." He waited until the sedative took effect. Then he walked down the hall to where the policeman rested comfortably in a large upholstered chair he had brought from the living room.

Grinning, the policeman got to his feet. "This ain't such a tough assignment, Sarge."

"Did Sammy give you something to eat?"

"And how." He licked his lips. "It was worth the price of admission."

"Did she complain of being sick?"

"No, Sarge, except she sneezed a few times. *Is* she sick?"

"When did she decide to lie down?"

"About a half-hour before you came back. Something wrong?"

Nelson shook his head. "Questions are just a habit with me. I suppose if anyone had called or telephoned while we were gone you'd report it without my asking?"

The policeman looked sheepish. "Well, as a matter of fact, Sarge, nobody phoned, but there was a fellow rang the bell just a few minutes after the chief left. He didn't come in, though. Sammy spoke to him at the door. He was asking for a Miss Martens, and when he found out she wasn't here he blew in a hurry."

"What did Sammy say to him?"

The policeman gulped. "Search me. As soon as I saw it was all right and he was friendly I went back to the eats. But I got his name. Gene Holden. And I can tell you what he looks like. A thin nice-built guy with dark hair and eyes."

"Did you get his address, too, and did you ask him to show proof that Gene Holden wasn't a name he picked out of a grab bag?"

"Gee, Sarge, I—"

Nelson practiced control. "Remember to do that next time." He took a slip of paper out of his pocket and wrote a number on it. He gave it to the wilted policeman. "That's my home telephone. I'm going there now. Phone me if it's necessary—if Miss Martens turns up, for example. And have Sammy phone me as soon as she wakes. Stay put until you're relieved."

"Gee, Sarge, you won't—"

"No, I won't."

"Gee, thanks. I'll be on my toes after this."

Nelson drove to his apartment in the East Fifties. After he had taken a shower only a few hours warded off daylight, so he decided that bed was an impracticality. He shaved, dressed, made some coffee, took it into his pleasant living room, seated himself, and tuned the radio to an all-night program of recorded music. With singular inappropriateness Ysaye's *"Reve d'Enfant"* unwound an accompaniment to the grim assembling of his thoughts.

Charles Cotter comes home on furlough. Charles is sick. Enter Captain Shay. Exit Captain Shay. Charles's sickness is tentatively diagnosed as encephalitis lethargica, a disease of the brain. A disease known in some cases to bring about mental changes ranging from general weakness of intellectual powers to definite dementia and insanity. Dementia and Charles versus Captain Shay!

Nelson muttered, "I don't believe it." He thought of the man he knew who had recovered from a bout of encephalitis lethargica. An upright man whose moral fiber had slowly but markedly disintegrated.

He lit the reading lamp behind his chair and reached for a volume of an encyclopedia. He turned the pages until he found what he sought. His eyes traveled quickly, eliding as they went.

"Onset ... sometimes extraordinarily sudden, the patient falling asleep almost without warning ... delirious ... general symptoms are not in themselves distinguishable from those of other conditions. Headache is common ... temperature variable.... A persistent rise is a serious sign. Some cases are apyrexial throughout ... no characteristic eruption. In the mild abortive types the condition may suggest influenza and the nature of the illness can only be recognized by the development of late manifestations. Diplopia, or double vision, also occurs in the majority of cases and is due to some form of paralysis of the ocular muscles. Other ocular manifestations may occur, such as ptosis. At the onset the patient can usually be aroused and may then act with unexpected clarity ..."

Nelson closed the book with a snap and let it drop to the floor. He thought, Never. Not if I have to dream up a new and incontestable means by which Shay strangled Shay behind his own back.

He turned out the light, leaned back in the chair, and closed his eyes. A studio operator of catholic tastes had replaced *"Reve d'Enfant"* with Schubert's *"Der Tod and das Mädchen."* Nelson muttered, "That's a help," and conjured up a shadowy faceless image of Kyrie Martens, the "now-she's-here, now-she's-gone" figure of the night's events. Why had she run out at the time of Shay's appearance, not pausing to arm herself with either compact, cigarettes, or money? Why had she not returned?

He put his hand in his pocket. Then he remembered that after his shower he had changed clothes from the skin out. He switched off the radio, went into the bedroom, and found the lemon-colored slip of paper and the ration book in his recently shed suit. He studied the slip again. "Mr. Holden called." So it looked as though there actually was a man named Holden, or at least one who used the name consistently. Gene Holden. Nelson was glad he had not borne down too heavily on the well-fed policeman.

He glanced at the bedroom clock. Its hands were crawling toward five. He wondered if, in spite of conditions imposed by war, night service still endured at the Hotel Gascony. He went to the phone and discovered that it did.

A powerful voice, undaunted by the hour, rushed at him. "Hotel Gascony. Good morning."

"Is a Miss Kyrie Martens registered there?"

"Just a moment."

He waited. The voice returned and said, "Miss Martens checked out this evening."

"Are you sure she didn't check in again?"

"I have no record of it. I can give you her forwarding address if you wish. Care of Mrs. Charles Cot—"

"Thank you." Then he said hurriedly, "Don't hang up. Is there a Mr. Gene Holden?" Her answer surprised him. He had fully expected to draw a blank.

"Yes. Room 1403. I suggest that you call back. I wouldn't wish to disturb Mr. Holden unless it's an emergency."

"It's an emergency. Please connect me with his room."

"Very well."

Mr. Holden was a light sleeper. Or he was no sleeper at all. One short ring and his "Hello" sounded, fearful and breathless, as though he had come on the run. "This is Nelson of the Homicide Squad."

"Nelson of the— My God!"

"Hello, are you there?"

The answer came faintly. "I'm here. Tell me—"

Nelson said quietly, "Just what were you expecting?"

There was a pause at the other end. Gene Holden seemed to be taking time out. After a moment or two Nelson, speaking very distinctly, sent his home address through the mouthpiece of the telephone. "Have you got that? Remember, the name is Nelson."

Gene Holden repeated name and address mechanically. Then

his voice firmed. "What is this?"

"I want to talk to you. You have the option of paying me a visit alone or with a police escort."

"What do you want to talk about?"

"A girl named Kyrie Martens."

Gene Holden shouted, "If anything's happened to her I'll — How do I know this isn't a trap? How do I know you're not—?"

"Come and find out." Nelson replaced the receiver and went back to the other room. I'm getting better and better, he thought. I tipped him off. If he has anything on his conscience, instead of coming here he'll disappear so fast and so completely that Missing Persons will have to drop all previous commitments to flush him out. He could see Inspector Furniss wearing his most reproachful face, hear his reproachful voice. "Why didn't you go to the hotel, Grid, instead of phoning—or at least why didn't you put a tail on him? I've warned you that your unorthodox methods would land you in the soup someday."

He lit a cigarette, strode to the window, and stared out at the gray dawn. He was not really worried. He believed that presently there would be a ring at the bell to herald the arrival of Gene Holden, but he did not look forward to the interview with any great hope. He fervently desired that Gene Holden, whom he had never seen, would turn out to be a plug-ugly, a villain whose appearance alone would instantly dissolve the aura of suspicion clinging to Charles, Kyrie, and, yes, even Louise. Even Sammy. Yet the voice he had just heard did nothing to nourish the conception of a plug-ugly. Wishful thinking. And he knew it.

To pass the interval of waiting he began to plan his activities for the forthcoming day. They must begin with a complete investigation of every fact extant concerning Orrin L. Shay, starting as far back as the first World War, ending with his rudely nipped career on the radio, his visits to Washington, his—

"Washington," Nelson said aloud. He considered the thought that had just come to him and decided that it was a far more likely hypothesis than the one he had presented to Louise. Kyrie had been working in Washington. She had met Captain Shay under unpleasant circumstances. She had recognized his voice in the Cotter apartment and, rather than face him, she had lit out. Unpleasant circumstances. An elastic term. Unpleasant enough to cause her to creep up behind him—strangle him? How strong was Kyrie physically? That she was headstrong he knew, unless she had altered beyond recognition since childhood.

He said, "Damn it!" He did not like the thought. He wished that it were possible to tear up thoughts as one tore up words committed to paper.

The bell rang. Before he went into the hall to press the buzzer Nelson armed himself, not because he felt that it was necessary, but as a sop to Inspector Furniss and his orthodox methods of procedure.

It appeared that Gene Holden was practicing his own brand of caution and that entrance by stealth was no part of it. He had pushed every bell in the vestibule. An eruption of buzzers and enraged sleep-heavy voices plagued the hall. Holden climbed the stairs ostentatiously, pausing to establish his presence on every floor. "Excuse it, I rang the wrong bell. I'm visiting Mr. Nelson."

Nelson grinned as the belligerent figure reached his landing. He stepped forward and said softly, "All right—you've created enough witnesses. Do you want to get me a dispossess in the bargain? You can be certain that if they find your dead body they won't have the slightest doubt as to where the responsibility lies."

He saw that Gene Holden had his hand in his pocket. His long fingers reached out suddenly, wound fast just below the bent elbow, and pressed down. "Relax and bring your hand out empty."

Holden looked murderous. "What's to prevent me from shooting through my pocket?"

"Nothing but the fact that your witnesses will become my witnesses—and this." Nelson's automatic shone dully in his left hand. "Come into my parlor and we'll try to determine reasonably whether there is any real need for these heroics."

Holden brought both hands to shoulder level. Nelson relieved him of the gun. "I hope you have a permit for this. Don't look so disgruntled. If you *did* use it I'd be mean enough to make a very silent corpse, and your errand would be entirely fruitless." He stepped aside. "You first. The second room on the right." He shut the door and followed his visitor.

In the living room Gene Holden whirled to face him. "Where is she?"

"That's what we're here to discuss. You can lower your hands." Nelson opened a desk drawer and dropped both guns into it.

Holden stared at him, his dark young face drawn and puzzled. Then he looked around the room, taking in the good masculine furniture, the rows of books.

Nelson said, "Exactly. No self-respecting thug would spend a moment here, but if you're still in doubt, read these." He handed him his police credentials, complete with photograph.

Holden moved over to the lamp. As the light struck the dark face Nelson searched it for traces of viciousness or weakness, or traces of anything that would render it suitable for casting in the role of Shay's murderer. He could see nothing but a rather attractive young man stamped with an unhappy expression that might indicate a recent quarrel with his girl or with his job, but hardly with the law. Again he heard the chief's voice raised in protest. "The trouble with you, Grid, is that you expect all criminals to be marked by lack of chins and ear lobes and brows. You never credit the fact that as often as not they've been marked by their close resemblance to noblemen and saints." But Gene Holden resembled neither a saint nor a nobleman. Wearing an Arrow collar or stripped to the waist, he might have posed as a composite specimen of average American manhood, with no sign of overemphasis to show that he *was* posing. He had good coordination. The better part of his brain was probably employed to govern his muscles. Yet his face was far from stupid.

Holden raised his eyes. He put the credentials on a small table and nodded.

"Let's sit down to it," Nelson said.

He watched Holden's legs fold, lowering him to the lap of the large chair. He seated himself directly opposite, offered a cigarette, put one between his own lips, and noted that the match Holden extended was quite steady.

Holden veiled himself in smoke. He said, "Just why has Kyrie Martens become the concern of the New York Homicide Squad?"

"I've proved my own status. It's only fair that you return the courtesy. Who are you besides being Gene Holden? How does Kyrie happen to be *your* concern?"

Holden said defiantly, "I met her in Washington. We worked in the same building. We became friends, and I managed to make my vacation coincide with hers. I knew she intended to come to New York, so I arranged to come too."

"Before you go I'll expect you to write down the address of the building in Washington where you and Kyrie are employed."

Holden said impatiently, "All right. You'll find that it checks. Now will you please—"

"Why did you call on the Cotters late last evening?"

"Miss Martens said I could. I had lunch with her, and she told me she was going to move out of the hotel to stay with her cousin. I asked her for a dinner date, but she said she would have something sent up to her room because she had a little packing to do. She had said before that she'd like me to meet the Cotters, and I asked if I could drop around tonight—I mean last night. And she said yes, if I didn't stay long, because Mr. Cotter was home on leave or something and she didn't want her friends to intrude on the reunion between him and his wife."

"But you phoned her room at about five-thirty?"

"Yes, I thought she might have changed her mind about dinner, but there was no answer." Then he said resentfully, "How did you know that?"

"Did it strike you as odd that when you rang the Cotter bell a policeman answered?"

"Certainly it struck me as odd. It struck me as odder that no one was home except the cook after I'd been—well, even if I had practically invited myself. But the cook told me that Mr. Cotter had been taken sick and sent to the hospital in an ambulance, so I figured the policeman was just left over from the general excitement, especially since he had his mouth full, and that made his hanging around understandable."

"The cook didn't tell you anything else?"

"No—was there anything else? Kyrie—?"

"She didn't tell you that Captain Orrin Shay had been murdered in the Cotter apartment?"

Holden leaned sideways and stubbed out his cigarette with more than necessary care. He said tonelessly, "No, she didn't tell me that." His difficulty in restraining a spate of additional words was manifest to Nelson.

"You know Captain Shay?"

"I'm not on speaking terms with him."

"No one is at the moment. He's dead. Was Kyrie Martens on speaking terms with him?"

"Why don't you ask her?"

"I'm asking you."

"I'm not her keeper."

"But you'd like to be."

Holden gripped the arms of the chair. "Did you bring me here to pry into my love life?"

"I brought you here for several reasons. One is to act as proxy for Kyrie."

"Miss Martens doesn't need a proxy. She's quite capable of thinking and acting for herself."

"When, as, and if I find her."

"What?"

"She's disappeared. I think that's not news to you. You look like a man who has spent a sleepless night. When I called your voice showed no evidence that you'd been rudely awakened—none of the huskiness or daze that characterizes a man dragged from his bed in the small hours. Perhaps you can explain that."

"Yes," Holden said readily, "I can explain that. A while after I came back to the hotel I called the Parkside Hospital. I thought it was only decent that I inquire about the state of Mr. Cotter. Of course I got nothing but the usual 'patient-is-doing-nicely' stuff, and when I asked if his family was with him the answer was no. Then, by coaxing a bit, I found out that Mr. Cotter had not been accompanied by anyone, nor had he received visitors since admittance. So I began to get uneasy. If Miss Martens wasn't at the hospital and she wasn't home, where was she? And just about ten minutes before you got in touch with me I rang the Cotter apartment again. I realized it was late, but I couldn't help it. The policeman answered, and I knew he couldn't still be hanging around for the sake of the meals he might cadge. He said Miss Martens wasn't in and began a sort of quiz, and I hung up. That's all there is to it."

"Why should you be uneasy about Kyrie? By the way, I have a right to her first name. We came from the same hometown. I assure you that I wish her well."

"You do?" Holden regarded him without warmth. He said bitterly, "She's a popular girl—she's often told me. Why shouldn't I be uneasy about her? She's alone in New York. I—"

"It won't wash. She's not alone. She has relatives."

Holden ignored that. "What was Captain Shay doing in the Cotter apartment?" The question seemed torn from him, escaping his rigid control.

"He was an acquaintance. He just dropped in for an informal visit."

Holden muttered something that sounded like "Damn funny."

"What's funny?"

"Huh?" Then he said tensely, "How—how was he murdered? Who did it?"

Nelson raised his broad shoulders.

"Was Kyrie there when—when he dropped in? Had she talked to him?"

"She was there. But she wasn't there when the body was discovered or when the police arrived."

Holden's jaw dropped open. He forced it back into place. He said hoarsely, "Now look here, Mr.—Mr. Nelson—" and seemed unable to continue.

Nelson said, "I presume you can account for your own movements up to the time of the killing?"

"Then you presume wrong. I don't know the time of the killing and I didn't bother to establish an alibi because I'm not gifted with second sight, but if it's any comfort to you, Shay was no loss, and if you let his death go down in police annals as an unsolved crime you'll be doing everybody a service."

Chapter 11

Nelson got up from his chair. He did a little jig step to flex his long legs. He said, "Don't you think it's time we really began to work with each other? I'm keeping an open mind about you. I'm keeping an open mind about Kyrie too. But I know she's been in Washington and I know that Captain Shay made frequent trips to Washington. It seems possible to me that he met Kyrie there—a possibility that leads to certain conclusions."

If Holden was a good actor this was one of his off moments. His laugh was an inferior performance. "Washington's crowded with people who never meet."

"All right. What kind of a job do you do there?"

"Clerical work."

"Is that how you developed those muscles?"

Holden set his mouth stubbornly.

"Are you a draft evader?"

Holden mimicked his tone. "No, I'm not a draft evader. Some clerical work is considered important enough to warrant deferment."

"I suppose you carry identification papers?"

Holden was silent. He seemed to be having a debate with himself.

Nelson said, "I think Kyrie's disappearance is a serious thing. We know she's not at the hotel, and if she'd returned to the Cotter apartment I'd have been notified." He gave that time to sink in. He walked over to the lamp behind Holden's chair and turned it off. "We don't need this anymore. It's morning." He looked at his watch. "Exactly seven o'clock. There's work to be done."

Holden's dark face was bleak in the weak cold light. He said hopelessly, "We haven't a single clue as to where she might be. How can we start?"

"We?"

Holden said, "They told me to cooperate with the local police if I had to. I guess I have to. I'm not carrying identification because I might go places where it would do me more harm than good. But it will be simple for you to verify the fact that I'm a member of the FBI."

Nelson nodded without surprise. "Does that go for Kyrie too?"

"Yes."

"And she uses the name of Madge Carter?"

Holden stared at him. "It's no wonder we've failed if you've been able to dig that up so fast."

Nelson smiled. "I didn't exactly dig it up. I pulled it out of a convenient hat. There's more coming. Captain Shay fell under suspicion, and the two of you were set to watch him." He sat down again on the edge of the chair. "I'm afraid that's about all I can produce without assistance."

Holden said, "Fell under suspicion is right—just suspicion—based mostly on the company he kept. We had no proof and we haven't been able to get any, though we've tried every trick we know, including an engineered street brawl to get possession of his wallet which contained nothing at all incriminating. We didn't believe he was the ringleader or that he had any interest in the matter beyond a financial one. He is—or was—a great spender—women and stuff—and although he had been making more money on the radio than he'd ever seen before, his talent for splurging seemed to develop along with his income. So our premise was that he wouldn't be averse to extra cash if opportunity knocked—even opportunity with a dirty nose. One or two incidents in his past bolstered that theory."

Nelson said, "If you'll tell me what particular guise opportunity wore it might help me to solve Shay's murder."

Holden shook his head. "Sorry. I can't tell you without permission from my bureau. Shay was only part of the job. The fellows behind him are the ones we really want, and, with all due respect to police methods, blundering would be fatal. Any sign that we're wise to what's going on would be all the tip-off they'd need to make them pick up their marbles and skip. Besides, they didn't kill him. If we're at all right, he was too valuable to them. Crooks with the contacts he had don't grow on trees."

"I see your point. I wish I didn't."

"Now don't go getting the idea that because they didn't kill him Kyrie did."

"That's just one of my ideas," Nelson said pointedly. "Of course if either you or Kyrie *were* responsible, I doubt if you'd be tried for it. However, you *do* think *they* might be responsible for her disappearance?"

"It's possible. She's supposed to be off the job for the time being, but maybe she stumbled into something."

"Where? in the Cotter apartment?"

Holden said angrily, "Well, why not? Shay was calling on the Cotters, wasn't he? Doesn't that make them as much involved as—as anyone else?"

"No." The syllable sounded overly vehement to Nelson's own ears. By way of canceling its effect on the startled Holden he elaborated: "The reason for Shay's call was perfectly innocent. He'd become acquainted with the Cotters by way of their rather famous jewelry repair shop, and as a result he visited them occasionally. That much I'm sure of." He paused. Worry was the only thing legible on Holden's face. He felt rather sorry for him. He said, "I'd suggest that you go back to the hotel and wait. It's quite likely that Kyrie might try to reach you there." He went over to the desk and took out Holden's gun. "Here—I hope you find a good use for it. I'll get in touch with you if anything happens from my end. I'll expect you to do likewise."

The two men shook hands. As soon as Holden had been ushered out Nelson went into the bedroom and called Furniss. The old man mumbled in answer but took on alertness as soon as he recognized the voice of his favorite assistant.

"What's up, Grid? I hope you're not disturbing my rest just to say good morning. I still had almost an hour to go."

Nelson told him of the interview with Gene Holden. "You have a drag with the FBI, Chief. You were hand in glove with everyone from Hoover to the janitor last winter before the case of Booming Beulah pulled you back to your own duties."

"Never mind the impudence." Furniss did not choose to remember that episode in his career. "I take it you want me to check Holden's story and find out the details of Shay's snide activities. Why don't you do it yourself? You've a perfectly good desk at headquarters, and long-distance phone calls are on the house."

"I won't be at headquarters this morning, Chief."

"Oh yes, you will. I have plenty I want to discuss with you."

"But you said you wouldn't give me much time to crack this thing. So I've got to crack it my way." It was a lie about not going to headquarters. He intended to arrive there before Furniss to examine Charles's pajamas for whisky stains. After that his plans were vague, but they did not include a conference with his superior officer.

"Hmmm." Furniss gave in with suspicious willingness. "All right. Maybe I'll get more accomplished if you aren't around. See you later."

"Chief, you're not planning to have Louise on the carpet again! You promised. And, besides, with this FBI angle—"

"I'll keep my promise, Grid, but not forever. Goodbye."

Nelson hung up, conscious suddenly that fatigue had moved in upon him. He went to the bathroom and splashed his eyes with cold water. He came out and reached for his hat and coat. Then he heard a key turn in the outside lock.

Sammy's voice said, "You home, Mr. Grid-dely?" She appeared at the bedroom door with a small package in her hand. Her eyes fastened upon the coat thrown over his arm. She said firmly, "No sir, you not going nowhere without your breakfast. I bound to have it all ready for you in five minutes."

"I drank a cup of coffee, Sammy." Nelson looked at her. She was heavy-eyed and something else. Embarrassed? Angry?

"Coffee ain't enough. You going to swallow a solid meal to stick to your ribs." She glanced at the untouched bed. "You didn't have no sleep."

"But you did," Nelson said. "Is your cold better?"

Sammy's eyes met his levelly. "I fixing to explain about my cold. Maybe we save time if you come in the kitchen while I put on your eggs."

"Not a bad idea." He meant the food and whatever else she so obviously needed to feed him. He became aware of a hollow of hunger in his stomach as well as a hollow of curiosity in his head.

On the way to the kitchen Sammy stopped to pick up the coffeepot and the cup. She said nothing while she put the small package on a shelf, fastened her apron, and went to work. Presently a good smell of bacon warmed the room.

"Don't bother to set a place inside. I'll eat here." Nelson sat down at the kitchen table. "What was it you wanted to explain, Sammy? I really am in a hurry."

Sammy laid a cloth on the table and set it rapidly. "I going to talk while you eating. I in a hurry my own self 'cause I want to get back to take care of Mrs. Cotter. Drink your juice so I can dish out."

She served Nelson with eggs and bacon and toast and poured coffee for him. He began to eat. The food tasted wonderful. His spirits lifted.

Sammy took the little package off the shelf and brought it to the table. She unwrapped it carefully. It was a bottle, less than half filled with brown liquid.

Nelson put his fork down. "What's that?"

"Keep on eating. It cough medicine."

He looked at her questioningly.

Her voice was resentful. "Leastways that what the ticket on it say."

He took the bottle from her hand and read the label. "Prescribed for Mr. Cotter by Dr. Purcell. Where did you get it?"

Her words came out at twice their habitual tempo. "Last night when you went away with Mrs. Cotter and Mr. Chief, he went away with Mr. Sugs, I fix myself and that policeman a bite, and after I wash up I look around for something else to busy me and I find poor Mr. Cotter's luggage bag and unpack it and put his clothes away. And I come on this here bottle and another one with the same ticket on it, only empty." She cleared her throat. "I sneezing and I don't reckon Mr. Cotter, he going to fret much if I dose up with his medicine. So I drink some big spoonfuls and hope it do me good." She looked at the bottle reproachfully. "But the next thing I know I plain dozing on my feet and I go lay down for a nap. But it ain't no nap. When I wake up again I got trouble to open my eyes 'cause they don't want to pay me no mind even if it daylight. I bothered, Mr. Grid-dely. I ain't never do that-a-way before when I got reason to stay awake, but I think they something mighty funny about this medicine."

A thought struck Nelson with such force that the shock of reception communicated itself to his hand. He almost dropped his coffee cup. He jumped up, pushing back his chair. He said warmly, while his long deft fingers rewrapped the bottle, "You don't have to be troubled or ashamed of yourself, Sammy. You did a perfectly sensible thing in taking that medicine for your cold." His tone said, A perfectly splendid thing.

"You ain't disappointed in me, Mr. Grid-dely?"

"Not a bit." He became somewhat incoherent. "Of course when a doctor prescribes medicine for one person it isn't always good for another—and it isn't always wise to go around sampling stuff—but in this case I think it's going to be good for everybody."

She was bewildered. "You mind saying that over? Seems someway I—"

"Not now." He gripped the bottle firmly. On the way to the door he stopped. "Do you feel all right?"

She nodded. "The same minute I got me some air I start improving. I about natural now."

"Good. Take care of yourself. Eat a big breakfast."

"But you ain't finish yours, Mr. Grid-dely."

"I'll make up for it another time. Good-by, Sammy. Bless you."

He drove straight to headquarters, climbed the broad stone steps, and strode down a narrow corridor to a small office. He sat down at his desk, took the bottle out of his inner pocket, and gave it a place of honor in front of him. Then he picked up the phone and called the police laboratory.

"Who's this—Kenny? ... Nelson speaking. Send one of the boys to my office. I've got something here I want analyzed.... I don't know—a drug of some sort.... Yes, as soon as possible. I'll phone for the report."

He sat back for a moment and contemplated without eagerness the bottom drawer of his desk. He had to steel himself to open it. The bundle was there all right. He took it out, untied the knot made by the conscientious Miss Hartshorn, removed the brown paper that had seen other usage, and reluctantly examined the pants of Charles Cotter's striped pajamas. There was a faint yellowish stain on the hem of one leg. When he bent his head to it he smelled the distinctive odor of scotch whisky. He said, "Hell," and looked betrayed. Because although Sammy's prize package might mean that matters had taken a rosier turn in regard to Charles's health, Charles's future loomed black.

A shadow was thrown over the desk and a hand stretched out for the pajamas. Involuntarily Nelson snatched them out of reach. Then he looked up and grinned at the laboratory messenger.

"Oh, it's you."

"Isn't that what you want me to take, Sarge—or have you been sleeping on the premises these nights?"

"I haven't been sleeping at all. The pajamas are just a souvenir of better days. This is yours. Be careful—it's a bottle. Ask Kenny to hurry it up."

"O.K. He won't like it—he's up to his ears—but he'll do it for you." The messenger walked out whistling.

The sound grated on Nelson's nerves. Guiltily he returned the pajamas to the drawer, shoving them back out of sight. The battered clock on the desk told him that it was a quarter to nine. That would give him time to make one phone call without risking a meeting with Furniss. Furniss usually arrived punctually at nine unless a case took him afield. Nelson drew the telephone toward him and asked for an outside line. He called Louise's number.

The policeman answered sourly. Evidently the delights of the assignment were beginning to wear off. He had nothing to report except that Sammy was missing. Nelson cheered him by promising to send a relief man over in short order. Then he asked to speak to Louise.

Her voice came prompt and husky. "Hello, Grid."

"Did I wake you?"

"No, I woke myself about ten minutes ago. Did you put something in that milk? I slept like a log."

"You were tired. By the way, if you're curious about Sammy, she's doing a double shift. She'll be there any minute to give you breakfast."

"She needn't have bothered. I can get something at the drugstore on the way to the hospital."

"You wait for Sammy. Regular visiting hours at Parkside don't start until ten-thirty. Chances are they won't let you see Charles before then."

"Grid, until I found the policeman here this morning I kept telling myself that I'd had a bad dream. Are you—are you getting anywhere? Kyrie hasn't come back. Did you call the hotel?"

He said cheerfully, "In answer to the first I think I'm getting somewhere. And I did call the hotel about Kyrie, but it was late and the operator was new and uncertain. So I'll call back today. But don't worry. I met a friend of Kyrie's who seems to know where she is.... No, don't ask me. It's a secret."

"You're not making this up just to—?"

"What a doubting Thomas. Look, Louise, you know how irrelevancies have always bothered me. Well, they're at it again—worse than Gremlins. All night I was haunted by something you said about cough medicine that Charles asked for when he was at camp. Did you send it?"

"Yes—two large bottles—so he could keep one on hand for emergencies." Then she said, "Never mind the Gremlin build-up. I'm old enough for a man-to-man talk. Why are you interested in cough medicine?"

"Did you mail the package yourself?"

She thought for a moment. "No, Mr. Loth was going to the post office, and he offered to take it for me."

"Oh. Well, I'll see you later."

"Grid—please—what's it all about?"

"I don't know. I've been doing some thinking, and it occurred to me that the medicine might have something to do with Charles' condition. Those things often contain drugs, and maybe he was impatient and overdosed himself."

"Grid, the prescription's mild. He's been taking it for years and it never hurt him. Dr. Purcell wouldn't—"

"But sometimes an allergy's set up, and what's good one year is poison the next. Forget it. It's beginning to sound thin even to me. Good luck, Louise." He hung up.

Sammy's tale and the conversation with Louise had drawn a line that seemed to point away from his intended course. He had thought, while waiting for Holden, that his day would begin with a study of Shay's life, but Holden had given him facts enough to make this unnecessary, at least for the time being. It was true that the new line wavered considerably, but in spite of that he decided to follow it. He left the building and drove to Cotter's. There was no parking space in front of the shop, so he left his car on the corner and walked to the entrance.

The eighteenth-century bonnet-top clock had been removed from the small window. In its place was a corpulent spindly-legged tureen dressed in a new coat of silver. Inside he found other changes. The gnome had also been replaced. A tall, thin old man was rearranging the shelves behind the counter. He turned as the door opened and greeted Nelson with smiling courtesy.

"Good day, sir. What can I do for you?"

Nelson smiled back at him. "I'm afraid I'm not a customer—just a friend of the Cotters."

"A friend?" The wrinkled face drooped mournfully. "Perhaps you haven't read the newspapers, sir. Mr. and Mrs. Cotter are having quite a bit of trouble, and if ever a pair deserved it less—"

Nelson said, "That's why I'm here. Mrs. Cotter asked me to look in to see that things are running smoothly. Not that she's worried. She told me that you'd be on the job. That is, if I'm correct in assuming you're Mr. Ben Seeger. She's often spoken of you. And I believe I was introduced to you when I visited her once."

The old man beamed. "I never did have a good memory for faces, but now that you mention it I believe you're right. So she's spoken of me, has she? Bless her. Yes, I'm Ben Seeger and I've been working at Cotter's, man and boy, for over forty years."

"You don't look old enough for that."

"And do you know why? Because I keep busy. Busy people never have the time it takes to grow old. Would you mind giving me your name again, sir?"

"I beg your pardon. Nelson. I come from the same town as Mrs. Cotter."

"Do you?" He regarded Nelson as though coming from the same town as Louise was a feat of great cleverness. "She's a fine woman. I was as pleased as the boy's own father when young Charles chose her for his bride. Have you heard how he is? I'm most anxious. I look upon him as a son. A terrible blow for his good name that a guest—and a patriot at that—meet such an end under his roof. I hope they find the scoundrel who did the deed."

Nelson said, "The doctor doesn't believe Charles' illness is serious." He thought that further preliminaries could be dispensed with. "As long as I'm here I'd like to have a few words with Mr. Loth."

That produced no good effect on the old man. A cloud settled upon his face. "Mr. Loth is not here. Much as I hate to put a man's character in jeopardy, there's small doubt in my mind that he's read the papers and taken advantage of the young couple's ill fortune to idle in bed while others do his share of the work. I sincerely hope that he'll be given his walking papers when Alex returns to the job. Do you know Alex, sir? An excellent fellow. The place doesn't seem the same with both Alex and Mr. Cotter away."

"Alex is the one who met with an accident. I don't quite remember how—"

"A hit-and-run driver. He might have been killed, but as it was he escaped with a fractured leg. A strange day and age we're living in, Mr. Nelson, when even a careful man like Alex isn't safe on the street."

"It *is* a strange day and age. But I'm interfering with your work. Where does Mr. Loth live?"

"He does himself proud at a fine hotel—the Murray."

"I see. Well, if you don't object I'll go inside and wait for a bit. Perhaps he'll turn up after all, with a good excuse for being late."

The old man said darkly, "He'll have a good excuse. That much is certain. Will you find your way, sir? I'll have to ask you to sit in the common workroom. Mr. Cotter is a bit fussy about his tools, so we're keeping his private quarters locked until the good day when he returns."

"Yes, I'll find my way. I know the place quite well." Nelson walked to the rear of the shop, pushed the door inward, and closed it behind him. He stood for a moment in the narrow hall that led to the workrooms. The common one, large and well lighted, was half open. He heard the sound of hammer taps, looked in and saw the two silversmiths busy at their work. They were engrossed and unaware of his eyes upon them. Quietly he moved on to the door of Charles's private quarters, a room used by his father and his grandfather before him, and specially equipped for the pursuit of his varied interests.

Nelson routed about in his pockets and took out a key with most of the bit filed away. He worked it around in the lock, turned the knob, and pulled. The door gave without a creak of protest. Thoughtfully he shut himself in the room.

Surprisingly little dust had settled there, and although the one large window was fastened tight the atmosphere was not stuffy. A dark rug covered part of the floor, spotless except for a sprinkling of ashes and here and there flecks of ingrained powder, residual, probably, of the grindstone on the workbench. The ashes reminded Nelson to light a cigarette. He dropped the match into one of several clean ash trays.

There were many shelves in the room, a rolltop desk, a small bookcase filled with technical volumes, several chairs, and three powerful lamps. In one corner stood a long pine table covered with the outmoded tools that had belonged to Charles's grandfather, a diamond cutter in his youth. There were, at a glance, rusted screw clamps, lathes, saws, lapidary sticks, a large cast-iron wheel, and a refractometer that was a museum piece. Prominent in the opposite corner, modernity, in the shape of the radio that Charles had built, bulked under a protective cloth of heavy stuff. Nelson lifted the cloth and peered beneath. He replaced it, stubbed out his cigarette, lit another, and sat down at the desk.

He raised the top and picked papers at random from the various cubbyholes, as though he were taking a cross section of the desk's contents. He riffled through bills and letters and notes, all directed to or written by Charles Cotter. Finally he let the top slam back into place.

His sad, deep-dug brown eyes lit upon a length of telephone wire, and he followed it to where the telephone rested on a small metal stand. He thought, I might as well call the lab while I'm waiting, and rolled the stand toward him. Then he thought, No, I'll have to go out to do it. This isn't an extension. It's Charles's private wire, and I guess Louise had it disconnected after he left. She's a practical soul. But when he lifted the receiver tentatively the dial tone sounded. He called the laboratory.

"Have you got it, Kenny?"

"You didn't give me much time, but I can tell you enough."

"Go ahead."

"That doctor must be a quack. A hell of a fine cough medicine—worse than the soothing sirups they used to feed to babies. *Tinctura camphorae composite*—"

"Speak my language."

"Paregoric to you—double the usual quantity of one fourth of a grain of opium or one thirty-seventh of morphine in each dram. Not fatal, of course—it needs at least four grains of opium to do a man in. Still, taken three times a day over a period of time, this stuff would make a rundown adult pretty sick. Will that do you? The rest seems to be usual—that Purcell had no reason that I can see to add paregoric to a perfectly—"

"Thanks, Kenny, thanks." Nelson broke the connection, thumbed through the telephone book, and dialed Dr. Purcell's number.

Chapter 12

The blond man said, "She's shamming again. They never learn." He swooped and gave her hair a vicious tug.

She couldn't stand the pain. She opened her eyes. "Haven't we met before?" she said.

"Sure. And I knew at the time you'd break down and have a date with me someday." He began to shout at her, pausing between questions for answers that did not come. "What did Shay tell you? What was the purpose of your arrangement to meet him at the Cotter apartment? What tricks did you have up your sleeve that made him decide to sell out?"

"I don't know anything."

The blond man shrugged. He lowered his voice. "Maybe that's true. Maybe she doesn't know anything." He turned to the comic strip character, whose appearance no longer held an element of humor for Kyrie. "What do you think about it, Max?"

"I think maybe yes she knew nothing when she came in, but

she knows enough now to make her release impossible."

"Who said anything about release?" The blond man grinned down at Kyrie. His grin made her nauseated. "What did you hope to gain by playing dead? You didn't think you'd ever be free to peddle what you overheard, did you?"

Kyrie said gamely, "I didn't hear a thing. I was too busy having a headache to listen."

"Your headache couldn't have come from the few playful little licks we gave you. Conscience, no doubt. It was naughty of you to murder Shay. He was so very, very fond of you. Do you know?— We thought at first that Mr. Cotter would have to take the rap for Shay, but we're glad that the evidence points elsewhere. After all, we've nothing against Cotter. In fact, we're grateful to him."

Kyrie sat up. She bit her lip to keep from crying out because everything hurt, including the separate hairs of her head. Her hot eyes strayed to the end of the bed and took the hurdle of the footboard. She saw with horror that her companion in misery was attempting to raise his head. She looked away and said quickly, "All right, I murdered Captain Shay. Where does that lead us?"

"It leads you to suicide."

"You're wrong. I'm not built that way."

The blond man's comprehensive stare conjured up a series of physical indignities upon her person. "You are built perfectly. It's a pity your life must end in such an ignoble way."

She kept talking to divert them from what was taking place on the floor at the foot of the bed. "If my life ends it won't be because I ended it. You can't make me. You'll have to do your own dirty work." She thought with wonder, I'm marvelous. I really sound brave.

"We'll do our own dirty work—with pleasure. But it will be suicide just the same, when the police get around to naming it. Of course they'll be aided in forming their opinion by the confession they find on you."

"I can't write," Kyrie said. "I'm a case of arrested development. Would you give me a drink of water? I'm sure you couldn't bear to have me die of anything so humane as thirst."

The blond man laughed. "She's very funny, isn't she? I'm going to miss her, but business is business." He spread his hand over her bruised face and shoved. "Lie down, sister, and rest for a minute. No, we're not going to let you die of thirst. We're going to shoot you. But first we're going to teach you to write in ten hard lessons, or maybe less, depending on how smart you are." He called out, "Walter, bring that artistic confession I scribbled, and bring a pencil and paper and a book."

The driver entered the room. "What do you need a book for?"

"So the lady can lean the paper against it while she writes."

"Well, I haven't got a book. Let her come inside to the table."

"Do it your way. Max and I are going out for a while. I'll expect to have the confession all signed and sealed by the time we get back. Be sure to burn my sample as soon as it's copied. If she's stubborn you know what to do. Not where it shows though. When the police find her they're going to have enough trouble trying to figure why a suicide's face should be so roughed up. Maybe I'd better put in a P.S. saying that Shay beat her."

Walter said, "Why don't you get her to write the note before you go, so's we'll be finished with the whole thing? Using my place wasn't in the bargain. I want it to myself again."

"Don't be a fool. You can't stay here even after we get rid of the bodies. It's too dangerous. Somebody might remember something. You'll have to move."

"Nuts." The driver was disgusted. "Next time you got people to bump off take them to a hotel or something. I had a girlfriend all lined up to come here today, and by the time I find a new flop she'll be cooled off and—"

"Shut up. Look at all the money you're earning and the fun you're having. Is your girlfriend as good-looking as that?" He pointed at the bed.

"No, she ain't, but—"

"Then what are you kicking about? If you only had sense enough to grasp your opportunities, a skirt in the hand is worth a frill off the street any—"

"I can't stand any more of this." The unexpected voice rose from the floor, powerful, as though every bit of force the injured man could muster had gone into its production.

Kyrie groaned, struggled to sitting posture again, and saw the white-knuckled hand reach up to grip the footboard. Why didn't he have sense enough to wait until they'd gone? she thought despairingly. With only the driver left we might have— Then, as the upper part of his body appeared above the bed, she saw that his face was on fire and that his eyes had a mad glint.

"Well, what do you know about that?" Walter said. "I guess you didn't hit him good, Max."

"You try your hand," the blond man ordered. "Not too hard. My grandmother always told me never to have a corpse around until the moment I was ready to get rid of it. That's right. That will hold him."

Kyrie heard the blow, cringed from it as though it had been aimed at her own aching head.

The blond man watched her. "Don't worry. We'll put you out of your misery soon. Just copy what I wrote, and when I get back you won't have a care in the world. Come along, Max."

Max said, "I wish you would wait until tonight. I do not like this. It is too risky."

"I've got to risk it. We missed out last night, didn't we? One thirty-three knows more about what's going on in this country than the President. He'll give me a new prospect to contact, and I won't have to waste time feeling around for one and maybe run into another snag. Besides, that old fool should be easy to handle. You're over him, and he'll take orders. All you have to say is that under the circumstances you're taking it upon yourself to close up for the day. So what are you afraid of? I'll wait under cover, and when the coast is clear I'll—" The voices were cut off abruptly by the slam of the door.

The driver placed his big hands on Kyrie's shoulders. For the first time he looked at her with interest. "Up on your feet, babe. We'll get the chores done first."

Nelson was surprised to discover that he had been sitting at Charles's desk for more than an hour, sorting his thoughts to the tune of muted hammer taps and, at intervals, the sound of the silversmiths' voices. Then he heard voices from another direction, one of them loud and angry. He got up quietly, closed and locked the door behind him, and stood listening in the narrow hall.

Ben Seeger was saying stubbornly, "Until I hear to the contrary from Mrs. Cotter, we stay open as usual. Not in the forty-odd years that I've been employed here has Cotter's ever—"

The angry voice climbed high. "Listen to me, old man; I have been noticing for a long while that your usefulness is outlived. In the absence of Mrs. Cotter I am in charge. If you do not choose to honor my orders I shall suggest that you be retired on a small pension."

Ben Seeger said remotely, "First you'll have to find somebody stupid enough to heed your suggestions. I doubt if either Mr. or Mrs. Cotter will fill that bill."

Nelson made his entrance. "I've been waiting for you, Mr. Loth."

The brown nutcracker face pivoted toward him, seeming to court the danger of snapping off at the thin neck. But the words that followed were addressed to Seeger. "Since when do we permit people to wait in the workroom and interfere with the smiths?"

Nelson said, "It's quite all right. I'm here at the request of Mrs. Cotter."

"At the request of—" Loth's sharp eyes stabbed at his face, at his white hair.

"Yes, we've met before," Nelson stated calmly. "You recognize me. I came in one day when the unfortunate Captain Shay was here."

"You're a policeman," Max Loth said flatly.

Seeger was surprised. "Well, now, I didn't know that. You told me you came from Mrs. Cotter's hometown."

"Policemen have to be born somewhere."

"I never had any quarrel with the law myself," Seeger said slowly. "Why, I can remember—"

He had to be cut off. His leisurely pace was giving Loth time to think things out. "I'm sure you've always been a model citizen," Nelson said conclusively and meant it. But it was too late.

The gnome had accomplished a right about-face. His next speech was well buttered. "Perhaps you can advise us, sir. I was suggesting that, with Mr. Cotter stricken so sadly and with a close friend struck down in his prime, it would be a mark of respect if we closed the shop for the day."

Nelson said, "The suggestion does you credit, but it can be discarded on two counts. First, Mr. Cotter has not been stricken so sadly, and second, Captain Shay was not a close friend."

Loth made a sucking noise, tried to look as though he had made no noise at all, and said, "Is that so? I was led to believe that Mr. Cotter's condition was serious."

"Who led you to believe it?"

"Why, I did what anyone interested in the welfare of Mr. Cotter would do. The moment I saw the paper this morning I called the hospital and got all the information I could."

"Which wasn't much, I imagine. I called, too, and received the stock answer that the patient was resting nicely."

Mr. Loth said airily, "Ah, but I wasn't satisfied with that—I mean I was glad to hear it, naturally, but I wanted more reassurance and not, as you put it, the stock answer. So I asked to be connected with his room and learned that it was, alas, not so simple after all."

"Well, you can be entirely reassured now. I presume you spoke to his nurse—a charming woman but inclined to look on the dark side. I went even farther. I spoke to his doctor—not the one who called last night; he seems to have dropped out of the picture—but the family physician. He tells me that in some strange way opium had been added to a cough medicine which he, himself, prescribed for Mr. Cotter, who took it unwittingly and with disastrous but far from fatal results. By this time, however, his stomach has been washed out and he's being treated for drug poisoning. The doctor predicts a speedy recovery."

Max Loth coughed. "A pharmacist's mistake, no doubt. Lucky that the doctor discovered it."

"Very lucky."

Ben Seeger smiled happily. "That's good news. Yes sir, I couldn't be better pleased if that boy were my own son."

Loth said, "I suppose that Mr. Cotter will have to spend most of his furlough in the hospital?"

"I hope he'll have at least a few days in which to enjoy himself," Nelson said.

Loth fidgeted with his tie. Nelson watched his hands. "Did I understand you to say that you were waiting for me, Mr.—er—"

"Yes. That's what I said."

"You have a message from Mrs. Cotter, perhaps?"

"No."

Loth looked at him. "What was it you wanted, then?"

Nelson said pleasantly, "I just wanted to talk to you."

"Well, I am at your service, unless it is something you wish to discuss in private." He transferred his gaze to Ben Seeger.

The old man muttered, "I'll just step into the back—"

Nelson stopped him with a gesture. "No need of that, Mr. Seeger. I wanted to talk to Mr. Loth and I have talked to him."

Loth said, "I confess I am at a loss. Perhaps I missed the significance of our conversation, but it hardly seemed important enough to warrant your waiting."

"In the face of your anxiety concerning Mr. Cotter's welfare I don't see how you can say that." Nelson's voice was reproachful. "Wasn't it important for you to hear that he's out of the woods?"

"Of course—of course—and I appreciate your coming here just to set my mind at rest. Now if you'll excuse me—" He headed for the door.

Ben Seeger said, "Are you taking a holiday anyway?"

"No, I'll return. But there is a small errand I must undertake first—a business errand—*with your kind permission.*"

Nelson said, "I'll stay and keep you company for a while, Mr. Seeger. Mrs. Cotter said she would call me here after she's seen her husband." He bowed to Max Loth. "With *your* kind permission."

Loth gave it hastily. "Make yourself comfortable. Any friend of Mrs. Cotter's—" That was his exit line. He opened the door and walked out with controlled dignity.

Under his breath Nelson counted to ten. Then he smiled at Ben Seeger. "I find I'm out of cigarettes. I'll see you again." He went to the door, drew it toward him, and stood on the threshold. He looked up and down the street. He saw Max Loth on the curb several doors away. He saw him lift his hand to hail a taxi. The taxi drew up and he entered it, but before it rolled off another man sprinted out of a nearby drugstore and climbed in.

It was Nelson's turn to sprint, and his long legs readily lent themselves to the undertaking. He reached the corner, jumped into his car, and got under way.

Traffic was surprisingly heavy in view of the fact that gas was at a premium, but he had little difficulty in keeping the taxi in sight and in preserving enough distance to prevent possibility of suspicion from its occupants. His difficulty lay in another direction, far back in his brain. He had to plow through a welter of extraneous matter to bring it into the open. His glimpse of the second man had brought instant recognition. And that was strange. For Nelson had believed he was speaking literally when he told Loth that Dr. Randolph was out of the picture. He had neither gone to Parkside to see how his latest patient was progressing, nor had he been at his home or his office when Dr. Purcell tried to contact him. Dr. Purcell had also volunteered the information that Randolph's housekeeper sounded rather disturbed about him. She needn't be disturbed, Nelson thought. For her employer is safe and sound in a taxicab with a man named Loth. Or is he?

After the war, Nelson thought, the electron experts will have to get busy on a device for cops, so they can tune in on their suspects under conditions like this. He would have given much to learn what was taking place between Loth and his companion.

He was driving down Seventh Avenue now, a good safe distance behind the cab. Traffic signals worked with him as if by plan. Each time another vehicle shut off his view the red light showed, and when it changed again he was able to pick up the trail.

At Thirteenth Street the cab turned west. Nelson crawled until he reached the corner. He saw it a block away and followed after. It came to a halt before a low building in the center of the Eighth Avenue block, and the two men got out. It was Randolph who paid the driver, Loth standing by with his nasty face averted. Then he and Randolph started to climb the steps of the building. But as soon as the cab had rolled away they reversed their course.

Caution, Nelson thought. Good. It proves I'm onto something. He turned off the ignition, pocketed the key automatically, and left the car. He began a shambling saunter, managing to look as though he had been part of the neighborhood for years.

A small boy came catapulting out of a doorway, collided with him, picked himself up, and began to swear.

Nelson said, "Want to earn a dime, fellow?"

"Maybe."

"I need protection. All you have to do is walk along with me until I say 'enough.'"

The little boy eyed him suspiciously. He was eight at most. "My old lady didn't raise no dopes. Let's see the dime."

"Here it is."

The boy snatched it. "All right, but I ain't going on no hike in the woods for a dime. You better say 'enough' quick." He walked along at Nelson's side.

Now, Nelson thought, if they happen to look back they'll see pop and the kid out for a stroll. But it was unnecessary camouflage. They did not look around.

"What are you staring straight ahead for, mister?"

"It's always a good idea," Nelson said.

"Have you got another dime?"

"What for?"

"I want to buy some butts for my big brother."

"Is it his birthday?"

"Only sissies got birthdays."

"Let him earn money to buy his own cigarettes."

"He could lick you."

Nelson said absently, "I'll take him on sometime." The pair ahead were crossing the street at Ninth Avenue. They passed a corner saloon and turned in a few doors beyond it. Nelson said, "Enough." Weakly he tossed a coin into the air. His convoy caught it and was off like a shot.

Nelson quickened his pace and crossed the street. He slowed up again, hunched his shoulders, and shambled on. The first door after the saloon led to a tailor shop, the second to a pizzeria, the third to a house, the fourth to a stationer's. Out of the corner of his eye he saw that the vestibule of the house was empty. He walked up the stone stoop and took a quick glance at the tarnished bell plate set in the stuccoed wall.

"Dreher—Vespiglio—Sternfels—Tilstrom—Binniker." All the names but Vespiglio's were penciled in, which told Nelson only that Vespiglio was or had been a businessman at some time in his life. And this he added to his collection of useless information. He discovered gratefully that there was something wrong with the lock on the door. It did not fasten. He grasped the knob, pushed, and entered the dark high-smelling atmosphere of the hall. Somewhere in the upper regions he heard a slam. Maybe, he thought. But I'll be thorough.

So, starting with the ground floor, he listened at every door on the way up, the sum total of his garnering being a child's sick wail, the whir of a sewing machine, an old voice raised in song, and the sudden rushing sound of cheap plumbing. With the exception of the first apartment, which apparently ran through, there were two doors on each floor. This made his task risky, but he reached the third floor without being surprised from the rear. And there he received a dividend in the form of Loth's thin utterance.

"It was a mistake to bring them here in the first place." That was Loth.

"You said it, Max." That was unidentified. From it Nelson reconstructed a brute with coarse lips set, for the moment at least, in lines of passionate conviction.

"Shut up, both of you." That, strangely enough, was Randolph exhibiting the stronger half of a dual personality.

"But I ask you, how will you carry them out of here in daylight?" Loth again. "You must listen to me. I was right when I advised you not to go to Cotter's. I am right this time too."

"Pull yourself together," Randolph said and laughed. "Very well, I took a chance and lost. But I made precautions against losing, and so no harm has been done. You let that dick get under your skin. He was bluffing. I sized him up last night. If I'd come into the place with you there'd be something to worry about. But I didn't, and I'm still playing it smart. Why do you think we've let them live this long? The answer, as I said before, is you never know. We're going to put that dead meat back on the hoof, and then he and the lady will march out of here with pal Walter and you and me to keep them company. Just a nice friendly group on the way to the country for target practice. It's quite simple."

There was a silence. And then came a new voice. A plaintive, weary voice that plucked at Nelson's spine. "Perhaps you gentlemen would like me to adjourn to the drawing room while you talk shop."

Nelson's first impulse was to leap. Sweating, he repressed it. My gun, he thought with agonized longing. My gun—in the desk drawer! Then he stiffened. Only his eyes moved, seeking a hiding place. But there was no hiding place. And there were footsteps climbing with infinite stealth to where he stood.

Chapter 13

That stealth presaged no good intention. He turned sharply, girded for battle. When he saw who it was he dropped his fighting stance and tamely placed a finger on his lips. He was bewildered, suspicious. Friend or foe? And if friend, how had the man found his way to this place? While he wondered he acted, descending four steps to grip the arm of Gene Holden, whispering, "Hush," imperatively, pulling him down the rest of that flight, down all of the next, not pausing until the ground floor was reached.

Holden spoke, low-voiced and fast. "She's here. Kyrie's here. How did you know?"

"I tailed a man. How did you know?"

"I got a message—a note she'd dropped out of the window—weighted by her ring. It landed on the sill of an apartment beneath. The woman had a box fastened there where she kept her butter and milk. She saw it when she was starting to fix breakfast early this morning, but she didn't bring it until a little while ago. Couldn't get away sooner. Kyrie had promised that whoever delivered the note would receive a reward of money, and when I paid the woman she told me the address and the name of the tenant above her—top floor—Walter Hinkle. From her description of him, just a hireling." He added softly, "If Kyrie's hurt I'll kill him."

"There are at least two other men in the apartment besides him. Have you your gun?"

"Yes."

"Give it to me. You get help. Call Inspector Furniss at—"

"No, I'm going up. I'll keep the gun. I'm a good shot."

Nelson saw that argument would produce no result. Holden looked ready to lay siege to a city. He looked like a pale knight, drenched in fanaticism. Briefly Nelson debated the advisability of going for aid himself. But, considering Holden's state, that would be tantamount to fostering a one-man crime wave. The group upstairs might wait for a while before they emerged. On the other hand, they might appear at any moment. He had to make the best of it. He had to stay.

He whispered, "Well, anyway, I'm glad to see you've changed your tactics since this morning. I shudder to think of the results if you'd barged in on them the way you did on me. Try to continue being just a little bit reasonable. I was listening while you crept up so cautiously. I heard a woman's voice, presumably Kyrie's, and I heard enough to assure me that she's in no immediate danger. They plan to walk her out of here. If you break in you'll do her no good. There's not a vantage point on that floor—nothing to duck behind. Our best bet is to camp here under the stairs and wait—" He broke off. "We start camping now."

Unresistingly Holden allowed himself to be drawn beneath the stairs. He had caught the sound too. A lumbering descent. He crouched at Nelson's side.

Both men stuck their heads out a fraction just as the large figure went through the door. Nelson, still gripping Holden's arm, could feel the muscles hardening for a leap. He hung on, and Holden stayed with him, timing his words with the door's closing. "That's Walter Hinkle. From the woman's description I'm sure of it. Oversized and flashily dressed."

"I hope you're right," Nelson said. "There couldn't be two like that under one roof. Well, the odds are lessened against us. He'll be back, though. Probably getting a car." He shrugged. He took the lead. "Come on. We'll chance it."

On the second floor their path was crossed by a little girl carrying a shopping bag. She looked at them without curiosity, and they looked back. Nelson grinned in passing because Holden's face was so suspicious of her and she was so authentic.

Just below the third-floor landing they paused by common consent. Through the rear apartment seeped the ugly noise of something being dragged across the floor. Loth's voice whined, "If this hasn't revived him nothing will. We must wait until it is dark. I tell you that he will not be able to walk out of here."

Then vigorous slaps commingled with the splashing of water and Randolph saying with fine humor, "If we could wake him for a moment he'd tell us what to do."

Nelson muttered, "Oh," and saw light. Holden raised a warning hand because the next voice was Kyrie's.

"Can't you see you're only making him worse? Let me—"

It needed neither ears nor eyes to judge what followed. Randolph shouted angrily, "Max, you fool! Haven't we got enough with one dead weight? Do you want to put her out too?"

Simultaneously Nelson and Holden took the remaining steps and tried to force the door. Nelson regained his presence of mind in time to say hoarsely, "It's Walter." He matched his shove to the lock's release and he and Holden were within, and Max stood before them, a pasty, gasping replica of his gnomelike self.

Kyrie cried out, and Holden's eyes were drawn to her. He changed color. He looked down at the gun in his right hand, then shoved it at Nelson. "Hold this," he said, and, rid of it, his clenched fist rose and pounded against the side of Loth's head. Loth fell screaming. Holden muttered, "Get up. Get up and fight."

Nelson saw Kyrie's dry swollen lips move. "He's not important, Gene. It's this one." But Holden was drowning in his own rage. He did not hear.

She was seated at the table, a blank sheet of paper before her. Her eyes looked out of dark encircling shadows and fixed upon Nelson. Suddenly she got up. He moved toward her, but she warded him off. She stumbled into the next room. He heard water running.

He was holding the gun. He was pointing it at the blond stocky man who, last night, had been Dr. Randolph. Incredibly the man was smiling. He seemed about to launch into speech. Nelson waited to hear what he would say. It was hard for him to wait. Still pointing the gun, his eyes roamed to a corner where lay a huddled mass of torso and limbs.

The man who had been Randolph said blandly, "If you're here in your official capacity I gather that things are not what they seem."

"Things are exactly what they seem," Nelson answered. Behind him Loth screamed again, hit the floor again. He rejoiced. That lovely delicate girl! He would have welcomed the opportunity to get in a few blows himself. He brought his attention back to the blond man. "You were saying?"

The blond man peered around him at the hysterical Loth. "He summoned me to treat a sick man. A doctor finds himself in some strange situations, but he rarely questions them until his work is done."

"Is your work done?"

"No. The poor fellow you see lying there unconscious is suffering from concussion. He must be moved to a hospital."

"Moving people to hospitals seems to be your favorite occupation," Nelson said. "It strikes me that as a happy medium you should have moved him long ago—to a bed or a couch. He doesn't look very comfortable." Behind him he heard a thud that sounded final. He said over his shoulder, "You've had your innings, Holden. I'll take it from here while you watch out for Walter."

Kyrie came from the other room carrying a pillow and a glass of water. She looked at Loth, then Nelson. She said, "He's got a gun in his waistband. Get it, or likely as not he'll recover enough to shoot one of us in the back."

Holden knelt and found the gun, handling Loth as though he were a discarded garment. He arose and said, "Kyrie, are you all right? Your face."

"They didn't break anything. I'll recover." She was trembling, but her voice was steady. She sat down on the floor beside the inert body in the corner. She slid the pillow under the battered head and tried to force water between the slack lips.

Nelson said, "Don't do that. He might choke."

She put the glass down and began to chafe the man's wrists. "Gene, who's your boyfriend?"

Nelson swallowed a lump that rose out of nowhere. "I was your boyfriend long before I met Holden. I'm Grid Nelson."

"Grid Nelson." She turned toward him and smiled a heartbreaking smile. "Fancy meeting you here after all these years."

"Can you talk while we're waiting?" She's beautiful, Nelson thought. Even like this she's more beautiful than anyone I've ever seen.

"Must we wait? The place palls after a while. And this man needs help."

"I know. We'll get out as soon as we can. But we don't want

Walter to come back to an empty house."

She caught her breath. "I forgot about Walter. Be careful, won't you? He's a monster."

Holden said, "Did he hurt you too, Kyrie?"

"He tried."

"And this one?" He pointed to the blond man.

For the first time the blond man lost his smile.

Nelson said, "Save him for later, Holden. Just go over him once lightly to see if he's armed."

Holden obeyed, but not to the letter. His searching hands were anything but light. "If he's got a gun he's swallowed it."

"Of course I'm not armed. I'm a medical man. As I told you—"

"Then dose yourself for this," Holden said and hit him across the mouth.

"I know what kind of a medical man he is." Kyrie was attempting to straighten the limbs of her adopted charge. "I know a lot about him, including two of his names. Edward Long doesn't count—but Eric Lessner does, because he shut Loth up when he called him by it—"

"Eric Lessner," Holden repeated. Then he said quickly, "Don't talk now," and looked at Nelson.

Nelson understood. He shook his white head. "There's no point in trying to maintain secrecy, Holden. Kyrie will have to talk sooner or later—to the police—and so will these men, if you can find it in your heart to leave them mouths to talk with. But I promise you that the police will cooperate with your bureau and that the story won't break until your pals in Washington give the word."

Kyrie said, "Relax, Gene."

"Why did they bring you here?" Nelson asked.

The blond man, or Long, or Lessner, wet his lips. "I never saw this girl before in my life until I set foot inside this place. But it doesn't even take medical knowledge to judge that she's under a strain. She's obviously received a blow on the head and is hardly accountable for—"

"It's a good thing it doesn't take medical knowledge to judge that," Nelson said. He felt Holden's advance. He staved him off with his left arm. "By the way, do you usually come visiting unprepared? Where's your black bag?"

Kyrie's patient groaned. She said helplessly, "He's in pain and I don't know what to do for him." She rose to her feet.

Nelson pushed a chair toward her. "Sit down. At least he's alive." He said to Lessner, "You should have planned better. A few dead witnesses would have worked wonders for you—offered no dispute to your unlikely story. Then perhaps we'd have let you free to lose yourself among your numerous professional duties. Because Dr. Randolph is a reputable physician, and the dumb police you sized up last night couldn't be expected to hold him on suspicion."

The sudden moan from the corner was low but distinct. "I am Dr. Randolph."

"I know," Nelson said gently, "and you're among friends now. You're going to be all right."

Lessner said doggedly, "He's delirious, poor fellow."

Nelson's fingers itched. "Holden, open the door a crack so we can hear the approach of Dr. Randolph's colleague."

Holden kicked Loth out of the way. He opened the door. The blond man made a lightning dash for it, falling with a curse over Nelson's outflung foot.

"Were you going on an errand of mercy, Doctor?" Nelson lifted him by the slack of his coat.

"Just put the gun down." Lessner was beside himself. "Just put that gun down and give me the pleasure of smashing your—"

"Gladly." Nelson handed the gun to Kyrie. "Well, what are you waiting for?"

"She'll shoot me. You know she'll shoot me if I get the best of it."

"I will," Kyrie said clearly, "but I'll just make it painful—not fatal—because I'm going to need you to fill in the gaps about your Washington cohorts."

Holden said, "Quiet—I hear something." He shut the door softly.

Lessner roared, "Walter, come in shooting—the cops are here." He ducked behind Nelson.

Nelson said, "They're wearing skunks in front this year," and brought him around as a shield, pinning him into place with the crossbar of his arm. Then he maneuvered so that his back protected the injured man in the corner. He called to Kyrie, "Give me the gun—go into the bedroom." Kyrie rose but seemed planted, and he did not have time to repeat the command. Lessner was struggling frantically to free himself. He bent and heaved, almost succeeding in lifting Nelson off his feet. He did succeed in twisting so that he faced his opponent. And in the same move he flung his arms crushingly about the taller man's middle. But Nelson yielded to the grip with surprising suddenness. He pitched forward loosely, and Lessner fell under his weight. He had no time for another try. Nelson lifted the yellow head and banged it against the floor decisively.

He climbed to his feet. Kyrie was staring at him. Color came into his set face. "Just stunned," he said in an embarrassed voice.

She nodded. "Anticlimax—and no Walter. Do you think he heard that shout and turned tail?"

"I don't think so—unless he was right outside the door. Holden had closed it before the shout, and very little penetrates to the lower floors."

"He wasn't outside the door," Holden said. "I thought there were steps coming up. Maybe they weren't his at all." He added nobly, "You could take Kyrie home and send an ambulance for the sick guy. The odds are even now. I'll fix Walter."

Before Nelson could answer Kyrie said, "I'm all right. But I've grown fond of my fellow victim, and the sooner he's taken care of the better I'll feel. Only—you haven't seen Walter, Gene. I'm afraid he'll—"

Holden said stiffly, "I'm not exactly in the puny class. I can manage."

A knock on the door decided it. The three who remained on their feet exchanged glances. The knock was repeated and joined by "It's me, boss. The coast is clear."

Holden whispered, "For God's sake, duck, Kyrie." He flung the door wide and pinned himself behind it. He seemed to be standing on tiptoe because his hand, gripping Loth's small pistol, reached far over the top of the door, ready to descend on the giant who stood framed on the threshold. Framed, I hope, Nelson thought. He did not think much of Holden's position, though he realized that the young man meant well. He moved in front of Kyrie, blocking off her view. He braced himself for attack.

Walter Hinkle did not take in the situation at a glance, nor did he step forward within reach of the poised gun. He looked stupidly from the heap that was Loth to the heap that was Lessner. Then he said, "Hey—what goes on?" and as his eyes climbed to Nelson a glimmer of understanding settled upon his great expanse of face. His meek follow-up was ludicrous in view of the preparations that had been made for his reception. "Understand—I'm only his chauffeur. I don't want trouble." With that he turned tail.

Holden sprang from behind the door, lunged, and grabbed a handful of lozenge-patterned coat. There was a sound of ripping cloth. Walter stepped into the room of his own accord, his voice grieved. "My best suit. What did you want to do that for? Well, all right—" Belatedly he reached into his pocket.

"Drop it," Holden said. "Put up your hands."

Walter's hands flew up, but they became fists in transit. One of them caught Holden's gun and sent it spinning across the floor. The other caught Holden's chin. He managed to roll with the blow, but his eyes clouded. Nelson, watching, forgot Kyrie and started to the rescue. Kyrie's loud and sudden "Help!" pulled him up short. He wheeled, thinking, Lessner had come to life. That put him out of the line of fire.

So it was Kyrie who fixed Walter, shooting him just below the kneecap. The room shook as he crashed. Then Kyrie went down, too, her slim body providing a faint and sorrowful echo.

Chapter 14

Nelson stood in the doorway of his own kitchen. His hands were jammed into his pockets, and he rocked back and forth on his heels. He took a few deep breaths, and his pointed olive-skinned face assumed a look of beatitude.

Sammy waved a spoon at him. "That your best clothes and you going to get the pockets baggy."

"What are we having, Sammy?"

"We having the same kind of dinner I cook for Mr. and Mrs. Cotter. Only this time it going to be lucky."

"I'm not sure it wasn't lucky then, Sammy." He thought, A cop condoning murder. Fine! And added almost belligerently, "Shay was no loss."

Sammy said practically, "That no reason why Mrs. Cotter have to suffer 'cause he get choked in her house."

"She'd have suffered more if you hadn't." He was sorry he had brought that up. Cough medicine was scratched from Sammy's list for all of time. Any reference to it disturbed her.

Sammy said, "You got no call to hush your mouth. I done the wrong thing at the right time. I guess I good at that, but I ain't fretting no more."

"You did the right thing and you're good. Period."

She was pleased. "Mr. Chief, he right sorry he suspicion me that-a-way. He send me some new stockings. He pick them out his own self. I baking that pecan pie he favor for dessert."

"See that he doesn't hog everybody else's share."

"Don't you worry none. I going to put a big piece on Miss Kyrie's plate. And I going to see that Mr. Cotter eat himself fat too. You say Mr. Holden, he coming?"

"Yes—he's coming."

"Don't you be no fool, Mr. Grid-dely. Miss Kyrie know her own mind." His expression did not halt her. "It nice to have ladies around here. Course Mrs. Cotter, she a lady, but she married."

Nelson said, "They'll be arriving soon."

"Not for a solid hour—if they on time."

"You're sure we have enough chairs? Let's see. There's the chief, Louise, Charles, Holden, me, and—"

"And Miss Kyrie," Sammy said happily.

"Yes," Nelson said. He went into the living room. Everything there had been washed and swept and dusted with extra care.

The long ash table was set for six. The curtains were drawn, and flowers reached for the soft lamplight.

He was restless. He sat down. He got up. He wandered around, making small pointless alterations in Sammy's arrangements. The bell rang. He shouted, "I'll get it, Sammy." He went to the door. It's sure to be Furniss. He's always ahead of schedule for meals—Sammy's meals.

He opened the door, but it was not Furniss who stood there. It was Kyrie—alone. A gold willow tree standing slim and tall, her fairness startling above the black of her coat. "Come in," he said. "Welcome."

"I bring Gene's apologies. He was called back to Washington this afternoon."

"Called or sent?" Nelson asked in spite of himself.

Her lips curved. He searched her face. The only trace of anything that should not be there was a small mark high on her right cheek.

"You look well," he understated. "Let me take your coat. I'm afraid they left out the powder room when they built this place. Would the bedroom do instead?" Then he reddened. Stop being sophomoric, he told himself. You're over thirty. What's all this about? You've been in mixed company before.

She was poised and cool. "I didn't come very far, Grid, and I don't think I need any last-minute touches."

"You don't," he said grudgingly. He led her to the living room. She seated herself, choosing the most comfortable chair with unfailing instinct. She said, "This is nice—the room, I mean."

He agreed. He did not mean the room. "Cigarette?" He lit one for her. Sammy came in with cocktails. She said in her deep, peaceful voice, "We glad to have you here, Miss Kyrie."

She set the tray down. "You help yourselves," and went out quietly.

The smile called forth by Sammy stayed on Kyrie's lips. "I'm early, Grid, on purpose—"

Nelson gave her a glass. Took one himself. "You want to get things straightened out before the others come—things they needn't hear."

"I want to thank you for everything—the flowers, the visits. I know I didn't seem to be registering much when you came, but—"

"It's swell we managed to keep Shay's dereliction from the public," Nelson said hurriedly. "When they find that one god is shattered they begin to look around for flaws in the other figures they've been worshiping, and often they get overzealous and start a witch hunt."

"Grid, do you remember when we were kids and I hit you over

the head with a cookie dish? You haven't changed an awful lot since then."

"You mean you still have the same impulse? All right. I won't bore you with any more of my own interpolations. I'll get on with it."

"Do," she said. She sounded half cross, half amused. She settled back in the chair and sipped her cocktail.

He was slow to start. His eyes were on her mouth. He tore them away. He said desperately, "You found plenty of questions to ask when you were recovering and the doctor didn't want you to talk. What's the matter—have you lost interest?"

"No, I've gained interest—in everything. Want me to cue you? All right. One of the things that bothered me was that I knew Gene had found his way to that wretched place because of my note. When I learned that you hadn't come with him but strictly on your own I wondered. So take it from there."

"Sammy gave me the right steer by sampling Charles' cough medicine with curious results. Then Louise told me that Loth had mailed the package containing the medicine to Charles. Conclusion—Loth had doped the medicine. Query—why? Tentative answer—he knew Charles was coming home on furlough and he didn't want him prying into affairs at the shop. What affairs? So I went to the shop to see Loth. And Loth turned up with the man I'd thought was Dr. Randolph. And the two of them led me to you."

"Are you glad?"

"Naturally." Nelson's voice was businesslike. "Because while waiting in Charles' private quarters I stumbled onto something. I figured that if anything out of order were taking place it was taking place there—and that was confirmed by the fact that the room didn't smell as though it had been locked up for months— and by a few other little signs. By the shining new improvements on Charles' ham radio set, for example. He'd built it a long time ago, and the original parts showed wear and tear. Then while tailing that taxi I had time to do a little sorting out. The phony Randolph had not impressed me favorably the night before, but I hadn't stopped to analyze it. When I did it became quite clear— clearer when I was listening outside the door and overheard a remark he made. It was obvious that he was trying to revive someone. He said, 'If we could wake him he'd tell us what to do.' I had decided on the way that he was impersonating the real Dr. Randolph. And when he said that it dawned on me that he'd kidnaped the poor man." He paused. "But I'm ahead of myself. You see, you and Holden were on the trail of Shay, and even the lice he was in cahoots with were always on his trail, too, because they didn't trust him. They'd got onto you in Washington, hadn't they?"

Kyrie nodded. "Yes. Eric Lessner—to give him one of his right names—spotted me. He didn't accept what he saw and visited my boardinghouse to check. He didn't find anything there, but later he met me in the street and contrived to relieve me of some letters. One of them was from Louise, relaying a bit of family advice—and all of them were addressed to Kyrie Martens, not the name I'd been using. So the jig was up so far as I was concerned. That same night I had a date with Shay—Rex." She twisted her mouth at the memory. "He'd asked me to call him Rex. The *L* in his name stood for Lionel, and someone at school had nicknamed him facetiously, but he didn't know that. He liked it. Anyway, Lessner tipped him off and—" She raised her shoulders. "That's another story. Its outcome was that I came to New York on vacation. I hardly expected Cotter's to be the scene of Shay and Company's activities. When I heard his voice in the apartment I was panicked. I bolted out the back way and landed smack in the clutches of Max Loth." She ended forlornly, "A hell of an undercover operative I am."

"And I'm a hell of a policeman—sometimes."

"You're wonderful, Grid."

"That depends on which side of the fence you are. My chief wouldn't think so if he knew all the facts. I thought for a while that you'd killed Shay."

She made a shameless bid for sympathy. "You might have found my dead body with a confession on it to prove I did."

Nelson did not look at her. "Then I received almost absolute evidence that Charles had done him in, but I forgot where my real loyalties lay to the extent of disregarding it."

"What evidence was it?"

"A whisky stain on Charles' pajamas to show he'd left his bed and gone to the hall where Sammy had dumped the bottle of scotch. Yes, and it meant suspecting Sammy of collusion, the theory being that she'd witnessed Charles doing the deed and dropped the tray in horror. It meant that Louise was guilty, too, because it contradicted her story that she was with Charles at the time Sammy discovered the body."

"How *did* the stain get on Charles' pajamas?"

"Lessner. He'd dropped his handkerchief in a puddle of the scotch and transferred it to his patient."

"Grid, you *are* wonderful. Anyone else would have accepted that. You went on to find the truth."

Nelson's voice was harsh. "Not exactly. If necessary I would have manufactured another murderer out of the whole cloth to spare Louise."

Kyrie's voice dwindled. "You always loved Louise. Why didn't you—?"

Nelson went on: "Fortunately all of that is irrelevant now. As I said before, Lessner didn't trust Shay, knowing the way he was about women, not even though Shay had sworn he wouldn't see you again. Lessner got the vine that you were coming to New York, and he didn't believe it was on vacation. He assigned Walter to keep an eye on you—even had him call Louise to see if the name 'Madge Carter' meant anything to her. He knew you checked out of the hotel and he knew you were going to stay with Louise. Your relationship with her made him nervous. Cotter's, with its established reputation, was a perfect setup, and he meant to keep it that way. He wasn't going to have you put a bee in Louise's bonnet."

"And the funny part of it was that the FBI had no inkling at all of the Cotter angle," Kyrie said. "There had been a serious leakage of war information to the Axis—information that Shay had access to because of his position. They thought he might be sending it over his shortwave broadcasts, even though recordings of his scripts had been minutely examined by all the experts in captivity. Suspicion had fastened upon him because in spite of elaborate precautions he was spotted with Lessner several times—and Lessner is a man with a past."

Nelson nodded. "Yes, a man with no political convictions—he wasn't even a Nazi. He just wanted money and he didn't care where it came from. Late in 1940 he worked with a Gestapo-controlled ring in the Gerais province of Brazil, smuggling industrial diamonds to Germany. He was caught carrying a pound candy box filled with stones valued here at five thousand dollars but commanding two hundred thousand dollars on a market open to the Axis." He paused reflectively. "That's how hard up the Axis is for precision tools to make Messerschmitts, Skoda tanks, torpedoes, and all the other implements of war since it's been cut off from the European sources."

Kyrie said, "Let's not go into that. I typed so many reports on bort and carbonado while I was waiting for Shay to nibble that even the gem diamonds I've seen since seem to leer at me. Finish your story, because there are a few things I'd like to tell *you* before the others arrive—if you don't mind."

Nelson did mind. He slowed up deliberately, his ear cocked for the doorbell. "Well, Lessner jumped eight thousand dollars' worth of bail and lay low until—"

"Until he went on the Axis pay roll again as agent 103," Kyrie said. "I overheard that much while I was held in durance vile.

Apparently Lessner eavesdropped on Shay's last telephone conversation—heard him say 103—and got the wind up. Go on."

"Where was I? Oh. Lessner's man, Walter, kept tabs on you, and at the same time Lessner was keeping tabs on Shay. He hardly let him out of his sight—dogged him all the day of your arrival. While Shay dined at the club Lessner and Loth dawdled in a bar across the street until he came out. I think it was pure impulse that made Shay visit Louise. Maybe he was lonely. You'd let him down, and Louise is a beautiful woman. Maybe he had ideas. Anyway, Loth and Lessner had you placed at Louise's. And when they saw where Shay was bound they were sure he was meeting you by prearrangement and that he contemplated some kind of a sellout—either because he'd begun to be afraid of the role he was playing and thought he could buy immunity if he turned informer, or just because he couldn't resist your charms."

Kyrie muttered, "Can you say the same?"

"Walter was parked outside the apartment house in the car. He told them that you'd come running out a few moments ago and turned into the corner drugstore. They told him to stand by. They entered the lobby. It was fairly crowded. Loth lost himself easily among the people there, and Lessner went upstairs to get a line on what was cooking. He walked up to avoid being seen in an elevator. The door to the Cotter apartment was propped open by your luggage, and everyone was more or less occupied with Charles. Lessner slipped into the little dressing room off the hall, and he heard Shay calling Dr. Randolph. Only he didn't know it was Dr. Randolph and he didn't know that the number 103 concerned Charles' temperature. He naturally applied it to himself, with the result that his fears were confirmed."

"So without pausing to think much about it he crept up behind his buddy and socked him on the noggin and strangled him before he had time to come to."

"Yes. What worried him was that he didn't know how much information had been given out or who had received it. He ran downstairs and rounded up Loth. The two of them stood as near to the desk as they dared without attracting attention and carried on an animated conversation about the weather until a man arrived and asked for the Cotter apartment. The man gave his name, but someone got between them and the desk at that point and they didn't catch it. Nor did they attach the right significance to the fact that he was carrying a small black bag. They got him outside on some pretext or other, shoved him into the car, and conked him. Only after they'd searched him and discovered that he was one Dr. Randolph did they put two and two together and get the right answer. To wit—someone was sick upstairs, and

Shay had called a doctor. That someone was probably Charles. Hadn't they arranged for him to be sick by sending him the drugged medicine so that he wouldn't stick his nose into his workroom at the shop and find out that something had been added to his radio? Shay wasn't in on that bit of play and—well, the joke was on them. They made the best of it. Lessner had a flair for drama. Besides, he was most anxious to know what interpretation the police would put upon the murder. So, in spite of all that the nervous Loth—a real Nazi, by the way, a Swiss jeweler by birth—could do to dissuade him, he went through Randolph's papers, memorized a few salient facts, such as Randolph being on the staff of the Parkside, armed himself with the black bag, and returned to the scene of the crime. I should have been wise to him on several counts. No wonder he had so little respect for my qualifications as a detective. When the ambulance came for Charles he pretended he had a cramp and hid in the bathroom—just in case one of the interns knew the real Dr. Randolph by sight. But when he emerged he gave no evidence of having gone through an unpleasant seizure. And then he said he'd been Shay's physician for years. Yet that statement, in view of his age, meant that he finished medical school a beardless prodigy. Furthermore, when our own Dr. Perry went into consultation with him, it was Perry who did all the talking without eliciting a single medical term. Perry himself didn't notice, being too carried away with the joy of having a real live patient for a change. Perry diagnosed encephalitis lethargica without batting an eye, because not only was he slightly rusty, but his subconscious cried out for some rare disease to mark the occasion. And of course Lessner agreed because he couldn't have dreamed up anything that would suit his book more. But did I twig? Oh no. Or maybe I did at that. But I was too busy trying to avert suspicion from my friends to bother with the obvious."

"Obvious, my hat!" Kyrie's voice went husky. "Even if you were the dope you're trying to say you are, it wouldn't matter in the least to me. This—this—whatever it is I feel about you—"

He scowled at her. "Whatever it is—is right. I'm not that much of a dope." He leaned forward suddenly and took her by the shoulders. "Take your games somewhere else, Kyrie. To Holden, maybe. He'd give his teeth for a chance to play."

She said, "I've never encouraged Gene. I haven't any guilt about him." She was completely relaxed under his hands, her head tilted back to study him.

"You never had any guilt about anybody." He took his hands away. He looked at them. "As a kid you were the bane of my life—"

"Because I loved you and you wouldn't notice me. Grid, it sounds corny, but it happened again the moment you came into that sordid place. I didn't see Gene at all—just you. You saw me, too, the same way. I could tell. You looked at me and you trembled."

"Shuddered is more like it," Nelson said. "Your face was a mess."

Kyrie went on, "And while Gene was knocking the stuffing out of Loth your hands clenched as if you—"

"Loth," Nelson repeated. The name was a saving straw, and he grasped it desperately. "I haven't finished explaining. Don't you want to know how Loth entered the picture?"

Kyrie groaned. She covered her face with her hands.

Nelson rushed along. "Shay had discovered the potentialities of Cotter's inadvertently when he came in one day to have a watch repaired and struck up a conversation with Charles in which mutual interests came to light. He was invited to Charles' private room, and Charles proudly exhibited his radio. Lessner had already approached Shay with the proposition that it would be well worth his while if he dropped a few hints to the Axis now and then over his scheduled shortwave broadcasts. Shay had declined because he dared not risk it. But he was tempted, and Charles' radio hit him between the eyes. Charles had put a great deal of money and all of his considerable ingenuity into the building of that set. And who would ever suspect that anything snide was taking place behind Cotter's eminently respectable doors? And Charles was going into the Army. Perfect. So Alex, Charles' assistant, was injured by a hit-and-run driver. Walter was the driver, and it was no accident. With Alex out of the way, Loth applied for his job, provided with full references supplied by Shay out of his many contacts." He paused for breath. "Matter of fact, Loth looked peculiar to me the first time I saw him. He asked me if I'd brought a watch. By his own admission he was expecting a Nazi friend, and 'watch' was the password."

Behind her lovely long hands Kyrie muttered, "You talk too much."

He stared at her, horrified, because her shoulders were heaving. "Kyrie, stop it. You don't fool me a bit. You're not really crying."

She took her hands away. "No, I'm not. I thought tears might move you, but I couldn't even muster one. Just not a weeper, I guess."

"What do you want of me, Kyrie?"

She seemed to weigh the question. Then she said, "Well, for a starter I've been wondering how it would feel to be kissed by a tall, striking guy with white hair. After that I don't know."

His heart was thumping. He said grudgingly, "I don't mind kissing you," and pulled her out of the chair into his arms. In the moment before he kissed her he said to himself, You're a cop—

just a plain cop. You couldn't hold this woman for two minutes. After he kissed her he was silent. He looked at her helplessly. He did not hear the doorbell.

She broke the silence. "So now I know—and now you know."

"Kyrie, you're from my hometown. Your family and mine—well, if you were just another girl it would be all right, but I can't; I'm a confirmed bachelor—" The stumbling speech sounded insufferable and smug to him. To make it worse, she was laughing. He hated her. And he tightened his arms around her.

"Grid, I'm not propositioning you. I swear it. My intentions are honorable, and you needn't worry about that bachelor business. It's been known to wear off before."

"Stop it," he said and released her.

There were sounds in the hall: Sammy's voice, and the resonant bass of Furniss, and Charles's lighter tone, and Louise's charming laugh. All of them came into the room together. Louise and Furniss were chatting away as though they had been friends for a lifetime.

Nelson played host in a dazed but efficient way while Sammy produced more cocktails. He presented Furniss to Kyrie, and Furniss regarded her with bright blue appreciation.

"So you're the missing girl? It hasn't seemed to do you any harm."

Kyrie answered sweetly, "Because Grid came to my rescue in the nick of time."

"The white-haired boy, eh? If all the murders in this town involved his friends they'd be solved at the drop of a hat. What do you think of a fellow who breaks a case before his chief has a chance to take the first roll of red tape out of the box?"

"I think he's marvelous."

Furniss' eyes twinkled. "Look out, Grid."

Nelson went over and sat beside Louise and Charles. Charles was a changed man, clear-eyed and relaxed. He and Louise were drinking a toast to each other. Their happiness had color and substance.

Nelson said gloomily, "You're looking swell, Charles."

"Thanks to you. Did I ever mention that you could have my right arm if the whim seized you?"

Louise smiled up at Nelson. "I can't spare it and, besides, Grid doesn't want to hear that kind of talk. It makes him blush."

"Any more bulletins from Dr. Randolph?" Nelson asked.

"He's getting along fine," Charles said. "He's in my room at the hospital, and Miss Hartshorn's in seventh heaven clucking over him. Incidentally, you made quite a hit with her. She kept asking about you all the while I was there."

Kyrie called across the room, "He makes a hit with all the

ladies."

Furniss said, "Always has. He's rotten spoiled."

"I am too," Kyrie said. "We'd make a good pair."

Furniss chuckled. "*You'd* make a good pair with anybody."

If Furniss approved he was sunk. Nelson said hopelessly, "When are you due back in camp, Charles?"

"I have three more days. Louise is going with me. Alex is back, and he and Ben Seeger can run the place without us for a while." His face darkened. "Imagine those rats using my shop and my radio for their dirty business! As soon as the trial's over and the radio stops being Exhibit A, I'm going to start a bonfire with it."

Sammy appeared. "Get to the table, folks. I going to serve now. You sit here, Mr. Chief. You on the other side, Mr. and Mrs. Cotter. And, Miss Kyrie, you sit right next to Mr. Grid-dely." She gave Kyrie a conspiratorial look.

Nelson groaned. He was sunk all right.

THE END

www.ingramcontent.com/pod-product-compliance
Lightning Source LLC
LaVergne TN
LVHW021807060526
838201LV00058B/3277